**"You are really something, Claire.
Do you know that?"**

She knew a lot of things. She knew she was pretty, because she'd been told so her entire life. She knew she wasn't stupid, even if school hadn't always interested her.

But Ford was seeing other things. Things she'd thought were invisible. The things that fought to be noticed.

I'm strong. I'm capable. I can take care of myself.

He took off his hat, and there were those eyes. Nearly green at this time of day. And they stared right at her.

Right into her.

"I see you," he whispered. His lips were so close.

She dropped the rope. Ford's Adam's apple bobbed as he swallowed. She rose on her toes and their lips touched in a soft and hesitant kiss. Claire held back, hoping he'd be the first to pull away. God knew she didn't have the strength.

But he didn't pull away. He deepened the kiss, so intensely that Claire could hardly breathe.

Who needed oxygen when this man's lips were made of everything she needed to survive?

Praise for
Big Bad Cowboy

"Sexy, smart, sensational!"
—*New York Times* bestselling author Lori Wilde

"*Big Bad Cowboy* is sweet and sexy!"
—*New York Times* bestselling author Jennifer Ryan

"Fans of Susan Elizabeth Phillips will delight in this funny, optimistic, quirky contemporary."
—*Publishers Weekly*, starred review

"A smart, sizzling read."

—*Entertainment Weekly*

"Heartwarming, hysterical, and completely sexy & charming, *Big Bad Cowboy* was an outstanding start to the Once Upon a Time in Texas series. A series that I expect to be a huge hit with rom-com fans."

—Harlequin Junkies

"A remarkable love story."

—Fresh Fiction

COWBOY
come home

ALSO BY CARLY BLOOM

Big Bad Cowboy
It's All About That Cowboy (novella)

COWBOY
come home

A ONCE UPON A TIME IN TEXAS NOVEL

CARLY BLOOM

FOREVER

NEW YORK   BOSTON

Copyright © 2020 by Carol Pavliska
Rocky Mountain Cowboy copyright © 2018 by Sara Richardson
Cover photography by Rob Lang. Cover design by Elizabeth Turner Stokes.
Cover copyright © 2020 by Hachette Book Group, Inc.

Forever
Hachette Book Group
1290 Avenue of the Americas, New York, NY 10104
read-forever.com
twitter.com/readforeverpub

First Edition: March 2020

Forever is an imprint of Grand Central Publishing. The Forever name and logo are trademarks of Hachette Book Group, Inc.

The publisher is not responsible for websites (or their content) that are not owned by the publisher.

The Hachette Speakers Bureau provides a wide range of authors for speaking events. To find out more, go to www.hachettespeakersbureau.com or call (866) 376-6591.

ISBNs: 978-1-5387-6347-6 (mass market), 978-1-5387-6346-9 (ebook)

Printed in the United States of America

OPM

10 9 8 7 6 5 4 3 2 1

To Jasper.

You and this book share a birthday
(albeit sixteen years apart).

Yours was the easier delivery.

Acknowledgments

꘎

I think a couple of ghosts helped me write this book. Actually, that might be a stretch. I think a couple of ghosts laughed their asses off while I wrote this book.

My granddaddy, Jim Weaver, was ranch foreman and manager for the B.B. Dunbar Cattle Company until the day he retired to Uvalde, Texas. You can read stories about him and his horse, Coco, in old copies of *The Cattleman* magazine. It is said he was one of the finest cowboys in the country, and I think folks are referring to the entire country, not just the country of Texas.

I'm sorry I never met my uncle Worth (I only know him from a photograph), but my uncle Gene was all the uncle I needed. Like my grandfather, he was a ranch foreman and manager. He taught me to two-step, had a cowdog named Son (short for Son of a Bitch), and never wore his Stetson in the house (or set it on the bed). I never saw him in a short-sleeved shirt, even on our trips to the Texas coast, where he scuffed up the deck of my dad's boat with his cowboy boots.

In addition, I enjoyed support from a few of the living, most of whom probably wished they were dead by the time

I typed "the end." I simply can't thank Madeleine Colavita, my editor, enough. She wrangled a very wild and unruly manuscript, somehow turning it into a book. I'm pretty sure she regularly screams into a pillow. And God bless my agent, Paige Wheeler. I know she gets tired of telling me I'm pretty, but she does it anyway (it's her job—another day, another dollar/existential crisis).

Thank you to my copyeditor, Lori Paximadis, master of math, Spanglish, and the space-time continuum. Thank you to Bob Castillo for his patience, and thank you to Estelle Hallick for promoting my books with such boundless enthusiasm (she's my favorite Disney princess).

Thank you to authors Amy Bearce, Alison Bliss, Sam Tschida, and Erin Quin for their support. Writing is hard, but these women understand that I like to think it's harder for me. And thank you to Jessica Snyder, who is very good at pretending I'm fine.

Thank you to Carolyne, Anne, and Gemma for entertaining my Facebook readers' group, Carly's Bloomers. And thank you to the Bloomers for their encouragement and loyalty, especially Natasha, who named Baby Blake! Thank you to my family for believing in me and loving me and never telling me it's time to get dressed. Special thanks to Camille for helping me tweak a Cinderella moment by saying "Nobody loses a whole ass boot!" But most of all, thank you to my readers. Big Verde was just a place in my weird imagination until you turned that first page and put it on the map.

COWBOY
come home

Chapter

One

❧

Claire Kowalski gazed across the table at Chad, her latest Sizzle match, and wished she'd swiped left instead of right. It wasn't his looks, because he was tall and trim with a full head of brown hair and a sexy Prince Charming cleft in his chin. It was literally everything else.

They'd suffered through enough stilted conversation during the appetizers to last Claire a lifetime.

You sell respiratory equipment? How exciting!

She'd worked hard at keeping her eyes from glazing over. He seemed equally unimpressed by her job at Petal Pushers, a nursery and landscaping business owned by her best friend, Maggie. But her rock climbing seemed to have piqued his interest.

"When you say rock climbing, you mean those walls in fitness centers, right? There are a few of them here in Austin." He winked at her and grinned.

She dabbed the corner of her mouth with a linen napkin,

trying not to show her irritation with Chad, who really hadn't done a thing wrong other than be himself.

"I use walls for training, but I climb real rocks. Big ones. I'm the president of the Texas Hill Country Rock Climbers Association."

Chad raised his eyebrows. "So, like, you climb up sheer rock walls and stuff? I thought you had to be pretty strong to do that."

His eyes dipped down to Claire's ample cleavage. She shouldn't have forgone the "Sunday safety pin" she often used with the pretty blue wrap dress.

She didn't have the typical lean, athletic build of a rock climber. She was tall and curvy, and with what her mother referred to as a "shock" of red hair, she was easy to spot on a cliff. But looks aside, climbing required strength and agility, as did loading saplings and shrubs onto flatbed trucks, or holding down a calf who'd managed to get a strip of baling wire wrapped around its leg, which she'd done on her family's ranch earlier today.

Claire placed her napkin back in her lap, noticing the small angry puncture the baling wire had made in her palm. Her hands were the only things that might offer a hint as to her toughness. They were definitely not as soft and flawless as her carefully moisturized face, but her nails were freshly painted.

She picked up her fork, took a bite of dry salmon, and downed it with a substantial sip of merlot. "I'm no expert, but I've done some class five climbs."

She waited for him to ask what qualified as a class 5 climb. That's how this worked. *It's your turn.*

"I'm a runner," he said.

They were back to Chad's favorite subject: himself. That's pretty much all he'd talked about for the past twenty minutes.

"I see a lot of trail runners when I'm climbing," Claire said. "Do you run on trails?"

"I run at the gym," he said. "And I do CrossFit, of course."

"Of course." She squinted over her wineglass, which had miraculously worked its way back to her lips and concluded (a) he was everything she'd chalked him up to be, (b) his healthy glow came from a tanning bed, and (c) she might have to fake a text from her dying grandmother.

"This is Kobe beef, you know," Chad said, pointing to his plate. "You should have gotten the steak."

"That's not Kobe," Claire said. Kobe was extremely rare, and most places that claimed to sell it were outright lying. They got away with it because there were an awful lot of people willing to be duped if it made them feel special.

Including her.

Two years ago, she'd fallen for a sexy, wandering cowboy named Ford Jarvis. He'd made her feel so stupidly special that she'd thought he might actually settle down. Ha! Zebras didn't change their stripes. Especially if they were dumbass cowboys, and even if they'd taken you home to meet their mother.

Ford had told her he'd never settle down. Not in a town. Not on a ranch. And not with a woman.

Put that on a bumper sticker, cowboy.

She'd been duped, and then she'd been dumped.

Now Ford was back in town. More specifically, he was back on *her* ranch.

Temporarily, of course.

Claire only had to survive the next six weeks. How hard could that be?

She desperately needed a distraction. Unfortunately, the only thing distracting about Chad was a bit of arugula stuck in his teeth.

Chad took a sip of wine. Would it free the arugula? He swallowed and smiled. Nope! That piece of lettuce was holding on like a grasshopper on a windshield wiper.

"Well, a guy from the gym told me they serve Kobe here. And I'm pretty familiar with what constitutes a fine cut of beef." Chad picked up his knife and poked at his steak. "Look at this beautiful marbling."

"Marbling is just fat, and it's usually the result of corn feeding, which is not very good for the animal or the person consuming it. Have you ever been to a feed lot? Have you ever *smelled* one?"

"You act like you grew up on a ranch."

Claire sat up straight, pride swelling in her chest. "That's because I did. My family owns Rancho Cañada Verde."

The ranch had been in the Kowalski family for five generations, and at twelve thousand acres, it was no small family farm. In recent years, it had become a household name among the growing organic, grass-fed market, and Claire's expertise—she had a degree in fashion merchandising— had played a big part in it. It didn't matter whether you were pushing pencil skirts or skirt steaks, it was all about branding and positioning. She was good at marketing. Because of her, the ranch's brand was even gracing grocery store shelves on the labels of salad dressings, salsas, and marinades.

"Never heard of your ranch," Chad said. "Where is it?"

"It's in Big Verde, which is about an hour southwest of here."

Big Verde was barely a pinprick on the map, but thanks to the beautiful Rio Verde and its various springs and swimming holes, it attracted a fair number of tourists.

"I think we rented a cabin there once," Chad said.

"Really? Do you know who owned it?"

Chad shook his head, as if he could barely remember the cabin, much less the owner.

"There's an adorable little Airstream trailer on Rancho Cañada Verde that we used to rent to tourists," Claire said. "But I live in it now."

She'd optimistically moved out of her parents' ranch house in the hope that she'd need privacy for herself and the Prince Charming she'd find on Sizzle. But so far, the only person to experience the new Egyptian cotton sheets and their ridiculously high thread count in the trailer's newly renovated loft bed was her.

"You live on your parents' property? In a trailer?"

"The ranch is twelve thousand acres."

Chad stared blankly.

"It's a fifteen-minute drive from my trailer to my parents' house," she said. "It's hardly a camper in the backyard."

Claire didn't go into how the refurbished trailer, which she'd named Miss Daisy, had appeared in a magazine spread featuring unique Texas getaways. And although it wasn't anywhere near her parents' house, it was pretty dang close to the foreman's cabin.

Claire's eyes were on Chad, but every cell in her body vibrated like a tiny traitorous compass pointing toward Ford. She could literally *feel* the man's pull.

He was probably already done unpacking his measly belongings—Ford bragged that everything he owned fit in the back of his pickup with room to spare—and not thinking about her at all.

"I wouldn't have pegged you as a small-town country girl," Chad said. His eyes dipped down to her chest again, as if small-town girls were also expected to have small boobs.

Claire gently tugged at her neckline and gave Chad the

steely gaze she'd learned from her father. Big Verde men might not have fancy gym memberships, but they knew not to stare at a woman's chest.

Chad cleared his throat. "Do you have cows and stuff on your ranch?" he asked, shoveling another bite of steak into his mouth.

Cows and stuff were what turned a chunk of land into a ranch. "Yes. And I typically don't eat anything with four legs unless I knew it by name. Or at least its tag number."

"That's kind of...morbid, isn't it?" Chad shuddered a little.

Maybe a little, and it was probably why she tended not to eat beef. "I consider myself a pescatarian, for the most part."

"Pescatarian? Your profile says you're Baptist," Chad said. "I'm pretty sure they eat meat."

Claire lifted her wineglass. "It's drinking they don't do."

She checked the time. How had it only been six minutes since the last time she'd looked? She set her phone down only to see Chad pick his up. He was probably looking at more Sizzle profiles.

Yep. His thumb swiped right.

Claire cleared her throat, and Chad hastily set his phone down. "Sorry," he said. "A message from my grandmother."

Claire raised an eyebrow. She'd offer a few more discussion prompts for Chad before politely declining dessert, coffee, and—if she was reading him right—fellatio. Then she'd chalk him up as another Sizzle "fizzle" and be on her way.

Chad cracked his knuckles. Maybe he would be the one to end the date early. "I was thinking we could go back to my place after dessert."

Claire folded her arms across her chest and placed her

napkin on the table. "This has been fun, Chad, but I really need to be getting back—"

"What for? What could possibly be happening in Little Big Town that you need to get back to?"

Somebody really wanted his blowjob.

Claire could have explained that Big Verde was in for some weather tonight—thunderstorms coming from the east—but instead, she dug in her purse and pulled out two twenty-dollar bills. She dropped them on the table and then slammed back the last of her wine. "Dang," she said. "That's a decent merlot."

* * *

Thunder rumbled through the Texas Hill Country as Ford Jarvis leaned back in his kitchen chair, balancing on two legs. It had been raining on and off all day and, according to Gerome Kowalski, had been doing so for the better part of a week, making the ranch soggy as hell.

Beau Montgomery, head herdsman, was taking credit for it. He'd killed two rattlesnakes in one day and hung them on the fence.

You've got to put them belly-up if you want it to rain.

Cowboys were a superstitious lot when it came to the weather. Heck, they were a superstitious lot *period*. And although Ford liked to poke fun, he was no exception. When he'd seen two heifers in the creek-side pasture running with their tails up this afternoon, his first thought had been, *Here comes a flood.*

And the first thing he'd done when he'd moved into the cabin was turn the horseshoe over the door right-side up, because everybody knew an upside-down horseshoe was bad luck.

He glanced out the window and thought about those heifers. The ground was saturated, the creeks were full, and if the sky opened up, they might, indeed, see some flash flooding. He checked the weather radar on his phone.

He let out a low whistle that earned him a glare from Oscar. While some guys had friendly dogs to ride in the back of their pickups, Ford had a mean, bony cat.

"Damn," he said. "Things are about to get worse."

Oscar pulled his tiny ears back tightly against his head.

The scraggly cat had shown up on a stormy night much like this one while Ford was living on a ranch outside of Sonora. He hadn't wanted to take the nasty creature with him when he'd left for Wichita Falls, but he'd been afraid the other ranch hands would let the poor thing starve. Same story when he'd moved to El Paso, and from El Paso to Big Verde.

Four ranches in two years; five if you considered he'd hit Big Verde twice. He didn't have many belongings, so packing up and heading out was easy. It was just him; his trusty adopted wild mustang, Coco, who he'd broken himself; and Oscar.

Of all the ranches he'd worked, Rancho Cañada Verde was the finest. It wasn't the biggest or the fanciest, but it was the gem of the Texas Hill Country, and Gerome Kowalski was a rancher any cowboy would be proud to work for. Nevertheless, Ford had been very firm with Gerome about this stint as ranch foreman being temporary. He'd committed to a roundup in West Texas in six weeks.

He didn't like staying in one place for too long.

There was something about the newness and excitement of going from ranch to ranch that agreed with him. And he liked leaving folks behind while he could still tolerate them, before they'd had much of a chance to wear on his nerves.

He especially enjoyed knowing that the ones who did wear on his nerves would soon be nothing more than an image in his rearview mirror.

Six weeks. Surely, he could last that long. All he had to do was keep his mind, eyes, and hands off Claire Kowalski, aka the rancher's daughter.

How hard could it be?

He swallowed. Twelve thousand acres wasn't *that* big. And he and Claire had a history together that involved their clothes falling off any time they were within ten feet of each other.

She'd been nowhere to be seen when he'd visited Gerome's office at the ranch house earlier. Beau—the rattlesnake slayer and resident busybody—told him that Claire had moved out of the ranch house and into a silly little Airstream trailer practically within spitting distance of the foreman's cabin. Well, maybe not spitting distance. Ford couldn't see Claire or her little tin can from here.

He swore he could feel her, though.

That tug. Whenever he thought about Claire—and he'd thought about her plenty over the past two years—it was as if someone was yanking on an invisible band attached to his midsection. The first time it had happened, he'd thought he was having a damn heart attack.

He was used to it now. The feeling kind of went along with the other chronic aches and pains of cowpunching.

Had he fallen in love with Claire?

Maybe.

Was the condition permanent?

Most definitely not.

Jarvis men didn't fall in love and stay that way.

The Jarvis curse.

Some of the men in his family took it seriously. As in,

they literally believed in a curse. His family's colorful history included a story about Ford's great-grandfather messing with the wrong *bruja*.

Ford didn't believe in witches, Mexican or otherwise, and he found the idea of a curse to be utterly ridiculous. But whether it was the result of a *bruja* or a family disposition, the fact remained that Jarvis men were cursed with being incapable of settling down. And when they tried, bad luck always came knocking.

Ford's dad, Johnny Jarvis, was a retired rodeo bull rider who'd earned the nickname Johnny Appleseed because he'd fathered nine kids with eight women. All of them, except for Ford, were named for the cities they were born in.

There was his oldest brother, Dallas, who'd been only two when their dad had met a woman in San Antonio, which resulted in Tony. Two years later, he'd met and married his "real" soul mate in Laredo, producing Larry. Like clockwork, it was two more years before a pretty little rodeo queen—Ford's mom—attracted Johnny's attention in Dallas.

Nine months later, Ford was born. And since there was already a Dallas in the family, he'd been named for the literal place of his conception, the backseat of a Ford Fairmont.

That union lasted the longest, and in two years the little family had moved to Abilene, where Abby, Ford's only full sibling, was born. After his parents' divorce, Ford gained four more half-siblings: Houston, Austin, Odessa, and Worth (they'd left off the "Fort"), who was the baby of the family.

Spreading "seed" here, there, and everywhere wasn't a lifestyle Ford aspired to, and he was disappointed that some of his brothers had already followed in their father's footsteps.

Curses were hard to break.

Nobody knew if Jarvis women were afflicted with the same curse. Odessa was twenty-two and seemed hell-bent on independence. And Abby had died when she was only ten years old.

She'd drowned in a creek when a flash flood had come out of nowhere.

Ford was supposed to have been watching her. And he *had* been. Just moments before...

That's why they called it a *flash* flood.

Lightning lit the sky again, and the rain picked up. A shiver ran up and down Ford's spine. Wailing Woman Creek felt a little too close for comfort.

Chapter

Two

༄

Claire stamped her feet on Maggie's muddy welcome mat and hesitated briefly before knocking on the door. It was nine thirty—possibly too late to show up unannounced on her best friend's doorstep—but the gate to Happy Trails ranch had been open, and if Claire didn't vent to someone, she was going to erupt.

She felt like giving up. Maybe it was time to stop searching for Prince Charming since all she could find were frogs and toads—and since this was Texas, most of the toads were horny.

With comedic timing, a toad hopped out from behind an overturned cowboy boot nestled in the corner of the porch. Claire stifled a squeal, but her pulse raced like the engine of her shiny new car. She raised an eyebrow at the toad as he hopped away, blissfully unaware of how close he'd just come to being impaled by a stiletto heel.

She started to knock on the door again when she clearly

heard laughter coming from inside the house. She tried the knob. It turned, so she pushed the door open a few inches and hollered, "Knock, knock! Anybody home?"

"In here!" Maggie shouted.

Claire walked past the staircase to the den, where Maggie was doubled over in laughter. Her husband, rancher Travis Blake, was sitting on the couch with his head between his knees. Alice Martin, the town's librarian, hovered by the coffee table while clutching a book to her chest. Her brown eyes were wide with concern. "I'm so sorry, Travis," she said.

Claire couldn't possibly imagine what Alice needed to apologize for. "I thought you were going to stop saying you're sorry all the time," she said.

"In this case, I need to," Alice said. "Poor Travis!"

"I don't care about people saying they're sorry," Travis said, lifting his head from between his knees. "But I could do without the *poor Travis* business."

He was as pale as an oyster, or as at least as pale as someone who'd just eaten one and hadn't much cared for it.

Maggie straightened up, cheeks still pink from laughing. "Alice, all you did was bring over some pregnancy books. It's not your fault that Travis opened one up and had a fit."

Maggie, who was about four months pregnant, looked like she might laugh again.

"This one is about labor and delivery," Alice said to Claire, squeezing the book even more tightly, as if it housed an evil entity. "And look what it did to poor..." She winced. "Sorry." Then she stomped her foot, causing her ponytail to swing frantically. "Dang it!"

Maggie ruffled Travis's hair. "And to think that just this morning Travis bragged to the doctor about how prepared he is for the birth because he's"—Maggie made air quotes with her fingers—"*pulled plenty of calves*."

"Oh dear," Alice said.

Claire gasped. "Travis Blake, you did *not* compare child-birth to pulling calves."

Travis stood up, a slight bit of color returning to his cheeks. "It's actually very similar, according to that damn book," he said. "More similar than I was expecting."

He looked at Maggie and went a tad pale again. Maggie leaned into him and rose up on her toes, an act that didn't do much to add to her five feet and two inches of height. With her short hair and small stature, she looked like a little blond pixie. But she was tough as nails.

"I'm not the first woman to give birth," she said softly while stroking Travis's cheek. "I'll be fine."

Travis sighed. "I know. And I'll be there for you." He swallowed audibly and gave Maggie a squeeze. "Always."

This. This is why Claire hadn't given up on finding her own Prince Charming.

"You ladies shouldn't stick around too long," Travis said, letting go of Maggie and heading for the stairs. "We're in for a downpour."

As if on cue, it started to rain again.

"I'm not staying long," Claire said.

Travis furrowed his brow. "There are two low-water crossings between here and Rancho Cañada Verde."

Travis was right. And once Claire got onto her family's ranch, she'd have to go through another one to get to Miss Daisy. But she wasn't stupid, and she knew how to take care of herself. She'd driven in the rain a million times.

Seven-year-old Henry appeared at the top of the stairs. "Dad, I'm scared."

Travis was Henry's uncle, but he and Maggie had adopted

him when he was six years old. Soon, a baby girl would be joining their little family.

"I'm coming, buddy. We'll count the seconds between the lightning and the thunder."

Claire's heart started to melt as she watched Travis ascend the stairs, and it didn't stop melting until it came to the tiny, frozen nugget of jealousy in the center.

She wanted this. Or some version of it, anyway. She was the freaking "Cupid" of Big Verde. If it weren't for her, Maggie and Travis wouldn't even be together. Why couldn't she find someone for herself?

She'd turn thirty later this year. According to a book Alice had shared with her, only twelve percent of her eggs remained viable. What was the point of being the sole heir of a ranching empire if the empire would die with her?

"Come and sit for a few minutes," Maggie said, pointing at the couch. "How did your date go?"

Claire sighed and sat. Something sharp poked her in the butt, and she yanked a toy tractor out from between the couch cushions.

"Sorry," Maggie said, snatching it up. "Tell us everything. Was there spray-on hair involved? Did he have red wine trapped in his Invisalign braces?"

Claire shivered. She'd encountered both of those situations on previous Sizzle dates.

"His name was Chad, and he sells respiratory equipment to hospitals."

Maggie shuddered. "How dreadful."

Claire nodded in agreement. "Chad likes sushi and fine wine, and he's super smart. I know he's super smart because he told me so. And he does CrossFit."

"Of course dudebro does CrossFit," Maggie said, nodding. "Maybe you need to stop trying to hook up with city slickers and stick closer to home," Alice suggested. "It doesn't seem like you've had much in common with any of your Sizzle dates."

Claire wanted to point out that she didn't see Alice dating any local Big Verde guys, but she wasn't sure Alice ever dated *anyone*. She was cute, smart, and independent. And she seemed perfectly content to remain that way. Claire, however, wanted what her parents had, and what Maggie and Travis seemed to have. And she wanted it yesterday. Was that asking too much?

As if Maggie had read her mind, she said, "A watched pot never boils, Claire. Maybe if you stop trying so hard—"

Claire sighed. "I've dated every single man in Big Verde, and none of them have tickled my fancy."

"If I remember correctly," Maggie said with an impish grin, "Ford Jarvis tickled it three times in one night."

Alice gasped. "Really? Three times?"

Claire's cheeks heated up. *Yes, three times.* But sex was all Mr. Fancy-Tickler cared about. It was probably why he was so dang good at it.

Alice stood and headed for the door. "I'm going to ruminate on that when I'm in bed tonight."

"Heading out?" Maggie asked.

"Yes. I've got a library board meeting in the morning. I need to hit the sack."

Maggie started to rise.

"I can let myself out," Alice said. "You sit tight."

Maggie sank back into the chair and rested her arms on her belly, even though her baby bump was barely visible. "Maybe I'll bring Henry to story time. He really loves it."

"Isn't he getting a little old for that?" Claire asked.

"Nobody is ever too old for *once upon a time*," Alice said.

Claire wondered if they got too old for a happily-ever-after.

With a little wave, Alice headed out the door.

"I should probably get going too—"

"Wait a minute," Maggie said. "I have something to discuss with you."

Claire leaned back against the cushion. "What is it?"

"You know how busy I've been with landscaping projects lately."

Claire nodded. Maggie was a landscape architect.

"And Happy Trails is taking off. Our website orders have doubled within the last six months, and our calendar is booked solid with field trips and tours."

Happy Trails, the small ranch Maggie and Travis owned, raised organic poultry, pork, and beef, which they sold directly to consumers. They also had bees and an apple orchard.

"I don't know how you're finding the time to grow a human."

"Me either. I feel pulled in a million different directions, and the baby isn't even here yet." She paused for a moment and took a sip from a water bottle on the coffee table. Then she focused her big brown eyes on Claire. "I need to prioritize."

Claire nodded. She completely understood. How had Maggie been holding it all together?

"First is my family. And next is my landscape architecture business."

"Of course," Claire said. "You worked long and hard for that degree, and you've built something to be proud of. What more can I do to help you with the rest?"

Maggie cleared her throat and dropped her gaze to her pregnant belly. She was clearly nervous, and that made Claire nervous, because Maggie was almost never nervous.

"Claire, I've decided to sell Petal Pushers."

It took a few moments for the words to connect in her brain. Had she heard Maggie correctly? "I'm sorry. What did you say?"

"I just can't keep it," Maggie said.

"But you inherited it from your grandmother! And it's..."

Where I work.

"I know," Maggie said, biting her lip.

Claire felt selfish, but all she could think about was herself. What would she do without Petal Pushers? It was the hub of her world. Heck, along with the Corner Cafe, it was the social hub of Big Verde.

But she understood Maggie's predicament. She was only human, after all.

"I hate to let it go," Maggie said. "It's been keeping me up at night. That's why I was thinking that maybe you'd like to buy it."

Claire felt her mouth drop open. "Me? Buy Petal Pushers?"

The idea sank in with incredible speed, and by the time Maggie started to speak again, Claire's mind had changed the question into an exclamatory sentence.

She was buying Petal Pushers!

"You wouldn't have to keep it as a garden center," Maggie said. "The possibilities are endless. A boutique. Or a gift shop maybe. It doesn't matter, because I swear you could sell a bicycle to a legless man."

Claire's imagination started humming.

"It's already such a sweet little country shop," she said. "And there's so much room. What could I do with the outdoor nursery? A patio, maybe. Or a tearoom..."

Suddenly, Claire's lame Sizzle date was ancient history. Her body tingled. Her mind raced. Her despair had been replaced with a sense of purpose.

A loud clap of thunder made them jump.

The skies opened up, and the rain clattered so loudly on the roof that Claire barely heard the pounding of Travis's feet on the stairs as he came rushing down.

"Claire," he said, adopting a stern fatherly expression that went adorably well with the *Little Red Riding Hood* book in his hand. "If you don't leave right now, you're going to have to stay the night. I don't like the weather, and you've got those two low-water crossings..."

Three, actually.

Claire hated to leave now. She wanted to scheme and plan with Maggie. But Travis was right. She didn't dare stay another minute.

"Yes, Dad," she said, throwing in an eye roll. "Leaving now."

"We'll talk later," Maggie said. "Be careful driving home."

Claire hugged Maggie and grabbed her umbrella from the porch on her way out. She popped it open and ran to her car, barely feeling the rain that battered her unprotected legs. Her mind was going a mile a minute, which was probably faster than she was going to be able to drive in this weather.

* * *

Ford sighed and shifted in his seat. That damn tugging sensation had become worse ever since his boots had hit Rancho Cañada Verde's soil. He should have turned this gig down. But it was hard to say no to Gerome Kowalski, especially since he'd sounded just a hair shy of desperate.

Another glance at the weather radar showed a threatening cloud of red and hot pink just to the north, and it was headed straight for Big Verde. If they got a downpour,

Wailing Woman Creek would swell, and the crossing would be under water. That meant he'd be cut off from the rest of the ranch until the water receded. As would the other two inhabitants this side of the creek—a hermit named Ruben, and Claire.

Ford's right eye twitched. His thumb hovered over his phone. *Don't do it, dipshit.*

He did it. Clicked on the Sizzle dating app and logged in. Because yes, he had a fucking login for a fucking online dating site. Hell, he'd never used any form of social media. Had snubbed it, in fact. And here he was with a Sizzle profile. A password, username, the whole nine yards. It was embarrassing, and he wasn't even looking for a date. But he couldn't see Claire's profile if he didn't have one of his own.

He wished he didn't even know about Claire's profile. But Beau had gleefully spilled the beans about it. It was clear that Beau had been hoping to get a rise out of Ford, but it hadn't worked. Why should Ford care if Claire was dating?

He wasn't jealous or upset or concerned in any way. He didn't have the right to be. At most, he was mildly curious.

He looked at Oscar, who stared back through squinty eyes that seemed to say, *Curiosity killed the cat.*

Ford clicked on Claire's profile. His heart stuttered, and he dropped his chair back to all four legs at the sight of Claire's smiling face framed by that mass of auburn hair. Bright blue eyes stared back at him. No, *through* him. He shook off the sensation that she knew he was looking, that he was doing something wrong or invading her privacy. Hell, she had put it out there. Obviously, she wanted people to see it.

Username: Glass Slipper
Age: 29
On weekends you'll find me: Shopping for ALL the shoes. Rock climbing by day, two-stepping by night, and enjoying everything the beautiful Texas Hill Country has to offer.
Looking For: Prince Charming (NO PRESSURE LOL)

Ford had read these words probably ten or thirty times (who was counting?), but they still settled in his stomach like a block of concrete.

Claire's Sizzle profile identified her as an "active" member. What did that mean? He sure hoped it didn't mean she was out on a night like this. Especially since Beau told him she'd recently traded in her ranch truck for a bright red, impractical chunk of low-clearance tin called a Mini Cooper. Beau said she'd thought it was cute. *Cute!* Ford didn't care if it had dimples and a lollipop, mini *anythings* were not safe. This was Texas. People went big in Texas, and that included vehicles. If a truck, or even a goddam deer, smacked into a mini whatever, it was going to do some serious damage. That bit of obviousness, combined with the fact that Claire drove her car even faster than she ran her mouth, worried the shit out of him.

And it shouldn't. Because she wasn't his to worry about, and God knows he was no Prince Charming.

That boot didn't fit.

Chapter
Three

❧

Claire was not going to panic. Her car had stalled. That was all. And she was maybe a mile from her trailer. She didn't relish walking in this weather, though, so she checked her phone for a signal again.

Nada. Coverage was spotty on the ranch, and nonexistent in low-lying areas, which is where she and her adorable new Mini Cooper currently sat.

Lightning flashed, illuminating the sign identifying Wailing Woman Creek. She opened the door to see how much water was flowing across the concrete surface of the low-water crossing. It looked to be about the same as the last time she'd checked, just a few inches. She hated to ruin a perfectly good pair of heels. Maybe someone would come along...

Nobody would be out driving around in this, and the only people on her side of the creek were Ruben and—she gulped—*Ford.*

She strummed her fingers on the steering wheel and chewed her lower lip. It was raining so hard she could barely see. She pressed her nose against the window as dread crept up her spine.

She shook her hair and rolled her shoulders. Wailing Woman hadn't seen a flash flood in years.

About time for one.

The creek was usually no more than a trickle, and the low-water bridge going across it typically dry. But every ten years or so—on nights like this—the crossing earned its designation as a flash flood zone.

She turned the key in the ignition one more time, just for grins.

The car did not start. It had either stalled in the few inches of water she'd stupidly driven into, or...

The low fuel light was on, but the operator's manual said the Mini Cooper could go another hundred miles after it lit up. Surely, she hadn't run out of gas. Only idiots did that!

She was pretty sure she'd run out of gas.

She smacked the steering wheel, and the car shuddered.

A bit of panic set in. Had her car just moved?

Claire cracked the door again and peeked out. The water looked higher.

She held her breath. Would the car shake again? Maybe she'd imagined it.

Nope. It shook again. Actually, it shimmied. She put her hand on the door handle. Abandoning her new car in the dead of night seemed dramatic. But so did clinging to a tree like a drowning possum.

She gritted her teeth. Like it or not, she was going to walk.

Huddling beneath her umbrella, Claire slammed the car door with her hip. It made a sturdy, solid sound. But floodwaters could lift her little car up like a toy and carry it downstream, smashing it into trees and bridges and the cars of other idiots. She looked down at the water rushing across her Laurence Dacade heels.

Shit was getting real.

Claire tiptoed through the rising water while the wind whipped at her hair. Relief washed over her when she made it to the bank. Now all she had to do was hike a mile in wet stilettos.

No problem.

Her heel snapped on the third rocky step. She toppled over, smashing her umbrella and dropping her purse.

Dammit! She stood up on shaky legs—the shoe was broken beyond repair, so she tossed the heel—and looked back at her Mini Cooper.

It was rocking. Violently. She squinted, shielding her eyes against the rain with her hand, just in time to see her precious lifted up and carried away! Anguish bubbled up like globs in a lava lamp, but it gave way to panic as the wind became deafeningly loud.

Only the sound wasn't wind.

It was water. And Claire hadn't cleared the flood zone, not by a long shot.

With her heart pounding, she kicked off her shoes—$348 on sale—and ran for her life.

She could do this.

And she would have, had her foot not caught on a root. Down she went again, smacking her chin on the ground. She hadn't yet reached the top of the knoll, and the sound of the water was all-encompassing. She swallowed the knot in her throat and tried to get up while turning to look back at Wailing Woman Creek.

She didn't need to look very far. It was at her feet.

* * *

Ford finished his bowl of soup while tucked away nice and dry in his sturdy cedar cabin. The rain pounded the metal roof, its clattering tempo chasing Oscar under the couch until only the tip of his twitchy black tail poked out.

"Scaredy cat," Ford muttered.

A big bolt of lightning struck somewhere nearby, and the smell of ozone filled the air.

There went the lights.

Ford flipped his emergency radio to battery mode and went back to listening to the Big Verde police and county deputies chatter back and forth.

He sure was glad they'd gotten the herd off the river property this afternoon. This was the kind of weather that washed cattle away.

He rinsed his soup bowl and set it in the rack to dry. The radio was seventy percent static and thirty percent intelligible conversation. Deputy Bobby Flores made periodic reports as he patrolled the low-water crossings. His voice broke through the white noise. "Flash flood at Wailing Woman…"

Ford raised his eyebrows. There it was. Just what he'd feared.

But he had nothing to worry about. He was safe. The cattle were safe. There was no reason for the stirring sense of…what was it? Panic? Whatever it was, it was making his skin feel too tight.

Claire. Why couldn't he stop worrying about her? She might be exasperating, but she was smart. Sure, she had a high tolerance for adrenaline and was a bit of a thrill junkie. But she wasn't stupid. Hopefully she was where she should be on a Friday night during a severe thunderstorm warning—at home in that little tin can. And if she wasn't? She'd grown up in Big Verde. She wouldn't drive into a low-water crossing during a flood watch. She'd know to go the Harper's Hill route and come across the bridge at the east entrance to the ranch.

He slammed his hand on the table. She *couldn't* do Harper's Hill in that stupid little car.

He picked up his phone, but he hesitated to call. She was a grown woman, and she'd most likely cuss him out and remind him that she wasn't his business anymore.

As if a woman who set your heart on fire like a never-ending case of indigestion could be referred to as *business*.

Deputy Flores's voice crackled over the radio. "Can't get across, but Wailing Woman looks clear. I'm setting up a barricade on this side."

"You probably should have done that earlier, pal," Ford muttered.

Ten minutes later, Deputy Flores's voice broke through the radio again. "Car floating…"

Ford turned up the volume. Flores was breaking up, and Ford could barely hear him. But two words came through loud and clear: *Little* and *red*.

The blood in his veins turned to ice. Without another thought, Ford grabbed his hat and rushed to the closet, where he grabbed a spotlight. He might need it to scour the creek's banks and trees.

He opened the door. The rain hit him in the face, but he barely felt it as he ran to his truck. With shaking fingers, he turned the key in the ignition, and then he peeled out.

The rain hit his windshield like a wall of water, rendering his wipers practically useless. It was a bit over a mile to

Wailing Woman Creek. In good weather, it was maybe a five-minute drive.

Ford made it in two, and then sat in his truck, staring in shock. If it seemed like he'd come up on Wailing Woman too quickly, it's because he had. It was a raging torrent of swirling brown water, well outside of its bank. He got out of the truck and walked as close as he dared. Claire's car—and it *was* Claire's car, he just knew it—had been seen *floating*. It would be way downstream. Claire would be trapped inside, unless she'd climbed out. People tended to panic and climb on the roofs of their vehicles when stranded at water crossings. What if she'd done that?

He turned to search the bank.

He felt crazed, and his thoughts came in images that tore his heart out. What if she was trapped in debris underwater? Or lying cold and lifeless along the shore?

He shut his eyes. Clasped a hand over them. But it didn't stop what he saw.

Watch Abby while I'm at work. Don't let her go down to the creek.

He didn't have time for flashbacks. He forced his eyes open. He had to remain in the present.

A hand clasped his arm, and he spun, eyes wide.

"What the actual hell?" Claire yelled. "You drove right past me!"

She was soaking wet. Her hair was a tangled mess. She had a dirt smudge on her face, a bloody lip, and smeared makeup. He grabbed her and pulled her close, feeling the intense shivers that wracked her body. "Are you okay?"

"S-s-seriously, Ford. I was on the s-s-side of the road waving you down. I had to freaking ch-ch-chase—"

He squeezed tighter. She was half-drowned, possibly hypothermic, probably in shock, and one hundred percent pissed off that she hadn't been able to hail a pickup truck in the middle of a flash flood with the delicate lift of her finger.

Warmth spread throughout his body, even though the springtime rain was cold.

"My car is g-g-gone!" Claire wailed.

"Good," he said. "It was a stupid car."

Claire gasped and pushed him away. Her nostrils flared, her eyebrows dove down in a menacing glare, and dammit, she was sexy as hell.

"You," she said, with a measured pause, "are a j-j-jerk."

Probably. But she had no business driving that little car. It was most likely tangled up in a tree somewhere...*and she could have been in it.* Was her life so full of rainbows and unicorn farts that she didn't understand what could have happened?

Claire's life was untouched by tragedy. Hell, it was untouched by *unpleasantness.* She probably couldn't fathom the reality of what she'd barely escaped. She lived in a fairy tale.

"What were you thinking trying to cross the creek during a flood watch? Did the piece of crap stall out on you?"

"It's not a piece of c-c-crap and I'm not sure it s-s-stalled out on me. I might have run out—"

She shut her sweet little pie hole like a steel trap and stared at him defiantly.

"You ran out of *gas*?" Shit. Who ran out of gas? Like, who *did* that? "Get in the truck," he ordered.

"No."

He recognized the tone, and he wasn't in the mood for it. He wanted away from this water *now.* This was no time for Claire to dig in her heels.

A sharp pain stabbed him between the eyes. She knew he

couldn't leave her here. It wasn't like anyone else was coming along. She was literally up Shit Creek without a paddle, or a car, or shoes, for that matter. "Claire. You're cold, wet, and barefoot. You've got no car. Get in the truck."

"No."

The last drop of patience left his body. Without another word—from him, anyway—Ford bent over and grabbed Claire just below her ass, straightened up with her over his shoulder, and while she did the classic *beat man on back with fists of fury* move, he carried her to his pickup.

Chapter

Four

☙

The man had hoisted her over his shoulder like a sack of flour. And then he'd plunked her on the seat of his truck before buckling her in like a child and angrily shutting the door.

He was a horrible rescuer. Would it kill him to offer any amount of comfort after she'd nearly died?

She'd entertained many reunion scenarios over the past few days. She'd practiced speeches, lectures, and various tirades, along with expressions of aloofness, as if she were trying to remember where she'd met him.

Ford Jarvis? The name does ring a bell...

He'd definitely rung her bell. Multiple bells. And that was all fine and dandy. But he hadn't stopped there. Oh hell, no. He'd taken her home to meet his mother. Was she crazy for thinking he'd been serious about their relationship? Most men didn't take a woman home for Thanksgiving just because they were currently ringing her bell. Did they?

She'd fantasized about ignoring him. Slapping him. Kissing him.

She had not prepared for any scenario where Ford saved her from a flash flood while calling her car stupid and indicating it was something she and it might have in common.

"Lift up your legs," Ford said.

She lifted her legs, and Ford dug around beneath the seat before pulling out a blanket. He put it around her with a gentleness that didn't match his voice, and Claire felt a bit of resolve melting and pooling around her feet.

Ford started the truck and backed it away from the raging creek. Claire let out a ragged breath. She was ready to put distance between her and Wailing Woman.

The truck's headlights illuminated fallen branches through the onslaught of nearly horizontal rain, but they barreled right over them, heading to higher ground.

Claire risked a glance at her savior. His wet hair shimmered in the dim light of the truck's dashboard. Water dripped off the brim of his worn cowboy hat. Strong chin, straight nose, and full, luscious lips.

They were still silent when they arrived at the fork in the road. Ford's cabin was to the right, her little trailer to the left. "I've moved into—"

"Beau told me."

Claire had known Beau and his twin brother Bryce her entire life. They'd been raised right here on the ranch. Their daddy had been the foreman for Rancho Cañada Verde for twenty-seven years. Since his retirement, they'd had trouble finding another reliable foreman.

It was hard to get ranch hands to settle down, even on a ranch like theirs.

"Beau was gossiping about me?"

"Like a clucking hen."

"What else did he say?"

"Nothing important that I can remember."

Claire narrowed her eyes. If Beau had told Ford about her Sizzle dates, she was going to strangle a cowboy.

Ford turned left toward Miss Daisy. "Why on earth are you camping in a trailer? Your parents' house is huge."

"I'm not *camping*. I live in Miss Daisy."

"Miss Daisy?"

"My trailer."

Ford looked at her like she'd grown a second head. "Did you name your car, too?"

"No."

Yes. Poor Rosie!

"But *why*?" Ford asked.

Why did she name inanimate objects? Or why had she moved from her parents' house?

"None of your business."

"Okay. I was just making conversation. I don't really—"

"I needed privacy," she snapped.

Ford raised an eyebrow but didn't say anything. He didn't need to. For a guy with approximately three facial expressions, he sure could express a lot with that dang eyebrow. He was wondering what she needed privacy *for*.

When they'd had their…*thing*…Ford had lived in the bunkhouse. No privacy whatsoever. And Claire had lived in her parents' house, where there were plenty of doors with locks, but it would have been awkward as hell to waltz down for breakfast in the morning with a ranch hand in tow.

They'd had to get creative. Hay barns. Horse barns. The bed of Ford's pickup truck. Their favorite spot had been the ruins of the old stone chapel.

Ford shifted in his seat and yanked the brim of his hat down low.

"I can't believe you might have run out of gas. Don't Mini Coopers have dummy lights? Or do their owners think they're too smart for those?"

She glared at him. He was drenched, but he didn't shiver. In fact, it looked like he had steam rising off his slick arms as he turned down the short lane leading to her trailer.

Claire resisted the urge to ask him what was chapping his ass. Did it matter? Nope.

"I'm not used to the gas mileage the Mini Cooper gets, and I miscalculated."

Ford shifted gears and the truck groaned. "Where the hell were you anyway? You know better than to go out on a night like this."

"I had a date," she said.

Ford stopped the truck. "I can't believe it."

"Oh, you can believe it all right. I've had *lots* of dates—"

"Claire, shut up and open your eyes."

She opened her eyes, but she was unsuccessful in shutting her mouth. There seemed to be a small river between them and her trailer. There'd never been a small river there before.

"What is that?" she asked.

Ford got out and walked to the front of the truck. He stopped and looked around for a minute or so, shaking his head the entire time, and then climbed back in.

"Well?" Claire asked. "Can we get across it?"

"I can't see how deep it is, but by the way it's moving, I'd say it's a pretty good cut."

"What does that mean?"

"It means you're not going home tonight."

"That's ridiculous. It's just a bit of runoff."

He began backing up.

There were risk takers, and there was Ford.

"Can you just take me to my parents'?" she asked.

"They're on the other side of Wailing Woman."

"I know that," she snapped. "Let's go up Harper's Hill."

"It won't do any good. With Wailing Woman that far out of its banks, the bridge past Harper's will be underwater." Ford sighed. "You're coming home with me."

Her heart pounded as she tried to come up with an alternative plan. But everything he said was true, and there wasn't one.

Excitement ran circles around irritation and worry. Because even after nearly being washed away in a flood, her body reacted strongly to the idea of spending the night with Ford.

But she could never go down that road again. All he'd wanted was a good time.

And she'd fallen in love.

* * *

Ford hoped his exterior didn't match his interior, which was a jumbled mass of nerves and adrenaline.

They were *not* going to have sex tonight. He had to keep his wits about him. And his clothes on.

Easier said than done around Claire.

He'd hoped time and distance would lessen the intensity of the attraction, but he glanced at the seat between them, and it seemed he'd unconsciously scooted closer to her.

It's like his charge was negative and hers was positive.

Although, Claire was hugging the door. Maybe he was the only one feeling the tug.

He followed the winding path through the cedar trees to

the foreman's cabin. A side glance at Claire confirmed that the chatter he heard was her teeth. He'd get a fire going as soon as they got inside.

He wanted to gather her up in his arms. But he couldn't. If anything, he needed to be brusque. A little harsh, even. Otherwise Claire would melt all over him, and then he was in trouble.

The woods thinned to a small clearing, revealing the cabin sitting in the center. The windows glowed. "The lights are back on," he said.

"That's a good sign, right? Maybe things are letting up."

"Maybe."

If he was going to spend the evening with Claire Kowalski, he'd prefer to do it in a well-lit room.

The rain had slowed, and Ford got out of the truck to check the rain gauge nailed to a fence post. He was curious as hell to see how much rain they'd gotten, and he wasn't anxious to get inside the cabin with a wet, sexy Claire. His hands were damp, and he couldn't tell if it was rain or nervous sweat.

Ford squinted at the gauge. They'd gotten two inches in about an hour. He got back in the truck. Claire shivered like a cartoon character whose limbs had turned to ice. She glared at him from beneath her matted mass of wet hair. "Must you lollygag so?"

Ford didn't know what that meant, but he had a sneaking suspicion, so with a barely concealed grin he closed the door, buckled his seat belt, adjusted the heater vents, and drove slowly through the gate, which now that he thought about it, really didn't need closing.

He put the truck in park.

Where was she going to sleep?

He opened his door and climbed out of the truck.

What the hell was she going to wear after getting out of those wet clothes?

He closed the gate.

Should he check the rain gauge again?

A door slammed. Claire's bedraggled figure, illuminated by headlights, stomped its way up the lane.

Ford ran after her. "Hey! You're barefoot. Get back in the truck."

Claire spun and faced him. "I wouldn't want my hypothermia to interfere with your meandering around checking on things."

"You're going to step on a mesquite thorn. Stop being silly and get back in the truck."

Her nostrils flared at the sound of *silly*.

"I'm halfway to the cabin," she said. "It makes no sense to walk back to the truck on my poor delicate feet when they could take me to the porch in the same amount of time." She started back up the lane, but Ford jumped in front of her.

"There's only one thing to do that makes any sense." He'd already done it once tonight, might as well do it again. He took a step toward her.

"Don't you dare."

They were way beyond dares, and Ford had her over his shoulder in two seconds flat. She did more than beat on his back this time, and an errant foot grazed his crotch. He grabbed her ankle. "Stop acting crazy."

It was a good thing she'd lost her shoes. Otherwise he'd have said that about five octaves higher.

She quit fighting and went limp. Then she shuddered, and Ford thought she might be crying. Well, hell. He couldn't put her down barefoot, but he didn't have to carry her like a sack of potatoes, either. He shifted and she slid down his chest. He stopped her just before her feet reached the ground and pressed her against the front of his body.

Instead of kicking him in the shins, Claire wrapped her arms around his neck.

That felt nice.

She gazed at him with a little sigh.

"Ford," Claire whispered. "What are you doing—"

"This," he said, putting her down so that her bare feet rested on the tops of his boots. Then he leaned over, crooked his arm behind her knees, and lifted her in a more dignified manner.

He'd just dodged the first bullet of the evening. And dammit, he'd fired the shot himself.

Chapter Five

🥀

Claire was being carried through the doorway. *Across the threshold.*

She'd imagined the moment many times, only in her stupid fantasy she'd been dry, warm, and perfectly draped in a Vera Wang wedding gown. The same fantasy had Ford making love to her on a petal-strewn mattress surrounded by candles instead of plunking her unceremoniously in the middle of the room.

"I haven't been in the foreman's cabin since I was a teenager," Claire said.

Ford removed his hat and tossed it on the table. His dark hair was mostly dry, but the rest of him was wringing wet.

He gazed at her with his hazel eyes, which were often the only feature to hold any expression on Ford's typically stoic face. He could laugh without cracking a smile. He could question everything you thought you knew with a single raised eyebrow. He could say *I love you* with a glance.

Except he never had said it. And she'd only imagined having seen it.

If there was one thing Claire had learned from her relationship with Ford, it was that she was horrible at reading people.

Ford's eyes traveled the length of her body. Her nipples, perky from the chill, were clearly visible through the wet blue silk, and they hardened even more from the heat of his gaze.

When his eyes made their way back to hers, they seemed darker and more intense. There was a slight flush beneath his scruffy five o'clock shadow.

Suddenly, he grabbed a towel off the counter and dropped it on the floor. "Here, stand on this," he said gruffly.

A small puddle had amassed at her feet.

Ford shed his flannel shirt, revealing a white T-shirt plastered to his chest. "I imagine you'll be needing a warm shower."

Or a cold one.

Ford's chest was as familiar a landscape as Rancho Cañada Verde's back forty. Claire's mind traced its angles and planes just as thoroughly as her fingers had once done. She swallowed, thinking about how firm and fit those abs were, and although she couldn't see it now, she knew there was a delicious trail of hair dipping into the waistband of his clinging jeans.

"Is it smaller than you remember it?" Ford asked. "Or bigger?"

"*What?*" Claire asked. Was there a cartoonish thought bubble floating over her head?

"The cabin," Ford said. "Bigger or smaller than you remember it?"

"Oh." She looked around at the sparse surroundings. A

single couch. A small table and two chairs. Faded curtains. "Smaller, I guess."

When the Montgomery family had lived here, the cabin had been cheerful and cluttered, yet somehow, even with the two rowdy Montgomery twins wrestling all over it, it had seemed much larger.

Claire stepped onto the towel, irritated by how quickly her thoughts strayed into the danger zone. But there was some kind of weird sexual chemistry between her and Ford. Two years ago, she'd thought it was something more than chemistry, but she'd been wrong.

Ford turned to hang his wet shirt on the coat rack in the corner. Claire watched the muscles of his back flex. She thought about how he'd effortlessly picked her up—even though she wasn't exactly a dainty wisp of a thing—and the silky warmth that had taken over her body focused all of its attention between her legs.

Ford walked briskly to the bathroom and turned on the shower.

Lightning flashed.

Storms like this were surely triggers for Ford, even though it had probably been two decades since his little sister had drowned.

"You're shaking like a leaf," he said, coming out of the bathroom. "You might be in shock."

He tossed a log in the fireplace and stared at it like he could light it with his eyes. "You just came pretty close to dying. You know that, right?"

"I almost had to swim," she admitted in a low voice. "Although, I doubt I'd have stood a chance in that current..."

Ford drew in a sudden breath. "No, you wouldn't have. Now go take a hot shower. Just toss your clothes out, and I'll throw them in the dryer."

"It's silk," she said.

Ford stared blankly.

"It's ruined. Do you have something I can wear?"

Ford nodded. "I'll grab you something."

She headed for the bathroom, thinking about how stupid she'd been. Tonight could have ended very badly. How could she have forgotten to check her gas gauge? What had she been thinking about when she drove into that low-water crossing with the needle on *Empty*?

The store. She'd been thinking about Petal Pushers and fantasizing about the many possibilities...

Fantasizing. She'd also been thinking about Ford.

And it had literally nearly killed her.

She'd been warned time and again about flash floods. From the safety of a high bluff, she'd once seen the typically calm and meandering Rio Verde turn into a torrential wall of destruction. Her dad had taken her there specifically for that purpose, having predicted the event based on a week's worth of thunderstorms.

See that, princess? That's why you don't ever mess around with low-water crossings.

The radio screeched and stuttered and Ford's head whipped around. He went over and began fiddling with various knobs.

Claire went into the bathroom and started the business of peeling off her wet clothes. The silk dress was ruined, so she dropped it into the trash. Then she stepped into the shower and beneath the warm spray with a sigh.

By the time she'd gotten rid of the chills, the water felt a tad cooler than it had when she'd started. The water heater was small, and Ford would probably want a hot shower, too. She turned off the water, grabbed a towel, and dried off.

Ford knocked on the door, and she jerked so suddenly that her head spun.

"Yes?"

"I have a flannel shirt you can borrow."

"Thank you. That'll be fine."

The door opened a crack, and Ford's arm popped in with the shirt. Claire snatched it, and Ford yanked his hand back and slammed the door.

He hadn't even sneaked a peek.

Claire picked her panties up off the floor. Like everything else she'd had on this evening, they were soggy wet. Still, she made a go of it and slipped a foot in a leg hole. The fabric stuck to her skin and generally refused to cooperate, so she draped them over the side of the tub. She'd have to go commando.

Clutching the soft flannel shirt by its hem, she held it snugly in place and stepped out of the bathroom just as the room went dark. "Ford?"

A beam of light hit her in the face. She let go of her shirt to shield her eyes. "What the hell?"

"Sorry," Ford said, lowering the beam. "Electricity is out again."

He stuck the flashlight in his armpit and worked to light the mantle of a small propane lantern. Once that was taken care of, he motioned for Claire to sit on the couch.

Smoothing the tail of the shirt against her rear end, she sat and looked around the room, now bathed in the glow of the lantern and the roaring fire.

Lightning flashed and she jumped.

"Everything will be okay," Ford said in a soothing voice.

"I'm fine," she said. "The lightning startled me."

"I was talking to Oscar."

Claire rolled her eyes as Ford awkwardly patted the

wincing cat. "Leave that poor thing alone. He can barely tolerate that piss-poor display of affection."

"It's not affection. It's pity."

The side eye he gave her made Claire wonder if he'd meant the statement in regard to her.

She picked up a cushion and crushed it against her chest. "I like what you've done with the place," she said.

Ford looked over with a glint of humor in his eyes.

Ranch foremen weren't known for their decorating skills, but Ford was particularly hopeless.

"Are you hungry? I can heat up some corn chowder on the gas stove."

Claire's stomach growled. She hadn't finished her salmon before abandoning the date.

"I don't know," Claire said. "I ate on my date." The *ha!* she wanted to add was drowned out by another horrific growl from her stomach.

One corner of Ford's mouth turned up. "Is that a yes?"

"Maybe I'll have a—"

"And I'm sorry your date sucked."

"What makes you think my date sucked? It was *ideal*. The guy was really cute, very successful, and he took me to a super expensive steak place."

"Since when was a super expensive steak place *ideal* for a woman who doesn't like to eat meat? And as for how I know your date sucked, you've been to Austin on an *ideal* date, driven all the way home to Big Verde, survived a flash flood, and then used up every drop of my hot water"—he looked at the clock over the stove—"all before midnight."

"It was our first date," she muttered.

"Must have been a doozy," Ford said. "Our first date sure as hell didn't end by midnight."

Claire controlled her facial features with difficulty. Their first *date* had ended at six in the morning when the wrangler walked into the stable to find her and Ford wearing nothing but hay, smiles, and an Indian blanket.

* * *

Ford's heart pounded in his chest as he watched the memory of their first date play across Claire's face. She never could hide what she was thinking, and he never could resist watching the fascinating facets of her thoughts. Damned near everything about her was fascinating.

"Going out with him again?" he asked, hoping it sounded like he didn't care.

"You're quite curious."

So, no, then. If Claire had a second date with the guy, she'd have said so with glee and a middle finger. He stole a glance at her as he ladled chowder into a small bowl. The glow of the fire lit up her face and made her hair dance.

He put her bowl of soup on the table, already feeling his resolve to remain distant and brusque melt away. It was so easy to fall into a familiar pattern of chitchat with Claire, even though he typically wasn't much of a talker and the topic was making his blood boil. "Where'd you meet this guy? The one who tried to feed you meat."

He knew where she'd met him. Sizzle. But would Glass Slipper admit it?

Claire stood up and stretched, raising her arms above her head. He only had a side view, but it was a good one. Her breasts stretched the limits of his flannel shirt. And the hem rose higher and higher until...

No underwear. The woman wore no underwear.

Claire suddenly dropped her arms and grasped the shirt's hem, plastering it against her legs. Ford turned toward the sink as if he hadn't seen anything, and really, he hadn't. Just creamy thigh and smooth hip and...

Claire daintily cleared her throat behind him, and he heard her scoot the chair to the table. "Well?" he asked. "You meet him at a bar?"

"No," Claire snapped. "Who has time for that?"

"Church?"

He grinned as Claire sighed loudly.

"It was a blind date."

"Who set you up? Anyone I know?"

"I don't think any of this is your business," Claire said haughtily. "And aren't you going to eat? Saving a damsel in distress must make you hungry."

"You saved yourself," he said. "And I already ate. I do want a shower, though. You need anything else before I get in?"

"No," she said, picking up the spoon. The steam wafted up and she inhaled deeply, closing her eyes. "I've really missed your chowder."

But then, as if remembering all the things associated with him that she didn't miss, she opened her eyes, furrowed her brow, and dipped her spoon into her bowl.

"You miss anything else?" he asked.

Jesus, why had he asked that? Maybe he was a glutton for punishment.

Claire paused, spoon halfway to her mouth, as if pondering the question.

"Yes," she said. "I miss poor Oscar. And I hate that you're all he's got for company."

Ford glanced at the corner where Oscar was currently licking his asshole. It seemed that Ford was the one in poor company, not the other way around.

Sensing he was being discussed by a beautiful female

and not fully comprehending his lack of balls, Oscar jumped his scrawny butt up onto Claire's lap.

"Shoo," Ford said, moving to knock Oscar off those luscious legs.

"Leave him alone," Claire said, rubbing the cat's head. "And this is how you pet a cat, by the way."

"I know how to pet a cat, darlin'."

He hadn't meant that to sound dirty. But he'd had absolutely no trouble making her purr.

"I thought you said you needed a shower."

Boy, did he. A cold one. "If you want to lie down, you can take the bed. I'll take the couch."

Claire shrugged and spooned some more chowder into her mouth, and Ford responded with a grunt before heading for the bathroom, where he closed the door and leaned against it in relief.

Maybe he could just sleep in here. It was kind of cozy. He could put a blanket on the floor and if he curled up just so, there was enough space between the shower and toilet—

Something pink and lacy was draped over the tub.

Ford picked up the small slip of silk and lace. Claire's panties. He swallowed. The woman liked her fancy underwear. He hung them up on the shower curtain rod, and then he stepped into the shower spray, unleashing a torrent of curse words when the icy cold water hit his back.

She'd used up all his hot water.

Twenty minutes later he emerged, satisfied that every part of him had been thoroughly prunified and rendered useless. He hadn't thought to bring any clean clothes in with him, so he wrapped a towel around his waist and quietly eased the bathroom door open.

He tiptoed out. The door to the bedroom was closed. He jiggled the knob.

Locked.

He turned and looked at the short, uncomfortable couch. With a frown, he grabbed a blanket from the closet. Then he shunned the couch and sat on the floor in front of the fireplace. After a few minutes of watching the flames dance, he stretched his cowboy ass out right there on the ground.

He shifted on the hard floor.

Maybe coming back to Rancho Cañada Verde was a mistake. He laughed out loud.

Of course it was.

Chapter

Six

❦

Claire awoke to sunshine and birdsong. She yawned and stretched. It was Saturday, and she didn't have to be at Petal Pushers until noon.

Maybe she'd sink back into the silky sheets...

Her eyes flew open. The sheets did not feel silky.

She sat straight up. *Not her sheets.* She looked around. *Not her room.* She peeked through the window. *Not her outside.*

Memories smacked into her like a freight train—bad date, stalled car, flash flood, pissed-off cowboy—and she groaned. Not a pleasant way to begin the day.

She looked at her phone. Still no signal. The tower had probably been hit by lightning. She flipped the switch on the lamp, and nothing happened. Either the lightbulb was toast or the electricity was still out.

She tossed off the non-silky sheets and padded to the window. Brilliant blue sky. No sign at all of last night's destruction, except for some massive puddles and a few tree limbs on the ground. She absolutely loved the Texas Hill Country after a good soaking, and part of her longed to open the window and inhale the crisp air. But last night they'd received more than a good soaking. This was no time to fling open windows and sing like a princess.

With a sigh, she unlocked the door.

Judging from the sun, it was well past seven. Ford rose before dawn and tended to look down his nose at anybody who didn't. He'd probably already had his breakfast and assessed the damage from the storm, and if Wailing Woman was passable, was already hard at work somewhere on the ranch.

But there was no coffee aroma when she opened the door. All the blinds were shut up tight, and it was dark in the room.

Claire looked down, and *oh!* Ford lay stretched out on the hard, stone floor, either dead or sound asleep (from the soft snoring sounds it was the latter) and naked as a jaybird. Oscar was curled up on his stomach, rising and falling with every deep breath Ford took.

Should she go back in her room and wait until Ford woke up and got dressed? That was probably best. She turned to head back to the bedroom, but her bare foot squeaked on the rock floor. It was enough to startle Oscar, who jumped and ran as if a gun had gone off.

Ford sat up with eyes as wide as saucers, adorably mussed hair, and a stubbled chin hanging open in confusion.

He did not seem to realize he was naked or that Claire was even in the room.

She cleared her throat, and he looked in her direction. Slowly, his eyes focused.

"Jesus. What are you doing here?"

Claire ticked off the acclimating facts. "Rancho Cañada Verde. Flood. Rancher's daughter."

Clarity took over Ford's features, hardening them to their usual stony-faced mask. He stood swiftly, and when he did, everything was all out there in the open, radiating enthusiasm because Ford's crankiness hadn't worked its way south.

Ford gasped and comically spun around to hide himself, giving her a glorious view of his backside, which was no less impressive than the front side. Horseback riding made for some nice thighs and buttocks.

He grabbed a towel off the floor and tossed it up. He caught it in one hand and wrapped it snugly around his waist while glancing over his shoulder. "You could turn around."

"It's not like I haven't seen it before."

Oscar poked his head out from beneath the couch, looked at Ford's glowering face, and ducked back under again.

Ford stomped to the kitchen sink and filled the coffee carafe with water. "What time is it?"

Claire opened a blind to let some sunshine in. Maybe it would chase away the storm cloud simmering over Ford's head. "Somebody wakes up cranky, and I have no idea what time it is. Also? The electricity is still out, so good luck with that coffeepot."

"Shit," Ford said. He glanced at the clock above the stove. "It's nearly nine o'clock."

"When's the last time you slept this late?"

"Never." The towel slipped a bit as Ford reached into an upper cabinet. "I saw an old stovetop percolator up here somewhere..."

Oscar slinked out from beneath the couch and rubbed against Claire's ankles. Next, he visited Ford's, but he was shaken off with muttered curses.

Oscar wasn't having it. He quivered, assumed the attack

position, and then pounced on a stupidly unsuspecting Ford, snagging his claw on the towel.

The percolator made a horrible clatter when it hit the floor, and Oscar exploded in a mass of claws, fur, and terrycloth towel. He ricocheted off the walls, dragging the towel behind him. And in the middle of it all stood a very naked Ford, clenching his jaw and making no attempt to cover himself.

Claire masked a giggle with a fake sneeze. At least, she tried to mask it.

"You think this is funny?"

She snorted.

Ford reached over just in time to catch a lamp as Oscar shot past, towel snapping every which way. "Would you try and grab him?"

Claire made a grab at Oscar as he shot under the couch, missing him by a mile.

The towel poked out from beneath the couch, and Ford rushed over and stomped on it. Then he bent and slowly pulled it out, dragging the cat with it.

"Dumbass cat," he said, picking the animal up by the scruff of its neck and unsnagging his claw.

Claire leaned over to pet Oscar just as Ford straightened, and it brought them dang near nose to penis.

Claire froze.

Ford froze.

And then one part of him moved with enthusiasm.

* * *

He could feel her warm breath on his cock.

Move, asshole. Take a step back. Then another. And then run for the hills.

Every hair on his body stood at attention. Every nerve ending was lit up in anticipation of what might be coming. His skin literally vibrated.

If he were to gently place a hand on Claire's head right now, he'd be enveloped by heaven. His mind would go blank. His thoughts and worries would disappear. Claire would reduce him to a mass of nerve endings and pleasure receptors incapable of reason.

He felt himself slipping away...

His brain was disengaging from his physical body...

Claire moved suddenly, and *boom!* She shoved him. *Hard.* He took two steps back and stomped on Oscar's tail.

The cat screeched and shot across the room.

Ford's consciousness landed rudely back in his body and he covered himself with his hands as blood vacated his penis to invade his cheeks. Oscar had the nerve to slink back over and rub against his ankles. Ford gave him a slight shove with his foot.

Claire gasped. "What did you just do?"

Ford couldn't form words. And anyway, which action was she referring to? The one where he'd shoved the cat with his foot? Or the one where he'd unwittingly lined himself up for a blowjob?

This was no way to begin his stint on Rancho Cañada Verde.

Claire glared at him, and his cheeks heated up even more. But whatever the hell he'd just been doing, he hadn't been doing it by himself.

"What about you? What did you just do?"

"Shoved a naked man out of my face."

"I wasn't in your face on purpose, and it took you a full ten seconds to do it, which was unnecessary, because I was about to back up."

Two of those three things were true.

It was clear that whatever attraction he and Claire had had for each other—the one that rendered both of them incapable of reasonable thought—was still here. They'd both just gone loco.

Now Claire's cheeks were pink.

Her eyes darted to where his hands cupped his goods, and goddammit, the goods started to react. His dick was like a teeter-totter around Claire...*up and down, up and down.*

He leaned over, picked up the towel, and wrapped it around his waist. Then he spun on his heel to march into his bedroom and find the nearest pair of jeans.

Unfortunately, he tripped over the cat.

Claire probably got an eyeful of cheeks and balls as he went down. Maybe that's what made her gasp. Or possibly, it was the horrible sound his head made when it hit the floor because he couldn't break his fall without dropping the towel.

Did Claire see clouds of stars floating in the air, too? Or was it just him?

Claire knelt at his side. "Are you okay?"

He caught a glimpse of smooth thigh and realized she wasn't wearing much more than he was. Still gripping the towel, he pushed himself up into a sitting position. "I'm fine."

"I'm not convinced," Claire said.

Fine was subjective. Was he able to climb five flights of stairs right now? Probably not. Could he crawl to his bedroom and put on some goddam pants? Yes. And that was his current definition of *fine*.

Claire sucked in a deep breath. "Your lip is bleeding."

She touched it with her fingers. Her blue eyes were

filled with genuine concern, and Ford swore everything was starting to feel better just from her fingers brushing against his skin.

"That's because I just kissed a rock floor."

Oscar sat in the corner, twitching his tail and looking fairly satisfied with himself.

"How many fingers am I holding up?" Claire asked, wiggling two fingers in front of Ford's face.

He waved her hand away. "Stop it."

"Let me help you up at least."

Ford rolled his eyes, but he didn't jerk his arm away when she grasped it, and he let her help him stand.

"Can you manage to get yourself dressed?"

Ford stilled. Gave her the side-eye, and quietly said, "Are you offering to help me?"

Claire's cheeks turned even pinker. "No. I don't really think I should."

This was not going to be an easy six weeks.

Ford limped into his bedroom, which still smelled like Claire, and glanced at the indention in the pillow where her head had been. He stood in the silence for a moment, just feeling her. It's like she'd left an echo in the room.

He shook his head. Shrugged it off. It was damn near ten o'clock. The water had surely receded enough to get over the bridge at Harper's. Everyone on the ranch was probably already hard at work.

And what was Ford's excuse for being late?

He'd spent the night with the rancher's daughter before oversleeping and then getting into a literal catfight.

They hadn't *done anything*—thank God—but Gerome wouldn't know that. What a way to make an impression.

He wandered over to the dresser and pulled a pair of

jeans out of a drawer. He snapped them three times in the air (scorpions always came in threes) just in case an unwelcome visitor had made itself at home. He stepped in with his left leg first, because doing it the other way around was bad luck. And he'd had enough of that already.

Chapter Seven

❦

Claire pulled at the hem of Ford's flannel shirt. It wasn't like she could go anywhere like this. "Can you lend me some jeans?"

Ford sighed and yanked open a drawer, grabbed a pair of jeans, and tossed them to her. Then he opened another drawer and snagged a white T-shirt. "Here," he said, tossing that, as well.

"I hate to ask, but I lost my shoes—"

He nodded at a pair of boots in the corner. "They'll be too big, but they'll do until you get home."

Claire held the waistband of the jeans out. "Speaking of big…"

Ford grabbed a belt off the dresser and pulled a knife out of his pocket. "This is an old belt. I'll poke an extra hole or two in it."

Two minutes later, Claire was alone in the room. She turned so she could see her derriere in the mirror over Ford's dresser. The jeans actually weren't that bad. Big in the waist, but the rear view was pretty decent.

She tightened the belt, rolled the jeans up at the ankles, and finished the look by putting the flannel back on and tying it in a knot. She struck a couple of poses. All she needed to complete the sexy farmer's daughter look was a stick of straw to suck on.

Although if she sucked on anything right now it would probably cause Ford to have an aneurism.

Their sexual attraction was still there. Just as big as ever. And speaking of big, they'd had a stupidly close call. And Ford was right on the money about her hesitation when his penis had ended up mere inches from her mouth.

She'd hesitated, all right.

It would have been so easy to give in to temptation. She could remember exactly what Ford felt like in her hands, what he tasted like on her tongue. But mostly, she remembered the sound of his breath catching at the thrill of his release. The melting that followed.

She'd never felt about anyone the way she'd felt about him. And this meant that her heart was still vulnerable in his hands. He'd crushed it once. She couldn't let him do it again.

Distance. They needed distance.

Buying Petal Pushers would definitely give her something to do that would keep her away from Ford. There was so much to do! She'd need financing, suppliers, a marketing plan...

It was exciting, and none of it involved a cowboy or being in the presence of a cowboy or accidentally landing on top of (or beneath) a cowboy.

She squared her shoulders, breathed in a big old whopping sense of purpose, and walked happily outside, oversized boots slapping on the ground like flippers. The air was cool and the sun was shining bright. There was even a rainbow!

Rainbows were good luck.

Ford stood at the stable gate. Coco was on the other side, and the two of them looked up as if she'd just interrupted a conversation. Ford's eyes drifted above her head. "That damn horseshoe over the door won't stay upright. Do you mind flipping it over?"

Claire straightened it. There wasn't a cowboy alive who could tolerate an upside-down horseshoe, with or without a lucky rainbow.

"Hop in the truck," Ford said. "We'll head to your folks' place."

Claire climbed in. She was anxious to get to Petal Pushers and scheme with Maggie, but she might have to spend the day dealing with piddly-assed insurance details over her car instead. And she'd need a new set of wheels.

She sighed. Maybe the Mini Cooper wasn't the most practical decision she'd ever made. But after a lifetime of driving ugly white ranch trucks around, she'd wanted something fun and sporty.

"Listen, I've been thinking," Ford said.

He was wearing the hat she liked. The one with the turned-down brim that made him look like a badass. But she wasn't going to think about his hat or the way his jeans stretched tightly across his muscular thighs or the way the morning sun turned his hazel eyes green.

"I heard about your car getting washed away from Deputy Flores," Ford said. "Over the emergency radio scanner. And I'm wondering if he came to the same conclusion I did."

"That people who drive small cars are stupid?"

"No. That it was *your* car. Because, you know, not too many people around here drive little red Mini Coopers."

Claire's heart nearly stopped. "Does that mean—"

"He would have told your parents."

A wave of nausea rolled through Claire. Her parents probably thought she was dead! She pulled out her phone and stared at it. Useless.

"We still don't have cell service," Ford said. "And I don't like the way Coco was acting. He kept looking in the direction of the creek, like maybe he sensed something was off."

"What are you saying?"

He glanced at Claire. "I think this might have been more than a bad storm."

"Oh, Ford, please hurry."

"I am, darlin'." Ford's jaw was clenched. And his knuckles were white from gripping the steering wheel. He sounded calm and in control, but it was obvious he was just as anxious as she was.

"Do you think the crossing is still underwater?" she asked.

"Yes," Ford said. "I'm headed to Harper's Hill. It's higher."

The seconds felt like hours as they drove the backroads to Harper's Hill. The truck struggled with the muddy inclines, and water stood along both sides of the road. Judging from the debris—some was even stuck in the trees—the water had been very high.

They came over a hill, and Ford screeched the truck to a stop. The road in the dip below was completely underwater.

"Shit," Ford said.

"Can we get through it?" Claire asked. "We've got high clearance in this truck."

"Nice to know you learned your lesson about driving into water," Ford said.

"But Ford—"

"What would be the point of getting through that? Look at the bridge, Claire."

Claire looked in the direction Ford was pointing. The brown, muddy river water swirled in the distance, way out of its bank. Shouldn't she be able to see the iron trusses of the old bridge from here? "I don't see anything," she said.

"That's because it's gone."

Claire sat up and leaned into the windshield. This couldn't be right. "Maybe it's past the next hill," she said. The landscape, covered in water, looked so foreign.

"Nope," Ford said. "That's the river. And the bridge is washed away."

"But that can't be—"

The whirring sound of a helicopter drowned out Claire's words. She stuck her head out the window and looked over the treetops. A news helicopter hovered above them.

Ford started to back up.

"Ford, if the Harper's Hill bridge is out, there's no way we can get across Wailing Woman."

"We're going to Wailing Woman anyway."

"But why?"

"That's where they'll be looking for you." He reached over and squeezed her hand. Just once. "I can't stand the thought of it."

His Adam's apple appeared to get stuck when he tried to swallow. Surely, his mind was wandering to Abby's drowning, and how they'd searched for her.

Claire squeezed his hand back, and Ford nodded before putting the truck in drive.

"Even if we can't get across, they'll see us," Ford said. "They'll know you're safe, and that's what matters."

* * *

It wasn't often that things were actually worse than Ford expected them to be—he wasn't a ray of sunshine by anyone's standards—but this was one of those times. Seeing the bridge washed away at Harper's Hill had been a shock. That old bridge had no doubt withstood many a flood.

But not this one.

Claire shivered next to him. Damn, he knew the agony her folks must be experiencing. He'd had to see his own mom go through it, with a much worse outcome.

It didn't take long until they came to the waterline of the flood.

"Holy cow," Claire said. "Ford, if you hadn't come along when you did—"

Ford swallowed. He hadn't *come along*. He'd headed straight for her like a bat out of hell. With his heart pounding and his mind racing and... He could still taste the relief. Still feel the way his knees had struggled to hold him upright at the sight of her.

He cleared his throat. "I think we're as close as we can get. I'm going to pull off here, and we'll walk the rest of the way."

Claire threw her door open. The creek was just down the hill. They could hear it. "Hold up," Ford said.

She waited for him, blue eyes nearly frantic. "There's no way to get across?"

"Not without a boat."

They walked up over a rise and the swirling waters appeared, muddy and ugly, in front of them. Across the creek was a sheriff's vehicle, a fire truck, and five pickup trucks.

Several people stood around. One looked up, and that's all it took. Everyone began waving their arms and shouting.

Before Ford could stop her, Claire ran for the creek. His heart leapt. "Wait! Don't get close to the water."

On the other side of Wailing Woman, Lilly Kowalski broke free from the arms of a deputy and ran toward her daughter.

"Mama!" Claire called. "I'm fine!"

Ford caught up with Claire and grabbed her by the waist. "Close enough," he said. "She sees you."

Lilly Kowalski had been likewise restrained. She was shouting something, but they couldn't make it out. The sound of the water was too loud.

Ford gave the thumbs-up sign to Lilly and the others standing on the bank. Lilly looked as if she was both laughing and crying, and everyone began hugging each other in celebration. Ford couldn't imagine the relief and joy they must be feeling. He reached over and squeezed Claire's hand.

"I don't see my dad," Claire said.

The hum of a motor preceded the sight of the game warden's boat, moving slowly upstream toward them. Sitting tall behind the warden was Gerome Kowalski, a walkie-talkie up to his mouth. He looked right at them, but unlike his wife, there was no show of emotion beyond a slight nod. But then, as the boat drew near the shore, Gerome made his way to the front, put one long leg over the railing, followed by another, and as the game warden shouted and made a grab for him, he jumped.

Claire gasped, and Ford had to hold her tightly.

The swirling water was chest-high on Gerome, but thanks to a pile of debris forming a small dam just upstream, the current wasn't strong, and he managed to wade ashore. The old fool hadn't even gotten his hat wet.

Ford let go of Claire and she rushed to her father.

"You're going to get wet," Gerome said, holding her at arm's length for about two seconds before drawing her in for a voracious hug.

While Claire still clung to him, Gerome held out his hand to Ford. "Much obliged," he said simply.

Ford accepted Gerome's hand. It was shaking, but Ford didn't let on that he noticed. "Didn't do much. Dried her off. Fed her some chowder."

Got naked but nothing happened.

Gerome nodded. "Check on the pastured herd on the east forty. It's high ground, but we've never seen anything like this."

"Yes sir."

Gerome released Claire from the hug and looked her up and down. He probably noticed she was wearing Ford's clothes.

"You might want to check on Ruben," Gerome added. Then, with another nod, he took his daughter's hand. "Let's get you back to the house."

The game warden had brought the bow of the boat onto the shore, and Claire headed for it. But then she stopped, and looked at Ford. "Thank you. For everything."

He nodded. "You're welcome."

She turned slowly, almost reluctantly, as if she had more that she wanted to say but had decided to keep it to herself.

Gerome climbed onto the boat first and then helped her up. The warden handed her a life vest, and as she struggled to put it on, Gerome tipped his hat at Ford.

Unlike Ford's family's worst day, the Kowalskis were getting a happy ending to their nightmare.

Ford sure was glad to be a part of it.

Chapter
Eight

Claire stared at the scrambled eggs in front of her. It had been two days since the flood, and sixteen-year-old Alison Mendoza was missing. Who could eat at a time like this?

Her mom plopped three strips of bacon onto her plate.

"Oh, no thanks—"

"It's from Happy Trails," she said. "Organic, free-range pork, so you can feel good about eating it."

Maybe Claire *could* eat at a time like this.

"Toast?" her mom asked.

Claire nodded as her mom put a jar of fresh apple butter on the table. It, too, came from Happy Trails. Hopefully, Maggie and Travis's apple orchard had survived the flood.

"Eat up," her mom said, sitting across the table from her. "There's a lot of work to be done today. Some ladies are coming by to help make food for the deputies and firefighters."

Act One of *Claire's Not Dead* had consisted of tears and hugs. Act Two had consisted of *What were you thinking?* and *We thought you were smarter than that.* Act Three consisted of everybody going on about their business.

The flood was the worst anyone in Big Verde could remember, and the loss of her Mini Cooper wasn't worth mentioning when four houses along the Rio Verde had been lifted right off their foundations. Luckily, the Schmidts and Hendersons hadn't been home and were accounted for. The other two were vacation homes, and everyone was hoping their owners were safe and sound. But nobody had seen Alison since she'd left her friend's house at nine o'clock on Friday night. There were no low-water crossings on the route she'd have taken to get home, but if she'd been anywhere near downtown and the river park, where lots of teens often hung out…

Her poor parents were going crazy.

It wasn't a good time to bring up Petal Pushers, although even now, Claire was dying to share her ideas.

Heavy footsteps came down the hall, along with deep, male voices. Casey Long stepped into the kitchen, followed by Claire's dad, two deputies, and Beau and Bryce Montgomery.

Casey removed his hat. "Miss Lilly," he said. "How are you holding up?"

Claire's mom reached up and patted the sheriff's cheek. "Better than you, I imagine."

"I'm fine," Casey said. "And Jessica said to tell you that Chateau Bleu would like to help your efforts at feeding everyone."

"Oh, what a dear!"

Jessica Acosta was Casey's fiancée, and she'd recently moved home to Big Verde to manage the only fancy restaurant in town, which was owned by a celebrity chef in Houston. People came from all over to eat there, and it had been a huge boon to Big Verde's small downtown businesses, which were now soggy and water-damaged.

"Sit, Casey," her mom said, pulling a chair out.

Six feet and four inches of Texas lawman did exactly as he was told.

"The rest of you, too," her mom said. She opened the cabinet and grabbed coffee mugs, filled them, and set them on the table. "I've got enough bacon and eggs for everyone."

Casey silently stirred some sugar into his coffee, glancing up at Claire. She knew he was going to light into her about driving into the low-water crossing. It was just a matter of time.

He took a sip, closed his eyes, and swallowed. "Good coffee, Miss Lilly."

"There's plenty more where that came from."

His eyes landed on Claire's. And he didn't blink.

"Really?" he said. "You tried to get through Wailing Woman during flash flood conditions?"

"It wasn't flooding when I drove into it."

"That's where the word *flash* comes in."

"And there wasn't that much water over the low-water crossing. I'm not even sure I stalled out. I might have run out of—"

Oops.

"You ran out of gas?" Casey stared at her like she was a complete and total moron.

"I'm not sure. The needle on the gauge was pretty low..."

They'd known each other their entire lives, and she could literally see the words *dumb* and *ass* connecting in his brain.

"Jesus Christ, Claire. You should know better."

"That's what everybody keeps telling me."

Her dad stepped forward. "Claire, I don't think Sheriff Long—"

Claire snorted at the formality. This was Casey's second term as sheriff, but she still hadn't gotten used to it. Casey had been the town's teenage hooligan—drinking, fighting, shooting up road signs—and now here he was with a badge and an attitude.

Her dad touched her shoulder. "Sheriff Long hasn't had much sleep since the night of the flood. He was up all night looking for you the first night, and since then he's been searching for Alison."

Casey's eyes were red, his jaw was unshaven, and there was a slight tremor in his hands. The truth was, he was a good sheriff and an even better friend. "Oh, God, Casey. I wasn't thinking. Thank you for everything you've done." She reached across the table and touched his hand. "I mean it."

"No need to thank me. I'm just glad you're okay. Hopefully, the same can be said for Alison."

"I'd like to join the search party."

"Oh, now, Claire," her mom said. "You've had a harrowing experience. Why don't you stay at the house and help me cook?"

"Actually," Casey said, "we could use the help. And nobody wants to survive a flood only to die from Claire's cooking."

* * *

Ford stared at the landscape. He hadn't grown up on Rancho Cañada Verde. Hell, he'd only spent one season on the place. But what he saw jarred him to the bone. Places that were typically green and dry were either submerged in standing water or covered in brown sludge. Cattle huddled together on the higher, dry mounds, and there was plenty of bawling going on among heifers and calves.

There was still no electricity. He and Oscar had spent a romantic night dining by the light of the lantern, and he'd only had fitful bouts of sleep. Lots of water dreams. Flood dreams.

Nightmares about Abby.

He adjusted his hat. Pulled the brim down low and stared down at the eastern valley to continue counting cattle. Now wasn't a good time to think about Abby.

Was there ever a good time?

Ford closed his eyes and an image of his wild-eyed mother filled his mind. *Where is Abby? Ford, you were supposed to be watching her—*

He hated how it could still knock his feet out from under him. After all these years, he was still bowled over, carried away, rolling and tumbling out of control as if he'd been smacked by a wave while miles from the seashore.

He opened his eyes and got his bearings. Then he began to count heads. *Eleven on that mound… nine on that one…*

An hour later he and Coco had finished surveying the back two-fifty. He pulled out a small notebook and recorded the numbers, and then he and Coco went through the east gate to survey the next quadrant. A lot of fences were down. Some of the missing cattle had probably gone into the limestone hills to escape the water. There wasn't much to eat up there, so getting them back down wouldn't be too difficult. It was a lot of land to cover, though. He'd have to get some guys on it soon, otherwise they were going to end up with cattle in the nearby state park.

Gerome had asked him to check on Ruben, so he figured he'd better do that next.

Ruben lived on a bluff called Oak Meadow in a small house that was reportedly well over a hundred years old (and looked every minute of it). Gerome said it had been on the property when his great-great-great-granddaddy bought the place in 1853. Eight members of the Luna family, none of whom recognized borders, fences, or the legitimacy of the deed August Kowalski had held in his hand when he'd come knocking at the door, were living in it at the time.

There'd been at least one Luna living in it ever since, and Gerome had sold it and the surrounding five acres to Ruben for a pittance (it was rumored to be a hundred dollars). So, the old scoundrel officially owned what was probably the prettiest damn spot on the entire ranch. But Gerome had said it was only fair. The land had belonged to the Luna family, whether they'd bought it or not, long before the Kowalskis ever set foot on the soil.

Ruben was good with animals. Gerome said he was part veterinarian and part *curandero*. Ford doubted Ruben had ever been to veterinary school, but he'd saved more than one birthing heifer when the vet hadn't been able to make it in time. And Miss Lilly said he was good with tinctures and whatnot for both animals and humans.

There was a road on the other side of the hill, but Ford preferred the trail that wound through the juniper trees. He inhaled the sharp scent of cedar and noticed it was tinged with smoke. He looked to the top of the bluff. There was a steady spiral of white smoke meandering into the air. Ruben must be burning something, but what?

It only took about fifteen minutes to get to the top of the bluff and the source of the smoke. Ruben stood in a small clearing in front of his house stacking green branches of cedar and sage atop a crackling fire.

Ruben nodded briefly and then continued on about his business as if Ford wasn't there. One of Ruben's mongrel mutts came out and sniffed around Coco's ankles, but then he also lost interest.

Ford dismounted and sauntered over to where Ruben was fanning the fire. It wasn't easy to keep green things burning, and it was smoking like hell.

"Good morning, Ruben. What's with the fire?"

"I'm just putting things in order," Ruben said.

Ford looked around. He didn't see any evidence of brush clearing. "Looks like you came through the flood just fine."

"Yep. Gerome got you out working?"

"Sure does."

"He's sick," Ruben said.

"Oh?" Ford hadn't seen Gerome since he and Claire had made it to Wailing Woman. And he doubted Ruben had made it across the creek to the ranch house, either. "How do you know that?"

"Boo," Ruben said simply.

Ford raised an eyebrow. Ruben was nuts.

Ruben called an ugly white dog over. "This is Boo," he said.

Things were making only slightly more sense. "Anyway—"

"Boo knows when people are sick. I think he can tell by smelling, but I don't know for sure. If someone is ill, he'll whine and try to sit on their feet. He's done that to Gerome for the past year or so."

"Well, did you tell him?" Ford asked, even though it was all a bunch of bullshit.

"Yes. But he wasn't ready to hear it."

The dog came over and sniffed around Ford. He was relieved when the dog circled him a few times and wandered off. "Whew," he said. "He didn't sit on my feet."

"No, but he circled you two times going counter-clockwise."

Ford swallowed. "What does that mean?"

"It means you're cursed," Ruben said simply, adding another green branch to the fire.

Ford laughed. "I already knew that."

"Did you?"

"Yeah."

Ruben eyed him for a few seconds, then went back to what he was doing. Ford figured he might as well tell the Mexican witch tale. It had amused many a cowboy over the years. "The story goes that my great-grandfather—"

Ruben put a finger to his lips. "Shh."

Ford looked to where Ruben gazed into the woods. At first, he didn't see it, but then a small motion brought it to light. A doe. And a little fawn.

"The smoke is working," Ruben said. "You just missed a raccoon and a skunk."

"I'm glad I missed the skunk," Ford said, shaking his head. "What is it exactly that the smoke is supposed to do?"

"It's welcoming back all the creatures who were displaced by the flood. Letting them know it's safe to come home."

"Don't they already know that?"

"Some animals are too frightened. Others are just too dumb to know where they belong. The juniper smoke is their guide."

"What about the sage?"

"Cleansing. Gets rid of things that have no business being here."

He hadn't said *animals*. He'd said *things*.

Ford shivered. He'd heard about folks burning sage to get rid of evil spirits, and he couldn't help it. He looked over his shoulder.

"I've never heard of juniper smoke being used for welcoming," he said. "But then again, I'm allergic to it."

He sneezed.

"Watch out for that snake," Ruben said, calmly, as a black rat snake Ford hadn't even noticed slithered lazily past. Ford jumped out of its way with a start.

"Shit," Ford said. "He crawled right next to me. I've never seen a snake do that."

"That makes seven," Ruben said.

"Snakes?"

"No. Seven animals, including the snake, who have followed the smoke home."

Doe, fawn, raccoon, skunk, and snake. That makes five.

"What were the other two animals?"

"You and Coco," Ruben said placidly.

Ford laughed out loud. "Ruben, man, you are something else."

Ruben shrugged. Added another branch.

"And I haven't been displaced by the flood," Ford said, with a grin. "My cabin stayed high and dry, just like yours."

"You followed the smoke, didn't you?"

"Yeah, but..." There was no point in arguing with Ruben. This was crazy talk, plain and simple.

"Welcome home," Ruben said. Then he put another green limb on the fire.

Ford shook his head and got back on Coco. He could mark *touch base with crazy Ruben* off his list. He glanced down the trail in the direction of the creek. He needed to get to the ranch house and talk with Gerome. He'd done about all he could do by himself on this side of Wailing Woman.

Water levels often dropped rapidly after flash floods. The low-water crossing would still have water on it, but he and Coco could probably pick their way across.

He wasn't much for water. Didn't like to swim in it. Didn't like to fish in it. And didn't relish trying to wade through it on horseback.

The tugging started.

Ford rubbed his chest just above his diaphragm. Claire was safe and sound at her folks' house. But he wouldn't mind laying eyes on her. She'd had quite the ordeal, and it was only natural for him to want to check on her.

Tug, tug, tug.

He hadn't intentionally done anything to urge Coco into a trot, but the horse had picked up on Ford's emotions—the creature was damn near psychic—and they headed briskly in the direction of the creek.

Chapter
Nine

❧

Claire leaned back and put her feet on the coffee table. Her boots were on the porch, muddy and wet. She'd ridden for two hours with Beau and Bryce along the creek while Casey and Bobby Flores searched the riverbank. They all planned to go back out again after lunch.

The ranch house was serving as a hub for the search. Rancho Cañada Verde had more river land than any other property in the county, so it made sense. There were busy people coming and going, and under any other circumstances, Claire would enjoy having all the company. But there wasn't much time for socializing, and a nerve-wracking anxiety hovered in the air.

Alison's parents had come by while Claire was out. She was sorry she'd missed them, but also a little relieved. She wasn't sure what to say to folks in such distress. The best thing she could do was continue searching for Alison.

The men had plates loaded down with sandwiches, potato

salad, and homemade pickles. Claire wasn't quite ready to eat yet. She never had much of an appetite when she was tired, and she was downright exhausted. Searching was physically tough—it was hot and humid and the mosquitos were already out—but mostly it was emotionally draining.

Her mom came out of the kitchen, wiping her hands on her apron. She scanned the room, and when her eyes met Claire's she smiled warmly. "Honey, could you follow me upstairs for a minute? Dad and I want to have a chat with you."

"Of course, Mom."

Maybe the insurance guy had called about her car. Or maybe there was news about Miss Daisy, and Claire could get back in her little trailer. Not that it was a huge inconvenience to stay with her parents. Her mom was a great cook, and due to space restrictions, Claire kept a lot of clothes here anyway.

She stood, stretched, and followed her mom up the stairs to her father's study. The door was open, and her dad sat behind his huge desk. An aura of haggardness hovered over him, yet he was clean-shaven and wore his typical white starched shirt, the same Western style with a yoke that he always wore. When Claire thought of her father, two images came to mind: a straw Stetson and shiny mother-of-pearl snap buttons.

He stood and gave her a hug. His arms were strong and warm, and he smelled like coffee and sunshine, same as always.

"You've been out searching?" he asked with a gravelly voice.

Claire nodded.

"That's my girl," he said.

His voice had been hoarse for weeks, which he kept

attributing to oak pollen. But the dunk he'd taken in the creek yesterday really seemed to have aggravated things. "Dad, your voice sounds awful. I think maybe it's time to see Dr. Martin."

He sat down and motioned for Claire to do the same. Her mom stood behind her and gently rested a hand on her shoulder.

"I saw Dr. Martin a couple of weeks ago."

A sense of unease crawled up Claire's spine, and by the time it arrived at the base of her head it was something closer to panic. Her dad was never sick, and he'd sooner consult the ranch's visiting veterinarian than make a trip into town to see Dr. Martin. He thought going to the doctor was something ladies did, like having brunch or getting their hair done.

Claire racked her brain. When had his gravelly voice *really* started? And why hadn't she known about the trip to the doctor? "What did he say?" she asked.

"He sent me to another doctor."

"What kind of doctor?"

"Ear, nose, and throat."

Claire relaxed a little. Ear, nose, and throat doctors treated sinus and allergy issues, didn't they?

"Well, what did *he* say?"

Her dad shrugged. "Princess, don't get upset, but I've got a little bit of cancer in my throat."

The panic at the base of Claire's skull bloomed into something just shy of hysteria. "Cancer?" she squeaked.

"Just a bit. The biopsy results—"

"Can you have *just a bit* of cancer? And when did you have a biopsy? Why didn't I know about it?"

"You've been busy with your socializing and your job in town and whatnot."

Gulp. He didn't say it in a judgmental way. Just matter-of-factly. But it still hurt.

"And all the marketing for the ranch," her mom added.

Her dad grinned. "That reminds me," he said, digging in his drawer. "You got some mail from a leather company…"

Junk mail? He'd stopped the Bad News Delivery Train to give her some junk mail?

"Here you go," he said, handing her an envelope from Bosco Leather.

She took it without looking at it.

"There wasn't much point in bothering you with any of this until we had something to say," her mom said. "We were hoping it would turn out to be nothing."

"We're a small family," Claire said. "You need to keep me in the loop. What's the treatment plan?"

"Surgery is in a couple of months," her mom said. "And then he'll have some radiation."

"Why can't they do the surgery now?" Claire asked.

Her dad gave a slight shrug. "It's calving season…"

Claire sighed.

"It's not aggressive," her mother said reassuringly.

"No chemo?" Claire asked.

"The doctor thinks it won't be necessary," her dad said. "But I won't be up to snuff for a few weeks, or possibly longer, regardless."

So that's why he'd asked Ford to come back to the ranch. He needed someone responsible who knew the ropes. Someone who'd worked here before who wouldn't need training and attention.

"Thank goodness for Ford," her mom said. "Although I'm worried about what we'll do after he's gone. He could only give us six weeks."

"Nobody needs to be worrying about a thing," her dad

said. "I've always taken care of this family, and I'll continue to do so, one way or another."

"And I'll be around to help out more," Claire said.

"Maggie needs you at Petal Pushers right now," her mom said. "She's going to have a baby."

At the mention of Petal Pushers, Claire's heart plunged down to her gut in a fabulous belly flop. There was no way she could bring up her plans now.

Disappointment must have shown on her face, because her father reached across the desk for her hand. "Princess, I realize the news is a blow. But the doctor said our bad news would be good news to quite a few of his patients. Let's keep that in mind." He gave her hand a squeeze and then leaned back in his chair.

Perspective. Her dad was right. He was almost always right, and she was just about to say so when Beau hollered from downstairs.

"Hey! Big Verde is on TV!"

* * *

"Oh God," Bryce said. "Bubba is behind the reporter."

Sure enough, Melanie Neubauer of KTBC was in front of the camera, and behind her stood Bubba Larson, photobombing the news with a huge grin and an upturned thumb.

Watching TV felt wrong, since most of the area still had no electricity. But her parents' house and the bunkhouse shared an emergency generator. They had air-conditioning, lights, and annoying twenty-four-hour news coverage.

"They're calling it the five-hundred-year flood," the reporter said. "And as you can see, downtown Big Verde has sustained considerable damage."

The camera scanned the debris-strewn street. Sally

Larson, Bubba's mother, pushed mud through the Corner Cafe's door with a broom.

Casey stood in the center of the room, rubbing a hand across his face. "Is that harebrained reporter even going to mention that we have a missing girl? I faxed a picture out this morning. And speaking of Alison, we sure could use another guy on horseback to continue searching the riverbanks."

"We've got Kit and Manuel checking on fence lines," Beau said, "but as soon as they're done—"

The screen door slammed, and little footsteps pounded their way in from the kitchen. Henry exploded into the room, followed by Maggie and Travis.

"Big Verde flooded!" Henry yelled.

Maggie ran straight to Claire. "We heard your car washed away. But then Bobby said you were okay, and I—"

Maggie's eyes were wide—she was clearly trying not to blink out a tear—and her dark eyebrows had disappeared into her bangs. "It was just really awful for me," she finally said.

"Imagine how awful it was for me," Claire said.

Maggie swallowed loudly. "I think it was worse for me."

Claire grabbed her up in a hug. "I'm fine."

"Promise?" Maggie asked, her voice muffled by Claire's chest.

"Promise. I wasn't even in the car when it was swept away, and Ford came along and gave me a ride—"

Maggie's head snapped up. "What kind of ride?"

She'd lost interest in Claire's near-death experience in light of this new development.

"What's this I hear about needing another guy on horseback?" Travis asked.

"We're searching the riverbanks for any sign of Alison Mendoza," Casey said. "We could use all the help we can get."

"I brought Junior," Travis said. "He's in the horse trailer."

"We need to search the dam," Beau said.

"We got to where we could see it from the bluff," Bryce added. "But we couldn't get our horses down there."

The scene on the television switched to an aerial view. "There's Rancho Cañada Verde!" Beau said.

Claire stared at the TV. Everything but the house was nearly unrecognizable.

"The Rio Verde crested at three twenty a.m. on Saturday morning," the reporter said.

"At least it's going down," Claire's mom said. "We're over the worst of it."

The aerial footage showed the eastern part of the ranch and the crossing at Wailing Woman. The exact spot where Claire's car had been washed away.

"Someone's riding a horse through Wailing Woman," Travis said.

Claire sat at attention, heart pounding. "Where?"

"Right there. See?" Maggie said.

Sure enough. Far below the helicopter was the muddy creek, and a man was halfway across. On horseback.

"It looks like we might have a man in trouble," the reporter said dramatically.

Claire squinted at the screen.

"That's Ford," Beau said with a grin.

The water had receded, but it was still up to Coco's flanks.

Claire gripped the sofa cushion. Ford and Coco were in the middle of the creek, the deepest part. The water wouldn't get any higher…unless the low-water crossing had washed out.

"He's fine," her mom said softly. "See? They're coming across slowly."

"Coco is a mustang," Bryce said. "They're sure-footed and cautious."

Claire's dad cleared his throat from the doorway. In all the excitement, nobody had heard him come down the stairs. Her mom put a sandwich in his hands. "Eat."

He took a bite and looked at his watch. "Ford should be here in about fifteen minutes, give or take."

"What a spectacle, folks!" the reporter said. "Both man and horse have made it through the floodwaters safely."

The camera zoomed in on Ford just as he glanced up at the helicopter.

He tipped his hat.

"What a show-off," her dad said, turning to go back up the stairs. "Send him to see me when he gets here."

Only Gerome Kowalski, a man who considered a full-sized smile an outlandish display of emotion, would call Ford Jarvis a show-off.

Chapter
Ten

❦

Claire followed Casey to the porch. "I can't believe how bad things are in town. People lost their homes."

"Most of those houses were cabin rentals or vacation homes. If this had happened on a holiday weekend . . ." Casey shuddered. "But as a whole, Big Verde was very lucky. And I hope that luck extends to the Mendoza family."

Claire swallowed. "Don't you think we'd have found her by now? If she was okay, I mean."

Casey shrugged. "Hard to say. There are all kinds of crazy and unlikely survival stories, and I'm going to assume that's what we're dealing with until I'm forced to accept otherwise. That means Alison is depending on us."

Claire looked down the lane that led to the creek. Ford should be riding up any minute. He was going to insist on joining the search for Alison, and given his family's history, it would be agonizing for him.

She and Casey were both quiet for a moment, lost in their

thoughts. And then Casey said, "You haven't already taken up with Ford Jarvis, have you?"

Claire crossed her arms. "You are not about to stand here lecturing me about cowboys, Casey Long. I am not a child—"

"Just one specific cowboy," Casey said. "And I'm well aware that you are not a child."

His eyes briefly flitted up and down her body. "If you were a child, this conversation wouldn't be necessary."

"It's not necessary now, but to answer your question, no, I have not *taken up* with Ford."

"I'm surprised your dad asked Ford to come back, considering."

"Considering what?"

"Considering your history with him."

Casey was really pissing her off. "First of all, I love my dad, but he doesn't dictate who I date."

"He might not dictate to you, but believe me, every ranch hand and cowboy on these twelve thousand acres and all surrounding acres and basically all of Texas knows they can't date Gerome Kowalski's daughter."

"Well," Claire sputtered, "even if that were true—"

"Oh, it's true."

"Dad doesn't know that Ford and I ever—"

"Messed around? A lot? All over the place?"

Claire held her finger to her lips. "Shh."

"For someone who doesn't care what her daddy thinks, you sure do seem to care what your daddy thinks. Also, I'm pretty sure nothing gets by him. Not a goddam thing. Believe me, he knows, or thinks he knows. So, all I'm saying is he must be pretty hard up for a foreman."

"Don't you have official business to attend to somewhere? We're having a natural disaster."

"Don't get attached again, Claire. Ford Jarvis is not going to settle his spurs here, or anywhere. I know his type. Met a lot of men like him on the rodeo circuit."

Claire leaned against the porch railing. "I'm not an idiot."

Casey raised an eyebrow as if he were looking at someone who'd recently driven her Mini Cooper into a low-water crossing during a flash flood.

So maybe she was a little bit of an idiot. But not where Ford was concerned. He was determined to wander the Texas countryside like some sort of tragic, romantic figure from a spaghetti Western. Why would she want to get involved again with a man like that?

Casey looked down the lane. "Speak of the devil."

Claire squinted into the glare of the noonday sun at the familiar silhouette of Ford and Coco. Her feet suddenly had a mind of their own and started down the steps. She managed to stop at the bottom, but her heart beat frantically against her rib cage, as if it were an object determined to remain in motion.

Coco halted in a cloud of dust, and for about five seconds Claire and Ford just stared at each other.

She tried to read his face and couldn't. Was he happy to see her?

Ford shook his shoulders and dismounted, slapping at his chaps, which were wet and coated with mud.

Nobody looked as hot in a pair of chaps as Ford.

Ford nodded at her. "Claire."

Claire's pulse was pounding, but she nodded her head right back and said, "Ford."

She hoped it sounded formal and clipped and somewhat sarcastic because, seriously? They were nodding-and-naming now? But she probably sounded breathy and desperate.

Because that's how she felt around him. *Desperate and out of breath.*

Her mind was made up about Ford. But her body hadn't gotten the memo and was responding like a full-blown traitor.

Ford removed his hat, wiped his hand on his shirt, and held it out to Casey. "Sheriff."

Casey smiled. "How does it feel to be a television star?"

"Pardon?"

"Your treacherous crossing at Wailing Woman," Casey said. His lips twitched and his eyes twinkled.

"There was a camera on me?"

"Yep. Good thing you didn't decide to stop and take a piss."

That got half a grin out of Ford. "Maybe I should have."

"Would have served them right," Casey added.

Ford's face melted back into its usual seriousness. "Anybody missing?"

Casey slumped and sighed. "A sixteen-year-old girl. Last seen at her friend's house wearing red shorts with white polka dots."

Ford went pale. "Oh, Jesus."

"We're searching the banks of the Rio Verde and the creeks," Casey said.

Ford's head snapped up. "I'll help."

"Figured you would," Casey said. "We need someone with a good horse to get down to the dam. Neither Beau nor Bryce wanted to try it. Said to wait for you and Coco."

Ford nodded. "Is Gerome around?"

"Yes, and he wants to see you," Claire said. "He's in his study."

Ford looked at his chaps. "I'd better get these off before I go in the house."

He quickly removed the chaps and draped them over the

porch railing. There was a definite squishing sound as he walked up the steps.

"Are you harboring any fish in those boots?" Claire asked.

"Maybe," Ford said, pulling one off and turning it upside down. Water poured out (no fish). Next, he peeled off his socks, wrung them out, and hung them on the railing next to his chaps.

Beau and Bryce stepped onto the porch. "Hey, Ford. Saw you on TV. Can we have your autograph?" Bryce asked.

"Shut up," Ford said.

"It was like watching Tom Cruise in *Mission Impossible*," Beau said.

"We were really biting our nails," Bryce added.

Ford ignored them both and looked at Claire. "Am I okay to go in like this?"

"Yes, you're..."

Fine. Perfectly acceptable. Incredibly hot.

"There's the outdoor shower if you want to strip down to your skivvies," Beau said. "Claire's super familiar with it."

Good grief! The twins were irritating. And now they were going to tell one of their favorite stories—

"We had a Peeping Tom case here on the ranch a few years back," Beau said.

"*Many* years back," Claire said. "And Ford's not interested in a shower so—"

"I might be," Ford said with a glint in his eye. "Are you talking about the shower behind the bunkhouse? The one next to the pump shed?"

Sometimes, when the cowboys were particularly filthy, they showered off before going inside. The shower was private and enclosed, but they occasionally exited the dang thing completely nude, dirty clothes in hand, and walked the ten or so yards to the back door of the bunkhouse. Anybody standing at the alcove window on the second floor of the ranch house had a clear view, a fact Claire had discovered when she was a teenager.

"I never leave that shower without waving at the window," Bryce said.

"Just in case Claire's watching," Beau added.

"I am *not ever* watching."

Beau laughed. "That's only because your mama had a shutter put up."

"I'll pass on the shower," Ford said, opening the screen door. He looked at Claire. "After you."

Claire stepped through the door, cheeks aflame. "Thank you."

"Pervs first," he added softly, causing Beau and Bryce to break into raucous laughter.

* * *

The stairs creaked beneath Ford's bare feet as he followed Claire up to Gerome's study.

When they got to the second floor, he glanced at the shuttered window at the end of the hall and grinned. Claire caught him and rolled her eyes.

"Come on," she said, yanking on his sleeve.

They stopped outside an ornate wooden door, and Claire knocked firmly. Ford automatically straightened up and squared his shoulders.

Gerome's voice came from the other side. "Come in."

Claire opened the door, and there stood Gerome, behind his desk.

Gerome was an intimidating presence, even if you hadn't slept with his daughter. Which Ford had. On numerous occasions.

Ford entered the room and shook Gerome's large hand.

"Have a seat," Gerome said. Then he looked at Claire. "We're just going to talk rotation schedules. It'll bore you."

"I should probably listen. Especially now that I'm going to be helping out more."

That sounded like a good idea to Ford.

"Later, sweetheart. I've got a lot to discuss with Ford, and not much time to answer questions."

Claire's mouth fell open. She clearly wasn't used to being shut down by her father, and frankly, Ford was surprised by it too. He squirmed in his seat while Claire and Gerome stared at each other with identical stubborn chins and furrowed brows.

Claire blinked first. "Okay," she said, almost managing a smile. "I look forward to talking to you later then."

She didn't even glance at Ford before leaving the room. Maybe she was embarrassed. Maybe Ford was just so insignificant that she'd forgotten he was even there.

She was embarrassed.

Ford crossed his arms. He had nothing but respect for Gerome Kowalski, but he shouldn't embarrass his daughter that way. Claire was smart. She was strong. And she didn't deserve to be dismissed from the room like hired help.

Hell, *he* was the hired help.

Gerome's face relaxed ever so slightly at Claire's exit. Ford only noticed because he tended to control his features in the same strict manner. Just a lessening of tension around the eyes...

"We're going to have quite a bit of fence work to do..." Gerome said hoarsely. He closed his eyes for a moment, and then cleared his throat before adding, "I'm going to let you do most of the talking. Tell me what you got."

Gerome made a circular motion with his hand that indicated Ford should start talking, so he did.

"All the fences in the low areas are down. I'm guessing we've got cows over at Happy Trails and vice versa. We're missing quite a bit of the herd in the back quadrant, but they could be up in the hills."

"They might be in the state park too," Gerome said.

Ford sure hoped not. It would be easier to get them down from the hills.

"Lots of gates are down. Roads are washed out or impassable from debris. Don't have a final tally on cattle loss."

Gerome nodded. "That's about what I expected."

The old rancher leaned back in his chair and sighed. Put a hand over his eyes.

"We've got a lot of work to do," Ford said. "But we can knock it out. We might need to hire a few more hands to get the fences up in a timely manner. That's top priority."

"It's going to take longer than six weeks."

That was probably true. "I'm committed to a roundup at the Sun-Barre in six weeks," Ford reminded Gerome. "Have you put some more feelers out for a permanent foreman?"

"What are you doing after the roundup?"

So, no, Gerome hadn't put any feelers out.

"I'm not quite sure. But there are a ton of ranches in West Texas. I figure I'll be on one of them."

Because none of them were surrounded by water or had a problematic redhead.

Gerome didn't say anything, so Ford decided to add a definitive statement. "I plan to summer in the desert."

The bone-dry and redhead-less desert.

"That sounds godawful," Gerome said. "Why would you want to cook in the Chihuahua Desert if you could spend the summer along the banks of the Rio Verde?"

That was a good question, and he couldn't answer it truthfully. Because the gist of it was, his heart was floundering around Claire. Fluttering like a damn butterfly. And on top of it, he seemed to be having a hard time keeping his pants on.

He'd broken her heart once, and it had gutted him. He wasn't going to do it again. Because even if he stayed through the summer—even if he stayed through the fall—he was not staying forever. And Claire was looking for forever.

"The money's good," Ford said weakly.

It was. The West Texas ranches paid more because everything cost more. It was hard living.

"You think I'm not paying you enough?" Gerome snapped.

It was very unlike Gerome to argue or beg. It made Ford uncomfortable, and a thick silence hung in the air while Ford considered what to say.

"I'm sick," Gerome finally said.

It was obvious that Gerome had a cold. And it was bad timing with so much going on, but that was no excuse for him to bully Ford into coming back to Rancho Cañada Verde. Ford couldn't extend his stay past the six weeks. The brush between Claire's mouth and his dick was proof of that. "I hope you feel better soon," he offered.

Gerome crossed his arms. Stared angrily at his desk, face blushing furiously, as if being ill were something to be ashamed of. "I've got throat cancer."

It took a second for it to register. And when it did, Ford felt as if the air had been knocked out of him. Damn.

"I'm having surgery shortly after you head out to West Texas. And there will be radiation after that."

"I don't know what to say, Gerome. I'm sorry to hear that you're ill."

"You don't need to say a thing. Words won't make the

cancer go away. But I need you to get the ranch in order, so I can get my affairs in order. Understand?"

Ford nodded. Then he cleared his throat so his voice wouldn't crack. Because Gerome Kowalski was talking about getting his fucking affairs in order.

"I'm facing my mortality, son. I was hoping that at the end of six weeks with you as foreman, this place would be in pretty decent shape. And that depending on what the surgeon finds, I'd be able to make a clear decision. But now we've suffered this setback—"

"Decision about what?" Ford asked.

"Beef prices are down, and I don't think they're coming back up. Folks are eating less red meat. Claire already saved our asses once—"

"Claire?"

"Hell, yes. Something called branding. And it's not the kind of branding that involves an iron. It has to do with marketing. She's carved out what they call a niche. Because of her, when folks think of organic grass-fed beef, they think of Rancho Cañada Verde."

Ford couldn't help it. Pride swelled in his chest, and from the look on Gerome's face, he felt the same way. It was like having a cocky marching band stomping around in your rib cage.

"And there's that other stuff," Ford said. "The salsas and whatnot. I can't get used to seeing it in the store."

Gerome grinned and shook his head. "Me either. I don't think we'll make a profit on them, but they probably won't sink us."

"I don't think anything can sink Rancho Cañada Verde, Gerome."

"That's what they said about the *Titanic*, and we all know how that turned out."

"But—"

"I'm a poor man sitting on a gold mine," Gerome said. "We limp along just fine, skirting back and forth between black and red lines. But it's a lot of work, and it's too much for Lilly and Claire to handle by themselves. I'm not leaving them with a burden."

"What are you saying?"

"Look, son. I'm not going to be around forever. It might be time to sell the ranch."

Ford could hardly pay attention to the rest of the conversation, and by the time he came downstairs, his heart felt like a concrete brick.

He was met by a lot of activity in the kitchen. Miss Lilly and another woman he didn't know were at the stove. Claire's friend Maggie was peeling potatoes, and all of them were chattering a mile a minute.

He attempted to scoot past the doorway without being seen. Failed.

"Well, hey there, Ford," Maggie Blake said.

Ford didn't know Maggie very well, but whenever she said his name, she stretched it out to two syllables in that particular way Southern women had. It had a slight flirtatious edge to it, but coming from Maggie, it was more of a tease. As if she were struggling not to laugh.

As if Claire had told her about him running buck naked through the cabin in pursuit of a cat.

"Hi, Maggie. It's good to see you again." She was either pregnant or had developed a beer belly. Ford had been raised by his mom, grannie, and Aunt Lucy, so he knew better than to ask.

Maggie grinned a grin that said *I have heard every last detail of your sex life* and went back to the potatoes. A kitchen chair moved, but nobody was sitting in it. Ford looked under the table and there sat a little boy, playing with a mess of toy horses.

"I'm Henry," he said. "And I'm bored."

"Did I hear somebody say he's bored?" Maggie asked without turning around.

"No ma'am," Henry sighed. He looked right at Ford and whispered, "If you tell 'em you're bored, they'll find some shit for you to do that's worse than being bored."

"Travis!" Maggie bellowed.

Travis came running into the room, eyes wide in panic. "Is everything okay?"

Maggie grinned. "The baby fell out while I was standing here peeling potatoes."

Travis paled and actually looked at the ground between Maggie's feet.

"Oh, good grief!" Maggie said. "I called you in here because your son just said *shit*. Again."

Travis ran a hand over his face. "Aw, shit, Henry. What did I tell you about that?"

"And therein lies the problem," said the other lady. She was probably in her mid to late sixties, and she wore skin-tight jeans with rhinestones on the pockets. She whipped around to face Travis. "Don't you think for one second that I won't wash that mouth out with soap, *mijo*."

"Ford," said Miss Lilly. "Have you met Lupe Garza?"

"She's Travis's nanny," Maggie muttered.

"Lord, isn't that the truth," said Lupe. "I also look after Henry, and I help out at Happy Trails."

"Couldn't live without her," Maggie said. "Especially now that I'm about to have my third child."

Third? Ford remembered that Maggie and Travis had adopted Henry. And now Maggie was pregnant. Had they had another baby while he was gone?

Travis smacked Maggie lightly on her rear. "Watch it, mama. I'm a fully grown man." He waggled his eyebrows. "And you know it."

"This doesn't need to go one bit further," Lupe said. "There is an actual child in the room."

Ford grinned. Maggie had meant Travis.

"I don't believe we've met," Ford said to Lupe.

"This is Ford Jarvis," Miss Lilly said. "He's our new foreman."

"Oh, I've heard all about Mr. Jarvis," Lupe said, stepping toward him with a raised eyebrow.

Ford held out a hand, but Lupe bypassed that and gave him a hug. Then she touched his cheek. "So handsome. A devil though, at least that's what I hear."

"Lupe," Maggie said in a warning tone.

"What? It's the truth."

She gave Ford a little pat on the cheek, followed by a wink, and went back to the stove.

Ford was left standing there, cheeks warm, watching the assembly line and wondering where Claire was.

Travis kissed Maggie on top of her head and put his hat on. "If you gals have everything under control here in the kitchen—"

"Hey! I'm in the kitchen, and I'm not a gal," Henry said.

"You're not actually doing any work," Travis said. "And if I were you, I'd focus on being invisible or they're going to give you something to do."

"Where are you headed?" Ford asked.

"Casey told me to ride up the creek. It should only take me a couple of hours, give or take. Beau and Bryce hit the riverbanks again, and Claire is headed out to the dam."

Miss Lilly spun around with a gasp. "The dam?"

"Yes, ma'am."

Miss Lilly sighed. "And she's riding Cinder?"

"Is that a bad thing?" Maggie asked, her voice edged with concern.

"None of the cowboys wanted to try and get their horses down there," Miss Lilly said. "They were waiting for Ford—"

"Don't worry, Miss Lilly," Travis said. "Claire's good on a horse, and she won't do anything risky."

Miss Lilly cocked an eyebrow and crossed her arms. "She's risk on wheels."

"That was Friday," Maggie said. "Right now, she's risk on hooves, and somebody better go after her."

Maggie looked at Ford, and he didn't need to be told twice. He was already halfway out the door.

Chapter

Eleven

❦

Claire rode Cinder fast and hard, and it felt good. She couldn't believe her father had kicked her out of his study. Right in front of Ford, too, as if they had "man things" to discuss.

She was a grown-ass woman. The sole heir to the ranch. And her dad didn't think she needed to sit in on a discussion about pasture rotation?

She hadn't really shown much of an interest in such things before, but maybe she should have.

Her dad was sick. Ford was only staying for six weeks. Who was going to take over after he was gone?

Claire urged Cinder to go faster. She thought better when she was on the move, and the faster—or higher— the better.

She'd received Cinder as a gift from her parents on her fifteenth birthday, and it had been love at first sight. It hadn't been long before the two of them were winning rodeo buckles in barrel racing, and Claire had loved every minute of it. She'd even been crowned Hill Country Rodeo Queen.

She'd given it up in college, but the adrenaline junkie in her had needed another outlet. She'd discovered the university's climbing club, and she'd been hooked ever since. Whenever she felt stifled or frustrated, she either rode fast or climbed high.

She and Cinder arrived at the bluff and slowly approached the edge to look at the Rio Verde below. It was usually crystal clear, but today it was like chocolate milk, and muddy water flowed over the top of the dam.

A steep rustic trail led to a spot where people often gathered to swim or fish, but it was a crumbly, washed-out mess. There was no way to navigate it on foot, much less on horseback. Maybe there was a better spot farther down.

Ten minutes later, after evaluating every possible trail, Claire dismounted and rubbed Cinder's flanks. "No can do, girlfriend. It's just too dangerous."

With a bit of smug satisfaction, she thought to herself that Ford and Coco couldn't do it, either.

She peered down at the riverbank below. Branches and debris were piled high. It was easy to imagine the raging wall of water that had blown through here.

She started to turn away when something red caught her eye. Was it fabric?

Alison had been wearing red shorts.

Claire broke out in a layer of prickly, panic-induced sweat as dread pooled in her belly.

She should ride back to the house and call Casey. But her heart wouldn't allow her feet to budge. She had to know what—or who—was down there.

There was a rope in her saddlebag. And she knew how

to rappel without a harness. Everyone in her climbing club had practiced it on short, safe descents. It wasn't hard if you knew what you were doing.

She was ninety-seven percent sure she knew what she was doing.

She grabbed the rope and played with it for a few minutes, pulling it up between her legs, wrapping it around her hip and thigh, crossing it over her chest and shoulder...

She remembered what to do.

She undid the rope and slipped it around a huge, sturdy cypress tree. Then she carried the two ends to the edge and dropped them over.

No problem.

Five seconds later she was rewrapped in her makeshift harness. Using her right hand as her brake hand, she backed over the edge. All of her concerns—her dad's cancer, her feelings for Ford, and even Alison—disappeared as she slowly and carefully descended. Every bit of her attention was focused on simply getting down safely.

When her boots hit the ground, she untied the rope. The entire process had taken less than five minutes.

She wrinkled her nose from the stench of trash and rotting things, and began picking her way across the sticks, branches, roots, and trash. She watched carefully for snakes, because floods brought them out, and the last thing she needed was to be bitten by a cottonmouth.

The red fabric was just a few yards away. She couldn't tell what it was, nor could she tell if the pile of debris it was in was on solid ground or floating on the water. She looked around for a big stick and found a cane pole. She poked it into the ground in front of her. It was sturdy, so she walked on, poking the ground with each step.

The splash of red could be clearly seen now, and Claire

took a big step toward it. But as she leaned into the pole, it began to sink.

She'd run out of solid ground.

She reached out as far as she could, intending to dislodge the fabric, or at least uncover it, before getting the heck out.

"Claire!"

The unexpected sound of her name startled her, and she lost her balance and fell forward, landing in the trash. It felt solid enough—she thought she might be all right—but when she tried to stand, she started to sink.

She'd read somewhere that lying flat and distributing your weight would help you escape quicksand. Would it work in floating debris? She leaned forward and tried to bring her feet up, but it was no use. Her boots were waterlogged and heavy.

As she twisted her body to see who the idiot was who'd called her name, her feet hit bottom. Or at least something relatively solid.

Good. She wasn't going to drown in a pile of trash.

"Claire, hold on! I'm coming!"

Holy shit. It was Ford. And he was staring at the rope like he was thinking about using it to get down.

"Don't you try that! You don't know what you're doing!" she shouted.

She didn't like thinking about what might be lurking or slithering around her boots, and she shivered and jerked as something brushed against her leg. A log shifted beneath her, and her right foot slipped off.

She tried to yank it up, but it was caught on something and wouldn't budge.

Dang it! She was stuck.

* * *

Shit.

What had Claire gotten herself into now? Ford had shown up at the bluff to find a riderless Cinder. He'd scratched his head, looked around, and then stepped on something he'd thought might be a snake. But no, it was worse than that.

It was a damn rope.

Tied around a tree.

With two ends going right over the side of a fucking cliff.

With a sense of dread and irritation, he'd picked up the rope—it was slack—and followed it to the edge, where he now stood, watching helplessly as Claire struggled in waist-deep, trashy floodwater.

"Claire!" he hollered again, holding the rope. She'd obviously used it to get down there. Why couldn't he do the same?

"Don't you dare," she yelled. Her voice echoed off the canyon walls, traveling up and down the river. "I'm fine!"

She was *not* fine. God knew what lurked in that muddy water. Broken glass, jagged metal, snakes... And what if something shifted and she went under and became trapped? It was almost as if she didn't understand that risk-taking was, well, risky.

Claire was watching him over her shoulder. "Don't you even think about it, you idiot! Just give me a minute to get my foot unsnagged."

Her foot was snagged? Ford eyed the rope again, but Claire was right. He had no idea what he was doing. So he stood there like a dummy, watching helplessly as Claire grunted and squirmed and grimaced.

And then...

"Aha!" Claire shouted. "It's free!"

Stress and strain leaked out of Ford like water through a sieve. But Claire still had to actually climb out of the river. However, instead of turning around and doing just that, she picked up a tree branch and reached across the debris to poke at something red.

Casey had said the missing girl was wearing red shorts.

Ford held his breath as Claire used the limb—still standing in waist-high water—to snag the red object. After just a few seconds, her shoulders slumped in relief, and Ford finally let out his breath as she dragged the object over and held up a bedraggled red umbrella.

* * *

Claire stared up the side of the cliff. She'd been in such a hurry to get down that she hadn't given all that much thought as to how she'd get back up. As far as climbs went, this one was easy.

With proper gear.

She sighed and kicked her remaining boot off. It would make for a horrible climbing shoe. "Ford!" she hollered.

She saw the brim of his hat first, then the toes of his boots. Both were peeking over the cliff, which meant he was standing way too close to the edge.

"Holy cow, back up, would you?"

He disappeared momentarily, then just his head appeared. He'd dropped to all fours.

"I'm going to need you to pull up one end of this rope, okay? And then wrap it around that tree again. Hold on to it as I climb up, but leave some slack in it."

"Do you want me to tie the rope to Coco and let him pull you up?"

Claire did not want to be dragged up the side of a cliff by a horse. She was banged up enough as it was.

"Thanks, but I think I'm better off free-climbing. Just keep a bit of slack in the rope, and if I fall..."

"I'll catch you," Ford said.

Even from down here she could see the steely glint in those hazel eyes.

After Ford was set with the rope, Claire inhaled. Exhaled. Looked up the face of the cliff. First, she intentionally scanned for footholds and patterns in the granite, her eyes darting here and there, her brain consciously calculating. But then the shift happened. It always did. The sensation reminded her of looking at one of those posters that appeared to be just a bunch of pixels, but if you allowed your eyes to lose focus, an image suddenly popped up, clear as day.

And just like that, the path revealed itself.

She reached up with her right hand and grabbed hold of a jutting piece of granite. Put her foot on a well-anchored tree root, and up she went. Ford did his part, keeping just the right amount of slack in the rope.

This was a really easy climb, the kind she would have attempted as a young teen without any gear or knowledge. And she'd have most likely made it up just fine without any awareness of the danger she'd been in.

But now that she had experience and training, she knew there was no such thing as a safe climb, and so she remained focused.

This was a green wall with lots of roots and trees and things to grab hold of. But any one of them could break free. So, she tried to avoid them, looking instead for jutting granite she could count on to support her weight.

Her left foot slipped as a root pulled loose, and she felt the tension on the rope increase. Ford practically jerked it, which wasn't comfortable, but at least she knew he was on the ball. She regained a foothold quickly and continued her way up, wincing from the pain of being barefoot.

When she reached the top, Ford extended a hand, and with seemingly no effort at all, he lifted her to the top of the cliff.

"Thanks," she said, proud to note she was barely breathing hard.

She unwrapped the rope from her body and tried to coil it up, but Ford clung to it with a death grip.

"You can let go of that now," she said.

"What?" he asked.

"The rope. Let go." She gave it a slight yank.

Ford looked as if someone had snapped him out of a daydream as the rope slid through his fingers. "You..."

Claire raised an eyebrow. "Mmm?"

"You just nearly died. Right in front of me. Again."

He was pale. What the heck was wrong with him? "Nearly died?"

What was he talking about? She'd been irritatingly uncomfortable and somewhat grossed out. Who wants to stand waist-deep in a pile of soggy trash? But she had been nowhere near—

"You fell in the river. You could have gotten sucked under all that junk."

"Oh, I was not going to let that happen, Ford." She'd felt in total control. The biggest problem had been her snagged boot, which she'd freed.

"And then you climbed up that"—Ford pointed to the edge of the cliff—"like fucking Spider-Man."

His eyes were huge. Was he even okay?

"You knew I climbed."

"But I've never *seen* it until today."

Claire finished coiling the rope and started for her saddle-bag. "So, what did you think, cowboy? Surprised to learn that ropes can be used for more than hog-tying a calf or roping a steer?"

Ford's hand was suddenly around her arm, yanking her back and turning her to face him.

"Goodness, Ford. What's wrong?"

He held her arm tightly—almost painfully—and it must have shown on her face because he loosened his grip.

"I told you I was fine. Good grief, get over it. I mean, I'm wet. And filthy." She lifted a bare foot and looked at the scratches. "And I might need antibiotics."

"You scared me," Ford repeated, squeezing her arm again. "And then you..."

She looked up. The angle of the sun lit up his face, but the brim of his hat cast his eyes in shadow. His lips were fully visible, however, and they were not smiling.

"And then I what?" She was not about to be lectured by a man who knew absolutely nothing about climbing.

"Amazed me," Ford whispered.

That was not what she had expected. And it wasn't what she was used to. She was used to being told to slow down or get down or hold on or—

Ford pulled her closer. Heat emanated from his body, and she wanted to melt into him.

He let go of her arm and slipped his hand around to her back, warm and steady.

"You are really something, Claire. Do you know that?"

She knew a lot of things. She knew she was pretty, because she'd been told so her entire life. She knew she wasn't stupid, even if school hadn't always interested her. But Ford was seeing other things. Things she'd thought were invisible. The things that fought to be noticed.

I'm strong. I'm capable. I can take care of myself.

He took off his hat and there were those eyes. Nearly green at this time of day. And they stared right at her. *Right into her.*

"I see you," he whispered.

His lips were so close.

She dropped the rope. Ford's Adam's apple bobbed as he swallowed. She rose on her toes and their lips touched in a soft and hesitant kiss. Claire held back, hoping he'd be the first to pull away. God knew she didn't have the strength.

But he didn't pull away. He deepened the kiss, so intensely that Claire could hardly breathe.

Who needed oxygen when this man's lips were made of everything she needed to survive?

Every inch of him was hard and unyielding. She remembered him naked, standing before her. So close…

Somewhere deep within her was the willpower she'd used to stop this nonsense when it had happened at the cabin. But she couldn't seem to muster it now to save her soul. She wanted the kiss to last forever. Because if it did, there would never be any consequences. No broken hearts.

This was the ticket. Just keep kissing.

Ford began to tremble. Then he groaned softly, and Claire responded by knocking his hat off his head and running her hands through his hair. Ford pulled her even closer, and sparks traveled up and down her spine like it was the fourth of July. But then Ford's soft groan turned into an angry growl as he let go of her and broke the kiss.

"I'm sorry," he said, before Claire even had a chance to open her eyes.

They both stood there, trembling and panting, in silence.

Cinder neighed as if she were fussing at Claire for losing her hold on reality. Because reality required staying away from Ford's lips since they, and the rest of him, were leaving in six weeks, and she could not get wrapped up in him again.

Claire straightened her shirt, which had climbed up her midriff when she'd wrapped her arms around Ford's neck. "Well, you should be sorry," she said, peeling some wet grass off her jeans and pretending she hadn't just tried to smother him with her mouth. And arms. And legs.

Rather enthusiastic response, Claire.

Ford shifted nervously from foot to foot and fiddled with the brim of his hat. "I lose my mind when I'm around you."

"Clearly."

"So, I don't think I should be around you. On account of how I, you know, need my mind."

"I'm not going to limit my movement around my own ranch," Claire said, walking to Cinder and slipping her bare foot into the stirrup. "Just because you can't hold on to your senses." She slid seamlessly into the saddle. "So, you'd better get a grip on yourself."

She snapped the reins and rode away as fast as she could, knowing full well that *she* was the one who needed to get a grip.

Her dad had told her there were more than five hundred million square feet on the ranch. Surely, she and Ford could avoid ending up in the same one for the next six weeks.

Chapter

Twelve

❧

Ford got out of the shower and stepped into a pair of jeans he'd borrowed from Beau. Or maybe it was Bryce. He couldn't tell them apart to save his soul. Claire could, but she'd grown up with them.

Bryce's face is a little thinner.

Beau's chin cleft is deeper.

Ford was staying in the bunkhouse tonight. He was bone tired and didn't have it in him to ride back across Wailing Woman. He hadn't much cared for riding through that rushing water this afternoon, and Coco hadn't seemed to enjoy it, either.

The creek should be easier to get through tomorrow, and one night in the bunkhouse wouldn't kill him. He'd set out some food for Oscar, and the cat probably preferred it when Ford was gone anyway.

As soon as he'd walked into the bunkhouse, he'd been given the news that Alison had just been found—alive and well—in San Antonio with her teenaged boyfriend. Ford had felt a level of relief that was probably uncommon for a man who'd never met the girl or her family, but floods did a number on him. He was thrilled she was okay, although she was probably in a heap of justified trouble.

The guys were going out to celebrate, so he'd have the place to himself for several hours. He gathered his dirty clothes and dropped them in the washing machine, and then he headed out to the porch, shirtless and barefoot, grabbing his hat on the way out the door.

He sat his weary ass in one of the rocking chairs and leaned back, putting his feet on the railing and slipping the brim of his hat just low enough to shield his eyes from the setting sun while still being able to take it all in.

The view before him was stunning. The giant live oaks rose majestically in the front pasture, set against what looked like an airbrushed sunset of orange, red, and burnt umber. It reminded him of melting sherbet on a hot summer day, or the mingling colors of an artist's palette, or...

Claire's hair cascading down her bare back.

The Hill Country sunset before him paled in comparison. How he'd loved running his fingers through Claire's hair while it magically changed colors depending on the light. It had been the color of a cinnamon stick when she'd ridden away this afternoon, leaving the taste of her kiss on his lips.

Watching her climb had been amazing. She'd been so focused and strong, and yet, she'd taken a dumb risk, and she'd done it alone. It made him shiver to think about what could have happened.

He had marks etched in his rough palms from holding that rope so tightly. Every muscle in his body had been taut with tension. Every brain cell focused on where Claire was going to put her feet and fingers next. And then when she'd made it to the top, the relief had knocked him senseless. Made him soft.

He'd lost his mind and kissed her.

Ford crossed his hands over his stomach and inhaled deeply. He'd known that coming back would stir old feelings, but he'd thought he would be tough enough to ward them off.

He'd had a lot of practice keeping his feelings under lock and key. Especially after Abby drowned. His mom had fallen apart often, so Ford had had to keep it together. The heartache, the goddam guilt...

It was easier when he kept moving. He'd left home to work on a ranch out west the minute he'd turned eighteen. And ever since then, if feelings surfaced, he dealt with them by riding or roping or hammering fence posts like he was driving a stake through the heart of a monster.

He'd thought he could do the same with his feelings for Claire, but so far, he was barely keeping a lid on them. The pot was simmering, just below a full boil, and the lid was dancing and rattling like the tail of a diamondback. Maybe tomorrow things would get back to normal. She'd go into town to work at Maggie's, and he'd start riding and roping and hammering fence posts. Work it all out of his system.

Nail that lid down.

He took a deep breath. The thick, honey scent of bluebonnets settled over his senses. The iconic Texas wildflower was just starting to emerge from its sleepy winter slumber. In another week or so, pastures everywhere would turn into vast oceans of blue waves.

Bluebonnets. The exact color of Claire's eyes.

He shook his head and tried to focus on the sounds around

him. If he did that, Claire's eyes would be forced out of the picture. His mind was a small place. Couldn't hold it all.

Crickets chirped, bullfrogs croaked, and tree frogs screeched, singing the ballad of the Hill Country. It all amounted to Mother Nature being horny. Sex was what kept the world spinning. The frogs and bugs were just trying to attract mates, and the wildflowers were putting it all out there for the bees.

Men were no different. They were just horny bullfrogs hoping for a bit of immortality, and places like honky-tonks were where they went to croak and prance about. The two-step was nothing more than a mating dance.

Ford had done his share of croaking and two-stepping in honky-tonks. Hell, he was a Jarvis, after all. Although, for the last two years he hadn't much felt like croaking.

Ever since Claire.

The screen door slammed, startling him, and cold droplets hit his arm. He looked up to see one of the twins holding out a beer. Ford accepted it and took a swig. It felt good going down. "Thanks."

"Sure you don't want to come to Tony's with us?"

Most of the downtown businesses, including the Corner Cafe and the Dairy Dream, had taken on water. Tony's sat just on the outskirts of town, nowhere near a river or creek, and it was open for drinks, dancing, and bar food. They'd be doing a booming business tonight.

"I plan to hit the sack the minute my clothes go in the dryer."

"We'll try to be quiet when we come in, then."

"Thanks. That's considerate of you—"

"I'm just kidding. We're going to be noisy as hell."

Ford laughed. That sounded more like it. Luckily, he slept like the dead when he was tired. They wouldn't bother him.

"Bryce!" the cowboy bellowed. "Get a move on."

So, this must be Beau.

"I heard you and Claire checked out the dam?"

News traveled fast on ranches.

"Yep," he said. "Didn't see a thing other than a bunch of trash, which we need to organize some kind of cleanup for."

He skipped the part where Claire nearly drowned— *again*—before climbing up the side of a cliff.

Beau shook his head. "I'm glad they found Alison. I can't imagine what her parents were going through."

Ford could.

It had taken three hours to find Abby.

The screen door slammed again as Bryce, Kit, Manuel, and Emilio stepped onto the porch.

Ford sneezed. "Jesus. You guys are wearing enough aftershave to choke a horse."

"I think it's me," Kit said. "I spilled some on my shirt."

"You're not getting in my truck smelling like that," Beau said. "Go in and change."

"Seriously?" Kit asked.

"You've got two minutes. Then I'm leaving."

"Shit," Kit said, rushing back inside.

Beau sat in the rocking chair next to Ford while Bryce and the others sauntered over to the truck and leaned against it. Beau eyed Ford, making him uncomfortable. "Are you really leaving for West Texas in a few weeks? It seems like this foreman position is the perfect job for you. I mean, Rancho Cañada Verde is a beautiful ranch, and Gerome Kowalski knows how to run it."

Ford still couldn't fathom the fact that Gerome was considering selling it. But he wanted to do what was best for his family. Wouldn't any man?

"I like West Texas," Ford said. And it was true. He

enjoyed the peace and solitude, two things he'd yet to experience since returning to Rancho Cañada Verde.

"But what about Claire?" Beau asked.

Ford nearly choked on his beer. "What about her?"

"Aw, come on, Ford. You guys might have thought you were being discreet the last time you were here, but everybody knew what was going on."

"Don't know what you're talking about," Ford said.

Kit came bursting through the door, tucking his shirt in and ending the conversation. The stench was only slightly diminished.

Beau stood and wrinkled his nose. "You're sitting in the back, and we're riding with the windows down."

He tipped his hat at Ford. "All I'm saying is we wouldn't mind you sticking around for a while."

Ford nodded. It didn't feel awful to have someone acknowledge your hard work, and to maybe indicate they even liked your company.

"And I'm sure Claire feels the same way," Beau added with a wink before heading to the pickup.

Ford doubted that.

She'd kissed him back, though.

As the men drove off, he leaned back in the chair again and lowered the brim of his hat. He closed his eyes and tried to listen to horny nature. What he heard instead was the sound of a four-wheel ATV coming down the lane.

* * *

Claire came around the curve in the Polaris, saw the familiar figure of Ford sitting on the bunkhouse porch, and dang near turned around. But she'd promised her mom she'd deliver supper to the bunkhouse.

She and Ford had avoided being in the same square foot for only three hours. She should have known he wouldn't go back across Wailing Woman tonight.

Her heart rose to her throat. She was not prepared to face him so soon after his lips had mistakenly made their way to hers, and she specifically wasn't ready for it while he was shirtless and bathed in the glow of a sunset.

Ford didn't look up as she approached, even though he surely heard her coming, and his hat was pulled down over his eyes as if he were sleeping, which he most definitely was not.

It had been a trying and emotional day. And now she had a shitstorm of *feels* racing around like a dang dirt devil on steroids. So why did the sight of Ford's bare feet, kicked up on the porch railing, calm her so? And why did it also make her pulse race?

Seeing Ford was like seeing a welcome mat after a hard day. It perked you up and settled you down at the same time.

If Ford was going to be around for the next few weeks, they were going to have to come to some kind of understanding.

Like no more kissing.

Because no matter how good a frog kissed (and this one kissed really well), he would not turn into a prince.

She turned the engine off and grabbed the two gigantic bowls of spaghetti her mom had prepared. She noted the absence of Beau's truck and the fact that it was unusually quiet. Was Ford here alone?

He didn't stir as she climbed the steps, nor did he look up when she stopped and stood right next to him. His hat was pulled over his face, leaving only his chin visible. No part of him acknowledged her presence.

"If you start fake-snoring I'm going to drop one of these bowls of spaghetti on your head."

The chin moved a bit, yanked around by a half-assed grin.

"I'm serious, Ford."

Ford sighed and raised his hat. He opened one eye and looked at her. "Is there something I can do for you? Pluck you out of a creek? Yank you up the side of a cliff?"

"I was already out of the creek when you came along, and I climbed up that cliff by myself, thank you very much."

"You're supposed to be avoiding me, remember?"

"I wouldn't have agreed to bring supper if I had known you were here."

Ford smirked and opened the other eye. The smirk turned into a smile as he took in her pink T-shirt with black lettering that said DON'T FLATTER YOURSELF, COWBOY—I'M ADMIRING YOUR HORSE.

Ford absentmindedly dragged a hand across his chest and down his stomach. "Did you say supper?"

Did he have any idea what it did to her when he rubbed his hand all over himself like that? She'd spent the ride back to the house and the thirty-minute shower and the time it took to help her mom with dinner rehashing all the reasons why another kiss absolutely could not ever happen.

But now, looking at Ford, she couldn't remember a single one.

Something about frogs.

"Spaghetti and meatballs."

He removed his bare feet from the railing and stood up. "Did you make it?"

Claire laughed. "What do you think?"

"I figure your mama made it." Ford took a swig from the beer bottle on the railing, and then took the bowls from

Claire's hands. "The guys are out, but be sure and tell Miss Lilly thank you."

He turned for the door.

"Well, good night then," Claire said. Because he clearly wasn't going to invite her in, and that was a good thing.

So, why did she feel disappointed?

Because she was a woman. And Ford was a man. And there was this thing called attraction, which she absolutely was *not* going to give in to. Ever.

Ford opened the door with one hand while he balanced the spaghetti bowls with the other. Then he paused. "Would you like to come in?"

Say no. Say no. Say no. Say—

"Maybe just for a minute."

Betrayed by her own voice.

Chapter
Thirteen

❦

Ford focused on shoveling spaghetti into his mouth while Claire fidgeted next to him at the table. Why the holy hell had he invited her in? Hadn't he told her earlier today that they needed to stay away from each other?

Her fault for showing up on his porch.

Of course, it wasn't *his* porch, and she hadn't known he'd be there. But still...

Why did you invite her in, idiot?

Because his mama hadn't raised a fool with no manners, that's why. Not that you'd know it by watching him wolf down his food. But as long as his mouth was full, he couldn't accidentally kiss her. Not without making a mess, anyway.

He was running out of spaghetti. What were they going to do when that happened?

"Would you like some more?" Claire asked. "I imagine the boys will eat at Tony's. And you seem to be incredibly hungry."

Ford swallowed and wiped his mouth on a napkin. "I don't think I could eat another bite."

That was the damn truth. He leaned back in his chair and put his hands behind his neck. Claire's eyes dipped down to his bare chest. Oh Lord...

"I bet my clothes are dry," he said, rising from his chair.

Claire rose, too. "I'd probably better get going. I mean, don't get me wrong, it was thrilling to watch you eat. But—"

"I'm sorry about your dad," he said softly. Because he was, indeed, very sorry about Gerome's illness. And also, because—*dammit dammit dammit*—he didn't want her to leave just yet.

"Is that why you agreed to come back to the ranch?" she asked. "Because Dad is sick?"

"No. I mean, I could tell something was up. But I wasn't sure what it was. Just knew he needed me." He ran a hand through his hair, remembering his earlier conversation in Gerome's study. "He just told me why today."

"He just told me today, too," Claire said. "I guess I'm glad you didn't know before me. That would have hurt even worse." Her voice cracked and her blue eyes got awful shiny.

If she started crying, it was all over. He was going to take her in his arms, and then he was going to comfort her the only way he knew how, and then they were both going to regret it afterward.

"Are you okay?" he asked. "I didn't know you just found out today. You've had an awful lot of trauma in a short amount of time."

He knew what that could do to a person.

"He seems confident, like always, and says it's a very treatable form of cancer."

"We just need to get him over this hump," Ford said. "And then don't you worry. He'll give up the silly notion of selling the ranch."

He knew it was a mistake as soon as he said it. There was no sign of acknowledgment on Claire's face. No comprehension. Just a blankness. But it didn't stay that way for long. While Ford's mind stumbled around, looking for a way out, Claire's jaw dropped. Her eyebrows rose. Then they dove down into a vicious frown as her hands found their way to her hips.

"What did you say?"

The phrase *Don't kill the messenger* flashed through his mind. Why the hell hadn't Gerome told him that Claire didn't know? Probably because Gerome didn't think he and Claire ever talked. Which they didn't. So how had this happened?

"Now, listen, Claire. There might have been some misunderstanding—"

"Oh, you're damn right there's been a misunderstanding. Dad would never sell Rancho Cañada Verde!" Claire walked to the counter, spun around, and walked back to the table. "It's been in our family for five generations! I'm the sixth. You're just...Ford, you're just wrong."

He wished he was. And he wished he hadn't opened his big, goddammed mouth. But he had, and the truth was out of the bag. Still, it wasn't set in stone. Gerome hadn't sounded completely intent on selling the ranch.

"It's nowhere near a done deal, Claire. He's just concerned is all. For one thing, beef prices are down, and nobody thinks they're coming back up. Lots of ranches are struggling."

Claire bit her lip. Wrung her hands. "Are we?" she asked. "Struggling?"

Gerome had indicated they might be. At least a little. But that was between Claire and Gerome. Ford hadn't seen the books, and he didn't want to. He'd gotten in deep enough already.

"I don't really know," he said. "But this is a big ranch. It's a lot of work. Gerome said he doesn't want it to be a burden for you and your mom if—"

Oh, shit. He hadn't meant to go there.

"If what?"

He swallowed. Hard. "I'm sure your dad is going to be fine. But he's facing his mortality. He's thinking about things. It's only natural. My mom did it when she had breast cancer—"

"She's still doing fine?" Claire asked, eyes huge and filled with concern. "I'm so sorry, I haven't even asked about her..."

"You've been busy nearly drowning and learning your own dad has cancer," Ford said. "And she's doing fine. She'll probably outlive us all. And..."

He looked down at his bare feet. Cleared his throat.

"What?" Claire asked.

"She said to tell you hi," he said.

Claire smiled and put a hand to her chest. "Bless her heart."

There were two ways to use that phrase, and Claire had just uttered it in complete sincerity, as Southern women most often did.

"Your dad is going to beat this, Claire. But someday, maybe a long time from now, this place is going to be yours. And like I said, it's a lot. Gerome runs it like a well-oiled machine, but the reality is sweaty, gritty, and detailed work on one end. On the other, it's like running a business and dealing with markets and subsidies and tariffs. It's not easy."

"I know that," Claire snapped.

Ford didn't say anything, because he didn't know if she really did. Claire could rope. She could ride. But did she understand pasture rotation? Did she know how to keep breeding records? Did she know how much of Rancho Cañada Verde's product was sent to Mexico? Did she keep up with the ever-changing laws in that regard?

She was watching his face, and even though most people had a hard time figuring out what he was thinking, he got the feeling she was reading his mind.

* * *

Ford wasn't lying. This much Claire knew. But was he mistaken? Had he misunderstood her dad?

Rancho Cañada Verde was her father's lifeblood. It was his anchor. His very reason for being. It was inconceivable that he would ever consider selling it. With the exception of his family, there was nothing Gerome Kowalski loved more than Rancho Cañada Verde.

Family.

Claire swallowed down a lump. Her dad would do anything for her and her mother. He'd said so over and over again. And while it was true that Rancho Cañada Verde was his lifeblood, it wasn't really his anchor.

Her mother was his anchor.

And Claire knew that she, Gerome Kowalski's one and only daughter, was her father's reason for being.

You're why God put me on this earth, princess.

If Ford was right, and the ranch was struggling...

Twelve thousand acres of Texas Hill Country with multiple sources of water was probably worth a fortune. In her father's mind, it would set her and her mom up for life, and they wouldn't be *burdened* by the very hard work of running a ranch.

For a moment, it felt as if the ground beneath her wasn't solid. As if it might shift and split and swallow her up. She might as well be back at the dam, trying not to sink. Or in the middle of Wailing Woman crossing, watching the water rise.

A sharp pain hit her right below the rib cage. She tried to inhale and found that she couldn't. A light sweat broke out all over her body. Good grief, was she having a panic attack? She'd never had one. What did they feel like?

A warm hand landed on her shoulder. "Breathe, Claire."

She looked into a pair of cool hazel eyes. *Calm eyes.* She took a shaky breath.

Ford rubbed her shoulder, and she focused on the weight of his hand. It anchored her, and the ground stopped shifting.

"This is my home, Ford," she said. "I'm Claire Kowalski of Rancho Cañada Verde. It's who I *am*. It is literally how people introduce me. And you're right. I don't know the first thing about running this ranch, and I don't even know how that happened."

Actually, she did know how it had happened. Rancho Cañada Verde was her home, and she loved roaming its valleys and climbing its limestone hills. She'd loved the summer days of her childhood spent swinging off rope swings into the Rio Verde, nights around a campfire beneath a blanket of stars, and the sheer delight of being a girl with a horse and twelve thousand acres. But while the beautiful landscape fed her soul, her heart and mind grew weary from the isolation. Claire, an extrovert through and through, needed people. So as soon as she was old enough to drive, she'd gotten a job at the Dairy Dream in town. And after college, she'd worked fashion retail jobs until Maggie had brought her on board at Petal Pushers.

The constant flow of folks in and out, the ever-changing faces and stories and juicy gossip... You didn't get that kind of energy on the ranch.

And speaking of people and how important they were, another thought struck her. "What about Beau and Bryce? And the others who work here full-time?"

Ford shrugged his shoulders. "It's unfortunate, but they're cowboys. There's always work somewhere."

"You don't understand," Claire said fiercely. "This is their home. Beau and Bryce have never lived anywhere else."

"I know their daddy was the foreman."

"For twenty-seven years," Claire said. "When he retired, Dad offered him the cabin and two acres."

"He didn't want it?"

Claire grinned. Even under these circumstances, the image of Mr. Montgomery wearing Bermuda shorts and a cowboy hat on the beach made it difficult to keep a straight face. "No," she said. "He always wanted to live near the Gulf. He and Mrs. Montgomery moved into a condo in Corpus Christi. They're having the time of their lives."

"See? People move on."

That might be true. But it was easier for some folks than it was for others. And Claire might be adventuresome, but she wasn't a *moving on* kind of woman. She was the kind of woman whose roots dug deep down into the earth and didn't let go.

Her father thought she wasn't strong enough to inherit the ranch. That she couldn't keep it going by herself. It wasn't often that Gerome Kowalski was wrong about anything. But he was wrong about this.

Claire looked up at Ford. "I want you to teach me how to

run this ranch. Dad doesn't need to keep up the search for a new foreman. I'll step into the position after you leave, and he'll see it's in good, capable hands and that there's no need to entertain silly notions like selling it."

Ford made the very serious mistake of grinning.

"You? As foreman?"

"Or...forewoman. Whatever you want to call it. And please wipe that grin off your face. You look ridiculous. Also, a little sexist."

Ford's grin disappeared. "You should know me better than that, Claire. I was raised by my mom, my grannie, and my aunt Lucy. They quite literally beat a healthy respect for women into me."

"But you don't think women should run ranches?"

"It's not the *woman* part of your suggestion that surprises me. It's the *Claire* part."

That was even worse! "I didn't think it was possible for you to be even more insulting, but look at you powering through."

"Now, listen. You've misunderstood me. I know you're—"

"Capable? Is that what you were going to say?"

"Yes, actually. That's exactly what I was going to say. But—"

"Nothing that comes before the 'but' matters."

That was something her dad always said, and it was true. Ford was about to say she was capable *but*, and then list all the reasons why she wasn't capable.

"Forget I said the b-word. You're obviously capable. But do you *want* to run this ranch? You're so happy working at Petal Pushers. Will you get the same joy from being a foreman?"

"It doesn't really matter what I want."

"I think you're wrong. It matters a lot."

"Maggie is selling Petal Pushers," Claire said. "So, it's a moot point."

"Oh," Ford said. "To who?"

"To anybody! Jesus, I don't know. Why do you care?"

Ford raised his eyebrows.

"I'm sorry—"

Ford put a hand up. "You don't owe me an apology."

"It's just that... Well, I'd hoped to buy it and make it my own. I'm disappointed. But it doesn't matter. What matters is that Rancho Cañada Verde is my family's home. And it's Ruben's home, and Beau and Bryce's home—"

Ford shook his head and stared at his hands. "Your dad is trying to do what's best for you. And I'm not sure you know what that is. But if you want to learn how to run this ranch, I'll do my best to teach you in the time I have."

"Great," Claire said. "When do we start?"

"The same time as always. At sunup."

Claire gulped. She'd seen her share of sunrises, but she'd almost always been on her way to bed at the time.

Chapter Fourteen

Lights glowed through the bunkhouse's kitchen window, and Claire could clearly see three figures standing there. They were probably laughing at her.

Whatever. She sat up straight in her saddle and squared her shoulders.

A girl needed chaps if she was going to chase calves and heifers through the brush. And the only chaps Claire owned happened to be the ones she'd worn as Hill Country Rodeo Queen. They were red, white, and blue, and patterned like the Texas flag with its lone star in rhinestones.

She'd worn them in arenas. She'd worn them in parades. Heck, they'd even appeared in a *Texas Monthly* photo spread called "Women on the Range." But she'd never worn them to work on the ranch.

She was excited. She hadn't ridden fence lines since she was a kid, when her dad would take her out, just the two of them.

Let's ride them fences, princess.

The rides, often at sunset, were some of Claire's sweetest memories. Her dad would take a blanket and a snack of cheese and dried summer sausage, which he'd cut with his pocketknife while telling her stories about the ranch. To this day, she didn't know which ones were true and which ones were made up. Had pirates really buried treasure in Quartz Cave? Probably (most definitely) not. But it didn't matter. They were Rancho Cañada Verde stories. They were *her* stories.

When had the sunset rides stopped? Most likely around high school. Suddenly, there'd been dances and football games and her afterschool job at the Dairy Dream. Then came college. She'd never forget her dad standing in the middle of her dorm room dressed in his fancy ostrich boots and straw Stetson that made him look even bigger than he was, and he was already larger than life. She'd been embarrassed and wished he'd worn cargo shorts and a polo shirt like the other dads.

If she could go back to that day, she'd rise up on her toes to give him a kiss instead of shrugging and rolling her eyes.

Dang it. She was going to start crying just as she arrived at the bunkhouse porch.

Shake it off, Kowalski.

The door opened and there stood Ford. With the light shining from the cabin behind him, she couldn't see his face or his features, but there was no doubt it was him. She recognized the way he held his shoulders, the tilt of his hat—brim pulled low—and the way his hips moved when he finally stepped through the door.

Her heart rushed out to meet him, leaving her breathless. Could you put a leash on your heart? Because hers needed one. It felt like an out-of-control slobbering puppy.

She didn't dare dismount out of fear she'd follow her stupid heart and leap right into Ford's arms, which would be especially embarrassing since he wasn't even looking at her.

"Good morning, Claire," he said, heading for Coco with the saddlebag. "You're right on time."

He was pretending he didn't see the chaps. "I know you want to say something, so go ahead and get it over with."

Ford messed with the buckles on his bag. "Say something about what?"

"About the chaps."

"You can't wear those," he said, without even looking up.

Oh, she was dang well going to wear them. "They're perfectly functional."

And custom made.

Ford turned to face her and the sun caught his eyes. Her heart began panting and quivering. It was going to leg-hump him if she didn't get it to heel.

"Functional for showboating, maybe. But not for working. Take them off."

No way. They were protecting her Guess jeans. "They're all I've got."

"There's a spare pair of chinks in the bunkhouse."

Chinks were a shorter version of chaps, and they were awful. They came mid-calf, and nothing that came mid-calf was flattering on anybody. "These are fine. Might as well get some use out of them."

Beau and Bryce came out of the bunkhouse, both grinning like idiots. For some reason, Beau saluted, and Bryce began singing, "The eyes of Texas are upon you..."

Ford walked over and stood right next to Claire's right leg. He touched a rhinestone. "These are going to catch the sun, and then no heifer in her right mind is going to let you anywhere near her."

Claire crossed her arms while Ford lifted some fringe.

"And this is going to get caught in brush and cactus. If it gets hung up on some barbed wire, you're coming off of your horse. But most importantly, if you're going to be the ranch foreman, you need to be taken seriously. And those two"—he pointed over his shoulder at the twins—"are going to start shouting *Remember the Alamo* any minute."

He was probably right about that.

"Your rodeo princess days are over, Claire. Go change."

The sunrise was casting everything in a yellow hue, and Claire hoped it covered the blush she felt creeping up her cheeks. Because Ford wasn't wrong. About any of it. And she *hated* that.

"Queen," she muttered under her breath.

"Pardon?"

"I was a rodeo *queen*," she said, getting down from the horse.

"Whatever you say, Your Majesty. Just get your royal ass into a pair of chinks. We're burning daylight."

"The daylight hasn't even gotten off to a decent start—"

Ford popped her on the behind with a rolled map. "Get a move on," he said sternly.

But she'd caught the grin. And it sent her reeling.

* * *

Ford wiped the sweat out of his eyes with the back of his sleeve.

Damn. He should have known Claire would make him eat her dust after being forced out of her fancy chaps. She and Cinder had taken off like it was the Kentucky Derby, and it was all he could do to keep up. He marked the map with the latest spot that needed new posts and wires, and then rolled it back up.

Beau and Bryce were out on ATVs with a drone, which would be able to nab a bird's-eye view of the fence lines that were harder to reach.

Claire was up ahead, working a calf out of the brush. The thing was bawling for its mama, and the mama was bawling back from the other side of the fence in the rye pasture. The calf had gotten out and couldn't figure how to get back in.

Inexperienced cowboys might start hollering and chasing the calf, but an instinctive one knew how to quietly round up a straggler and get it where it needed to go without stirring up a fuss.

Claire was instinctive. And holy shit, she could cut that horse on a dime. You could tell she and Cinder had competed in barrel racing. Earlier, Ford had just sat back and watched as they'd brought four heifers and three calves down from the limestone hills. One of the calves had been like a cat on a hot tin roof, running every which way, and then the other two would try to follow. Claire and Cinder stayed one step ahead of them the whole time. Neither one of them even broke a sweat.

And truth be told, Claire probably could have done it in rhinestones.

She liked sparkly things. Flashy things. High-heeled shoes and low-cut blouses. Red nails and shiny lips. This was nothing new to Ford. His mom and aunt never missed their Friday at the beauty shop, and they could work their way through a drugstore makeup aisle while blindfolded. But Claire's sparkly, fancy things were decidedly more expensive.

She was used to the finer things in life.

But finer things or no, like his own former rodeo queen mama, she was tough as nails. And she was smart. There was no doubt in his mind that she could learn how to run this ranch. But would it put a smile on her face the way working at Petal Pushers did?

Ranches weren't gardens that attracted social butterflies. Most cowboys were loners who wanted to be given a job and the freedom to go about doing it without having to talk to anybody but the cows. And it was sunup-to-sundown work. And often weekend work. There wasn't a lot of down time for socializing. Not that any of them wanted it.

But one thing he'd learned about Claire was that she thrived on social time. Good Lord, watching her with his mother and aunt and sister at Thanksgiving had been a hoot.

He swatted at a fly. Thanksgiving had been a mistake. If it hadn't been for his brother Worth setting his ass straight, things would have gotten even worse than they had.

Jarvis men didn't settle down. And they *really* didn't do it with women like Claire. Women who were like one of those big wrapped Christmas presents that had another wrapped box inside. And another. And another. A million little surprises nestled inside of each other like the Russian doll his grannie kept on a shelf.

Claire deserved a man who was going to stick around long enough to unwrap each and every gift. And take his time doing it. Not one who was only going to get through one or two bows before getting an itch to move on.

A voice from some place stupid in the back of his head said, *But what if you don't get the itch to move on?*

He snorted. Jarvis men always got the itch. The fact that he wasn't feeling it right now didn't mean a damn thing. And the itch was *good*. It's what got you moving before bad luck set in.

"Are you done napping over there?" Claire hollered.

Her hair had come down and she skillfully whipped it up into some kind of knot and stuck her hat on it.

"I was marking the map for Kit and Manuel," he said. "They're restringing wire along the highway right now. But they'll be hitting these spots next. And we need to get some hay out so these girls will stay put while they work."

Claire and Cinder trotted over. "Do we have hay in the eastern barn?"

"Don't know. This time of year, probably not. We'll have to get it hauled in this afternoon."

"I'm not going to be around in the afternoon," Claire said. "I have to get to Petal Pushers."

"I thought it was closing."

"Well, it's not closed yet. And I've got a craft session scheduled at two o'clock. I doubt many people will come considering the state of things. But I need to be there just in case."

Ford remembered how much she loved teaching those craft classes. He added *artist* to the long list of things Claire was good at.

"Hungry?" Ford asked.

"Starving."

"I'll race you to Comanche Hill."

He didn't wait around for a response. He and Coco took off. Claire could eat *his* dust for a change. Comanche Hill was nearby, and there was a huge oak tree they could picnic under. He didn't have to look over his shoulder to know she and Cinder were hot on his and Coco's heels.

He could feel the tug. Hell, it was like Coco felt it, too. Ford could swear the damn animal was holding back, either wanting the girls to catch up or maybe even let them win.

Traitor.

But they didn't win. He and Coco arrived at the giant oak first, and he dismounted and grabbed lunch out of the saddlebag.

He didn't look up when Claire and Cinder arrived on the scene a few seconds later, just set about laying out the spread.

"You cheated," Claire said.

"How?"

"You took off before I even agreed to race you! In fact, I didn't agree. This wasn't a race, so you didn't win."

"If you say so," Ford said, pulling out his pocketknife to slice the ring of summer sausage he'd brought.

"I do say so," Claire said, hopping down from her horse. "I got here first, though."

Claire punched him lightly on the arm before sitting on the grass.

She sighed and looked at the valley below. "Everything is perfect up here on the hill. You'd never know there'd been a flood."

"It's a real nice spot," Ford said, handing her a piece of sausage and a slice of cheese.

Claire smiled. "This is exactly the kind of meal my dad used to bring when we rode fences."

"Oh yeah?"

Claire nodded. "And this was one of our favorite places to stop."

It was one of Ford's, too.

Claire ran her hands over the grass. "If you dig, you can find arrowheads."

"Really? I've only ever found them in dry creek beds."

"This is a special tree. My dad said the folks who lived here before us used to sit beneath it to make their arrowheads.

The ones that weren't perfect were discarded. There were hundreds, maybe thousands, here once. When they became harder to find, we decided to stop looking for them. It just didn't seem right to find them all."

Ford nodded. It seemed better to let them lie. He sat down next to Claire while Coco wormed his way over to Cinder. He looked at the ground and thought about all those arrowheads. He was overcome with a feeling of permanence. And that was followed by a wave of impermanence.

It made him dizzy.

"Do you feel small up here?" Claire asked quietly.

Yes. That was exactly how he felt. Like he was nothing but a blip on a massive timeline that stretched out behind and in front of him as far as the eye could see.

"See that creek bed in the valley?" Claire asked. "Lots of fossils there. They look like snails and ferns."

"An ocean bed," Ford said.

"My dad used to take me down there. He'd make me close my eyes while he described the plants swaying in the currents and the animals swimming around us." She leaned back in the grass, arms behind her head, and closed her eyes. "Can you see it, princess?" she whispered.

It was so soft that Ford barely heard it. But he definitely saw the tear that slipped through Claire's lashes. He caught it with his finger.

Claire opened her eyes, and the blue was so crisp and clear in the shine of her tears. He dug the fingers of his other hand into the dirt and grass to anchor himself. Because he felt like he might fall into those eyes.

He wanted to tell her that Gerome would be fine. But the truth was, he didn't know for sure. None of them were here for longer than it took an angel to blink.

"I can't lose this place, Ford."

The finger he'd used to catch her tear trailed to a wisp of loose hair.

"We'll make sure you don't."

He was in no position to make such an insane promise.

"How?" Claire asked. "I can't possibly be ready to take over in just a few weeks. Dad will be recovering from surgery. You'll be gone. The ranch is a mess from the flood, and we've lost cattle, hay, fences, and infrastructure. Ford, my dad might really sell it…"

"I don't know, but I'll do everything I can to help you."

"You're heading to West Texas."

"We'll get as much done as we can, okay? I'm not going to just abandon you. I promise."

The statement had the effect of a gun going off unexpectedly. The words left an echo, crisp and clean, surrounded by a hazy feeling of shock and fear.

What the hell had he just done?

"Really?" Claire said.

"Yes," he said. The word was another stray bullet exploding from his mouth. "I'll even come back. If you want me to. Just until you're on your feet."

Forget the single bullet. He'd gone full machine gun now. Ridiculous nonsense just pouring out round after round like bullets from an ammo belt.

He didn't want this ranch broken up and sold off for God only knows what. An exotic hunting ranch, maybe? A Hill Country resort sprinkled with bright blue swimming pools? Both were an affront to the sacredness of this place. And yet, he didn't blame Gerome one bit for wanting to do what was best for Claire and Lilly. But if he could come back and get the place in as good a shape as possible, and get Claire ready to take over the reins, then Rancho Cañada Verde would stand a fighting chance.

"Okay, then," Claire said, relief relaxing her face. "You'll come back."

His finger toyed with that wisp of hair. He hadn't even known he was doing it. And when had he gotten so close to her? The brim of his hat was shading her face, and they were practically nose to nose.

She reached up and put her hand behind his neck. Pulled him even closer. There wasn't a cricket's hair between them now, and Ford swallowed.

"I'm glad you're coming back," she said.

Her breath grazed his lips, causing his head to spin. A million thoughts raced around, and he couldn't latch on to a single one of them.

"I can't remember whose turn it is," Claire said, her eyes dipping down to his lips.

"Whose turn for what?"

"For stopping this before it gets out of hand," she whispered.

"It's your turn," he said shakily. "I called it off last time."

"Oh," Claire said. "We're in trouble then."

She nipped his lip, and that was all it took. His body went into autopilot mode and pressed itself against hers, pinning her to the ground. He felt her go limp, then she opened her legs a little. He took advantage of that and slipped his thigh between them while deepening the kiss.

Her hand ran from the back of his neck all the way down to his ass, and he ground against her like a horny sixteen-year-old in the backseat of a car. His chaps rubbed against her chinks with such friction he feared they'd catch fire. Maybe it was already too late, and they were ablaze and sending up obscene smoke signals.

Claire's hand slipped between them and pressed against his cock, which was rock-hard and straining the fly of his jeans. He groaned. Would she go for the zipper? Maybe he should go out of turn and put a stop to things...

Nah. He was too far gone for that. Way too far gone. He didn't want to stop anything ever again. Enough holding back. Being measured. Always in control.

He was in one of the most beautiful spots on Earth with the woman who'd haunted his dreams and every waking moment of his life for the past two years. And he wanted her. He wanted her so damn bad that every cell in his body was humming and buzzing. He could literally *hear* his bones vibrating with need.

Claire broke the kiss.

No. No, no, no, no. She was going to take her turn after all.

"What's that sound?" she asked.

Ford raised his head. Could she hear his body going crazy the same way he could? The buzzing and humming and pulse pounding in his head?

"Oh, shit," Claire said, pushing him off and pointing at the sky. "It's a drone."

Ford was going to kill those twins.

Chapter

Fifteen

❦

Claire peeled off her dirty clothes—she'd left the butt-ugly chinks on the porch—and climbed in the shower. Oh, but the hot water felt amazing. She was in good shape, but her thighs and rear were going to be sore tomorrow. She might have ridden a little harder than she needed to, but she hadn't wanted to look like a wimp in front of Ford. He seemed to be taking her seriously, though, despite the rodeo queen chaps.

Truth be told, she'd had a great time.

Right up until the drone interruption.

She couldn't decide if she was grateful or irritated by it. A little of both probably.

She was so relieved that Ford was coming back. He wasn't going to stay forever. Nothing about him was permanent. But maybe he'd stay just long enough to save the ranch.

And not long enough to break her heart.

He'd kissed her senseless today. And Claire had a feeling he was going to do it again.

Ten minutes later, she flew down the stairs and into the kitchen, where her mom stood at the sink rinsing spinach leaves.

"There you are!" she said. "Where on earth did you go this morning? You were up before me, and I think that's a first."

Claire kissed her mom on the cheek. "I went out and rode fence lines with Ford."

Her mom turned off the water. "Oh? I thought you were working at Petal Pushers today."

"I'm fixing to head over there now. I've got my craft ladies coming in at two. We're doing wildflower arrangements."

Her mom dried her hands on a towel. "Sounds lovely. I hope you bring some home."

"You know I will."

"Would you like some iced tea for the road? I just made some."

"No thanks. But if Dad has already had all the coffee he wants, I'll take the rest in a travel mug. To be honest, I'm having a difficult time keeping my eyes open."

Her dad usually drank coffee into the early afternoon, and there was almost always a pot going.

"He hasn't come downstairs yet, but you can take as much as you'd like. I'll make him some more when he gets up."

Claire couldn't believe her ears. "Dad hasn't come down?"

Her dad was always up before the sun, working in the heat—or the cold—all day, and at his desk until well after bedtime every night. She'd been around seven years old the first time she'd seen him in bed. Until then, she'd assumed he didn't sleep.

"He's getting some much-needed rest," her mom said simply. She opened the refrigerator and put the spinach in a drawer.

"Mom, is his prognosis worse than what I was told?"

"We'd never lie to you about something like that, Claire. What would be the point? I insisted he get some rest today. He hasn't been feeling well, but I think it's more mental than physical. Folks around here treat your daddy like he's some kind of a god. But now he's learning the hard truth that he's only human, just like the rest of us."

"A mere mortal," Claire said with a grin. "I don't quite believe it myself."

"And then he thought he'd lost you, Claire. We both did."

"I'm so sorry, Mom. It was such a stupid thing to do—"

"He hasn't quite been the same since. It's like *he* was the one who had the brush with death. He insists that he finally has all of his priorities in order. That he knows exactly what has to be done to take care of his family, but—"

"He's thinking of selling the ranch."

Her mom gasped. "How did you know?"

"Ford told me," Claire said. "But don't you worry. It's not going to happen."

Her mom sighed and got a travel mug out of a cabinet. "I'm not sure it shouldn't, Claire."

Claire took a step back. "How could you say such a thing? This ranch is our home. It's been in the family—"

"The family is small now, honey. Your uncles didn't have children. It's just the three of us. And your father is thinking down the road, to when it might just be the two of us—you and me—or to when it's just you..."

The words hung in the air and stung on multiple levels. Nobody wanted to think about their parents getting old and dying. And nobody wanted to think about how they might be alone for the rest of their lives, because no matter how hard they tried, they couldn't find a partner.

When it's just you...

"Ford said he'd help," she said. "He's coming back after West Texas."

"Now that would be the first bit of good news we've had in a while," her mom said, pouring coffee into the mug and putting the lid on it. "But you'd better get moving if you don't want to be late to Petal Pushers. I keep meaning to make it to one of your craft classes again. I love my little fountain on the porch that we made out of terra-cotta pots."

"Well, you'd better hurry up. Petal Pushers is closing."

Her mom set the mug on the counter. "Oh my! Claire! I had no idea."

"I just found out myself."

"Goodness, honey. What will you do?"

"For starters, I'm going to save this ranch."

Her mom opened her arms, and Claire practically fell into them for a hug.

"I have no doubt that you can do anything you put your mind to, sweet girl. But I want you to be happy."

Claire gave her mom a squeeze before pulling away. "Thanks, Mom. But sometimes a girl just has to do what a girl has to do. And right now, a girl has to make flower arrangements."

"Don't forget your coffee, and make sure you take an umbrella."

Claire grabbed the mug off the counter and glanced out the kitchen window. There wasn't a cloud in the sky.

"Ruben says we'll be getting a light spring shower," her mom said.

Claire rolled her eyes. "Is that an official weather forecast?"

Her mom's eyes crinkled as she grinned. "He saw a dung beetle rolling its prize uphill."

Claire shook her head. "A beetle pushing poop means we're getting a spring shower?"

"A beetle pushing poop *uphill* means we're getting a spring shower."

Claire kissed her mom on the cheek and headed for the back door. "That's ridiculous."

"I know," her mom called out. "But there's an umbrella next to the washing machine."

Claire snatched it up on her way out.

* * *

Ford stretched in his saddle and admired the view from the highest spot on the ranch. He'd cowboyed all over Texas, and each region had its own beauty. The endless deserts of West Texas. The coastal plains of South Texas. The Piney Woods of East Texas. Even the endless prairies of the Texas panhandle, where the only things serving as landmarks were oil wells and windmills. But the Texas Hill Country was his sweet spot.

He looked below at the swollen Rio Verde. It already was coming to its senses and shrinking back within its banks. It looked muddy as hell, but usually it was a sensual green snake winding its way through limestone gorges and cypress-lined banks dotted with springs and swimming holes.

He didn't swim. But he could still appreciate the view of this majestic landscape. He could stare, hypnotized, at the Rio Verde all day. And all night, too. Because that's when the stars came out, big and bright.

And Big Verde was deep in the heart of Texas. Right smack in the center. There was something comforting about that.

Claire had gone on back to the house to get ready for her class at Petal Pushers. But her presence had lingered. He licked his lips. Damn, he could still taste her. Still feel her hair on his fingertips, the pleasant pressure of her breasts against his chest, and her hand rubbing against his hard cock. But even as those thoughts had him shifting a bit in his saddle, what he really wanted right now was somebody to enjoy the view with.

He was scared to admit it, but while he'd missed their sexy romps, what he'd really longed for was their quiet conversations in the bed of his pickup. The ones where she did most of the talking, but he still felt heard. She understood every one of his nods, grunts, or sighs. And every caress of his thumb when they held hands, silently watching for shooting stars.

He'd missed her laughter, her endless eye rolling, and even her daredevil streak that made his stomach churn and his heart pound.

Two years ago, he'd stood on this very hill and convinced himself that maybe Rancho Cañada Verde would be a good place to call home. And that maybe he'd do it with Claire by his side.

Forever.

Good Lord, he'd invited the woman home for Thanksgiving. And it had all gone great. His family had loved her. She'd loved his family. But their lives were so different. She came from a stable home. He came from one that was a revolving door of stepmothers, half siblings, and lately, sisters-in-law. Because his brothers, with the exception of Worth, were following in their father's footsteps, and dragging their drama home for the holidays.

He'd left her on New Year's Eve. And he'd pretended that he'd never intended to stay, even though he had.

A buzzing from his back pocket startled him, and he reached around and pulled out his phone, squinting against the glare of the sun to see who was calling.

He didn't get many phone calls.

It was Worth. Ford swore his brother had ESP. He always called when Ford was thinking about him.

"Howdy," he said. "Were your ears burning?"

"Hey there, Fairmont," Worth said. The little shit preferred using Ford's middle name. "Were you talking about me?"

"I was thinking about you. What's up?"

"I'm calling to make sure you survived the flood. It was all over the news."

"The place is a mess," Ford said. "But everybody survived."

Worth was a professional saddle bronc rider. There were ten years between the two of them, but they were close. In fact, other than Abby, Worth was the only sibling Ford had ever lived with. Worth and his mom, Lucy, had moved in with Ford's family when Johnny Appleseed had left them in a trailer park with no way to pay the rent. Most of the Jarvis ex-wives and girlfriends had found each other and formed a sort of support group that they called the "exes and hos."

He and Worth usually got along. Sometimes they didn't. But no matter what, they had each other's backs. And they were bound by their pact to avoid relationships and end the Jarvis curse—whether they believed in the damn thing or not.

"Where are you on the circuit, baby brother? Winning any money? Breaking any bones?"

"That's one of the things I'm calling about. I'm hanging up my spurs. Not going to compete anymore."

"What?"

"I'm retiring."

"Why?"

"It's just time."

"You're twenty-one—"

"Hey, now. I thought you'd be happy. You've always hated that I rodeo."

This was true. Bronc riding was dangerous, and Worth had already broken damn near every bone in his body. Ford couldn't even watch him compete. It was just too stressful. But he was concerned about this early retirement. Because rodeoing was the kid's life. He wouldn't give it up without a good reason.

Ford turned Coco around and headed back down the trail. It looked like it might rain, and besides, he wanted to get back to the bunkhouse and see everything the drone had recorded. (Well, not everything. He really didn't want to see aerial footage of his ass grinding against Claire on Comanche Hill, but he had a sneaking suspicion he was going to.)

"So, is everything okay? You're not calling me from a hospital bed, are you?"

Worth laughed. "Nah, man. It's all good. I'm in my truck heading south. But I am looking for a job. What ranches are hiring right now?"

"How about coming to Rancho Cañada Verde?"

"Seriously?"

"Yep. Nothing glamorous. I'm talking miles of fence work. But we could use the help."

"I don't mind. I need the money."

"When can you be here?"

"Weekend after next. I've got some business to tie up in San Antonio."

"I'll see you then."

"I'll be there with bells on, brother."

Ford hung up with a grin. It would be good to spend time

with Worth. He was a hard worker, and Ford was proud of him. In a way, he felt almost fatherly toward him. It wasn't like their dad had ever been very invested in the role.

Ford clenched his jaw.

Johnny Jarvis hadn't been around much. And the checks they'd depended on to pay rent and buy food were few and far between. Ford's mom had worked two jobs just to make ends meet. And that had meant Ford was often in charge of watching Abby.

And he hadn't been very good at it.

Coco had come to a stop. The animal did that sometimes when Ford revisited certain memories. He refused to believe the creature was psychic. But the horse definitely picked up on something. Maybe Ford's breathing changed, or his muscles tensed. Hell, maybe it was his heart rate. Whatever it was, at times, Coco would pause in his tracks. As if respecting a moment of grief.

Ford rubbed Coco's neck and urged him to continue down the trail. Carefully. Slowly. Deliberately. It was the horse's nature.

They were well suited for each other.

Chapter

Sixteen

༄

Claire sat at the counter organizing the supplies needed for the flower arrangements while Maggie perched on a stool and watched.

"You're really serious?" Maggie said. "I don't want to put Petal Pushers on the market unless you're absolutely certain you don't want it."

Claire bit her lip and sorted the bluebonnets from the Indian paintbrushes. "I want it, but I can't have it. At least not right now."

"Are you sure?"

The idea of buying Petal Pushers and turning it into a boutique still thrilled her, but the thought of losing Rancho Cañada Verde crushed her to the depths of her soul. "I'm sure," she said. "My family needs me."

Maggie sighed. "I don't blame you. It's just that you'd have a rocking awesome shop, and you know it."

Claire *did* know it, but what could she do?

"I wonder if anybody is going to show up today?" she asked. "Nothing is back to normal yet."

The bell over the door jingled. "Here we go," Maggie said, peeking over the cash register. "It's Alice."

Alice rushed in and headed straight for Claire. "Oh my God. Are you okay? I woke up on Saturday morning to the news that Claire Kowalski had been washed away at a low-water crossing! Then later, I heard you were okay, but that Alison Mendoza was missing. Then I heard that Alison was okay, but that my library was unsalvageable. It's been a roller coaster of emotions."

"It really has," Claire said. "When can we get off this ride?"

"Hopefully soon," Alice said. Then she looked Claire up and down. "You're sure you're okay?"

Claire leaned over and gave Alice a hug. "I'm fine. The only things that washed away with my car were my Laurence Decade heels."

"I don't even know what those are," Alice said.

"I imagine they're super expensive torture devices that could probably also be declared lethal weapons. Kind of like the ones she's wearing now," Maggie said, eyeing Claire's feet.

Claire held a foot out. "These aren't Laurence Decade. They're—"

"Impractical for working in a nursery and garden center," Maggie finished. "I keep telling you that. They're more suitable for working in a boutique, no?"

Claire produced a tiny pout.

"Sorry," Maggie said.

Claire could tell from Maggie's hopeful expression that she hadn't fully accepted the fact that Claire wasn't going to buy Petal Pushers.

"Did you have to walk all the way home?" Alice asked. "And barefoot, at that?"

Claire set out floral shears and wire. "No. Someone picked me up and gave me a ride."

"The someone has a name," Maggie said. "And it's Ford."

"Oh?" Alice asked, leaning against the counter. "The fancy-tickler?"

Claire tried not to grin. "The one and only."

Maggie crossed her legs, grunting with the effort. Then she raised an eyebrow and began bouncing her foot.

"What?" Claire asked.

"Has there been any tickling?" Maggie asked. "Of your, erm, *fancy*?"

Claire was absolutely not going to blush over a euphemism in front of a pregnant lady and a librarian. "My *fancy* has not been tickled, amused, or even mildly entertained," she said.

It was, however, slightly titillated. And whenever Ford was in the general vicinity, it was downright throbbing.

Her friends looked disappointed, and for a moment, Claire considered telling them about Oscar and the towel, the wayward kiss at the dam, and whatever the holy hell it was that had happened this morning before the drone had interrupted. But they'd respond with squeals and giggles, as if it were juicy gossip and fun times, when it was actually...

What was it?

She couldn't begin to know. But it wasn't silly. It was private. Personal. And Ford had looked her square in the eye and said he wouldn't let her lose the ranch. That *they* weren't going to let it happen. As in the two of them.

"What's going on in that head of yours?" Maggie asked, her eyebrow cocked suspiciously.

Time to change the subject.

"I'm thinking about the library. Were they able to save anything, Alice?"

Alice untwisted a tissue that had been balled up in her hand, flattened it out as best she could, and blew her nose into it. Her eyes were puffy and red. She'd probably been crying on and off since the flood.

"I feel so guilty crying over the library when people have lost their homes," Alice said. "But I just don't know how we'll replace everything. The books especially."

"You're a librarian," Maggie said. "It would be weird if you weren't terribly upset. You spend more time at the library than you do at home."

"I'm only here because I have nowhere else to go," Alice said softly. Then her face crumpled. "JD and Bubba are tearing it down today."

JD Mayes and Bubba Larson owned L&M Construction, and the aftermath of the flood would be keeping them plenty busy.

"The building?" Maggie asked. "Was it damaged that badly?"

Alice nodded her head and blew her nose again. Maggie reached over and patted her on the back. "There, there," she said. "Just think. A new library will be amazing."

Alice shook her head. "I talked to the city manager this morning. There's not enough money to build a new one."

"Oh no!" Claire said. This was horrible news.

"Why on earth not?" Maggie asked.

"The building was underinsured," Alice said.

Claire tried to imagine Big Verde without its library and simply couldn't. It was too important to the community. "What we need is a fund-raiser," she said. "A big one."

"And someone to chair it," Maggie said. "We're all too

busy. Who in this town has plenty of idle time on her hands and would love the attention?"

The little bell over the door jingled. Maybe someone else was coming to the craft class.

"Let me go see who that is," Claire said.

She walked to the front of the store, and there stood Annabelle Vasquez, also known as someone with plenty of idle time on her hands who loved attention. And she was shaking out an umbrella all over the floor.

Ruben had been right again.

"When did it start raining?" Claire asked.

"The minute I got out of my car," Annabelle said with disgust. "If I didn't have this umbrella with me, I'd have gotten soaked!"

"We'd hate to have you melt all over the parking lot," Claire said.

Anna narrowed her eyes.

"You know, like sugar," Claire added.

Or the Wicked Witch of the West.

"Your parking lot is a freaking mess," Anna said, wiping a clump of mud from her shoe onto Petal Pushers' pretty welcome mat.

Claire shrugged. "Sorry. We had a natural disaster."

Anna didn't pause long enough to accept Claire's apology on behalf of Mother Nature. "This horrible weather has knocked all the petals off my posies."

"Oh," Claire said. "How...tragic?"

"I need a few flats to replace them."

"They'll probably recover if you give them time," Claire said.

"I don't have time. I'm hosting book club soon. I want my yard to look perfect."

"Of course you do." If the woman wanted to spend

unnecessary money, Claire would sell her some posies. "Come out to the patio and we'll see what we've got."

Anna followed her out and then spent ten minutes being hypercritical of every leaf and petal on every plant before deciding on some flats of pansies that looked exactly like all the rest. Then she watched Claire load them on the cart and push the squeaky monster to the counter.

The bell over the door jingled again.

"Girls, I'm glad you're open," Bubba Larson said. "I need help."

* * *

Bubba was covered in kids who were covered in umbrellas. One smacked him in the face, but he hardly seemed to notice. He had a toddler in his arms and a medium-sized kid wrapped around each leg. Those two were using their umbrellas as swords, and one came precariously close to Bubba's crotch.

"Watch it," he said, dodging another smack to the head.

"Where's the other one?" Maggie asked.

"The other what?"

"Kid. You and Trista have four, and you're only wearing three."

"Aw, shit," Bubba said. Then he and his many appendages lurched back out the door, presumably to look for Kid Number Four.

"Would you like to stay and make a pretty wildflower arrangement?" Claire asked Anna.

Anna raised an eyebrow. "Are you sticking them in those tacky milk bottles?"

"We have other vases to choose from," Claire said.

Maggie reached beneath the counter and then plopped

a cheap glass vase down in front of Anna. "Here you go. Straight from Tiffany's."

Anna looked at it like it was straight from the dollar store. Which it was. "I guess I'll stay. It's not like there's anything else to do today, thanks to this dreadful flood."

"I wonder if Bubba found his other kid?" Maggie asked. Her brows were furrowed, and she walked to the door. Then she started laughing.

"What is it?" Claire asked, rushing to join Maggie.

Bubba was chasing a small child wearing nothing but galoshes. He still carried one, and the other two were jumping in mud puddles.

Alice joined them at the door. "Should we help? I mean, I'm not even sure I know how..."

"I don't think we want them back in the store like that," Claire said, watching as one child pushed another into a large puddle. That child retaliated by slinging a handful of mud.

Maggie shoved the door open. "Hey!" she bellowed. "Knock it off!"

All four kids, five if you counted Bubba, froze.

Maggie pointed to a spot in front of the door. "Y'all come line up right here."

Bubba, carrying the toddler, was the first one to obey. Next came the naked kid, and finally the last two climbed up out of the mud and took their places.

Alice ran to the counter and came back with a roll of paper towels, which seemed woefully inadequate for the job.

"Listen," Bubba said. "It's Trista's birthday."

"You need flowers?" Claire asked.

"Yes, and probably some other stuff."

"I like how you always plan ahead," Maggie said.

On any given anniversary or birthday, Bubba could be

found wild-eyed and covered in kids, desperately buying whatever item was nearest. If Trista was lucky, this meant an oversized nightshirt that said GIRLZ JUST WANNA HAVE FUN from Cathy's Closet. But in other years, it had meant an air freshener for her minivan (from the Pump 'n' Go) or a pair of leather work gloves (from the tractor parts store).

"You guys stay out here," Maggie said. "We'll handle this."

They went back inside Petal Pushers and started looking around. Trista was their friend, and they didn't want to let her down.

"I'll get some red roses," Claire said, heading for the flower cooler.

"I'll find a pretty wind chime," Maggie said.

"I wonder if he's considered a vasectomy?" Anna asked. "That would be the gift that keeps on giving."

Claire kind of wanted to laugh, but she didn't. For one thing, it was one of her cardinal rules to never laugh at Anna's jokes, even if they were funny, and for another, she happened to know that Trista and Bubba were as blissfully happy as two sleep-deprived humans knee-deep in diapers could be.

Five minutes later Bubba held a toddler, a dozen red roses, and a little gift bag.

"Thank you, ladies. You're lifesavers, every single one of you." He glanced over their shoulders to where Anna sat at the counter, mindlessly sticking flowers into her vase. "Well, three out of four of you anyway. Me and JD have been crazy busy, and this birthday got away from me."

Bubba's stubbled cheeks turned a bit pink, indicating he knew it got away from him every year.

"How is your parents' place coming?" Claire asked.

Bubba's folks owned the Corner Cafe, and it had been flooded.

"They're pulling the sheetrock out today. Got these big old fans in there drying everything out. Mom's kind of pumped over the insurance paying for new tables and whatnot. She's been wanting to freshen up the place for years."

Claire felt Alice wilt next to her.

"How much do I owe you?" Bubba asked, reaching for his wallet.

Maggie waved her hand. "Don't worry about it."

"Are you sure? Need any construction-type favors?"

Maggie shook her head. "Nah, we're good—"

"Actually," Claire interrupted. "I'm going to need a front-end loader to fill in a huge trench in front of my gate. I can't get to my trailer."

"That's easy. JD and I will get out there as soon as we can. It might be a week, though."

That was fine. She really wanted to be close to her parents right now anyway. "Thanks. I appreciate it."

"No problem," Bubba said. "Maybe it will cheer JD up to get out and play in the dirt."

"What's wrong with JD?" Maggie asked.

"He's been quiet and broody," Bubba said. Then he raised a hand to the side of his mouth and lowered his voice to a whisper. "Between you and me, there may be trouble in paradise."

JD and Gabriel Castro were newlyweds, and they seemed perfectly happy together. What the heck was Bubba talking about?

"Maybe he's not gay anymore," Bubba said. "And if that's the case, he's got himself in a real pickle."

"Oh, good grief," Maggie said. "It doesn't work that way."

Bubba raised an eyebrow as if maybe he knew better, which he most definitely did not.

Chapter
Seventeen

❦

Ford pulled in front of Petal Pushers and parked. It had been two weeks since the flood. Two weeks of working side by side with Claire. *Only four more weeks to go.*

He ran a hand over his shirt, noting the way his chest tightened uncomfortably at the thought of leaving Big Verde for West Texas.

"You're a pretty decent Uber driver," Claire said, pulling her bare feet off the dash of his truck and slipping them into a pair of high heels. "Although you could probably use an air freshener. Not everyone appreciates the scent of leather mixed with the subtle undertone of cow manure."

Claire wasn't picking her new truck up until next week, and so Ford had been playing taxi and not really minding it at all. He liked having her at his side, whether it was on the ranch or running errands.

"I've just got the one customer. Seeing as how she rides

with her bare feet on the dash, I figure she's not too offended by odors."

Claire gasped. "My feet don't stink!"

Ford raised an eyebrow and shrugged, repressing a grin. "If you say so."

After two weeks spent working side by side on the ranch, they'd become irritatingly comfortable around one another, and their conversations often slipped into ribbing and teasing.

"Thanks for the ride," she said.

"It was no problem. I needed to come into town to get some supplies anyway. Worth should be arriving at the bunkhouse any minute, but I can drive back in and get you if you need me to."

"I'll get a ride from Maggie. Or maybe Alice. She's been helping us mark down our stock and pack things up since the library is, you know, gone."

Damn. Claire must be tired. She'd been getting up at the crack of dawn, along with the rest of the hands, and working her sweet little ass off.

The outer perimeter of the ranch was secure. The guys were working on the interior fence lines. The cattle were sorted, and only a few were still unaccounted for. They had rotation schedules set for the next two months, and a truck was coming to haul some bulls to the processor tomorrow.

And throughout all the bustling activity, they'd managed to keep their clothes on.

Part of it was because they were too tired to even think about it. But the other part of it involved the fact that they'd been having fun doing other things. Claire had come by the cabin a couple of times under the auspices of checking on Oscar. On Thursday they'd ended up watching a stupid movie on TV. Saturday had found them partying down with a game of Scrabble. Claire had faked falling asleep after Ford came up with a six-letter word that earned him sixty-six points.

She'd rather fake unconsciousness than lose.

He'd covered her with a blanket, and she'd spent the entire night right there on his couch, fully clothed. And surprisingly, he'd slept like a baby in his own bed before fixing her breakfast the next morning.

Maybe they were moving past this insane sexual attraction. But these other feelings, the ones that he had when they were working and laughing and keeping their pants on, felt even more dangerous.

Claire yanked his rearview mirror around to examine her face.

He hated it when people fucked with his rearview mirror almost as much as he hated bare feet on his dashboard. So why was he grinning like a doofus?

He sighed, crossed his arms, and watched as she applied some kind of lip gloss that probably tasted like bubblegum. Then she puckered up her lips. He laughed, but the sight of that shiny mouth made his dick hard.

Not past the insane sexual attraction, then.

"What's so funny?"

"You made a duck face."

"I absolutely did not."

"Did too."

"I made a sexy face."

"To a duck, maybe."

Or to an exhausted cowboy fighting a raging boner in his Wranglers.

Claire huffed and brushed an imaginary strand of hair out of her face before turning his mirror back to the wrong position. He reached up and adjusted it.

"What's Alice going to do without her library?" he asked.

"We're not giving up on the library!" Claire said. "Insurance is going to cover at least some of the construction, and we're going to raise enough money for the rest. We're going to do a huge fund-raiser."

The woman didn't give up on anything. She was fighting tooth and nail to hold on to Rancho Cañada Verde, helping Maggie get the store ready to close even though it was breaking her heart, and now she was talking about a fund-raiser for the library.

Family. Friends. Community.

That's what Claire was all about.

"You've worked really hard," Ford said. "I'm proud of you."

"Thanks," she said. "Surprised?"

"Not even a little. And I heard you were schmoozing it up with bull buyers at the cattle auction on Monday. Travis Blake was impressed."

Claire was a natural. She might have thought she didn't know how to run the ranch, but she really did. It was instinctive for her. Like she was born to do it.

"If by schmoozing with bull buyers he means I was having coffee with a bunch of old ranchers while they talked about their aching knees and hemorrhoids, then yes, I was really schmoozing it up."

"You sold that bull, though. And Travis said it was for more than he expected."

Claire smiled and did a cute little shrug with her shoulders. She damn well knew she'd sold that bull for above market value.

It was just one more thing Ford was proud of her for. "Don't forget we're meeting with your dad tomorrow morning at nine. Why don't you sleep in a little?"

"I can't. I've got a ton of emails to send out." She gave him a secretive smile. "I've been working on a little something."

Ford leaned in. "Are you going to tell me what? Or do I have to guess?"

Claire bit her lip and looked at him as if she was trying to decide if she should share her secret. Then she nodded, as if she'd made up her mind, and took a bunch of brochures and letters out of her bag.

"If what you and Dad say is true, and beef prices aren't going to come back up, then we've got to think outside the box."

"And that's what you've been doing? Thinking outside the box?"

"Yes. I got an idea from some junk mail."

"Junk mail?"

"From Bosco Leather."

Ford had no idea where this was going.

"Product diversification," Claire said. "That's the key."

"Theoretically, I know what that means," Ford said. "But I'm still not sure what you're talking about."

"The non-beef items have been doing pretty well. I haven't seen the figures for the last quarter, but I do see the order reports. And that's with a single retail chain. They don't have exclusivity, so our products could be everywhere. And I don't want to be limited to food."

Ford raised an eyebrow. How could ranch products not be associated with food? Animals and crops. That's what ranches produced.

Claire popped open a catalog from an upscale department store. "Look at this."

Ford looked at a picture of leather travel bags and totes. He shrugged. They were nice, but what did they have to do with Rancho Cañada Verde?

"Look at the label."

He squinted and then saw what she meant. The bags were all stamped with the name of the legendary King Ranch.

"Our new product—in light of falling beef prices—is our brand," Claire said.

"You're going to sell luggage?"

"And boots. And cookware. And even personal care products. Online and in stores."

Ford removed his hat and scratched his head. She sounded crazy, but crazy like a fox.

"That's got to be a full-time job, darlin'."

Claire sighed. "It is. But it's one I've got to do. And I've also got to keep up with the ranch, because there's no point in having a Rancho Cañada Verde brand if there's no Rancho Cañada Verde."

Ford had some crazy words gathering in his throat. They were clawing and scratching their way to his mouth, and if they managed to make their way to his tongue, it was all over...

When I come back after the roundup, it can be for good. Back to Big Verde. Back to the ranch. Back to you.

He bit his bottom lip to keep his mouth shut as Claire stuffed all of her papers and booklets back into her bag.

When she was done, Ford tweaked the mirror again, turning it so he could see his own reflection. Then he made a duck face and winked.

Claire busted out laughing. "See? I told you it was sexy."

And then she gave him a kiss on the cheek before opening the truck door and hopping out as if kissing his duck face were the most natural thing in the world.

It rocked Ford to his core.

* * *

Oh, dear God. She'd kissed that cowboy on the cheek without even thinking about it. It was disappointing after successfully not making out for two weeks.

She headed for Petal Pushers' front door, bringing her fingers to her lips, where she could still feel the stubble from Ford's cheek and taste the salty, woodsy flavor of his skin.

She hadn't kissed him when he'd patiently bottle-fed a newborn calf that was too weak to suckle. She hadn't done it when his eyes had lit up and a little dimple of satisfaction had appeared in his left cheek over his stupid Scrabble victory. And she even hadn't kissed him when she'd felt his warm breath on her cheek as he'd covered her with a blanket.

She had to wait until he'd caught her off-guard by winking at himself in the mirror.

It probably had something to do with how excited she'd been to talk to him about her plans for providing a safety net for the ranch through diversification. Because just thinking about *that* gave her almost as big of a thrill as thinking about the way Ford's bristly cheek had felt against her lips.

Ford made her feel like she could accomplish anything. He believed in her. And that made her believe in herself.

What had he thought of the kiss? She hadn't waited around to find out. As soon as she realized her lips had connected with his cheek, she'd reached for the door handle like it was an eject lever and the plane was going down.

A car horn honked and dang near gave her a heart attack.

"Hey!" Maggie shouted from the window of Alice's Prius. "Didn't you hear us calling for you?"

No, she hadn't. What were they doing in Alice's car? Why weren't they in the shop? Claire shifted her bag to her other shoulder and headed over.

"You're too late," Maggie said. "We're quitting early

today. We got almost everything in the stock room inventoried and marked down."

"Oh, dang. Sorry." Claire looked down the road. Ford was long gone.

"We're heading over to the library site," Alice said. "Want to come?"

"Sure," Claire said, opening the back door. "Seeing as how I'm completely without a vehicle."

A short while later they were standing on a concrete slab, which was pretty much all that was left of the library after Bubba and JD had torn it down.

"Were you not able to save any of the books?" Maggie asked.

"What the water didn't reach, the humidity ruined."

"I'm so sorry, Alice," Claire said. "We really need to get on that fund-raiser. And I think you should ask Anna to chair it."

Loud beeps indicated Bubba was backing up his front-end loader. He was getting all of the lumber and soggy, moldy sheetrock gathered up to be dropped into one of the big dumpsters that lined Main Street.

Alice held her hand up. "I think that might be a hard no from me, Claire. I mean, nobody cares about the library more than I do. And nobody cares about it less than Anna."

"Oh, don't get me wrong," Claire said. "She doesn't care about the library. But she *does* love to feel important, and she knows how to throw a party."

Alice bit her bottom lip. Wrung her hands. "She did host that killer Halloween gala a couple of years ago. People are still talking about it."

"It was super killer," Maggie said. "That's where I met the Big Bad Wolf, remember?"

Maggie had gone to the party as Little Red Riding Hood

and Travis had shown up as the wolf. What started off as a very sexy *once-upon-a-time* had turned into a delightful *happily-ever-after*.

Claire twisted her hair around a finger and fantasized about a gala where she showed up in the world's most gorgeous gown and met her own Prince Charming...

He'd be in a cowboy hat, of course.

"What are you thinking about, Claire?" Maggie asked. "Your face is going through *all* the emotions."

"It is?" How embarrassing. "I was just thinking that we should bring up the fund-raiser at our book club. If we act like we want Anna to do it, it'll take the fun out of it for her and she'll say no."

"I'm not really good at being coy," Alice said.

Claire winked at her. "I am."

A cowboy hat caught Claire's attention, and her heart automatically began hammering. But it wasn't Ford. It was just JD, standing at the edge of the slab, talking on his phone. Although he'd obviously seen them, he made no effort to even wave at them, much less talk.

That was unusual. JD was usually friendly and chatty.

He stuck his phone in his pocket and then stood there, shoulders slumped, cowboy hat pulled way down low.

Bubba walked up and slapped a meaty hand on Alice's shoulder, nearly knocking her over. "I know this looks bad, but Big Verde is going to get its library back. I promise."

"Bubba," Claire said. "What's the matter with JD?"

"I don't know. I told you he's been a sourpuss. And it's not because of the flood. It started way before that."

JD spun around and headed their way, looking at the ground and walking quickly. Claire smiled and prepared to make small talk, maybe find out what was going on but...

He walked right past them. He didn't even say hello. And then he got in his pickup truck and peeled out.

"Yikes," Maggie said.

"See?" Bubba said. "I told you. Trouble in paradise."

"You don't know that. It could be anything."

Whatever it was, Claire hoped it wasn't serious.

"Goodness," Alice said, looking even gloomier than before. "It seems like there's a storm cloud over Big Verde. And it just won't go away."

Claire had a great idea. "Do you know what we need, ladies?"

"Books?" Alice asked.

"Well, besides that."

"What?"

"A night on the town. And it's ladies' night at Tony's."

Maggie patted her tummy. "I have a date with Travis's nasty recliner," she said. "That's how we do Pregnant Ladies' Night at the Blake house."

"Aw, really?" Claire said. "You don't want to get out and party while you still can?"

"I never thought I'd say this, but no. Y'all should definitely go and have fun, though. You both deserve it."

Alice furrowed her brow. "Tony's? I don't know, Claire. It's not really my kind of—"

"Too good for a honky-tonk?" Claire teased.

"What? No, of course not."

"Prove it."

Alice crossed her arms and jutted out her chin. "Fine. I'll pick you up at seven."

Chapter

Eighteen

ॐ

A gray Chevy Silverado pickup truck was parked in front of the bunkhouse. It had a faded bumper sticker that said BUCK OFF! and a silhouette of a curvy woman in a cowboy hat leaning against a fence post. There was also a HOMEGROWN IN TEXAS sticker, and one from the PRCA—Professional Rodeo Cowboy Association.

Worth "Baby" Jarvis had arrived at Rancho Cañada Verde.

He was known as Baby in the rodeo world on account of having gone pro at the ripe old age of seventeen. He was twenty-one now, but folks would no doubt call him Baby until the day he died. Once you'd been christened with a rodeo nickname, it would follow you all the way to your tombstone, where it would end up in quotation marks.

Kit's truck was also there. Ford looked at his watch and raised an eyebrow. Kit should be out working on fences. It was possible he'd ridden with someone else, but Ford had a sneaking suspicion that the kid was slacking off. Ranch hands came in two varieties: extremely hardworking and lazy as sin.

From what he'd seen, Kit was the latter.

The door to the bunkhouse opened as Ford got out of his truck, and Worth came bounding down the stairs with a huge shit-eating grin on his face. Unlike Ford, who liked his hair neat and trim, Worth wore his sandy blond hair long. The ladies said he looked like he'd just stepped off the set of *Legends of the Fall*.

The buckle bunnies of the rodeo circuit were nuts over him.

Ford braced for what he knew was coming, which was a jumping leap.

Oof! Worth damn near knocked the air out of him. Ford pounded him on the back a couple of times. "Okay, okay," he said. "Get off."

Ford tried to wipe the grin off his face before his little brother caught it.

"You settled in yet?" he asked, nodding at the bunkhouse.

"Yeah. They put me in with Kit Black. He's not feeling well today."

Ford crossed his arms over his chest. "Oh, really?"

"I can't believe this place," Worth continued. "I mean, holy shit! Who has actual bunkhouses anymore?"

Worth's face looked like it might hurt from smiling so hard. "Have you seen the horses? Hell, sure you have. Bet they're all beauties. This ranch is a dream come true."

Ford was overtaken by a misplaced surge of pride. This ranch wasn't his, but he sure loved it. No doubt about it.

"I met Miss Lilly already. But she said Gerome wasn't feeling well."

Ford leaned against Worth's truck. When Gerome wasn't

at a doctor's appointment, he was sticking around his study. The hands were used to seeing him out and about with his hand in everything. Big change. "He's having surgery in a few weeks," he said.

"I'm sorry to hear that," Worth said. "Anything serious?"

"Yes, but a good outcome is expected. Everyone has their fingers crossed."

"He's legendary," Worth said. "I hope I get to meet him soon. Miss Lilly said maybe tomorrow."

"Miss Lilly is a lovely lady."

"Speaking of lovely ladies…"

Shit. Here it came. Worth was going to bring up—

"How's Claire?"

Worth, like the rest of the family, had fallen in love with Claire when Ford had stupidly brought her home for Thanksgiving. And he'd been the one to yank Ford out of his delusion and bring him to his senses.

What the fuck are you doing, Ford? This woman is the marrying type. And you're a Jarvis. Get your shit together before you do something crazy.

Ford had looked around the room at his brothers, most of them with ex-wives and girlfriends or current wives and girlfriends…Living out of their long-haul cabs or motel rooms or man-camps in the oil fields and on ranches. Going from town to town, woman to woman, and juggling child support payments. Just like their father and grandfather and great-grandfather before them.

It would be one thing if Jarvis men kept their misery to themselves, but they almost never did. They shared it with women and children.

"Claire's fine," Ford said, staring his little brother directly in the eye. He was going to stick to simple answers until Worth petered out.

"Are you seeing her?"

"She lives here."

"But are you *seeing* her?"

"I just answered that."

"I don't think you did, though."

"You asked a question. I answered it twice. And now I'm going to check on Kit. You say he's not feeling well?"

He headed for the steps and Worth followed.

"I'd like to talk to you about Claire," Worth said. "I have some things to say."

"There's nothing to talk about. I'm headed to West Texas in a few short weeks. There's not a thing to be concerned about."

You don't need to know that I'm having crazy thoughts again, or that I can't fucking wait for the next game of Scrabble, or that I can't stop touching my cheek where she kissed me like I'm a love-struck teenager. You don't need to know a goddam thing.

That meant the less conversation and eye contact, the better. His little brother had shit for brains, but he was still fairly perceptive.

Inside the bunkhouse, the kitchen was a mess—the guys had been working long hours—and Ford made a mental note to talk to Beau and Bryce about it. They were the responsible ones. He went to the door of Kit's room and knocked softly, just in case the kid really was sick and was sleeping. There was no answer, so he turned the knob and quietly pushed the door open. Kit was lying in his bunk, but he wasn't sleeping. He had earbuds in and was watching something on his phone. A greasy bag of fast food was on the bed next to him.

Ford walked over and tapped him on the head. Kit jumped and yanked an earbud out. "Hey, Ford. What's up?"

"That's the question I was just about to ask you. You're supposed to be working on fences today."

As if suddenly remembering he was sick, Kit wilted right before Ford's eyes. In a soft, whiny voice he said, "Yeah, my stomach has been real upset today. I was having a hard time keeping food down."

Ford counted three hamburger wrappers. It looked like he was keeping things down just fine. There was an easy way to test Ford's theory. "That's too bad. Worth and I are going to Tony's to get a drink."

"We are?" Worth said.

Kit sat up. "Tony's?"

"Yeah. Too bad you're sick and can't come along. It's ladies' night."

Kit set his phone down. Ran a hand through his hair. "I'm actually feeling a lot better," he said. "I think maybe it was just something I ate."

Beau stuck his head in the door. "Did I hear somebody say *ladies' night*?"

The rest of the crew was coming in.

Ford motioned at Worth. "This is my brother, Worth. He's going to be helping out with fences, and he'll be staying here in the bunkhouse."

"Nice to meet you. I'm Beau Montgomery. You look a little familiar. Have you worked here before?"

"Nah."

"He's a saddle bronc rider," Ford said. "Or used to be, anyway."

"That's it!" Beau said. "You're Baby Jarvis. Man, you're really something. And so young! You've already retired?"

"Cool your jets. His head is big enough, and he'll be hammering fence posts with the rest of us lowlifes come tomorrow morning. I'd appreciate it if you guys could help him get settled in."

"No problem," Beau said. "But first, let's settle his ass on a barstool, see what's on tap, and give him a proper welcome."

* * *

Half an hour later, Ford sat at a table nursing a beer and watching his little brother. The kid was uncharacteristically quiet, no doubt trying to figure out a way to lecture Ford about Claire. The two of them had taken an oath to keep each other out of woman trouble, and they'd both had to fulfill that oath on more than one occasion.

But Ford wasn't in the mood for it tonight.

Luckily, Worth seemed preoccupied with his phone, which he'd hardly put down since they got to Tony's. It was weird, because he wasn't the kind of guy who had to be plugged in all the time.

Manuel, Beau, and Bryce hadn't gotten off the dance floor since they walked in the door, and Kit hadn't gotten off a barstool. Ford was keeping an eye on him. He was laughing and carrying on with a couple of hotheads Ford recognized from the Kelsey Ranch. He definitely didn't like the company Kit kept.

"So, you're hanging up your rodeo chaps for real?" he asked his brother.

Worth set his phone down. "Yeah, I am. Life on the road is hard. And it's only a matter of time before an injury causes me to have no choice. I'd rather walk out of my own free will and with my back in one piece. I do have one final go-round in Fort Worth in a few weeks. Lots of money at stake, so I'm going to see it through. But then I'm done."

Ford was relieved. Watching Worth ride was gut-wrenching. He always held his breath until the buzzer went off or Worth hit the dirt, whichever came first. He just couldn't understand daredevils, although he clearly seemed to be drawn to them.

"I'll drink to your back being all in one piece," he said, raising his bottle. "But I admit to being a little surprised. Are you going to survive without regular hits of fear and adrenaline?"

Worth raised his bottle and touched it to Ford's. "I'm still getting regular hits, brother. Just a different source."

Dear Lord. What had the idiot taken up? Motorcycles? Race cars? Skydiving?

"It's a woman," Worth said.

Ford set his bottle on the table. Worth had had his share of women, even at his young age. But why would he hang up his spurs for one? What the holy hell was going on?

Worth removed his hat and put it on the seat next to him. He ran a hand through his long, sandy hair, and then he slowly looked up. What Ford saw in his eyes was...

Pure delusion.

"I'm in love, Ford."

Ford shook his head. Even grinned a little. They could get through this. It wasn't the first time Worth had fallen for someone, and God knew it wouldn't be the last. Ford was just glad the kid hadn't gotten himself into *real* trouble.

"Let me get you another beer and we'll sort this thing out."

Ford looked around the room. Where was a buckle bunny when you needed one? A little attention from some rodeo groupies was probably all it would take to turn Worth around.

"I'm engaged."

Ford set his beer down. "What?"

"I said I'm engaged. You know, to be married."

After all the lectures Ford had given him, Worth had been careless. "How far along is she?"

Worth became very still. He glared at Ford with the intensity of a laser cutting through steel. "Don't make me hit you."

Ford leaned back in his chair. Goddammit. The kid had gone and done it. Tipped the first domino. More would follow, and he'd be walking in Johnny Appleseed's footsteps in no time.

And he was just twenty-one.

"Her name is Caroline Lopez, and she's not pregnant," Worth added through clenched teeth.

That was a relief. Maybe Ford could talk some sense into the kid yet.

"Where'd you meet her?"

Ford would bet his life it was—

"At the rodeo."

Bingo.

"She was on leave, and she and her friends had decided to hit up the San Antonio Stock Show and Rodeo."

"On leave?"

"Army. She's a nurse. It was her first rodeo." Worth grinned a little. "I mean that literally. It was actually her first rodeo."

This was not what Ford had expected to hear. He was speechless as his mind clicked along, trying to adjust its assumptions in the face of reality.

"I know what you're thinking. And it's true that we're both young, although she's two years older than me, but we're in love. We want to get married. And I'm willing to give up rodeoing so I can settle down. Her folks are in San Antonio, and I'm looking for a full-time ranch position nearby."

"And the curse?" Ford asked. "What about the curse?"

Worth looked him right in the eye. "That's what I wanted to talk to you about," he said. "The curse is bullshit, and I think you know it."

"But—"

"You can keep running if you want," Worth said. "But I'm done."

Ford couldn't even process what he'd just heard, much less his feelings about it.

A little bit of panic. A whole lot of concern.

And overwhelming relief.

What if Worth was right?

"I don't know what to say," Ford said.

"Most folks would say congratulations."

Ford shook his head. Took a deep breath. "Congratulations, Worth. I hope you know what you're doing."

Movement at the entrance to the bar caught Ford's eye, and his heart began stuttering like a faulty fuel pump. It was Claire. It had barely been two hours since he'd dropped her off at Petal Pushers, but it felt like an eternity. The tugging at his midsection started. It was so intense it nearly yanked him out of his chair.

Claire's head spun around, as if she'd felt it, too. Their eyes met, she smiled, and the ground tilted. Ford had to clench the edge of the table to keep from falling.

"You okay, Ford?" Worth stared at him with concern. "Can I get you a glass of water or something?"

"Huh? No, I'm fine," Ford said, taking a swig of beer and wiping his mouth on his sleeve. "Just fine."

Worth turned to see where Ford had been looking. When

he turned back around, he wore a huge, dumb grin. "I just saw what made all the blood drain out of your face."

"Knock it off," Ford said. "I don't know what you're talking about."

Worth picked up his beer and snickered. "And I bet I know where it went."

Chapter

Nineteen

☙

The familiar straw cowboy hat—brim curved down low—had caught Claire's eye as soon as she'd walked through the door of Tony's. The sight made her knees weak. Holy cow. It had just been two hours since she'd seen him, but she wanted to run across the bar and jump right in his lap.

Luckily, that was impossible. Tony's was absolutely packed. This was maybe not the best night for Alice's honky-tonk initiation, but it was too late now. They were here, they were going to honky-tonk, and they were apparently going to do it with Ford Jarvis.

The jukebox was blasting, and she spotted Bryce stirring up sawdust with...*a TV news anchor?* She grinned. They must have met during the flood. Next Beau blew past with Doris Estrada—he'd dance with every woman in the place before the night was over—followed by Manuel and a cute little blonde Claire didn't recognize. The Rancho Cañada Verde cowboys were out on the town.

"Come on," Claire said to Alice, grabbing her hand. "I see someone I know."

Ford stood up, followed by the other man at the table. Oh! It was Worth!

She dragged Alice over, and before she could even say hello, Worth grabbed her and lifted her off her feet, spinning her around twice before setting her back down. "Hey there, darlin'," he said. "You're sure a sight for sore eyes."

God. What a delightful flirt. "You're not so bad yourself," she said. "But are you even legal? What are you doing with that beer?"

"The rascal just turned twenty-one," Ford said, patting his brother on the back. "He's still a baby, though."

"Well, of course," Claire said. "Right down to the name." She pinched Worth on the cheek and was rewarded with an adorable blush.

"Did Ford tell you I'll be working for your daddy?"

"He did. And that is such great news, because we need the help."

"Oh, he's full of great news tonight," Ford said.

Was that a tinge of sarcasm in Ford's tone?

"I'm engaged," Worth said.

Claire put her hands to her cheeks. This *was* a surprise. Worth was so young, but gosh, his face was beaming. The boy was in love. "Oh my goodness! Congratulations, Worth."

"Thank you. Have a seat and I'll go get you a beer so you can join the celebration." He paused and looked at Alice. "Can I get something for your friend?"

Oh gosh! She'd been so thrown by seeing Ford and by Worth's announcement that she'd completely forgotten about Alice.

"I am so sorry," she said, looking at Alice. "I forgot my manners there for a minute. This is Worth Jarvis."

Alice blushed a little. Whether it was bashfulness or Worth's sparkling green eyes, Claire couldn't say. "Hi. I'm Alice Martin."

"Nice to meet you, Alice. Would you like a beer?"

"I would love a beer, and congratulations on your engagement!"

"Thank you." Worth motioned to his chair. "Why don't you have a seat?"

Alice started to sit, but then jumped right up. "Oops. There's a hat on the chair." She picked it up and set it on the table . . . *on its brim.*

Claire knew what was coming, as no cowboy in his right mind would ever allow a hat to sit on its brim. Worth grabbed it quickly and flipped it over.

"It's bad luck to set a hat down like that," he said, smiling nervously.

Alice laughed, but then it seemed to dawn on her that Worth wasn't joking.

"Oh, dear," Alice said. "I'm so sorry."

"It's okay," Ford said, giving his little brother a stern look while patting Alice's arm.

All cowboys were superstitious. If Claire's dad saw a cowboy set his hat down like that, he'd tell him to stay off his horse the next day. *Let that bad luck wear off.*

Rodeo cowboys were even worse. They wouldn't ride with change in their pockets. And they *all* rode with a lucky charm. As owner of the cursed hat, Worth still looked concerned. "It was only on the brim for a couple of seconds," he mused.

"There's a five-second rule," Claire said quickly.

Worth looked up. "Really?"

"Yep."

"Whew!" he said. "That was close."

He turned for the bar, but then reached back and grabbed his hat, eyeing Alice warily.

Claire sat down next to Ford, who was busy smirking at her.

"What?"

"There's no five-second rule."

"You don't know that for certain."

"Pretty sure I do."

Claire winked at him. "But Worth doesn't. And I don't think you've ever met Alice, have you? She works at the library."

"Well, I used to," Alice said sadly. "And honestly, I should have known about the hat. I've read an entire book on cowboy superstitions and folklore."

"It's nice to meet you," Ford said. "And don't worry about the hat. Worth's probably already forgotten about it."

That was doubtful.

"It's also bad luck to put a hat on the bed," Alice said.

Ford nodded. "The *worst* luck. I heard about a guy who set his hat on the bed, and on that very night his house caught fire and burned to the ground."

"Oh my!" Alice said. "Did he survive?"

"Unfortunately, no."

"Then who told the tale?" Claire asked.

Ford looked at her quizzically.

"If he set his hat on the bed and then promptly burned to a crisp, how did folks even know he set his hat on the bed?"

"Well, I don't rightly know—"

Worth set two beers on the table. "Y'all talking about that guy who set his hat on the bed and burned his house down?"

Claire rolled her eyes. "Never happened."

"Do you know the real reason cowboys don't set their hats on the bed?" Alice asked.

Worth sat down. "Because it will cause their house to burn down?"

Claire rolled her eyes *again*, this time with vigor. Cowboys loved stories, and they loved superstitions. They especially loved stories involving the tragic outcomes of ignored superstitions.

"No," Alice replied. "The origin of that superstition is most likely head lice. You see, back in the day, an awful lot of cowboys had head lice, and setting a hat on the bed meant sharing them with whoever happened to sleep there next—"

"Also, it's bad luck," Worth said, scratching his head.

Ford nodded in agreement. Then he removed his hat and scratched his head, too.

Claire refused to give in to the urge.

Alice took a sip of beer. "That book had a lot of interesting information in it. Do you know why cowboys won't wear yellow? Or where the saying *useless as a hind tit on a boar hog* comes from?"

"I know yellow is bad luck," Worth said. "But I don't know why. And I assume a tit is useless because a boar hog is a male?"

Alice had a captive audience in Worth, and Claire couldn't help but smile when her friend cleared her throat in anticipation of delivering her first honky-tonk lecture.

Ford's knee bumped Claire's beneath the table, but he took a sip of beer and gave no indication that he'd done it on purpose.

He had, though. So, Claire bumped him back and almost

got a grin as Alice chattered on happily about how yellow was associated with fear and some people thought *hind tit* referred to a testicle.

A piano melody floated through the air. It was the intro to "Bless the Broken Road" by Rascal Flatts, which was one of Claire's favorite songs. She and Ford had once danced to it inside the old stone chapel. A moonbeam had served as their spotlight.

It seemed like the only time she wasn't worried about the ranch or her father was when she was with Ford. She wanted his arms around her and for the world to shrink to just the two of them.

"Want to dance?" she asked.

Her heart fluttered. She broke out in a light sweat. What if he said no?

The corners of Ford's mouth turned up ever so slightly. "Well, I don't really want to hear Alice talk about tits on boar hogs, or on anything else, for that matter," he said. "So, let's dance."

* * *

Ford wrapped his arms around Claire, pulling her as close as he dared. They'd easily melted into the sea of swaying bodies, and now he just wanted to melt into *her*.

Her hair tickled his chin as they swayed, and he realized she was sweetly singing along with the song.

The song. It was the same one they'd danced to in the moonlight at the old stone chapel.

They had a song.

Did Claire remember? She stopped singing and looked up at him. "That's such wonderful news about Worth's engagement."

Ford couldn't fake the proper amount of enthusiasm. "Mm-hm," was all he managed.

"What?"

"Nothing. I just hope it works out is all. It probably won't."

"Aw. You're such a ray of sunshine."

He grinned. "It's what makes me fun at parties."

"He is rather young, though," Claire said.

Ford nodded, because that was definitely part of it. "She's a nurse. In the army."

"Really? She must have her head on straight then."

"I'd believe that if she weren't engaged to my brother."

"Oh stop. Worth is a sweetie," she said. "She's a lucky girl."

Oh yeah. All the women who married Jarvis men were "lucky girls."

"I sure hope so. She'll need all the luck she can get."

"Why is that?"

"Because . . ."

What could he say that wouldn't make Claire break out in laughter? Or run for the hills? He couldn't dare bring up the Jarvis curse. He was no idiot. He knew how bad it sounded. How *dumb*.

And yet . . .

The curse is bullshit. And I think you know it.

Was Worth right? Could it be as easy as just calling bullshit?

The song ended and he squeezed Claire tighter. He hadn't come here to dance, but if that's what would keep her body up against his, he'd do it all night.

Suddenly, he wanted to risk it. He wanted to tell her everything. About why he'd left the last time and how he never wanted to leave again. What would she say? What would she do? Did her feelings for him go beyond the physical? Ford felt like they did, but what if he was wrong?

It was hard to know, but maybe—

"Oh my gosh. Look!"

Ford lifted his head. "What?"

"JD is here."

Ford had only met JD Mayes a couple of times. Nice enough guy.

"Let's go say hi," Claire said. "Something's been bothering him."

Ford's body ached the minute Claire let go. He reluctantly followed her to the bar, where JD stood with his business partner, Bubba Larson. Whatever had been making JD out of sorts didn't seem to be a problem now. His eyes lit up at the sight of Claire.

Didn't everybody's?

"Claire!" he said. "I'm glad you're here! I was hoping to get everybody together."

"Everybody?"

"Maggie is on her way," JD said.

"Really? Because she had a pregnant lady date with a recliner the last time I talked to her."

"I told her it was a special occasion. She's bringing Travis."

JD's eyes were lit up like firecrackers. The man was seriously excited about something.

"Hey, Ford. Nice to see you again," JD said, holding out his hand. "I heard you were back in town."

Ford grasped his hand. "Nice to see you again, too."

"You're killing me," Claire said to JD. "Do we really have to wait for Maggie to get here before you'll spill the beans?"

"And Gabriel," JD said. "Until he gets here, I can't say a word."

Claire spun around to Bubba. "You can't keep a secret to save your soul. Spill it."

Bubba shrugged. "I don't know what he's talking about. He's been having mood swings. I think he needs to see a doctor."

"I am not having mood swings."

"There's medicine for it. I've seen it on TV."

"Shup up, Bubba," JD said.

"See?" Bubba said. "Mood swings."

JD sighed, but his bright smile popped right back up. "It sure is crowded tonight."

"We have a table," Claire said. "I think we can squeeze enough chairs around it."

They wove through the crowd to find that Maggie and Travis had already arrived and were seated with Worth and Alice.

"When did you get here?" Claire asked.

"Just now, and I'm not happy about it," Maggie said. Then she shifted her eyes to JD. "You'd better hurry up and tell me what all this fuss is about."

"Can't tell you yet," JD said. "Waiting for Gabriel."

Maggie rolled her eyes. "Fine. But somebody's going to get me some fried mushrooms while I wait."

"That would be me," Travis said, kissing Maggie on the nose. Then he whispered something in her ear that made her blush.

Worth stood up and offered a hand to JD. "Hi. I'm Worth."

"Nice to meet you. I'm JD, and this is Bubba."

"We're business partners and that's it," Bubba said, shaking Worth's hand. "I have a wife, but she's visiting her sister in Round Rock."

JD gave Bubba a stinky side-eye. "Believe me, Bubba. Nobody was wondering."

"This is my baby brother," Ford said, motioning to Worth.

"*Baby* brother?" JD asked. He furrowed his brow, as

if he'd heard something familiar. "And your last name is Jarvis?"

"Yep," Worth said, grinning.

"Holy cow. Is your daddy Johnny Appleseed Jarvis? The bull rider? And you ride broncs?"

"Yep."

"You're Baby Jarvis."

"I'm retiring. I've got one rodeo left in Fort Worth in a few weeks."

"Hot damn!" JD said.

"Here we go," Bubba sighed.

"I team rope," JD said to Worth. "I'm an amateur. And it's just roping..."

"Roping takes a shit-ton of skill," Worth said. "Nothing but respect, man."

"My roping partner is Casey Long. He used to be a bull rider. He couldn't come tonight because he's working. And anyway, now that he's the sheriff he's no fun in honky-tonks." JD was nervously rambling. He turned to Ford. "Does Casey know your dad is Johnny Appleseed Jarvis?"

Ford grimaced. "I don't really brag about it."

"The closest I come to rodeoing is when I'm the horse and my kids are the bronc riders," Bubba said. "I don't really get out much."

"He's got four little girls," JD said.

"I just look at Trista and she gets pregnant."

JD shook his head. "That's not how it works, and now I know why you seem surprised each time."

A tall man in a suit tapped JD on the shoulder. He was the only guy in the place not wearing jeans, but with a smile a mile wide and dimples in both cheeks, he looked perfectly at ease.

"Hey, Gabe," JD said, standing up. "How was work?"

The two men hugged briefly. "Better after I got that phone call."

"I bet."

The two stood there grinning at each other and bouncing on their heels like they might explode. But then Gabriel noticed Worth and Ford. "Hello," he said. "I'm JD's husband, Gabriel Castro."

Worth said his *howdy*, and then Ford did the same as Gabriel sat in the chair Bubba scrounged up for him. Then everybody stared. Waiting. Because Travis wasn't back with Maggie's mushrooms.

Beneath the table, Claire grabbed Ford's hand and squeezed. The suspense was clearly getting to her, and Ford squeezed her hand back. He didn't know these people, but for some reason, he was buzzing with excitement, too.

After a few moments, Travis finally made it back to the table with two trays of fried mushrooms and a tub of gravy. Everybody immediately dug in, including Ford, and *shit!* They were steaming hot. He looked up to see seven people fanning their open mouths, just like him. Gabriel and JD sat, stoic, waiting for everyone to recover.

Maggie spit her mushroom into a cocktail napkin and took a gigantic sip of water. Then she wiped her mouth and said, "Sorry, guys. Why don't you tell us your news while we wait for these to cool off?"

"Are you sure?" JD asked.

"Yes," Maggie said while everyone nodded in agreement.

JD leaned back in his chair and crossed his arms. "Because if y'all want to set yourselves on fire or do the ice bucket challenge or maybe take up hula dancing, we can just sit here and wait patiently to share the biggest news of our lives."

Bubba reached for another mushroom and Claire swatted his hand away.

"We're ready," she said. "You have our undivided attention."

The mushrooms still seemed to have Bubba's undivided attention, but at least he was being still and quiet.

JD and Gabriel took a giant breath in unison, looked at each other, and blurted, "We're going to be dads!"

Chapter
Twenty
♡

Everyone at the table was silent for about three seconds, and then they all started blabbing at once. Claire was out of her chair and practically in JD's lap. She was laughing, but she was also crying, and mascara ran down her cheeks. Even Maggie was dabbing at her eyes.

Bubba sat quietly for a moment, and then his eyes widened and he shouted, "It's a medical miracle!" before pounding JD frantically on the back. "No wonder you've been so moody! Trista is always moody when she's—"

"You realize neither one of us is pregnant, right?" JD said. "Believe me, Bubba, medicine has not advanced to that level."

Bubba nodded, but his big cheeks turned bright pink. "Of course, I knew that."

"We're adopting," Gabe said. "And it's been a rocky couple of months. We've had some bumps in the road, and this morning we got bad news about a child we were hoping for. But then, just this afternoon, we got the news we've been wanting. A birth mother has chosen us to be the adoptive parents of her baby."

"Oh," Bubba said, turning even more red. "Does that mean one of you has to...you know."

Gabriel's eyes widened, but JD just laughed.

"No, Bubba," Maggie said. "They're *adopting*. The woman is either already pregnant or she's already had the baby."

"Well, I bet that's a relief," Bubba said. "For everybody."

Gabriel somehow managed to keep a straight face. "She's pregnant. Second trimester."

Maggie reached across the table and took JD's hands in hers. "You realize our kids are going to be born around the same time, right?"

JD nodded. "They're going to get into all kinds of trouble together. Just like we did."

Damn. These people knew each other. Like *really* knew each other. The only people Ford was close to were family members, and heck, he wasn't even close to all of them. What was it like to make your own family? To share a history with an entire town?

"I'm a little worried," Maggie said. "What if we both get what we deserve? Just like our mamas always warned us?"

Gabriel laughed. "Let's hope that doesn't happen, because I haven't done anything to deserve it."

"How about a round of drinks?" JD asked.

"Yes!" said Claire. "We've got Worth's engagement and a Mayes-Castro baby on the way. So much to celebrate!"

"We're buying," JD said, standing.

"No way, man," Bubba replied. "Let me get it."

Gabriel pushed his chair back. "It's our night. We get to do what we want. And we're buying a round!"

Everyone applauded as he and JD walked off to the bar.

Ford couldn't help it. He felt light. Happy. Almost carefree. Things worked out for some people. A lot of people, actually. Why couldn't they work out for him and Worth?

The curse.

He shook his head to get rid of that nonsensical thought. Worth was right. The curse was bullshit.

Bubba suddenly stood up, scraping his chair loudly across the floor.

Something was wrong.

Bubba glared in the direction of the bar. Ford glanced over and spotted Kit, sitting on a barstool with a dumbass cocky grin on his face. He was staring right at JD, and JD was staring back with his fists clenched.

What the fuck had Kit said?

Gabriel set a hand on JD's shoulder, but JD shook him off. Gabriel might be coolheaded, but Ford would bet his uncle that JD didn't back away from a fight.

JD's jaw was clenched and his right hand was already balled up into a fist. The man looked like he could pack a good punch, and if Kit weren't so drunk, surely he'd see it. But instead of standing up and apologizing for whatever stupid remark he'd vomited, Kit gave JD a little push. The two guys from the Kelsey Ranch snickered and stood.

Everything happened in a flash. Gabriel grabbed JD by the shoulders and tried to pull him away, and Bubba shot across the room like a rocket. Ford was impressed at the speed with which the large man moved. Hopefully, Bubba would get there in time to put a stop to things. A man of his size would surely—

Bubba threw the first punch.

"Oh, dear!" Alice said.

"Ladies, let me escort you outside," Ford said.

"Oh, hell no," Claire said. "We're staying."

Maggie nodded, and Travis sighed in exasperation.

Kit punched back. Bubba easily ducked it. Unfortunately, JD was standing directly behind him, and Kit's fist connected solidly with JD's cheek. Worth hopped up with a stupid grin on his face and ran straight to the train wreck. First night in town and the idiot was going to get a shiner.

Gabriel, proving to be less coolheaded than Ford had thought, politely removed his suit jacket before taking a flying leap at Kit, while one of the Kelsey boys sucker-punched Bubba in the gut.

"Aw, hell," Ford said.

He removed his hat and handed it to Claire. Then he looked at Alice. It seemed she should also have something to do, so he picked up his bottle from the table and in a time-honored Texas tradition said, "Hold my beer."

Travis stood and Maggie grabbed his arm. "Don't you even think about—"

"Hold my glasses," Travis said, handing them to Maggie. Then he nodded at Ford and the two of them ran into the fray of scurrying boots and swinging fists.

It was over in about two minutes. Tony came out from behind the bar with a baseball bat, and his mom followed with a big wooden rolling pin. Most of the men seemed more frightened of Tony's mom, who was cursing like a sailor and telling them they should all be ashamed of themselves.

Kit, who could barely stand, had a bloody lip and a cut on his cheek. JD's eye was swelling, and Gabriel was holding his nose, as was Travis. Bubba didn't seem too much the worse for wear, but Worth was sporting an eye to match JD's.

Ford licked his bloody lip, savoring the copper taste while he waited for his pulse to slow down. He didn't even know who'd hit him.

JD was still staring hard at Kit, and it looked like things might heat up again in the parking lot if somebody didn't do something.

Ford didn't need to know the exact words Kit had uttered to start the fight. He'd heard words just like them all his life, and they made him fucking sick. How dare this mean-spirited, hateful little prick try to ruin what was obviously one of the best nights of these men's lives? What gave him that right?

He stared into Kit's drunken eyes and said, "You're fired."

"You can't do that!" Kit said. "I'm not at work. You're not the foreman of the entire town of Big Verde. And all I said to those freaks was—"

"I don't want to hear what you said. You're going to get in the truck with Beau and Bryce, and they're going to take you to the bunkhouse. In the morning you're going to gather your shit and get out."

"Guys fight in bars sometimes," Kit whined. "You can't fire a cowboy for doing what cowboys do."

"First of all, you're no cowboy. Secondly, I can, and did, fire you. And thirdly, it's not because you got drunk and started a fight. It's because you're a shitty, horrible person, and you don't belong on Gerome Kowalski's ranch."

God, it felt good to say those words.

"Yeah!" Worth shouted, while taking a step toward Kit and puffing his chest out like a brainless peacock. Tony's mom slapped the wooden rolling pin against his right butt cheek.

"Ow!" Worth wailed, rubbing the offended area.

"You deserved that," Ford said.

Bryce and Beau escorted Kit out of the bar, followed by the Kelsey boys, who glared and snarled over their shoulders. "No fighting in the parking lot, or I'm calling Casey to haul you all off!" Tony called.

Claire and Alice started tending to JD and Gabriel. Bubba had his hand on JD's shoulder, asking if he and Gabe were okay, and Ford knew he wasn't referring to their physical injuries.

What was it like to have friends who cared that deeply? The way Bubba had jumped up...

A pair of arms suddenly wrapped around his waist. He turned to see Claire's face, filled with emotion. "Are you okay?"

He nodded, trying to make out what Claire was thinking. What she was *feeling*.

There was definitely concern. Maybe a little irritation. Definitely some pride.

That made him feel the best, but he hadn't done anything for anybody to be proud of. He'd defended his friends. Who wouldn't do that? And also, when had he started thinking of these folks as his friends?

Claire touched his swelling lip, and then right there in front of God and everybody, she kissed him.

People were chattering away, either about them, or JD and Gabriel, or maybe the way Bubba had dodged that punch. Ford didn't care. Claire's lips were on his, and that's all that mattered.

If he were the kind of man to settle down, he might think that maybe these were his people, and that maybe Big Verde was his town.

And that maybe this could be his woman.

* * *

Claire's mind was blank. She couldn't form a thought. All she knew was that Ford had stood up for her friends, he'd been hit, his lip was bleeding...

And now she was kissing him.

In front of people.

And the people were whistling and making kissy sounds and she was probably going to regret this, but right now, she didn't care.

"Enough!" someone said.

But Claire hadn't had nearly enough.

"You folks need to get out of my bar."

Claire came to her senses and broke the kiss. Was Tony talking to *them*?

"Thanks for breaking up that fight," Maggie said to Tony. "It looks like the riffraff is gone."

"I said *out*," Tony said.

Maggie put her hands on her hips. "Pardon?"

Travis stood behind her, glasses crooked and a bloody napkin hanging out of his right nostril.

"You heard me," Tony said.

"But we just got here," Claire said. "It's supposed to be a celebration. And anyway, the bad guys already left."

"He threw the first punch," Tony said, pointing at Bubba with his bat. "I saw it with my own eyes. All of you out. Don't make me sic my mama on you."

Tony's mother smacked her rolling pin against the palm of her hand and eyed Bubba's backside like it had a bull's-eye on it.

"I can't believe you're kicking a pregnant woman out!" Maggie said indignantly, patting her tummy.

"I'm officially asking all the pregnant ladies involved in

the bar fight or whose idiot husbands were involved in the bar fight to get the heck out of my bar," Tony said. "You can come back next week."

Travis grinned. "Mrs. Blake, you have officially been kicked out of a honky-tonk."

"It's not her first time," JD said, and Travis raised an eyebrow.

"First time while pregnant, though," Maggie mumbled.

Alice raised her hand like a schoolgirl. "Excuse me, Mr. Tony—"

Tony sighed, but Claire thought he might have been holding back a grin. "Yes?"

"I'm the local librarian and—"

"You'll be leaving with the rest of the riffraff. Librarians, pregnant ladies..." He eyed Claire and added, "Beauty queens and whatnot. Out."

"What about lawyers?" Gabriel asked, as if he were afraid of being left out.

"*Especially* lawyers," Tony said, pointing at the door.

"Man, I'm sorry, everybody," JD said. "I feel like it's my fault for reacting—"

"It is," Tony snapped. And then his eyes softened a bit. "There are going to be assholes everywhere, JD. You'd better get a handle on that temper."

JD nodded and put his hat on his head. Then the group shuffled their way toward the door while folks waved and hollered and patted the guys on the back. Bubba waved like he was the grand marshal of the Big Verde Apple Festival Parade. Ford and Claire brought up the rear, followed by Tony's mom and her rolling pin.

The parking lot was filled with pickups, and a few had foggy windows from the activities of amorous couples. The sky was clear and the moon was full.

Claire looked around for Ford's pickup. She wouldn't mind fogging up some windows...

Maggie clapped her hands to get everyone's attention. "Why don't you all come back to our place? We've got cold beer in the fridge, the night is still young, and there's a recliner with my name on it."

"That's very kind," Ford said. "But I think Worth and I will be getting on back to the ranch."

What? Claire's heart plummeted. She was still flying high from the fight-fueled adrenaline rush, even though she didn't technically approve of fighting. And from the dancing that lit her up from head to toe and made her want to melt into a warm, gooey puddle. And the hand-holding that had unleashed a herd of butterflies in her stomach.

And the kissing that had made her forget she was in the middle of a bar surrounded by people.

Did Ford not feel any of those things? Was she feeling this by herself?

A wave of anxiety washed over her.

"But it's not even nine o'clock," Maggie said.

"And we're supposed to be celebrating my engagement," Worth added.

Ford stared at his boots, and then looked up at Claire. "Are you going?"

"Yes."

"Then I guess I'm coming, too."

Chapter
Twenty-One

ॐ

Ford followed the line of taillights up the lane to Happy Trails and Travis and Maggie's house.

"Would you stop that obnoxious whistling?" Worth said.

He was whistling? He never whistled. Weird. "Sorry."

"This is a nice little ranch."

It really was. "Last time I was here, it needed a lot of work and Travis was on the verge of losing it."

"Oh?"

"Gerome helped him out," Ford said.

"Gerome Kowalski is a special breed," Worth said.

"That he is."

They parked in front of a two-story white ranch house with a wraparound porch. Doors slammed as people climbed out of their trucks.

"Folks sure are friendly in Big Verde," Worth said. "I'm thinking that maybe it would be a good place to settle down. It'll depend on Caroline, of course."

Ford swallowed and fought the automatic surge of pessimism. He wanted to be happy for his brother. He loved the kid to death. It would be great if things could work out for him. And if they worked out for Worth, well, maybe they could work out for Ford, too.

And what exactly was he hoping would work out?

A Prius parked next to him. The passenger door opened and Claire got out.

"Damn," Worth said. "She really is beautiful."

"Hey, you're an engaged man, remember?"

"I still have eyes, idiot. And Claire is gorgeous, inside and out."

Claire knocked on the window. "Y'all coming in?"

He got out of the truck. Claire seemed to search his eyes. What was she looking for? Her hand drifted toward his, but then fell back at her side.

Oh, hell no.

Ford reached over and grabbed Claire's hand. She smiled, and they went up the porch steps together.

Lupe Garza stood in the doorway dispensing welcoming hugs as JD, Gabriel, and Bubba lined up behind Travis and Maggie.

Worth practically skipped up the steps like he'd been to Maggie and Travis's house a hundred times, and before Ford knew it, the kid was hugging Lupe like he'd known her his entire life.

They were brothers, but their personalities were as different as night and day.

When it was Ford's turn to greet Lupe, he leaned in for what he hoped would be a quick, impersonal hug, but no such luck. He had to hold his breath against the cloud of perfume as Lupe squeezed and patted and fussed over him.

"Come in, come in," she said. "It looks like a few of

you need some ice. I won't even ask why. I hope we have enough…"

She scurried into the kitchen as Ford glanced around the living room. There were toys piled in a corner, family photos on every surface, and although the furniture looked a bit worn, it was warm and inviting. A hint of something spicy hovered in the air.

"I made tacos for Henry," Lupe called from the kitchen. "All the fixings are still out—"

Bubba headed straight for the kitchen like he was a bull calf and Lupe had just honked the horn on a hay truck.

"He's always first to the trough," JD said.

"How about the rest of you?" Maggie asked. "Ready for a celebratory taco bar?"

"I sure am," Gabriel said, licking his swollen lips.

Mrs. Garza came out with an apronful of frozen vegetable bags. She handed peas to JD and corn to Gabriel. "What are we celebrating? And why are half of you beaten to a pulp?"

"We're celebrating a baby," Maggie said.

"And an engagement," Worth added.

"Also," JD said, tipping his hat, "you should see the other guys."

"Well, I knew about the baby," Lupe said, waving at Maggie's belly. "But who's engaged?"

"Not our baby," Maggie said as she squeezed past Lupe to get to the tacos. "And it's Worth who's getting married."

"Oh!" Lupe said, patting Worth's cheek. "Congratulations!"

"And we're having the baby," Gabriel said, putting an arm around JD.

Lupe's eyebrows rose up to her hairline. "You are?" Then her face lit up with a smile and her eyes began to mist.

Footsteps pattered down the stairs.

Everyone looked to see Henry, sleepy-eyed with mussed-up hair, wearing Spider-Man pajamas. He rubbed a hand over his face and yawned, but then his eyes widened and he jerked to attention. "Did Mama have the baby?"

"No, honey," Claire said. "Your mama is in the kitchen eating her weight in tacos. But JD and Gabriel are going to have a baby. Isn't that good news?"

Henry shrugged.

Bubba came out of the kitchen with a full plate. "And just in case you were wondering," he said, "neither one of them is pregnant."

"I know that," Henry said. "They're both boys. Who would think a dumb thing like that?"

Ford looked down at his boots so he wouldn't laugh.

"We're adopting," JD said.

Henry's face lit up. "I know all about adopting! Mama and Dad adopted me. So, if you have any questions, I can help."

"Thank you, Henry," Gabriel said. "It'll be nice to have someone to consult."

Henry's posture straightened with importance. Claire grinned at Ford, and he winked at her. The kid was cute. He was probably a pistol, though.

Maggie got Henry some water and sent him back to bed, and then Claire followed her into the kitchen while Lupe passed out the rest of the bags of frozen vegetables—Ford got okra—before heading home to her house in town.

Worth was already stuffing a taco in his face. Bubba walked by and smacked him on the back, knocking the taco out of his hand. Luckily it landed on the plate.

"Sorry," he said. "But you know what they say. A man who can't hold on to his taco can't hold on to his woman."

Bubba lowered his voice a bit and added, "I read that on the bathroom wall at Tony's. You'd better keep an eye on that fiancée of yours."

Worth laughed. "A man who compares a woman to a taco is not very good at satisfying a woman. I've never read that anywhere, but it's just common sense."

"I don't know about that," Bubba said, just as JD walked up. He eyed his pal for a second. "Hey, JD. What's the number one thing I'm good at?"

Without hesitation, JD said, "Eating."

Bubba winked at Worth. "It just takes practice, bruh. Trista's pretty satisfied."

Claire breezed over and handed Ford a beer. That was the only way to describe it, really. The way she walked. The way she talked. It was all like a breath of fresh air on a hot summer day. Breezy.

"Trista is pretty satisfied with what?" she asked, eyebrow raised.

Bubba's mouth hung open for a few seconds, but then he said, "The deck I just added to the back of the house."

"Oh? When did you do that?"

"A couple of months ago. JD helped me knock it out. Only took a day."

JD nodded vigorously.

Claire crossed her arms over her chest. "Speaking of the two of you knocking things out—"

"Can't we ever have a conversation with a woman that doesn't end with us having to build something or fix something or paint something?"

"No," Claire said. "And I'm still waiting on you guys to fill in that gigantic hole in front of my gate. I still can't get to Miss Daisy, and while I love my parents, we're all ready for a little distance."

"I think it's going to involve more than filling in a hole," JD said. "But we'll be out there to take care of it. Can we get a front-end loader across the low-water crossing?"

Claire looked at Ford and raised an eyebrow.

"I think so," Ford said. "Some county workers have fixed it up pretty good."

"How about tomorrow afternoon then?" JD asked.

"It's a date," Claire said.

She headed for the kitchen, and Bubba said, "Now then. Where were we? Oh, yeah. I was about to teach you boys how to satisfy a woman."

Worth had taken a bite out of his taco and now he dang near choked on it. Bubba pounded him on the back again and laughed. "I see we've got one that's still wet behind the ears."

Watching Worth rib with these guys as if he'd known them his whole life was weird. And knowing that Worth was thinking about staying in Big Verde, as in, *settling down with a woman* staying, made it even weirder. It's like Ford had accidentally stepped into an alternate universe.

And it wasn't half bad.

He tried to imagine Worth putting in a hard day's work on Rancho Cañada Verde and then going home to some little house in the country, one with just enough room for Caroline and a couple of horses. Ford swallowed. And maybe a kid, or two.

The scene played out pretty clearly in his mind. As a nurse, Caroline would probably work at the local hospital. On the weekends Worth would hit Tony's to watch a game with the guys, and Caroline might go to book club or some such nonsense with Claire and Maggie and Alice.

It sounded like a small, boring, and repetitive life

compared to the rodeo circuit, but for some reason, Ford had no trouble imagining Worth seamlessly gliding into it.

Ford took a huge gulp of beer and wiped his brow. Because while he was entertaining that scenario, he'd oddly started imagining himself in Worth's place. Only instead of a nurse named Caroline, there was a trail-blazing, rock-climbing, horse-riding redhead named Claire at his side.

What the hell was happening?

* * *

Claire and Alice stood at Maggie's stove and spooned Mexican rice onto their plates while Maggie sat at the table.

"Can we get you something?" Claire asked her.

"No thanks. Travis fixed me a plate. He's been taking such good care of me."

"And you know he's going to be great with the baby, too."

"That will make one of us," Maggie said as they carried their plates to the table. After they were seated, she whispered, "I'm terrified."

Claire took Maggie's hand. "Don't be. You've already got this mom thing down."

"Henry was six when we adopted him. I've never been around an actual baby."

"You're going to be fine. So are Gabriel and JD, for that matter. I mean, come on. If Bubba can do it, anybody can."

"Okay. That actually makes me feel better."

Claire grinned, and swallowed down the green monster of jealousy that was starting to rear its ugly head. *She* wanted all the excitement and hope that came with starting a family. But even if she never got it, she could be happy for her friends.

Raucous laughter drifted in from the living room, and they looked through the door to see Ford shaking his head at Bubba.

"I like the fancy-tickler," Alice said. "He's nice."

"Nice?" Maggie said. "Is that an abbreviation for tall, handsome, and sexy-mysterious?"

"Yes," Alice said. "And he's not bad in a fight. Not that I approve of fighting."

"No, no, me either," Maggie said as they all shook their heads to emphasize how very much they disapproved of fighting. "But Travis is definitely getting sex tonight."

Claire laughed. "I'm glad he thought to hand you his glasses."

"It wasn't his first fight," Maggie said. "But anyway, Ford seems to be fitting in nicely. And the two of you looked like a couple tonight. I saw you holding hands under the table."

"Oh, that's..." She struggled to find the right word. "Misleading. I was just so excited for JD and Gabriel. I grabbed his hand."

"You came in the house tonight holding hands," Alice said quietly.

It was instinct. Because when she was happy, she wanted Ford. And when she was worried or upset, she wanted Ford. And that meant grabbing his hand.

And a few other things.

"And there was the kiss," Alice added.

That one was harder to explain. "We're...friends."

This was true. They absolutely *were* friends.

"Ha! I'm friends with Alice, and we're not holding hands under the table."

"Or kissing in public," Alice said.

"In private, it's another matter," Maggie said with a wink at Alice.

Alice giggled, and Claire raised an eyebrow.

Maggie snorted. "Seriously, though. I know what it's like to be friends with guys. You and Ford are not friends."

Alice nodded in agreement. "It doesn't look platonic to me."

Claire sighed. "He's coming back after his roundup in West Texas, but he's not staying in Big Verde. He'll never settle down. He's just not capable of it. And he's said as much. Heck, he's *proven* as much."

"Remember when Travis first came back to Big Verde?" Maggie asked. "He was hell-bent on hightailing it out at the first available opportunity."

"But he didn't," Alice said.

Maggie nodded. "And Gerome predicted it. He knew Travis was a cowboy before Travis knew he was a cowboy."

Claire grinned, remembering her dad's voice—strong and clear before the throat cancer—saying, *Aw, that boy's not going anywhere.*

"Gerome Kowalski is never wrong," Maggie added.

Claire was afraid to let hope get the better of her. It just hurt too much when she was wrong.

"What's happening on Sizzle?" Maggie asked suddenly. "Any Prince Charming prospects?"

"I don't know. I haven't looked at it since—"

"Since Ford got here?"

"It's not like I've had a lot of spare time on my hands."

"Well, since you're not actively dating anyone, and you don't have time to pursue Prince Charming on that dreadful dating app, what would happen if you just decided to enjoy a handsome frog's company while he's here? It's not like you can avoid each other. And it doesn't seem like you want to."

Alice nodded. "And maybe if you keep kissing him, he'll turn into a prince."

Somehow, Claire didn't think it worked that way. But she really did like being with him. And he seemed to like being with her. Why *couldn't* they just have fun? Her heart was going to be crushed when he left either way. What if she set aside happily-ever-after to enjoy being happy for now?

Laughter from the living room drew Claire's attention. She caught sight of Bubba doing something weird with his tongue while Worth, Ford, and Travis watched. "Oh my God. What is he doing?"

They quieted down to eavesdrop and heard Bubba say, "You go through the entire alphabet that way."

Worth's eyes were huge. "Was that in cursive? I couldn't tell."

"Don't matter," Bubba said. "Just stick with it from A to Z. Guaranteed to satisfy."

Claire snorted. "They're talking about oral sex."

"If you make it all the way to Z, you're doing it wrong!" Maggie shouted.

The men laughed and then moved out of the doorway, presumably to continue talking about ways to please a woman without having to suffer critique from actual women.

"So," Maggie said with a grin. "What about Ford? He looks like a cursive guy, am I right?"

Claire's cheeks caught fire.

"Judging from that blush, I'm definitely right," Maggie said. "Travis, too. They don't teach that in school anymore, you know. We should count ourselves lucky."

Chapter

Twenty-Two

❦

It was Sunday morning, and Ford was out for a ride. He was satisfied with the ranch's progress. Things were getting back to normal. He and Claire had had their weekly meeting with Gerome, and it had gone really well. Gerome seemed pleased that things were running so smoothly, and he'd seemed especially pleased that Claire had so much to do with it.

There had been no more talk of selling the ranch, and Gerome had even mentioned how much he was looking forward to branding day, where neighboring ranchers and people in the community came out to help brand cattle and enjoy a nice barbecue.

Ford was looking forward to it, too, although he was also dreading it a little since every event or happening brought him closer to leaving for West Texas. There was not a lot of time to get everything in order so that Gerome could relax and rest up before his surgery.

Ford wasn't typically expected to work on Sundays, but he usually did because he didn't know what else to do. This morning he'd scheduled vaccinations, checked on hay fields and arranged for baling. Now he was at a loss as to what he should do with himself until three thirty, when he and Sheriff Long were supposed to head into the adjoining state park to round up some stray cattle who'd escaped during the flood.

Ford could have taken Beau and Bryce, but they usually had weekend plans, and Sheriff Long had all but begged Ford to take him and JD. They were about to find out that team roping in an arena was an entirely different experience than chasing heifers and their calves through a state park.

Should be fun.

A big pickup rumbled up next to him, forcing him and Coco to the side of the road. The back window rolled down and Claire leaned out. "Hey, Ford. What's up?"

At the sight of her beautiful face and songlike voice, lots of things went up (like his mood, his heart rate, and his teeter-totter of a cock).

"Nothing much," he said, tilting the brim of his hat up. "Just out checking on things. What are y'all up to?"

There was a front-end loader on the trailer behind the truck, so he figured they were going to finally attack that ditch in front of Miss Daisy.

Maggie poked her head out next to Claire's, and then the front window rolled down to reveal Bubba and JD. "We're going to fill in that big hole in front of Claire's gate. Want to help?"

Since Ford had been thinking about Claire nonstop since, well, forever, but especially since Tony's, he was happy to help.

She'd kissed him. In front of everybody.

"Okay. Sure."

Claire grinned at him. "See you in a few minutes."

He watched as the truck and trailer made its way slowly over the crossing before heading across himself. By the time he got to Claire's gate, Bubba was backing the big machine off the trailer while JD, Maggie, and Claire stared at the trench.

Ford dismounted Coco and went to join them.

"Well," Maggie was saying, "clearly it has to be filled in. But unless we divert the flow, I'm afraid it's just going to happen again."

A big pile of rocks had been dumped earlier, along with a huge corrugated culvert. Maggie started telling everybody what needed to go where, and Ford helped JD get the culvert in place. In under two hours, the whole thing was done, and JD was sitting in the truck while Bubba drove the front-end loader back onto the trailer.

"The lane was washed out pretty good," JD told him as they gazed at their handiwork. "We'll have to come out and grade it, but it looks like she can get a truck down it."

"Oh! That reminds me," Claire said. "The dealer called. My truck came in. Do you want to take me to get it tomorrow, Ford?"

"Sure thing," he said. Although he kind of liked driving her ass around.

"I shouldn't have any trouble getting my Jeep down your lane," Maggie said to Claire. "Don't forget I'm picking you up for book club later."

Claire gave Maggie a thumbs-up. "I won't forget. I haven't finished the dang book, though."

"Do you ever?"

Claire shrugged. "Not often, but this one was really good. And my copy is in the trailer."

Maggie and Bubba piled into the truck with JD. "We'll let you two get on with it," Maggie said. Then she winked at Claire, and the truck drove away.

What was that about? Get on with *what*?

"Want to get a grand tour of Miss Daisy?" she asked.

"Sure. I guess..."

The woman mounted his horse without asking.

"Hey, wait a minute..."

And then, with a grin, she trotted right past him.

He'd just been horse-jacked.

Coco swished his tail and then left it up, giving Ford a spectacular view of his asshole and leaving him with the distinct impression he'd been given the finger. Just in case he was wondering whose side his horse was on.

"Wait up!" he called, taking off after them on foot.

Claire looked over her shoulder and laughed, but then she slowed Coco to a stop and waited. When Ford caught up, she was leaning over and snuggling with his horse.

Or maybe they were conspiring. It was hard to tell.

"Want on?" Claire asked.

She pulled her foot out of the stirrup so he could get a leg up, but he didn't need it. He was going to impress her with a slick move he'd learned as a kid when he'd regularly hung out with bull riders and rodeo clowns.

Ford tapped Coco on his rump, took a few steps back, and called out, "Mounty up!"

"Oh my God. What are you doing?" Claire asked, looking at him over her shoulder.

Ford put a finger to his lips. He only knew one trick, and it was a good one. He took a deep breath and then took a running leap, mounting his pony from behind, Hollywood-style.

Coco didn't falter, but Claire emitted a high-pitched

squeal as he landed behind her. Actually, maybe that was him, because he'd just racked himself on the saddle.

He leaned into Claire, trying his best to curl up into a ball. "Damn," he wheezed. "I usually do that bareback."

"Are you okay?" she asked. "And why would you even attempt such a thing?"

"It impresses the ladies," he squeaked.

"Well," Claire said with a slight snort. "I'm mighty impressed. I just hope you weren't planning on having children."

* * *

Claire led Ford up the three porch steps to Miss Daisy's front door. She couldn't shake the *happy for now* seed Maggie and Alice had planted in her brain. Could she do that? Could she just live in the moment with this wayward cowboy who couldn't put down roots?

He was a fine man. A *good* man. And she was going to be heartbroken either way. Because she'd fallen for him again. She knew that as sure as she knew her left boot from her right.

What if there was no happily-ever-after in her future? What if there was just now? This summer, this week, this day, this moment.

She wanted whatever she could get of him. Which was *all* of him. Even if she couldn't keep him.

"You sure are quiet," he said. He looked gigantic on her tiny front porch.

"Am I?"

"Yeah. Thinking about your dad?"

Although her father was never far from her mind, no, she hadn't been thinking about him. She was now, though.

"He seemed happy at the meeting. And thank you, by

the way, for telling him everything I've been doing. I'm perfectly capable of tooting my own horn, but it felt nice to hear you do it."

"Everything I said was true."

"Do you think he's still considering selling it?"

"I think that depends on the numbers, and I haven't seen them."

Dang it. What good was all her hard work if her dad was just going to sell anyway?

"The water didn't make its way up here," Ford said. "Your little trailer seems just fine."

Miss Daisy sat on a bluff, surrounded by bluebonnets and buttercups. It had a small porch, built by Bubba and JD, just big enough for two chairs, a wind chime, and a humming-bird feeder. Claire had hung up twinkle lights. Nothing made her happier than sitting on this little porch with a friend and a cold beer, listening to the frogs in the creek below.

"Thank goodness."

"Are you going to invite me in?"

She remembered the way his arms had felt around her on the dance floor at Tony's, and the kiss that had followed, in front of everyone. And here he was. Asking if she was going to invite him in.

Happy for now. Happy for now. Happy for now.

She opened the door. "Welcome to my humble abode."

A musty odor hung in the air—Miss Daisy had been closed up for a while—and Claire wrinkled her nose while Ford opened the windows. "I've stayed in worse quarters," he said.

"I'll have you know this little trailer has been pinned on hundreds, maybe thousands, of Pinterest boards." Decorated in white and gray with pink accents, the place was adorable. Wood throughout, recessed lighting, a clever little loft bed she'd designed herself so she'd have room for a couch and a table. She wasn't much of a cook, so the tiny kitchen wasn't a problem.

"I don't know how to pin anything to a social media board, but this place looks like you, and I like it."

Aw, that was sweet. Especially since there was a miniature crystal chandelier resting on top of his cowboy hat.

He nodded at the little ladder leading to the loft bed. "You sleep up there?"

"Yep."

"It doesn't look like there's much room."

It *was* small. But it was perfectly comfortable for one person, and it would absolutely work for two people if they weren't very interested in high-quality sleep.

She'd thought about it plenty. The various ways two people would fit. The positions...

There were ways.

"It's big enough," she said. "And you are more than welcome to check it out if you don't believe me."

Ford kicked off his boots, set his hat on the little counter, and put a foot on the ladder. "Here I go."

Claire crossed her arms, shrugged, and tried to pretend she didn't care that Ford Jarvis was climbing into her bed.

He just went a couple of steps up the rungs until he was as high as he could go. "It's a nice little space," he said. "Cozy in that way that MRI machines are cozy."

Claire smacked his leg.

"I guess you have to kind of crawl in?" he asked.

"Not really—"

Ford's ass was in the air, and then... *Oof!* His feet hung over the side for a few seconds, and then he pulled them in, too. "There's absolutely no way two people could fit in this bed."

It was a challenge, and she knew it. The question was, would she accept?

She bit her lip. Chewed her thumb. Stared at the ladder.

A snort. Then a snore.

Oh, hell no. Ford Jarvis was not falling asleep in her bed before she'd even decided what to do with him.

She climbed up the ladder and poked her head over the mattress.

He was grinning. "Come on, now. I want to see you worm your way up here. Of course, I don't know where you're going to go if you do—"

She scampered right up, no problem, and found herself nose to nose with Ford.

"See? I fit."

Ford raised up on an elbow and glanced at where one of her legs hung over the edge.

"Partially."

"You could scoot over, you know."

"This bed doesn't seem to be made for people lying side by side."

His hazel eyes had been sparkling with mirth, but now they darkened slightly and drifted to her lips.

And he was right. She hadn't really been thinking of side-by-side sleeping arrangements when she'd designed this little love shack. "Spooning works."

"Yeah?"

She could feel his breath. The small space seemed to shrink even more, warming from the heat radiating off their skin.

"I'd think stacking works, too."

"Stacking?"

"You know. One on top of the other."

She swallowed.

"Want to try it?" he whispered.

Happy for now. Happy for now. Happy for now.

He pulled her on top of him, and the contact made her body hum like electric lines in a rainstorm. He was long, lean, and hard in more ways than one.

"You going to kick those boots off?" he asked.

Claire went to answer and realized she'd been holding her breath. She kicked off one boot, followed by the other. Both hit the ground with a thud.

His hands ran up her back and her erogenous zones sizzled and lit up like a Christmas tree.

Touch me here!

Ford knew where all her sensitive places were, and he followed those lights like a roadmap. Lips grazed below her ear. Fingers brushed against her ribs. A palm pressed the small of her back...

She couldn't help but move against him, and he responded to every motion with one of his own.

"Oh, Ford..."

His lips found hers and he moaned beneath her as he cupped her ass with his hands.

Thoughts and ponderings left as soon as they formed, dissipating into pure bliss. Her body had no misgivings over time or happiness or being present. It knew exactly what it was doing, and Ford's body was its personal Zen.

Ford softly bit her bottom lip. "Whose turn is it?" he asked.

"Yours," she mumbled, pressing her pelvis against his. "It's your turn to call things off."

He moved her hair out of the way to kiss her neck. "Really? I thought it was yours."

It was hard to think with his warm breath against her skin, but she was pretty dang sure it wasn't her turn. "No. I went last. At the oak tree."

She closed her lids and felt her eyes roll in the back of her head as Ford kissed her collarbone.

"No," he said. "That was the drone. You didn't say a word about stopping anything. And there's no skipping turns."

He slipped his hands beneath her shirt.

"I didn't skip. We were interrupted. And anyway, the end result was the same."

He pulled her shirt over her head and ran his warm hands across her back. Then he unclasped her bra with ease.

"You're forfeiting your turn?" he asked, licking his lips as she raised up just enough to give him a peek at her cleavage as the bra slipped down.

"For the last time, it's not my turn."

Her bra slid all the way down her arms, releasing her breasts from the cups. She wanted to reach up and cover them, to stop them from swaying or God forbid, *hanging*, because she was what her mother referred to as a "full-figured girl." But she couldn't sit up straight in this silly little loft, and she needed her hands to support herself as she leaned over Ford.

Ford's eyes went straight to her breasts and stayed there, going from left to right like he was watching a tennis match, because her breasts were indeed, slightly swaying. Was it possible for boobs to hypnotize a cowboy?

"Darlin', I don't care whose turn it is. I couldn't stop now if I wanted to." He covered each breast with a big, warm hand. "And I don't want to."

She gasped as he raised his head and flicked a nipple with his tongue before capturing it with his mouth. He sucked deeply while squeezing her other nipple with his fingers.

Claire panted like a puppy and rubbed herself all over him.

Ford released her nipple. "Unless, of course, you want me to stop."

She couldn't even handle that he'd stopped to get her opinion on the matter. "Are you going to lose that shirt, cowboy?"

He peeled his T-shirt off, revealing his own glorious chest.

Dang, but she loved a good chest. And Ford's was perfect. It wasn't overly muscular—she wasn't into boobs, herself—but it was sculpted. Tight. Hard. The result of real work.

A smattering of hair on his pecs narrowed into a trim little trail at his belly that dipped into his jeans. She knew where the trail went, and she was looking forward to hiking it with her fingers. And lips. And tongue.

She leaned over and kissed him softly, letting her nipples rub gently against his chest. The sensation of his rough hair against her sensitive skin lit a fuse that went straight between her legs.

He grabbed her hips. "Let's get these jeans off." He sounded breathless. "I want to touch every inch of you."

It was all she could do not to scream, *Okay, let's do that!* right in his face. Instead, she rolled off of him and unzipped her jeans. Then she started to peel them down.

She got them just past her hips and went to sit up, but dang it, she couldn't. Not enough headroom. She lifted her butt and shimmied the jeans down to mid-thigh, grunting sexily the entire time.

"Need help?" Ford asked.

"Nope."

"You sure?"

"Yes. But can you scoot over? I'm smashed against the wall."

"If I scoot over, I'll fall out."

Claire sighed. "I think we're going to have to crawl down the ladder if we want to get naked."

Ford rolled over and went down first. Claire tried to

follow, but she couldn't get down the rungs with her jeans at her thighs. She ended up hanging over the side of the loft, butt-side up.

"It seems you've gotten yourself in a pickle, Miss Kowalski," Ford said.

Claire chewed her lip. She was in quite the predicament. What could she say back to Ford that was sexy or witty or—

Whoosh!

Her pants had disappeared in one fell swoop.

"I swear," Ford said. "A cowboy has to do everything himself."

Chapter

Twenty-Three

❦

Ford's heart was pounding. Claire wore a tiny pink thong, and it was inches from his face. His hands trembled and his pulse raced. Hell, that had started as soon as she'd asked him if he wanted to see her trailer.

He'd known where it would lead, and now there was nothing between him and paradise but a wisp of fabric.

He was about to run his tongue across her perfect skin when she managed to get herself unstuck and climb the rest of the way down the ladder.

Was she going to take her turn after all? Call things off? *He'd die if she did.*

She put her hands on his shoulders, and her touch was warm. Gentle. Devastating.

"I'm okay with this, Ford. I know what I'm doing and who I'm doing it with and what the outcome will be... And I'm happy for now. Now is all anybody has anyway."

He didn't know what to say. He knew what he wanted to

say, but the words evaded his tongue. They floated around, disjointed, in his mind. Words like *forever*. Words like *love*. Words like *mine*.

He took a breath and tried again, but Claire put a finger to his lips. "Shh."

The finger entered his mouth, and all the words disappeared.

He sucked on her finger and watched as her eyes became glassy with desire...

Was it this easy for other men to turn her on? Or was this a reaction reserved just for him?

She pulled her glistening finger out of his mouth and dragged it down his chest and belly, all the way to the waistband of his jeans. She made a show of peeking inside before blushing beautifully. "Is that for me, Ford?"

"God, yes," he whispered.

She left the button alone and unzipped his fly. And then, as he stood like a statue with his arms at his sides, she reached in and extracted his throbbing cock. It stuck out like a flagpole, bouncing slightly with every beat of his frantic heart.

If she dropped to her knees, he was one hundred percent certain they weren't making it back to the loft bed.

Her warm breath grazed his chest as she delivered soft butterfly kisses. He broke out in goose bumps when she licked a nipple.

"Oh, Claire..."

You're my everything. My whole fucking universe.

She gave his cock a long, firm stroke. Then another.

Ford's head fell back. He swayed on his feet.

"Ford," Claire said. Her voice sounded distant and faint. "Look at me."

She stopped stroking.

He leaned forward to kiss her. He wanted to keep his eyes closed. It was too intimate in broad daylight to have her staring into his eyes and seeing...

The truth.

That he'd do anything for her. Be anything for her. If only he could. If only he weren't a Jarvis. If only he weren't so fucking scared.

His heart had ventured into unexplored territory.

"Ford," she whispered.

He opened his eyes, and slowly Claire's beautiful face came into focus. And then he fell right into her eyes.

Was it possible that she was just as lost in his?

He grabbed her face and kissed her with everything he had. He was insatiable, and he would never be able to get enough of Claire Kowalski. Not if he lived until the end of time.

"Let's get back in the loft," he said.

He was panting and gasping like an idiot, but he had the wherewithal to get Claire turned around and going up the rungs on the ladder.

He was right behind her, and when she got to the top and raised her leg to climb in, he lost the last bit of control he'd been clinging to.

He grabbed her hips and she stilled at his touch. He ran his hands over her sweet, round cheeks and then squeezed. The tiny strip of cloth that ran between her legs disappeared into her flesh. She gasped when he used a single finger to lift up the fabric and pull it over to the side.

He'd dreamed of this. Fantasized about it. Lain in bed and tried to remember exactly what she'd tasted like. Smelled like. Felt like.

He kissed her inner thighs, and she collapsed onto the mattress, raising her ass and opening up for him even more. He got his face as close to her as he could without actually touching her. He wanted her to feel his breath. His gaze.

His need.

He licked her softly, and she responded with a whimper. A tremor went through her body, and he wanted to turn it into a fucking earthquake. So, he licked her again.

For the next few minutes he worshipped Claire. Devoured her.

Loved her.

"Oh, God, Ford. I'm going to—"

She came like an avalanche, nearly knocking him off the ladder.

He held on, relishing the sight of Claire coming undone. And when she finally stilled, he leaned against her and whispered, "I'm not done with you yet, darlin'."

* * *

Claire thought the tremors passing through her body would never stop. It was almost embarrassing. Her legs felt like noodles, but somehow, she managed to climb the rest of the way into the loft bed, scooting up to the wall to make room for Ford.

She heard him step out of his jeans, and then he climbed in with the urgency of someone who hadn't yet gotten his fill. And for a man who'd been complaining about the cramped accommodations, he had no trouble at all sliding himself right on top of her.

Claire's legs opened of their own accord. She was out of her mind with desire again, even though she could still feel the aftershocks of her orgasm.

Ford breathed raggedly, and his lips trembled against hers. "I want you, Claire. All of you."

His fingers went to her nipples. His mouth was at her ear, and his penis was exactly where it needed to be. "Can I take you now?" he whispered.

"God yes," she said. "Now. Before I die."

He thrust himself inside and Claire grabbed his ass, letting him know that he didn't need to take it slow and easy. She was frantic with desire, and she wanted this cowboy to ride her, fast and hard.

But Ford had other plans, and he moved slowly and deliberately, hitting all the right spots. Soon, they were in perfect sync. And it felt like going home.

His body was so familiar, and Claire knew just how to move to set him on fire.

"Oh, damn," he said. "I want to go slow, but I just can't."

"You don't have to," she said.

He increased the pace, hitting new and deeper spots, and Claire felt another orgasm building. And it was coming from a place deep within. The low humming sound she heard was her own voice, and she barely recognized it.

Ford gasped. "I'm going to come."

Claire's eyes shot open. They'd been so overcome with desire that they'd made a stupid and immature mistake.

"Stop," she ordered. "No condom."

Ford froze. "Oh my God."

"You need to pull out," Claire said.

Ford gazed frantically into her eyes. "I don't think I can."

"What do you mean?"

"I'm so close. I can't move..."

"Really?"

"I haven't felt like this since I was a teenager with a hair trigger."

Claire shifted beneath him. This was ridiculous.

"Seriously, don't move," he begged. "Give me a minute to conjure up my grannie."

"Have you lost your mind?"

Ford's eyes were squeezed shut. "I saw her once in a threadbare, see-through housecoat. It's the image I use when I need to kill a boner. Be quiet and let me concentrate."

Claire started to laugh.

"No!" Ford said. "Don't laugh. It feels good when you do."

Claire tried to stifle a giggle, but she was mostly unsuccessful, even under such dire circumstances.

"Jesus, Claire."

"Maybe we should introduce some jokes into your sexual repertoire," she said.

"Grannie, Grannie, Grannie..." Ford mumbled.

Claire managed to be still and silent and Ford finally pulled out.

"Man, I'm so sorry," he said. "That was incredibly embarrassing."

"Just for you," Claire said with a grin.

"Thank you for coming to your senses. I can't believe I didn't think about protection. I've never gone bareback. Not even once."

Claire opened a little drawer on a shelf above the mattress and pulled out a foil packet. "Look what I have," she said, smiling.

He sat up suddenly and *wham!* He'd hit his head on the ceiling.

"Oh, Ford! Are you okay?"

"Do you hear birds?" he asked.

Claire brushed his hair off his forehead. He couldn't be very badly injured, because something moved against her leg, and she realized Ford had stopped thinking about his grannie.

"Oh, look who's perked up," Claire said. "I hate to proposition you while you have a possible head injury, but we're both naked, and you won't even have to work hard." She slung a leg over his thigh. "I'll get on top."

Ford snatched the condom out of Claire's hand. Ripped the package open with his teeth. "The hell you will," he said. "I'm on top."

* * *

Claire rolled over onto her back, wearing nothing but a devilish grin, as Ford slipped the condom on. She teased him by running her fingers down her smooth, soft tummy before dipping them between her legs.

Then she brought them to his lips and gave him a taste of heaven.

He entered her easily, and she moaned softly, eyelids fluttering. For every movement of his body, there was a reaction in hers. He could feel the tensing of her muscles, hear the hitches in her breath, see the fleeting expressions of ecstasy cross her brow. He played her like an instrument: this motion made her arch her back; that one made her fingers squeeze his upper arms.

His pleasure was rising, but he kept it in check. He wanted to draw this moment out forever.

Claire, however, was growing impatient. She dug her heels into his ass. She rocked her hips. "Ford, please..."

She'd asked nicely, so he thrusted deeper, harder, and faster, watching in delight as Claire started to lose it.

"Yes," she whispered. "Just like that. Oh, Ford, you feel so good."

His name on her lips was the sweetest song.

Claire whispered *yes, Ford* in rhythm with his movements.

Then she arched her back as her eyes flew open. Ford didn't stop. He rode her through it, until her eyes rolled back and her body buckled. And the most beautiful sight of all was the smile that spread across her face as she contracted around him.

He rose up to find his own release, but he hit his head on the ceiling again. And this time, he almost did see stars. Because at that exact moment, Claire began to laugh, teasing his cock with the tightest flutter of squeezes he'd ever felt.

He came to the sound of her laughter, and it was like hearing wind chimes in the middle of an earthquake.

She'd taken everything he had, and he collapsed on top of her.

She ruffled his hair. "You're going to need a helmet next time, cowboy."

He was still so awash in pleasure that he could hardly feel the knot that was probably forming on the top of his head.

He rolled over and settled Claire in the crook of his arm. It felt so damn right. All of it. The heat. The sweetness. The laughter.

For the first time in a long time, he relaxed completely. And as his mind drifted, his world shrank smaller and smaller until it was nothing but this ridiculously tiny trailer and the beautiful force of nature at his side.

Chapter
Twenty-Four
❦

Claire was in her Mini Cooper, sitting in the middle of the ditch that ran in front of her house. She was stuck. The car couldn't move forward or backward, and she didn't know what to do. But she had to do something, because a train was coming. And she knew it was coming because of its horribly loud and obnoxious horn.

A horn! Claire's eyes flew open. Ford's arm was around her waist. Her nose was pressed into the wall. They were spooning in the loft, and she could tell by Ford's steady breathing that he was sleeping through the horn blowing. What time was it? For that matter, what *day* was it?

She peeked out the window while nudging Ford. A yellow Jeep was parked outside, and Maggie was staring out the window at Coco, who was staring calmly back.

Book club! Shit. She'd forgotten. And she still hadn't finished the book.

"Ford! Wake up," she said, climbing over him.

Ford mumbled something that sounded like *curse* before rolling over and continuing to ignore her.

Claire looked out the little window again as Maggie laid on the horn.

Ford jerked and then, predictably, sat up. "Motherfucker!" he wailed, holding his head and plopping back down.

"We fell asleep," Claire said.

"No shit."

"Maggie's here."

"Why?"

"To take me to book club."

The exit strategy for the loft bed involved backing out and down the ladder. Which was unfortunate, because Maggie banged on the door twice and then opened it just as Claire's ass began its descent.

"Oh! Moon over Texas!" Maggie said. "Sorry!"

Claire grabbed the sheet, which left Ford completely naked. He started to sit up, but then he seemed to remember the low ceiling with whatever short-term memory he had left, and he plopped back down with a groan. He grabbed a pillow and covered himself with it.

"I'll go outside while you get dressed," Maggie said. "That is, if you still want to come with me to book club."

Claire would rather see if she could give Ford a couple more concussions. "Hmm, maybe—"

"I've got to hit the road with the sheriff," Ford said in a rough, hoarse voice. "We've got cattle in the state park."

"So, books over bang," Maggie said. "I'll be in the Jeep."

As soon as the door closed, Claire scurried the rest of the way down the ladder and grabbed her jeans off the floor.

Ford's face peeked over the edge, and he hungrily eyed her slipping into her clothes. "What time is it?" he asked.

"Maggie was supposed to pick me up around four, so I suspect it's around four."

"Shit, shit, shit," Ford said, tossing the pillow aside and squirming toward the ladder. "Sheriff Long was supposed to be at my cabin at three thirty."

Claire picked her T-shirt up off the floor with her toes—a special talent since childhood—and slipped it on without a bra. She couldn't possibly wear this to the book club, but at least it would cover her while she scrounged around for something else.

The ladder groaned as Ford came down, and warm desire pooled in Claire's belly at the sight. He really did have the best ass ever, and it was accentuated by a fleeting glimpse of what hung between his legs...

He bent over and grabbed his underwear, and when he stood up, she saw something flash across his face. Was it regret? Vulnerability?

She hoped it was the latter, because she felt it, too.

But no regrets.

Suddenly, the air was pierced by a sharp blast of a siren. Ford looked out the window and then frantically stepped into his underwear. "What is Sheriff Long doing here?"

"Looking for you, I imagine," Claire said.

"Go out there and hold him off while I get dressed, would you?"

Someone pounded on the door. "Police! Open up!"

Claire rolled her eyes. "Hold your damn horses, Casey!"

She slipped her feet into her boots, and just as Ford zipped up his fly, she opened the door to see Casey standing there grinning like a dummy. He glanced past her to look inside, but she stepped out quickly and pulled the door shut behind her.

"Hi," she said. "Ford and I were just discussing how

to implement Maggie's suggestions for handling runoff out here—"

"Discussing and implementing in the middle of the afternoon?" Casey shook his head. "And on a Sunday? You should be ashamed of yourselves."

"I think they discuss and implement *twice* on Sundays," Maggie said. "Also, Claire, your shirt is on wrong side out."

"Shit."

The door opened and Ford practically fell out, losing his hat in the process. His hair was a mess, his shirt was misbuttoned, and he'd missed at least one belt loop. He spun around to pick up his hat, plopped it on his head, and held out a hand to Casey.

"Good afternoon, Sheriff."

* * *

A half hour later, Claire and Maggie stood on Anna's porch, waiting for someone to answer the door. Claire shifted from foot to foot while juggling a big bowl of quinoa, kale, and cranberry salad that she and Maggie had picked up on their way. Her tattered copy of *Kilted into It* was in the bag slung over her shoulder. She'd read some on the drive over, but she still had about ten more pages to go. She was dying to open it back up, because she was *right there* at the part where everything was about to come together, only she didn't know how.

Maggie held a cheap bottle of pinot grigio. After what was known as the Salty Brownie Incident, she'd been relegated to booze-only status at book club, even while she was pregnant and couldn't drink.

The hollow sound of heels tapping on a tile floor grew louder and louder, and Claire braced herself for Anna. There would be a fake *happy to see you* greeting, followed by a backhanded compliment. And no matter how much Claire tried to prepare for it, she could never come up with a suitable response on the spot. She'd come up with brilliant humdingers once she was tucked away in bed later, but that never did her any good.

The door opened. Anna, dressed in a turquoise silk pantsuit that was really too much for book club, smiled brilliantly. Then she gave Claire a once-over. She took in the high-rise embellished jeans, white ruffled off-the-shoulder blouse, and sling-back Veronica Beard sandals. She smiled, which was never a good sign.

"Don't you look adorable," she said, leaning over for the fake *kiss-kiss* that literally nobody else in Big Verde did. "I had a pair of jeans like that in high school. They were in then, remember?"

Maggie snorted.

Claire smiled back. Painfully. *The embellished jeans cost over three hundred dollars, and they were all the rage.*

Maggie, who'd been chomping on gum the entire drive over, blew a gigantic bubble and let it pop. Anna ran her eyes over Maggie's outfit—maternity jeans and a T-shirt that said EATING TACOS FOR TWO—and smirked.

"Thank you, Anna," Claire said. "And don't you look…"

She tried to come up with something. Anything. Something with a double edge. *Did your grandmother die and leave you that pantsuit?*

"You look lovely. Is that silk?"

Damn it. She was just too polite.

"Of course," Anna said, taking the bottle of wine and salad bowl. "Come on inside."

They followed Anna into the kitchen, where she removed the lid from Claire's quinoa salad and wrinkled her nose.

"I'll put a spoon in this," she said. "In case anyone wants to eat it."

The doorbell rang, and Anna scurried off.

Laughter and chatter echoed from the foyer. Claire recognized the voices of Alice, Trista Larson, and Miss Mills.

Miss Mills came into the kitchen and set a homemade buttermilk pie on the counter. Claire had tried going full-blown vegan once, but it had been short-lived. There were two reasons for this: (1) cheese was the stuff of dreams, and (2) Miss Mills's buttermilk pies.

"That looks delicious," Claire said. "I might just skip straight to dessert."

Miss Mills looked at Claire's salad. "I wouldn't blame you," she said. "Although you might want to hold off on the pie. Those jeans are tight enough as it is. You young ladies don't leave anything to the imagination."

Miss Mills, bless her heart, wore a dress that could double as a housecoat, orthopedic shoes with compression hose, and a small ceramic pin that said SMILE! JESUS LOVES YOU! Claire didn't think she was leaving much to the imagination, either.

Miss Mills's primary occupation was organist for the First Baptist Church, and she'd never been *married nor nothin'*, as Trista liked to say with a wink. And even though Miss Mills no doubt believed Jesus was the final judge of folks' morals and behavior, she didn't seem to mind doing a bit of prescreening for the Lord.

Claire's off-the-shoulder blouse had slipped down a little, and she yanked it up to cover at least some of her cleavage.

"Don't do that," Alice said, placing a tray of fruit and veggies next to Miss Mills's buttermilk pie. "You look lovely, and besides, it's not your responsibility to cover up your body in order to make others comfortable."

Miss Mills raised an eyebrow and shook her head. "You'd think a librarian would understand the notion of modesty."

Alice, who was dressed very modestly indeed—gray blouse and black slacks—smiled sweetly at Miss Mills. Alice was one hundred percent sugar, but she had her opinions and she voiced them. "You might not know this, Miss Mills, but librarians, quiet as we may sometimes be, are often fierce feminists devoted to freedom of speech and expression."

Miss Mills reached in her purse and pulled out her daily devotional. "Some things ought not be expressed. Like feminism, for example."

She fluttered her daily devotional in front of her face like a fan.

Trista placed her dependable slow cooker of tiny sausages swimming in barbecue sauce on the counter and plugged it in. "Bubba would probably agree with you, Miss Mills. But that's just because he thinks feminism is something you treat with an ointment that comes with an applicator." She winked at Claire. "Aisle four, right next to the condoms."

Maggie laughed until her ears turned red, and then she lifted the cooker's lid and picked up a tiny wiener with a toothpick. "Ah, feminism," she said. "The *other F-word*."

"You will never catch me calling myself a feminist," Anna said.

"Why on earth not?" Maggie asked. "Don't you want to be treated the same as men?"

"Absolutely not," Anna said. "And besides, feminists don't wear bras."

Maggie opened her mouth to object, but then she seemed to notice that she was not, in fact, wearing a bra. Maggie had a small, athletic frame without an ounce of fat on her—even while pregnant—and it meant she could enjoy the convenience of often going without.

Alice furrowed her brow. She was probably trying to balance the lava of rage wanting to spew forth from her mouth like a thousand bees, with her extreme desire to be polite at all costs. It must be hard.

For the first time, Claire wondered about Alice's *perpetually single* status. Was it by choice? Did she get a little bit of *somethin'* now and again? Or was she like Miss Mills and *not married nor nothin'*?

"Pardon me," Alice said softly, "but modesty is a social construct whose sole purpose is the oppression of—"

"Good*ness*!" Miss Mills said, fluttering her devotional faster than the wings of a hummingbird. "The next thing you know you'll be burning your bra."

"I would definitely come to that party," Maggie said.

Miss Mills fanned herself more forcefully, no doubt thinking that a pregnant lady should behave more maturely and while wearing adequate undergarments.

Maggie rubbed her pregnant belly. "Y'all are lucky I wore any clothes at all. I'm hot. I'm cranky. And the waistband of my underwear has been trying to kill me for the past two months. I'm mostly going commando these days."

"I bet Travis doesn't complain," Trista said with a wink, setting a bag of chips and a container of dip on the counter.

"What on earth is *commando*?" Miss Mills asked.

"Sans panties," Trista said.

Miss Mills gasped.

"Just like our dreamy Scottish Highlander in his kilt," Maggie said, holding up her book.

"That was the custom of the times in Scotland," Miss Mills said, as if *Kilted into It* were a nonfiction historical document.

Anna poured wine into glasses. "I think it's still the custom in regard to kilts."

"It sure made it easier for that under-the-table hand job in front of the chieftain," Trista added.

"That scene was unsanitary," Miss Mills said. "Not that I remember it in detail. I skip the racy parts."

"I bet you got through the book super quick then," Claire said. "There were lots of racy scenes. Like the one at the inn where he tied her to the bed—"

"That was at the castle," Miss Mills corrected. "The inn is where they had that sinful food orgy. That is not what the good Lord intended butter for."

Miss Mills, as usual, had read every word of every scene, probably more than once.

"It gives a whole new meaning to buttered buns, doesn't it?" Alice said, cheeks turning a bit pink, before everyone started laughing.

"Listen," Claire said, yanking her book out and sitting on a barstool. "I have ten pages to go. I'll just get after it while y'all sip your wine. Give me five—"

"I can't believe he dies at the end," Anna said.

Claire's head snapped up. "What did you say?"

"Oh dear," Alice mumbled.

"I said I can't believe he dies at the end," Anna repeated while plopping an olive in her mouth.

"Spoiler alert," Maggie said. "Only really super too late."

"Don't worry," Alice said. "There's a twist—"

"Ha! Time travel!" Anna said. "Not dead because he hasn't been born yet. Plot hole you could drive a truck through. He's dead, he's not dead...Which is it?"

Claire snapped the book shut. Instead of reading the rest of it, maybe she'd read Anna the riot act. She was getting to the end of her nice-Southern-girl-manners rope.

Maggie walked over and whispered, "Fund-raiser. Don't piss her off."

Alice cleared her throat. "Well, hopefully, we'll be able to reopen the library soon. I know everyone will be anxious to request our next book club read."

"When do you think that will be?" Claire asked.

"It will depend on how soon we can raise enough money," Alice said.

"I can't remember the last time I was in the library," Anna said. "I just buy my books."

Way to be tone-deaf, Anna.

"There's more to the library than just checking out books you could buy at the store," Alice said. "For instance, we have children's programs—"

"I don't have kids," Anna said.

"And of course, we have reference books, historical documents, county registries…"

Anna wrinkled her nose.

"Computers, internet access, ESL classes…"

Anna crossed her legs and bounced her foot, clearly bored out of her mind by All Things Library.

"We need a fancy fund-raiser," Claire said. "Maybe a *gala.*"

Anna's foot quit bouncing. Nothing turned her on more than the words *fancy* and *gala.* She loved to host parties, and she was good at it. Claire had to give her that.

Claire winked at Alice, and Alice grinned and took a sip of wine. They'd dangled the bait. Now they needed to set the hook.

"If not a gala of some sort, maybe we could do a raffle," Alice said.

"A *raffle?*" Anna grimaced, as if maybe the word *raffle* meant *public execution.*

"Petal Pushers would be happy to donate something from our liquidation stock," Maggie said. "I mean, just imagine how excited folks will be at a chance to win gardening tools!"

Anna looked at Maggie as if she were crazy, and Maggie stared back with an innocent expression of earnestness.

"Maybe a bake sale," Trista said, joining in. "I don't have time to make homemade cookies, but I can donate something store-bought."

Miss Mills raised her hand. "I can't support a raffle—it's gambling and Jesus wouldn't approve—but I'll bake a pie for a bake sale."

Anna sighed loudly. She'd clearly heard enough. "Just how many books do you need to replace? *Ten?* Because that's all you're going to be able to manage with those lame ideas."

Only Miss Mills showed any indication of being offended.

"Maybe we should go back to the idea of a gala, then?" Alice said.

"Who could organize such a grand affair?" Maggie asked. "God knows I'm horrible at such things."

"Oh my God," Anna snapped. "You all must think I'm stupid."

"Not stupid," Maggie said. "Just self-involved and un-aware of other humans—"

"We'll call it Boots and Ball Gowns," Anna said, as if Maggie hadn't spoken. "And we'll have it at the Village Chateau."

"Well, I'm glad that's settled," Maggie said with a smirk.

Alice smiled sweetly, her ears going a bit pink with satis-faction. "I think that sounds fabulous. Now, who's ready to discuss our Scottish Highlander?"

Chapter
Twenty-Five
❦

A few weeks later, Ford pulled up to Miss Daisy and rolled his eyes over how he'd actually thought the words *Miss* and *Daisy* when he saw it. But then he grinned. Because Claire had a way of making you see things through her eyes, whether you wanted to or not.

It would never occur to him to name the foreman's cabin. But if he did, it would probably be a Burt. He had an uncle named Burt, and his mama always said he was plain on the outside and empty on the inside. Of course, that would be most of the places Ford had lived.

Claire's new pickup was parked under the oak tree. She could drive herself to branding day at her folks' place, but Ford liked having her in his truck. For one thing, she made it smell better.

He tapped the horn just as the trailer's little door opened. Claire stepped out wearing jeans and a white T-shirt that said DO NO HARM, BUT TAKE NO BULL in black letters. When she turned to shut the door, he saw the Rancho Cañada Verde brand on the back. Claire had been trying out various products—clothing, cookware, hand lotion—in an attempt to create what she called a "line" of branded retail items. She was working on a business plan to present to Gerome.

She ran to the truck and opened the door. No thick black eyelashes or shiny lips today. Just blue eyes, freckles, and mussy hair.

His heart damn near stopped at the sudden appearance of such beauty.

"I'm a mess today," she said, climbing in and shutting the door.

"No. You're—"

"But why dress up to torture cows, right?"

Claire was highly opposed to branding. She'd made a valiant plea to her father to switch to ear tags, but he'd rightfully stated that the heifers couldn't keep them on in the brush country. *Those girls can't hold on to their earrings*, he'd said with a grin. Claire had then brought up microchipping, which Ford thought was a good idea, but it was too big of an investment for the ranch right now.

"The cows have already been branded," Ford said. "We did it early this morning."

"What? Why didn't you tell me?"

He backed the truck up, turned it around, and headed down Claire's freshly graded lane. They'd be at her folks' house in about ten minutes, and Ford was looking forward to the barbecue. Branding was hard work, and he was hungry.

"I know it bothers you. I didn't want you to have to participate in it. I'm just here to pick you up for the party." He winked at her. "You're welcome."

He thought maybe she'd lean over and kiss him on the cheek. They'd been doing plenty of kissing lately, and he was looking forward to more, especially since he was leaving tomorrow for West Texas. She'd want to give him a proper goodbye—

"What the actual hell were you thinking, Ford?" she screeched.

Ford stopped the truck and looked at her. "I thought you'd be pleased."

"Why? Do you think this is a game?" she asked.

"A game?"

"I needed to be there. I am trying to hold on to this ranch, Ford. I'm trying to show my dad that I'm worth leaving it to. That I'm *enough*…"

Jesus. Her eyes were filled with tears. Her hands were shaking, and he grabbed them and held them tightly. He noticed the chipped nails. The calluses. The angry little scratches and punctures. He thought about how after giving her all to the ranch every day, she helped Maggie in the evenings, and worked on her business plan every spare minute in between.

Well, not *every* spare minute. Because she'd made time for him, too.

"Oh, my sweet angel," he whispered, bringing her palm to his lips. "You are more than enough."

Claire started crying, and it felt like someone was ripping his heart out. He'd only seen her cry once before, and it had been in his rearview mirror as he'd driven away like a fucking coward. "I just wanted you to have a little break. You've been working so hard."

She wrapped her arms around his neck and kept crying. He just held her, not knowing what to say.

After about three minutes, she pulled away, wiped her eyes, and said, "Done."

Ford raised an eyebrow. "You don't want to talk? Chew me out some more maybe? Because I deserve it."

"No, you don't. You were wrong, but your heart was in the right place. I'm exhausted, and I needed a good cry. I've had it. Now let's get going."

She couldn't keep this up. Doing all of it. Sure, she was capable of running the ranch. *Damn* capable. But if Rancho Cañada Verde was to keep going, what it needed was her ideas. Her branding and marketing. Because she was on to something, and the quarterly report had proven it. Rancho Cañada Verde needed something that only Claire, someone who loved her family and its legacy with all of her heart, could provide. And what she needed was time to prove it to Gerome.

But time was the one thing she didn't have much of.

He took a deep breath. "Claire, do you *want* to be the foreman of Rancho Cañada Verde?"

Claire sighed. "We've been through this. It doesn't matter what I want. My family needs me."

"You're right. They need you to work your marketing magic so this ranch can flourish long into the future, no matter what beef prices—"

"But someone has to actually run the ranch, Ford. And until we find a permanent foreman, that someone is going to have to be me."

The words were right there. All he had to do was open his mouth and let them pour out. Why was it so hard? He knew he could do it. He could run this ranch with his hands tied behind his back. He *loved* this ranch. And God help him, he still loved this woman. He'd never stopped.

But the word *permanent* gave him pause.

Jarvis men always kept moving. *Stay one town ahead of your problems, son, or bad luck will catch up.* That was something Johnny Appleseed Jarvis told all his boys.

As long as he lived, Ford would never forget his father's response to Abby's drowning.

I stayed too long in Abilene.

Like he'd had anything to do with Abby.

Worth was right. The curse was bullshit. It was just an excuse to be an asshole. And your problems always caught up with you. There was no such thing as staying one town ahead of them.

He licked his lips, feeling like a kid about to jump off the diving board for the first time. And then he just jumped.

"Claire, I'm coming back. To stay. I'll be the permanent foreman."

He was a Jarvis. And he'd just agreed to accept a permanent position. And it had come out so simply! So easily. As if he'd been meaning to say it since the day he got here. "If that's what you want, of course," he added.

Claire's jaw dropped. Her eyes, still shiny from crying, were as round as silver dollars. "But is that what *you* want?"

"I've never wanted anything so badly in my life," he whispered. Because he was afraid if he said it too loudly, Bad Luck would hear him.

Worrying about bad luck and curses would be a hard habit to break. It had been the cornerstone of his existence for thirty-one years.

"And maybe"—he was still whispering—"you could even buy Petal Pushers. Like you'd planned."

"Oh, I couldn't possibly buy Petal Pushers," she said. "There's still too much to do to make sure the ranch stays afloat."

That was disappointing. She loved it so much. She might be right, though.

Claire snapped her fingers and her eyes lit up. "Unless..."

"Unless what?"

"What if I turned Petal Pushers into a ranch store where

we'd sell all of the Rancho Cañada Verde products? I mean, we'd sell in other stores, too. Did I tell you I just got a department store to sign on to the cookware and bags?"

"No—"

"But we could have our *company* store right here in Big Verde. Tourists would love it. Locals would, too. Oh, Ford! What if this could work?"

He leaned over and kissed her gently on her lips. For the first time in his life, he had the feeling that anything was possible.

"I leave for West Texas tomorrow, and I think you need to put all these fancy plans into motion."

"I'll hold down the fort while you're gone."

"I have absolutely no doubt about that, darlin'."

Damn. They made a good team.

* * *

Ford stood at the barbecue station and stole another peek at Claire. Their eyes met, and she winked and blew him a kiss. It was a silly gesture. And a bit embarrassing, since the dumb grin on Bubba's face said at least one other person had seen it. But it made Ford's insides quiver and that familiar band around his midsection tightened and pulled, as if someone were yanking on it. It was all he could do to keep his boots in one spot.

Ford wasn't the only cowboy who had itchy feet. Worth couldn't seem to keep still to save his soul.

"Why are you so jittery?" Ford asked.

"I'm not. I'm just..."

Worth's voice trailed off as his eyes focused on a small figure walking up the lane. His face broke out in a huge smile.

"She made it!" Worth said.

"Who?" Ford asked. Whoever it was had parked at the end of the row. And she was carrying a big dish.

"Caroline," Worth said. "That's Caroline."

He took off with such a burst of speed that he lost his hat. And he didn't even stop to pick it up.

"Aw, hell," Bubba said. "The boy's done made a fool out of himself now."

"I'd say so," Gerome said. "Ford, go pick up your brother's hat before bad luck sets in."

It had landed on its brim, and Ford snatched it up, staring after his brother, who had stirred up quite a bit of dust. Worth hadn't even told anybody Caroline was coming. Maybe he wanted it to be a surprise.

A few minutes later, Worth walked up holding a bowl in one hand, and Caroline's hand in the other. Caroline was small, maybe just a hair over five feet tall. Her dark hair was put up in a ponytail high on her head, and it swung perkily as she smiled at everyone.

"This is Caroline Lopez," Worth said proudly. "My fiancée."

Caroline gave a little wave. "Hi, everybody."

Miss Lilly appeared out of nowhere. "Welcome to Rancho Cañada Verde."

"This is Miss Lilly," Worth said softly, as if whispering the name as a reminder. "And that's Gerome."

Gerome tilted his hat, and Ford realized that as much as Worth had been talking to all of them about Caroline, he'd been talking to Caroline about all of *them*.

"I'm so happy to be here," Caroline said.

She had dimples in both cheeks. Cute as a bug, as his grannie would say. No wonder Worth was acting like such a fool.

"I'll take that," Miss Lilly said, taking the bowl from Worth's hands.

"It's pinto beans with jalapeños and bacon," Caroline said. "I wasn't sure what to bring."

"Well, for someone who wasn't sure what to bring, you brought the perfect thing," Miss Lilly said. Then she looked at Gerome. "I bet that brisket has rested long enough. Why don't you bring it out to the table and let the ladies take care of it from here?"

"Yes, ma'am," Gerome said.

Introductions continued, with Ford being last.

"And this is my brother, Ford," Worth said, his voice tinged with nervous excitement.

Ford removed his hat. "Caroline, I've heard an awful lot about you, and it's a real pleasure to make your acquaintance."

Caroline smiled and offered a hand to Ford. "And I've heard a lot about you," she said, shaking his hand firmly. "Worth is lucky to have you for a role model."

Ford raised an eyebrow. First off, he was nobody's role model, and second, Miss Caroline Lopez had a mighty firm grip, a steady voice, and a dead-on gaze. She was a nurse. She was a soldier. And for some reason Ford couldn't grasp, she was in love with his brother.

Aw, hell. Ford liked her already.

"I don't know how lucky he is to have me as a role model, but he's damn lucky to have you as a fiancée."

Worth grinned. "I agree."

"And speaking of luck," Ford said, holding out Worth's hat. "You dropped this, dumbass."

Worth's face fell. "Brim-side down?"

"Five-second rule," Ford said. "I snatched it up just in time."

Worth smiled in relief and took his hat just as Claire joined the group.

"Did I hear someone mention the five-second rule?"

"Dropped my hat," Worth said.

Claire grinned at Ford in a way that said, *See how handy that is?*

Ford's skin warmed at her nearness, as if all the blood had rushed to the surface, ready to make his hair stand up and pay attention. He grinned back.

"Here," she said. "I fixed you a plate."

It was loaded down with two slices of brisket, potato salad, Spanish-style rice, and Caroline's beans.

"Thank you," he said, taking the plate with a wink. "Mighty thoughtful of you."

"I'm Claire," she said, smiling at Caroline. "Can I show you around?"

"That would be great," Caroline said. Then she rose on her toes and kissed Worth on the cheek. "Be back in a bit."

As soon as they wandered off, Bubba let out a low whistle and then proceeded to grin goofily at Ford.

"What?" Ford asked.

"Claire just fixed you a plate."

"Uh, yeah."

Bubba waved JD over. "Did you see that?"

"What?"

"Claire fixed Ford a plate."

JD grinned and shook his head. "Oh, you poor sonofabitch."

"What are you talking about?" Ford asked.

"Claire fixed you a plate," Bubba repeated, as if that hadn't already been decided.

"That means she tossed the rope out," JD added.

"And you accepted it," Bubba said.

JD nodded. "That's a dally for Claire."

A dally? That was a roping term that meant a calf had been successfully snagged and the cowboy had tied off his rope around the saddle horn.

"That's the most ridiculous thing I've ever heard," Ford said.

"Nope," Bubba said. "Ask any man about the beginning of the end and they'll all tell you it started at a barbecue or a wedding or some event where a woman not-so-innocently fixed them a plate. For me, it was brisket and potato salad at Trista's family reunion. Six months later I was standing at the altar."

"Has Caroline ever fixed you a plate?" Ford asked Worth.

"Tamales at her grandmother's birthday," Worth said. "That was the night I asked her to marry me."

Ford stared at his plate like it was a stick of dynamite.

Travis laughed. "They're full of shit. And as proof, you should know that I always fix my own damn plates."

"That's because you're married to Maggie," Bubba said. "She's not your average country girl."

"That's right," JD said. "She's more of your average scary girl."

Bubba nodded. "What about you, JD? Which one of you fixes the plates? I mean, which one of you is, you know…"

JD's face turned beet red, and Gabriel chose that moment to walk up and say, "Thanks for fixing me a plate, JD. Lupe sure does know how to make good barbacoa."

JD yanked the brim of his Stetson down and Bubba exploded in laughter.

"What did I say?" Gabriel asked.

"Nothing," Bubba said, trying to catch his breath. "And you might as well take a bite of that brisket, Ford. The damage is done."

"Yeah, well, I'm leaving for West Texas tomorrow, no matter who fixed me a plate."

JD smiled at him. "We'll leave the porch light on for you."

"Because you'll be back," Bubba said. "I mean, she might give you some slack..."

JD winked. "But you've definitely been roped."

Ford smiled and took a big bite of brisket. He looked at his brother and friends, all of them grinning like mindless idiots.

Dally up.

Chapter
Twenty-Six
❧

Is that the bunkhouse?" Caroline asked.

"Sure is," Claire said. "It's where Worth and the rest of the cowboys stay. Well, not the married ones, of course."

Caroline nodded. "I have no idea where Worth and I will end up. It'll depend on whether I reenlist, I guess."

"It must be hard, being apart," Claire said.

"I was reluctant to commit because of it, but Worth can be very persuasive," she said with a knowing grin.

"If you don't reenlist, will you stay in San Antonio? Worth says that's where your family is."

"Actually, Worth loves Big Verde. And I have to admit, it's a pretty little town, and the people sure seem friendly."

She offered Claire a bright smile, and Claire could suddenly see her fitting right in.

"It's a great place to live. I stayed in Austin for a while after college, and it was fun, but it wasn't home like Big Verde is home."

"Do you live in the ranch house with your parents?"

"No, I have a cute little retro Airstream trailer named Miss Daisy. It's on the other side of Wailing Woman Creek, not too far from the foreman's cabin."

"Well, that must come in handy," Caroline said, with a glint in her eye.

"Pardon?"

"Worth says you and Ford are a couple."

"Oh my. Really? Well—"

"I'm so glad these two are debunking that dumb curse. Aren't you?"

"Curse?"

Caroline furrowed her brow. "You know. The Jarvis curse. The one that supposedly prevents them from settling down…"

Ford believed in a freaking curse? It was hard to fathom, and yet…

A few things clicked into place.

"I can see he hasn't told you about it, and now I wish I hadn't," Caroline said. "I'm sorry."

"No, no. It's okay. Don't worry about it."

She tried to sound casual, but her mind was clicking along, connecting stray dots. Is this why he left two years ago? There was a big difference between worrying about an upturned horseshoe and believing in a *curse*.

"I thought Worth was kidding when he told me about it," Caroline said. "Honestly, it sounds nuts, and I come from a family that lights magic candles and puts eggs under their beds if someone looks at them wrong."

Claire laughed. "Well, you haven't been around many cowboys, have you? They're as superstitious as they come, but they're embarrassed and defensive about it because they also consider themselves so stoic and logical. And every single one of them has a lucky charm in their pocket."

Even her dad carried a rabbit's foot.

"Bronc riders are the worst," Claire continued. "When I used to rodeo, they drove me batty. *Don't bring peanuts in the arena! If you're going to keep that yellow shirt on, sit where I can't see you. You must have a death wish, because I saw you kick a paper cup.* That's what they were like. I'm not even kidding."

"Oh my gosh," Caroline said. "Worth won't let anyone eat peanuts in his truck if he has a rodeo event coming up! And we missed a movie once because he insisted on turning the truck around when a black cat stepped into the road."

Claire shrugged. "Sounds about right."

All this talk about superstitions made her a little edgy, and she jumped and squealed when someone sneezed *right into her hair* from behind. She spun around to find herself nose to large wet nose with Cinder. Ford was holding the reins, and he exploded in laughter.

Claire wiped at the back of her head—only slightly damp—as Ford continued laughing. He was joined by Caroline and Worth. And if Claire was really honest with herself, it looked as if maybe the horses were laughing, too. There were four of them, and they were all saddled up.

"Didn't mean to sneak up on you," Ford said, after he'd finally regained his composure. "It was pretty damn easy though."

"Funny ha-ha," Claire said. Then she narrowed her eyes at Cinder. "Gesundheit."

"We figured there was only one good way to show Caroline the ranch," Worth said. "And that's on horseback."

"Uh, hold up," Caroline said. "I've never been on a horse."

"That's why we saddled up Old Chester for you," Ford said. "He's as gentle as a dove."

"Yep," Worth said. "Unless he sees a squirrel."

"What?" Caroline said, eyes wide with panic.

"He's terrified of squirrels," Ford said.

"Well, what do I do if he sees a squirrel?" Caroline asked.

Ford and Worth looked at each other and winked. "You hold on for dear life," Worth said.

Caroline looked at Claire. "They're kidding, right?"

Mostly. "You'll be fine," Claire said reassuringly.

A few minutes later, they were mounted up and riding into the sunset. Claire followed behind Ford, watching Coco's tail twitch. Ford was going especially slow, most likely out of consideration for Caroline, who had a death grip on the reins while keeping an eye out for squirrels.

They'd come to the top of the ridge just in time to see the sky turn orange, and then they headed across the pasture so Caroline could get a good view of the Rio Verde.

Claire could feel that Cinder, like Coco, was twitchy. Open green pasture was an invitation to run, and the horses weren't used to their riders being so tempered. Both Claire and Ford liked to ride hard and fast.

The way Ford's hips moved in the saddle gave Claire an ache between hers. He was leaving tomorrow, and she'd want to give him a proper send-off.

She tried to shake off the sense of unease that had shown up about a week ago. Ford said he was coming back. For good. And she could tell that he meant it.

But she was no fool. What Ford wanted to do and what Ford was capable of doing were not necessarily the same thing.

She wanted to believe this time was different, and yet...

Caroline had mentioned that stupid curse.

"Hey!" Worth called.

Claire and Ford halted their horses as Worth rode up next to them.

"I'm thinking I might like to show Caroline the other side of Wailing Woman," he said.

"Really?" Claire said. "Why?"

"It might be fun for her to ride across the low-water crossing."

Ford raised an eyebrow. "There's not much there except for Claire's trailer and the foreman's cabin."

Worth's cheeks grew pink. "Yeah, I was thinking of showing her the foreman's cabin. Do you mind, Ford?"

Ah. Of course. Claire caught Ford's eye. There was a slight twinkle there, even though his face remained impassive.

"We haven't seen each other in weeks," Worth added in a low voice.

Claire glanced at Caroline. No doubt she was also anxious to see the foreman's cabin, but at the moment, she seemed mostly concerned with scanning tree limbs for squirrels.

Ford sighed. "It's unlocked. Have at it."

Worth smiled. "Thanks, brother."

"Don't let my goddam cat out," Ford grumbled.

"We won't," Worth said. "Erm, Ford?"

"What?"

"Will you be, you know, wanting to sleep in your bed tonight?"

Ford sighed and glared at Worth from beneath the rim of his hat. "Where the hell else would I sleep?"

Worth glanced sheepishly at Claire. "I don't know. Maybe…"

"Why don't you stay with me tonight, Ford?"

Ford crossed his arms. "Because I'm afraid I'll suffer permanent brain damage."

They hadn't spent a night apart since the Miss Daisy incident. But they also hadn't spent a night *in* Miss Daisy, because Ford had what he called a "proper bed" that didn't try to kill him.

They still spooned, though.

"Seriously, Ford?" Worth asked.

"How about I give you two hours in my cabin?"

Caroline, no doubt, had thoughts and opinions on the matter, but Old Chester had ventured off to sample a patch of sweet clover. "Oh no," Claire said. "Looks like Caroline could use some help."

Poor Caroline was yanking on the reins and swinging her feet back and forth in the stirrups, trying to get Old Chester to rejoin the group. But the horse knew a novice when he met one, and he wasn't having it.

They rode over to help her out.

"Ugh!" Caroline said. "I'm doing everything that y'all told me to do, but he's not budging!"

Worth looked frantically at Ford. "Seriously? Two hours? It's going to take over an hour just to get Old Chester to the cabin."

Ford shrugged. "I've got an early bedtime."

"Damn it," Worth mumbled. Then he got out of his saddle and easily pulled Caroline out of hers.

"Are y'all going to walk?" Ford asked.

"No," Worth said. "Although it would be faster than riding Old Chester." He pointed to the stirrup on his horse. "Here, Caroline. Let's get you on Lightning."

"Oh, I don't like the sound of his name—"

"He's a she, and she's as sweet as honey."

Worth helped Caroline into the saddle before effortlessly mounting behind her.

"We're not going to go fast, are we?"

"Nah, we're not going to go fast," Worth said, bringing his arms around Caroline to take hold of the reins.

"Whew! Thank—"

"We're going to go like the ever-lovin' wind."

Caroline's eyes widened in alarm, but before she could squeak out a word of protest, Lightning demonstrated how she earned her name.

Ford laughed as he watched them ride away.

"Two hours, Ford? You only gave them two hours?"

"It's plenty of time. He's twenty-one. It's about an hour and forty-five minutes longer than he needs."

"Ford!"

Ford turned and looked over his shoulder, eyes sparkling with mischief. "And speaking of time, I bet I can get to the old stone chapel before you."

"What about Old Chester?"

"There's a whole field of clover to keep him—"

Claire leaned forward in her saddle, clenched her thighs, and Cinder knew what to do.

Eat my dust, cowboy.

Chapter

Twenty-Seven

☙

Claire got to the chapel first, but only by a hair. She dismounted immediately and turned to face Ford as he hopped off of Coco. Then she threw her hands up in the air. "I win!"

For the past several hours she'd worked hard to keep her enthusiasm in check. She had socialized, made small talk, choked down what was probably delicious food, and met Worth's fiancée, all while wanting to scream that Ford was coming back *for good* and that she was going to get her store.

The gallop had gotten her blood pumping, and now she had more energy than she knew what to do with.

Ford walked over with a grin. "Cheater," he said.

That grin. You didn't get to see it all that often, but when you did, it was worth the wait. It was like a ray of sunshine sneaking through a rain cloud. And speaking of rain clouds, a tiny one was just overhead, darkening by the minute...

A droplet of water landed on her nose. She glanced up. No thunder or lightning. *No flood.* Just a light spring shower.

She laughed.

"What's so funny?"

"Somewhere there's a dung beetle pushing a ball of poop uphill," she said.

Ford raised an eyebrow and looked at her like she might be crazy.

"Ruben," she said.

"Ah," he said, nodding as if he understood. "He says some seriously ridiculous shit."

"He's almost always right, though," she said. "Him and that soothsaying dog of his."

Ford's face seemed to pale a bit.

"Are you okay?" she asked.

"Sure," he said. "Just tired."

The droplet of water turned into a sprinkle, and that quickly turned into a shower, and Claire squealed and held out her hand to Ford. Together they stepped through the doorway and into another time. The floor had long since disintegrated, and their boots crunched on rocks and dirt.

It was just a shell of a building, but it had part of a roof on the west side, and they huddled beneath it. Even though it was raining, the rays of the setting sun shone through, casting the room in a golden hue.

Claire crossed her arms over her chest. "I love this chapel."

Ford looked her over. "How did you get so wet in such a short amount of time?"

Claire shrugged. "Forgot my hat."

Ford clucked his tongue. "Forgot your hat? What kind of cowgirl are you?"

"The kind who crunches numbers and orders inventory," Claire said.

"And looks damn good in a pair of boots," Ford said. His eyes traveled up and down her body, and she realized she was wearing a white T-shirt. A *wet* white T-shirt.

"I have a blanket behind the saddle—"

"Oh? And what made you pack a blanket?"

"A cowboy is always prepared, Miss Kowalski." He winked and turned for the door, but then he stopped. Turned back around. "I think you should get out of those wet clothes."

"But—"

"Every single stitch," he said.

Claire watched him walk off and then she began doing exactly as she'd been told. She peeled off her T-shirt, removed her boots and socks, and yanked off her jeans. By the time she stepped out of her panties, the chill in the air had covered her in goose bumps.

"My God," Ford said from the doorway. "You are the most beautiful thing I've ever seen."

She needed to feel his arms around her. "Come here, Ford."

Ford wasted no time in walking over and quickly spreading out the blanket. Claire knelt on it, and then she reached for Ford. She could see how hard he was. How he strained against his jeans. She wanted to taste him. To devour him. But when she touched his belt, he removed her hand.

"Not yet," he said. "Go ahead and lie down."

Claire leaned back on the blanket, feeling its roughness against her bare skin. Ford lay down next to her, leaning on an elbow and letting his eyes drift lazily up and down her body.

"I wish I was a painter," he said, spreading out her hair like a fan on the blanket. "You are a sight to behold. Like a goddess."

She didn't quite know what to say to that. "Aren't you going to take off your clothes?"

"In due time," he said, running a finger over her breast, just barely missing her nipple.

He leaned over and kissed her, deeply and thoroughly, letting his body rub against hers. *His fully clothed body.* The chambray cotton of his shirt brushed her nipples, and the denim of his jeans rubbed against her thighs.

She longed for the warmth of his bare flesh, and yet...

His belt buckle grazed her sensitive mound. She gasped.

Ford moved his hips, lowered his chest, and spread her legs with his thighs. Being caressed by his clothed body, while she was completely nude, introduced delightful new sensations to her heated skin.

His mouth left hers and trailed down her neck to her collarbone. The button on his shirt pocket flicked across her nipple, and she nearly came undone. Ford moved so that it happened again.

The man was using his shirt as a sex toy.

She pulled at his hair to get his mouth back to her breast, where she wanted it, but he refused and playfully pinned her hands above her head.

"I'm in charge, sweet thing," he said, looking deeply into her eyes. "Okay?"

"Yes," she said.

Just get back to whatever it was you were doing.

His tongue flicked her nipple, then his mouth encompassed it, sucking and tugging. She couldn't tell who was moaning, him or her. Maybe it was both of them.

"You have the most perfect breasts," he said. "I love the way they move, the way they feel, the way they *taste*."

He moved to the other breast, giving it the same treatment as the first. He let go of one of her wrists and trailed his fingers down to her hip. He removed his thigh from between her legs and she moved to close them, but he lifted his head and said, "Keep them spread."

Claire opened her legs, wanting to pull him back on top of her to get that delicious friction going again, but instead, Ford parted the folds of her flesh with his fingers. He looked into her eyes while his thumb found her swelling nub.

Her eyes drifted shut. "Oh, Ford."

"I don't have a condom," he said.

Claire's eyes snapped open. "Again? What happened to a cowboy always being prepared? We can't—"

He thrust a finger inside, and her eyes opened wider.

"Oh, I'm fully prepared, darlin'. Get ready for the best orgasm of your life."

Claire wanted to say *Ha!* but he'd added a second finger, and it disengaged her vocal cords.

He crooked his fingers inside her and...*holy cow*. The pressure sent a tingling surge of pleasure all the way to her toes. Her eyes rolled back in her head.

Ford had hit the bull's-eye.

And he kept doing it, over and over, shaking her whole body while breathing heavily against her neck, or sucking on a nipple, or biting at her lips. She clawed at his arm, spread her legs wider only to close them again in a frenzy, squeezing his hand between her thighs and rocking her pelvis.

God, she was frantic. Ford was driving her up the side of a swell, and although there had to be a crest, it remained just out of reach. She panted and moaned and cried out his name as his fingers finally hit with just the right amount of pressure to bring her home.

"Oh my God," she sighed. "Ford..."

He kissed her neck.

"That was amazing."

He gently removed his fingers and flicked her nipple with his tongue.

But she was too sensitive. Her entire body was too sensitive. Every nerve was screaming *enough*!

Ford ran his fingers through her hair and smiled. "You didn't even miss my cock, did you?"

She wanted to melt. To just close her eyes and drift away. But if there was ever a man who deserved a reward, it was this one. And besides, he was wrong.

She missed it plenty.

"Get those jeans off, cowboy. I need a taste of you."

* * *

Ford's body felt heavy and warm. Claire had just outdone herself, and he could barely move. He didn't *want* to move.

He breathed in deep and slow, infusing his body with the scent of green things and with what could only be described as memories—prayers, tears, joy—that had seeped into the rock walls of the old stone chapel.

And flowers. He smelled them every time he inhaled. He didn't know if it was bluebonnets or Claire. She always smelled so damn good.

His stomach tightened beneath her trailing finger. She was going straight to that sensitive spot just inside his hip bone. The spot that made him—he grabbed for her hand but was too slow—*giggle*.

No, no. It wasn't a goddam giggle. It was more of a manly snort.

Claire giggled. And it was a soft, musical sound like a bubbling brook.

He squeezed her hand to keep it from more mischief and

grinned as his eyes drifted shut again. Endorphins, or whatever the hell it was that the body produced after sex, were dangerous. If a mountain lion showed up right now, he'd gladly lie here and let it eat him.

Claire's fingers made their way to his softening cock.

"Give it up, honey," he muttered.

"Never," she said, gently cupping his balls.

"It's already dark. The rain has stopped. We need to get going."

"It's a full moon. We're fine."

It was going to be a gorgeous ride back to the house.

He pulled her hand back up to his chest, covered it with his own. "Do you think Worth is out of my place yet?"

Claire sat up and looked him over with heavy-lidded eyes, mussed hair, and swollen lips. "I don't know. But if not, we can spend the night in my trailer."

"I have maybe three brain cells left. I think I should hold on to them. We're spending our last night at my place."

She stroked his face. "Last night?"

"Just for a short while. I'll be back before you know it."

"I wish you didn't have to leave."

"Me, too. But I promised Mr. Barre that I'd lead the roundup, and I don't break promises. It's only three weeks."

"I've half a mind to grab that rope you've got on your saddle and tie you up to keep you here."

Ford crossed his ankles and put his hands behind his head. He thought about Claire getting after him with a rope, and he wasn't entirely opposed to the idea. But not tonight.

"I'll give you ten more minutes here," he said. "Then we'd better get going."

"You're going to dole out minutes like candy?"

"Take it or leave it."

Claire folded her arms beneath her breasts, pushing them

up and out in a way that made him think maybe he could offer her thirty minutes or maybe twelve hours instead.

"I'll take it," she said. "What can we do in ten minutes?"

Ford thought about that.

"The clock is ticking," Claire said. "If you can't come up with something, then I'll have to."

"Sounds good to me. I'm pretty pooped. I think I'll just lie here and leave the activity planning to you."

Claire was as sweet and innocent as a cartoon princess… on the outside. On the inside, well, the woman had some dirty thoughts. She glanced at his cock with a raised eyebrow, probably trying to decide if she could resuscitate it in the allotted amount of time.

"I'm kind of hungry," Ford said with a fake yawn. "It's been a while since you brought me that plate."

"You'd better not ask me to make you a damn sandwich," Claire said. "Because that's not going to happen."

"A sandwich would be nice"—Ford looked around the empty chapel—"but it seems unlikely."

Claire rolled her eyes.

"I was thinking of something sweeter. Something I could eat while lying flat on my back."

Claire's eyes widened and then she blushed deeply in the moonlight. "I'm not going to do that, either."

Damn, it was cute when she got shy. Especially when it was right after she'd had a good old time sucking the life out of him.

"Come on, now. All you have to do is sit on my—"

"Ford!"

"What?"

She just kept staring at him. And blushing. "I've never done that before. Not from that…*angle*, anyway. I'll be so—"

"Exposed?"

Claire nodded.

The idea of that had him getting hard again. "Down to nine minutes now, buttercup. And I'd say I need at least seven or eight to get the job done. Although, heck, if you want to sit here wasting time, I might have to do it in five."

"Ha! You're too confident."

"Remember that night in the horse barn? You might not, since you were fairly out of your mind at the time, but I pulled that humdinger off in under five—"

Claire swung a thigh over Ford's head and rose up on her knees. He figured, if nothing else, she was trying to shut him up. And it worked. He was totally silent. Completely enraptured with the vision in front of him.

Claire leaned over, and her breasts tickled his abdomen.

"You okay back there, cowboy?" she asked over her shoulder.

"Damn, baby. I've got the best moonlit view in Texas."

And that was the last thing he said for the next half hour.

Chapter

Twenty-Eight

৵

Claire parked in front of Petal Pushers. For once, the big SALE! signs covering the windows didn't make her want to cry. Well, her eyes actually did sting with a few sweet tears of nostalgia, but mostly, she was just pretty dang excited.

Today was the last day that Petal Pushers would be in business. The next time Claire flipped the OPEN sign, it would be for her own shop!

She hadn't talked to the bank yet, or her dad. But she had a detailed business plan, and as soon as Ford was back on the ranch, it would just be a matter of ironing out the details.

She shifted behind the steering wheel as a little black cloud of unease took up residence in the seat next to her. Good Lord, that thing sure had enjoyed following her around the past few days.

Something was going on with Ford. She could freaking feel it. Cell coverage was spotty on the desolate Sun-Barre

Ranch, but he'd still managed to chat with her almost every day the first week. But by the third week, he'd been mostly radio silent, and when she had managed to talk to him, he'd seemed distant.

It was that goddam curse. She just knew it.

He was in an isolated spot, probably with a bunch of like-minded superstitious dumbasses, and he was succumbing to their nonsense. She almost laughed. The poor man was going to need reprogramming by the time he got home.

She got out of her car and straightened her shoulders. Shook off the bad feeling. Because by this time tomorrow night, her dad would be recovering from his surgery and she'd be in Ford Jarvis's arms, un-cursing him in every position imaginable.

There were several cars in the parking lot, even though there wasn't much left to buy but the fixtures. She grabbed a stack of catalogs off the seat of her truck and headed for the door.

The little bell jingled cheerfully as she entered, and Maggie's dog, Pop, barked his irritating high-pitched yaps until he recognized her. Then he turned on his heel and walked back to the counter, where Maggie sat.

"Look who's here!" Maggie said. "The future owner of Petal Pushers!"

"Shh," Claire said, setting her bag on the counter. "It's not a done deal yet. We don't need the whole town talking about it."

"Oh, I'm quite sure it's too late for that," Maggie said. "You know how stuff gets around."

"Possibly because you're shouting things like *the future owner of Petal Pushers!* every time you see me."

Bubba came around a corner, pushing a big flat cart with

nothing on it but two kids. "Who's the future owner of Petal Pushers?"

Alice popped her head around two big empty shelves. "Claire is!"

"I told you stuff gets around," Maggie said with a little shrug.

The bell on the door jingled again, and Anna walked in.

"Hi, Anna," Maggie called. "We don't have much stuff left, but that little fountain you had your eye on last month is still here."

Anna breezed in like a woman on a mission. "I'm not taking something nobody else wants. I just figured I'd have one last look around—"

"Aw, Anna. That's sweet!" Maggie said.

"Before a new owner turns it into something tacky."

Claire cleared her throat loudly. "Maybe you are the only person in Big Verde who hasn't heard, but I'm going to be the new owner."

"Oh, I heard," Anna said. "And actually, I don't care about any of this. I'm dropping off DJ quotes and menu pricing for the Boots and Ball Gowns Gala."

Alice scurried over to the counter. "Can I please have a look at—"

"I'm going with Cumbia Outlaw for the DJ, and you'll see that I've put check marks on the appropriate menu items on the catering brochure."

There was literally no reason for Alice to look at any of it. Anna had already made up her mind. And while it might be making Alice anxious, Claire was thrilled that Anna was taking charge and getting shit done. Because if one more thing were dumped on Claire's plate it was going to crack.

"So," Anna continued, looking at Claire. "What are you going to sell here? Farm equipment?"

Claire climbed onto a stool next to Maggie and plopped the catalogs on the counter. "Rancho Cañada Verde products."

Anna put her hands on her hips. "You're opening a meat market?"

"No," Claire said. "It'll be a ranch store, but our brand is going to be on all sorts of wonderful things!"

Maggie flipped through a catalog. "Look at this cookware. Cute!"

"Glazed cast iron," Claire said.

Anna raised an eyebrow. "That's high quality. And expensive. They've agreed to put your brand on it?"

"An exclusive line of Rancho Cañada Verde rustic cookware," Claire said. "They jumped on it."

"Will it have the actual brand on it? Like the ranch's brand?" Bubba asked.

"Yep. Everything from the cookware to the bluebonnet-scented soap to the leather bags made by Bosco."

"Very impressive," Alice said.

"I think we're hearing about the next big trend," Bubba said. "That's pretty neat, Claire."

"Thanks, Bubba. Did you find anything in the store today?"

"Just this super fun cart," he said, spinning it around to the squeals of his kids. "How much?"

"It's on the house," Maggie said. "But those kids are at least ten bucks each."

Bubba actually started to pull out his wallet before Maggie said, "Bubba! Get on out of here. We have girl talk to get to."

"My ears are probably going to start burning the minute I walk through that door."

"Not unless you happen to be a business loan," Maggie said. "Now scoot."

As soon as Bubba was gone, Maggie turned to Claire. "Still haven't heard from Ford?"

Claire shook her head. "No, but he's watching Worth's final event at the Cowtown rodeo tonight. That's nearly a ten-hour drive from West Texas. I'm sure he's just on the road."

The annoying cloud of unease plopped down on the stool next to her.

It was a stubborn little thing.

* * *

Ford pulled into the Fort Worth stockyards and looked at the clock on the dash. He'd gotten a late start this morning, and he wasn't having the best day.

The farther he'd gotten from the desert lands of West Texas, the more nervous and uncomfortable he'd become. Three weeks in the desert had put his mind in another place.

He'd spent a good bit of his time alone or with cowboys and ranch hands who wished they were alone. He didn't make friends with any of them, and they hadn't cozied up to him, either. He'd learned a couple of names, but for the most part, all the men kept to themselves. He didn't know if they had wives or girlfriends. He didn't know if they had kids or siblings or parents.

They were like Ford used to be.

Unattached. Unencumbered.

Without worries.

If any of them had cancer, he didn't know it. If any of them were being bullied or mistreated in a honky-tonk, he wasn't having to get involved. He hadn't had to search riverbanks or save anybody, or hold his breath while his heart climbed up the side of a cliff.

He still felt the band around his midsection, but it was squeezing instead of pulling. Making it difficult to breathe.

After only three weeks, Big Verde felt like a dream.

He'd been a different person there. A person with *big feelings*. And when you opened yourself up to big feelings, you opened yourself up to big disappointments.

He felt stupid and dumb and vulnerable.

Claire had texted him a picture of a blue ball gown for the library gala. Then she'd texted a picture of a Western-style tuxedo. *A tuxedo! The Ford Jarvis of Big Verde was a guy who went to fancy balls in a tuxedo!*

He didn't know himself anymore.

Being around Worth would help. For some reason, the kid centered him. Seeing his big goofy grin and hearing him go on about how much he loved Caroline and how everything was going to be spectacular and grand...Well, it would irritate Ford, but it would also rub off on him. It would push his Reset button, and he'd be able to shake this feeling of doom and gloom he'd been carrying since he left the Sun-Barre Ranch.

The Cowtown Coliseum parking lot was packed, and Ford was pulling a horse trailer. He was going to have to hoof it, because he was running late. He parked, checked on Coco, and then hurried to the entrance.

There was a line to get in.

Well, hell. He had no choice but to get in it, so he did. It was moving slowly, and he thought he heard the announcer say "saddle bronc riding." This was Worth's event, and it would be over in a flash. Ford shifted from foot to foot, impatiently staring at the front of the line.

When he finally got inside the arena, he looked over at the chute area and saw that Mike Gonzales was up. He was a good friend of Worth's. He came roaring out of the gate and made it to the eight-second buzzer. The crowd seemed happy with his performance, and Ford headed over to the chutes to try to catch him.

"Eighty-eight!" the announcer said.

That was a good score, and Ford waited while Mike accepted his accolades. He glanced around the arena, but he didn't see his brother anywhere.

"Hey, Mike!" he shouted.

Mike looked up, waved, and then headed over to where Ford stood, trying to stay out of everyone's way.

"Great ride," Ford said.

"Thanks," Mike said. "I've had a string of bad luck, but everything went right today. I wish I could say the same thing for your brother."

"He had his go-round already? I just got here, so I didn't see it."

"He missed his mark right out of the gate."

That meant he got a score of zero because he couldn't keep his spurs up high enough on the horse.

Ford's heart dropped. This was Worth's last rodeo. His big retirement night before settling down with Caroline. He should be living it up. Prancing around the arena. It should be a night of celebration, of going out on top. And Worth hadn't missed a mark since he was fifteen. What the hell was going on?

"You're kidding me."

"Nope. And then he wrecked."

"He fell?" A surge of adrenaline shot up Ford's spine. This was why he never came to watch. He couldn't sit still while his baby brother tried to hang on to the back of a bronco. It was the most helpless feeling on the planet.

Almost as helpless as watching someone get washed away in a flood...

"He was totally fine," Mike said. "Pissed as hell, though. Really upset. He still has two more go-rounds. You might want to try and find him and see what's going on."

"Any idea where he would have gone?"

"There was talk of going to Thirsty's later. Maybe he headed that way?"

Ford had been to Thirsty's. Their aunt June had worked there off and on for forever. He sighed. Pretty much the last thing he wanted to do tonight was go to a dance hall or honky-tonk, but he needed to find out if his brother was okay.

"Thanks, Mike."

What the hell could be going on with Worth?

The sense of doom thickened.

Pulling the damn trailer through more traffic to get to Thirsty's was a pain in the ass, and by the time Ford got there, he was actually looking forward to having a beer. He found a spot to park and apologized to Coco for leaving him in the parking lot. Then he headed inside.

It took a few moments for his eyes to adjust to the dim lighting. The place was packed, so he walked over to the bar. He hopped on a stool, ordered a beer, and started scanning the place.

Worth wasn't sitting at the bar. And Ford didn't spot him on the dance floor. By the time he'd finished his beer, he'd decided Worth wasn't there.

He checked his phone for messages again. Tried calling the idiot.

Nothing.

With a shrug, he heaved himself off the barstool. He had a reservation at a nearby motel. Hopefully, he'd hear from Worth in the morning. They were both driving back to Big Verde, and he'd hoped to caravan so they could stop and have lunch together.

His brother was a grown man—practically—and Ford wasn't all up in his business most of the time. Hell, he usually didn't see him except for every few months or so. But it wasn't like him to ignore Ford's calls, and it *really* wasn't like him to stomp out of a rodeo like a sore loser.

He headed to the parking lot. Maybe he'd spot Worth's truck.

He found it on the back row, not far from where Ford had parked his rig.

Ford turned to head back inside the bar. He hadn't checked the bathroom. And it was possible he'd missed Worth on the dance floor, although a man with a fiancée had no business dancing with a bunch of buckle bunnies.

He looked back at the truck to make sure it really was Worth's. Rodeo stickers weren't exactly a rarity in Fort Worth. He took off his hat and squinted at the rear window of the truck. It was Worth's, all right.

He started to head back to the bar when movement caught his eye. Was Worth sitting out here in the parking lot?

Ford walked briskly toward the truck, and as he got closer, he realized Worth was not alone. And the windows were slightly steamed.

He squinted to get a better look and...

That little shit. He was with a woman! Their arms were around each other, and the blond hair confirmed it wasn't Caroline.

Ford turned away. He couldn't risk Worth seeing him and stuttering out a bunch of sorry, stupid excuses.

A Jarvis was a Jarvis was a Jarvis. Even when he was the baby of the family and had dimples and a sweet little fiancée named Caroline. Even if he was *in love*, which Ford had no doubt Worth was. It didn't matter. He was already ruining it. Already setting Caroline up for heartache, just like Ford's mom and Worth's mom and their brothers' wives and ex-wives...

Worth wasn't going to settle down in Big Verde. At least, not for long. He already had one foot out the door, because Jarvis men didn't settle down. Period. Not in a town. Not on a ranch. And not with a woman.

Oh, Jesus. His world was spinning. Because if things weren't going to turn out for Worth...

Why had he blithely believed his stupid brother when he said the curse was bullshit? His father said they were cursed. His grandfather said they were cursed. Even Ruben's damn dog said they were cursed.

Ford spun around and spotted his truck and trailer. Then he stumbled in that direction, fists clenched—who did he even want to hit?—and pulse pounding.

A woman came out of nowhere, pushing a grocery cart full of junk and holding a bunch of light-up roses. "Want to buy a flower for your sweetheart? Maybe you'll get lucky tonight."

Ford stepped back, startled. "Get out of my way."

He must have looked and sounded awful, because the woman glared at him. For a moment, he thought she might spit at him, but she flipped him off instead, muttering something in Spanish. Then she grinned slyly, as if she was very pleased with herself, before pushing her creaky cart out of his way.

She'd given him the *mal de ojo*.

Ford laughed. Because this was seriously perfect. She could toss out the *evil eye* all she wanted.

"Too late!" he shouted. "I'm already cursed."

Chapter
Twenty-Nine

❧

This San Antonio hospital was a monster. Huge, cold, and impersonal.

Claire wished her dad had been able to have the surgery in Big Verde. She'd have been greeted by a friendly volunteer—they called themselves Blue Jays—instead of a menacing security guard. And nobody would be acting like Gerome Kowalski being in the hospital was business as usual.

Because it wasn't. He had freaking *cancer*, and the more people who acted like it was a dang emergency, the better.

The surgery had taken longer than expected, and Claire had run out to get some dinner. But her mom had texted that her dad was finally out of recovery and into a room in the post-surgical unit, so Claire had rushed back.

The elevator stopped on the third floor, and she got off and started looking at room numbers...*311, 312, 313*...

She stopped outside room 314. Squared her shoulders.

Hoped she didn't look like she'd been worrying, even though she had.

Worried about the surgery and why it was taking so long.
Worried about why Ford hadn't shown up yet.

She took a deep breath and pushed the door open.

Her dad lay in the bed, and at first, she thought he might be sleeping. But he was looking out the window. "Hey, Daddy."

He turned his head and smiled. She went over and hugged him. He hugged her back, and the strength of his arms was reassuring.

"You didn't have to stay here all day," he whispered. "I'm going home tomorrow."

"I just wanted to see you. And I'm pretty sure you're not supposed to be talking. Where's Mom?" Dang. She'd asked him a question. "Never mind. Don't answer—"

"Coffee," he whispered. "And don't look at me that way."

"What way?"

"Like I'm old and sick."

The door opened, and Claire's mom entered, cup of coffee in hand. She smiled brightly. "Well, look who's awake!"

Her dad waggled his hand back and forth, as if to say he was mostly awake, but not fully.

There was a light knock on the door, and the surgeon came in.

"Good evening, folks," he said. "How's our patient?"

"A little groggy," her mom answered. "But otherwise, just fine. We're looking forward to taking him home tomorrow."

"Well, now, you might have to cool your jets a bit. The surgery turned out to be a little more complicated than we'd anticipated. I think it might be a good idea for him to stay for another couple of days, just so we can keep an eye on him."

Her dad sighed loudly from the bed. "I'll be better off at home," he whispered.

"You're not supposed to be straining your vocal cords, and that includes whispering," the doctor said. "And while I'm one hundred percent certain that you would be more comfortable at home, in your own bed, I'd still like to keep you until about Wednesday. The nurses are excited, because they think you're cute."

That earned the doctor half a grin.

"Why did the surgery take so long?" Claire asked.

"There's been a bit of growth since the diagnosis, which is unusual for this type of cancer. It's normally not aggressive."

"But you were able to get everything, right?" her mom asked.

"Not quite," the surgeon said.

Claire's stomach took a nosedive. This was not what she wanted to hear. It wasn't what anybody wanted to hear. "But the radiation will take care of anything left behind, won't it?"

"That's a question for the oncologist, and he'll be by in the morning."

Claire grabbed her mom's hand and squeezed. Things were not going according to plan, and she hated it when things didn't go according to plan.

The surgeon looked her dad over, spoke a few more words that nobody listened to, and walked out the door.

"I'm sorry," her dad said.

Both Claire and her mom shushed him right up. "You have nothing to apologize for," her mom said. "Don't be silly."

"I'm making you worry."

"We're not worried," her mom said. "Because everything is going to be just fine. And you need to close your eyes and rest. I swear, Gerome, you've hardly said two complete sentences in the fifty years we've been married, but now that you've been told to be quiet you've got all kinds of things to say."

"Don't fuss at him, Mom."

Her dad grinned. "If it makes her feel better, let her do it."

"Hush, Gerome. I'm not kidding."

"You never are," her dad said.

Then he smiled and closed his eyes. Claire sat in the chair by his bed and took his hand in hers, noting the fragile, tissue-paper skin of his arms. They were pale, because he always wore long-sleeved shirts to protect himself from the sun.

He seemed so exposed in his hospital gown. Unprotected. And Claire didn't like it a bit. She wanted to put his shirt on and fasten the snaps, stick his hat on his head, and whisk him out the door. Instead, she squeezed his hand and studied the blue veins that ran just below the surface of his skin. It reminded her of the Rio Verde snaking lazily through the limestone landscape.

His face was weathered, despite the fact that he was never caught without his straw Stetson, and in the wrinkles and shadows and stubble she saw Wailing Woman, Comanche Hill, and Oak Meadow.

Gerome Kowalski was a legend who'd learned to ride a horse before he could walk. He'd shot his first buck at the age of seven and roped his first heifer the year before that. He'd ridden endless miles of fence lines, delivered countless calves, and pounded an infinite number of fence posts. His rough and calloused hands had yanked ropes, stretched wires, wielded branding irons, and cradled the head of a tiny redheaded baby he'd christened a princess.

It was unfathomable that he was lying here in this damn bed.

Her mom came over and stroked Claire's hair. "Ford sure picked a bad time to run off," she said quietly.

"What?" Claire whispered. "Why would you say that?"

"Because he's not here. And honestly, I was a little concerned he'd pull this."

Claire was speechless. Nauseated. Heartbroken.

She remembered what Caroline had told her at the barbecue on branding day and sighed heavily.

That God. Damned. Curse.

"I just can't believe it," she said.

Her mom shrugged. "I've known a lot of cowboys, honey. Some of them can't avoid doing abrupt U-turns when things are finally headed in the right direction. I don't know why they do it. I don't think they know why they do it. But Ford has done it before."

Yes, he had. "I should have seen it coming," Claire said.

"Don't be too hard on yourself. It's hard to see clearly when your heart's aflutter. And I'd hoped for the best where Ford was concerned. Your daddy did, too."

Her mom kissed the top of her head before sitting in the chair on the other side of the bed, where she began fussing with Gerome's sheets and smoothing his hair.

Her mom smiled at her. "When a cowboy is meant to come home, he always does," she said.

Claire met her gaze and tried to smile back reassuringly, even though her world was falling apart. "Daddy's going to be fine. He'll be back home by Wednesday."

"I know that, sweet girl. I was talking about Ford."

Claire crossed her arms over her chest. If Ford Jarvis

truly had tucked his tail between his legs and slinked off like a dog who'd been caught for the tenth time in the hen house, then he'd better not ever set foot on her ranch again.

Anger was already creeping in and displacing the worry and sadness. And she welcomed it with open arms.

* * *

Ford parked in front of the huge hospital and stared up at its glowing windows.

God, but he hated hospitals. Fucking *hated* them. He shivered. The last time he'd been in one was when Worth had punctured a lung after getting bucked off a damn horse.

He sighed and shook his head. Goddam Worth.

More like *Worthless*.

Ford still couldn't believe what he'd seen in the parking lot of Thirsty's. Worth had seemed so in love and smitten with Caroline, and yet as soon as he had a bad go-round, he'd fallen into the bosom of the first buckle bunny who opened her arms. The kid would probably tell himself it wouldn't happen again, that he'd just had a bad day and needed comfort, but Ford knew from watching his dad and brothers and a shit-ton of other cowboys that it absolutely *would* happen again.

A small voice in the very back of his mind said, *What has that got to do with you, Fairmont?*

And then a bigger, angrier voice told it to shut up, because it had everything to do with him. He was a Jarvis. He was cut from the same cloth. There was no getting around it.

And even if a Jarvis ever did manage to hold on to love, there was still the notion that if he stayed in one place long enough, bad luck would find him. It was better for everybody if he just kept moving.

Ford had been a fool to think he could make Big Verde his home. A selfish, naïve fool. And Claire deserved a prince, not a fool.

He'd gone to the foreman's cabin and packed up his stuff. Then he'd driven up to Miss Daisy, hands trembling and stomach churning, only to discover Claire wasn't there. He'd opened the door and slipped Oscar inside before driving to the hospital in San Antonio.

It was time to get rid of the cat, too. Let him go to someone who wanted him. Ford would fly completely solo from here on out.

An ambulance wailed nearby, reminding him that his wasn't the only life falling apart. It somehow made him feel even worse.

He sighed and tried to prepare himself for doing the hard work of explaining to decent folks why he couldn't do what he'd promised. He didn't often break promises, because he didn't often make them.

Should have stuck to that policy and he wouldn't be in this mess.

He dreaded facing Miss Lilly and Gerome almost as much as he dreaded facing Claire, who he suspected was also here. No, he knew she was here.

Tug, tug, tug.

He took a deep breath and got out of the truck. What would he say? Whatever he managed to vomit out was going to sound dumb as hell. He tried out several angles.

There's a curse on my family…

You see, a long time ago my great-grandfather met this witch…

So, I don't actually believe in curses, but there's this curse…

He broke out in a light sweat. His pulse started racing.

Then it felt like it stopped for a moment. Then it raced again.

He leaned against his truck and wiped his forehead. He couldn't go in there with a story like that. He couldn't believe how dumb it sounded even to *him*.

He tried to move away from his truck, to will his feet to start moving in the direction of the hospital. But they wouldn't budge.

After a few minutes of trying to stop thinking and start walking, he gave up.

And then, like the world's biggest goddam cursed coward, he got in his truck and drove away.

Chapter
Thirty

❦

The clock in the den ticked loudly. Had it always ticked like that? Claire didn't remember noticing it before, but now, as she sat in the silence of her parents' home, chewing on her lip while her mind raced around like a runaway train, it sounded like a dang jackhammer.

It was getting in the way of her thoughts, preventing her from settling on a single one.

Dad. Ford. The ranch. Ford. Petal Pushers. Ford. Boots and Ball Gowns. Ford.

Damn Ford.

She went into the kitchen and poured herself another cup of coffee, just as her mom and David, the home health nurse, came down the stairs.

"Well?" she asked. "Does he need to go to the hospital?"

Her dad had done really well the day of his first chemo appointment. Blew through it with flying colors. But now, several days later, he didn't seem so hot.

"He's doing awesome," David said.

That was a stretch. If you looked up the word *awesome* in the dictionary, you would not see a picture of Gerome Kowalski after chemo. He was ill and vomiting. Pale and weak. And all he'd done for the past four days was stare out the window or close his eyes with his arm over his forehead.

"You don't know what he's normally like," she said.

David rested a hand reassuringly on her shoulder. "That's true. I don't. But I do know what seventy-five-year-old chemo patients look like. And he's it. It doesn't matter if he spent the last ten years rocking in a rocking chair or the last ten years riding a horse—"

"Riding a horse," Claire said. "The last nearly seventy-five years of his life. Riding a horse."

"If he was active and healthy, then he'll bounce back sooner. So that's good. And even though he looks like shit on a cracker..."

Claire smiled. She liked David.

"It's exactly what I expect to see. His vitals are good. He's not dehydrated, although I'm keeping an eye out for that. The new anti-nausea med should kick in soon, and I'll be back tomorrow to reassess. Okay?"

Claire sighed. "Okay."

"Anything else?" he asked.

"It's just that, well, he seems really sad."

"And I expect to see that, too, Claire. You two," he said, looking from her to her mom, "need to take care of yourselves. Otherwise you can't take care of Gerome."

Easier said than done, and Claire suspected David knew it. But it was what people said in situations such as these. *The caregiver needs to take care of herself!*

But in addition to taking care of herself, Claire was also

trying to make sure her mom was okay, and there was that little side job of managing a twelve-thousand-acre ranch. She'd given up on buying Petal Pushers, but she was still working on the merchandising line. In her approximately zero spare time.

Her mom, who had been so cheerful, now looked beaten down. Exhausted. "Claire, I'll walk David out. You can go up and see your father. He asked for you."

"Sure thing. And thanks, David. We'll see you tomorrow."

David gave her a thumbs-up. "Remember to keep it positive."

Positive. She could do that. She'd give her dad a glowing and upbeat report on the ranch.

She pushed the door open and peeked in. Even though David had suggested they rent a hospital bed, her dad refused—*I'm not in goddammed hospice yet*—and he sat in his recliner by the window.

"Hey, Daddy. Mom said you wanted to see me?"

He faced her and smiled. And it was a tad disconcerting because it was a little too bright. Too forced.

"Have a seat, princess. I want to discuss something with you."

His voice was still hoarse, and Claire didn't think he should be discussing anything, but she sat down and took his hand. "What is it?"

"I've been thinking about the future."

Here it came. He was going to talk about selling the ranch.

"Just the general future? Or something in particular?"

"Yours and your mother's."

"What about yours?"

"That's a little uncertain at the moment."

"Welcome to the club, Gerome Kowalski," she said with a wink. "All of our futures are uncertain."

Her dad's eyes twinkled. "Don't sass me. And I'm serious. I need to talk about it."

He probably did. For his own peace of mind. But Claire wasn't going to entertain any of his silly notions. She squeezed his hand. "Have at it, cowboy."

"I've talked to George Streleki."

Yep. Here it came. George was a real estate agent.

"This ranch is worth a whole lot of money. There's some folks interested in it."

"But we're not selling, so we don't need to worry about who's interested or how much this place is worth." She patted his hand. "I've enjoyed our little chat."

"Claire, you need to hear me out. Beef prices are—"

"Down. I know. And I'm looking into ways of countering that."

"On the off chance that you can't actually control the beef market, or run this ranch single-handedly," he said, pausing to let it sink in, "we need to consider what life would be like if we sold at least *some* of this place. We could keep the house, of course, and a couple hundred acres. And you and your mom will probably be set up pretty well."

"What about you?"

"Set up or laid out."

Claire crossed her arms angrily across her chest. He meant laid out at the funeral home. "Dad—"

"What about your dream of having a shop selling fancy clothes and whatnot? You could easily buy Maggie's place, or any place, for that matter. Hell, you wouldn't even have to stay in Big Verde."

Claire stood up. "You listen to me, Gerome Kowalski. This ranch is my home. Not just the house, but the land. All twelve thousand acres of it. And I'm not giving it up for all the money in the world."

"Your home shouldn't be your prison."

This was crazy talk. "Why would you say such a thing? You've always said that the Rio Verde runs through your veins. What the hell do you think runs through mine?"

Her father smiled. And his eyes teared up.

"Sit down, princess."

"I don't want to sit down. I want to jump out this window and get on Cinder and ride as far away as I can, as fast as I can, until this conversation is far behind me."

They stared at each other for a few seconds, and then she sat.

He took her hand again. Squeezed it. "My three uncles died mean and alone. No wives or children. Your mama and I thought we would never be able to have children at all. You're our miracle. Our angel."

He lifted her chin and forced her eyes up to his. "*My princess.* And you can't run this ranch by your goddammed self. I never expected you to. That's why we sent you to college to learn all that business and marketing and clothing stuff you're so interested in."

"She won't have to run it by herself."

They turned to see Beau and Bryce standing in the doorway. Her dad gestured them into the room. "Howdy, sons."

They each shook his hand, and Claire could see that they did it firmly. They were not treating her dad as if he might break, and she wanted to kiss them for it.

"Gerome," Beau said. "We're not leaving this ranch. It's our home."

"I know that. And I'm going to take care of you boys. You don't have to worry—"

"We're not worried about a place to live," Bryce said.

"We're cowboys," Beau said. "We'll live anywhere we can hang our hats."

"But home is where your family is," Bryce continued. "For me and Beau, it's where *you* are. And you'll have to get a judge to kick us off this property."

Her dad snickered a little. Raised an eyebrow. And then turned and silently looked out the window. "The numbers aren't good. But we'll hold on to it as long as we can."

"Good," Claire said. "We've all had a lovely time socializing, but if you don't mind, we've got some hay to cut."

Her dad nodded. "And get those yearlings in the east pasture—"

"Separated," Claire said. "Did it this morning."

Without any more fanfare or chitchat, she followed Beau and Bryce out the door, where her mom was waiting in the hallway, wearing a big old grin.

* * *

Ford pulled up to the desolate cluster of trailers that housed the seasonal hands at the Sun-Barre Ranch. He and Coco were weary as hell. Sheer boredom would do that to you.

It wasn't that they didn't have enough work to do. Because they'd ridden fence lines, branded and castrated calves, hauled in feed and hay, and even sheared some sheep. But things were just... *boring*.

There were four other cowboys in the trailers, and predictably, they kept to themselves. Nobody worked out here because they were looking for company.

He checked to make sure there was hay and oats in the horse stall, because there wasn't much to graze on. That's why the West Texas cattle ranches were so damn big. You needed about seventy-five acres to keep a single heifer alive.

He wondered how the ranch—not this one, but Rancho Cañada Verde—was doing. Bile rose in his throat when he thought about how he'd fled San Antonio, leaving Gerome Kowalski up in his hospital room, sick and without a foreman.

Tug.

And Claire, with the weight of the world on her sweet shoulders. He'd been so sure he was doing the right thing, but now...

At first, he hadn't realized what this itchy feeling was. He'd just gotten to Sun-Barre. Why would he have itchy feet already? But then it dawned on him that he missed Big Verde. Plain and simple.

It would get better with time. He just had to wait it out, until Big Verde was just a memory like any other town and any other ranch.

What were Bubba and JD up to? Probably still pretty busy after the flood. Hopefully, downtown Big Verde was recovering nicely, and all the little shops and cafes would be as good as new. The Boots and Ball Gowns gala was probably coming along—Anna would make certain of it—and Alice would get her library back.

The Boots and Ball Gowns gala. He'd kept the picture Claire had texted him of that big, fluffy blue ball gown. It was going to look beautiful on her, and he wished he'd be there to see it. And that ridiculous tux she'd wanted him to wear! It wasn't suitable for a cowboy. She should have known better than to even try.

He grinned.

Claire Kowalski was used to getting her way.

She'd met her match with him, though. Where he was concerned, nobody got what they wanted. Good times.

He swung back by his truck and grabbed the mail off the front seat. As usual, there wasn't much. Junk and a bank statement. He'd look at the statement later. For a wandering ranch hand, he'd managed to squirrel a shit-ton of money away. He had no idea what he'd do with it someday. He had nobody to leave it to. Nothing he wanted to buy. He'd probably donate it to a charity like the Mustang Heritage Foundation.

He went into the trailer, flipping through the rest. Junk mail, junk mail, junk mail... A bright yellow envelope with a baby bottle sticker on it. Return address: Wayne and Trista Larson, 2010 C Street, Big Verde, Texas.

He hadn't heard from a soul since he'd left Big Verde. Not Claire. Not his brother. Nobody. Why were Bubba and Trista sending him a letter? And who knew Bubba's real name was Wayne?

What: Baby Shower for Maggie and Travis
And!!!
JD and Gabriel
When: 2:00 pm on Saturday, July 3rd
Where: Trista and Bubba's
*Bouncy Castle for the Kids
*Beer and Barbecue for the Grownups
*Lots of gifts (hint hint) for the parents-to-be

Who on earth had thought it was a good idea to invite him to a baby shower? And it wasn't like he wanted to go. He'd lived this long without ever having to suffer through a baby shower. Why start now?

It sure would be nice to see everybody, though. And he had to smile, and then laugh a little, when he remembered the night at Tony's when they'd all learned JD and Gabe were going to be parents.

He started to throw the invitation in the trash, but instead, he stuck the silly thing on the refrigerator.

The familiar sound of tires crunching on caliche drew him to the window. It was probably one of the other hands pulling up. Maybe they'd want to sit on the porch and have a cold beer. He moved the blinds aside and saw a very familiar pickup truck.

What the hell was Worth doing all the way out here? Probably looking for a job. Either Caroline had found out about his cheating, or he'd decided on his own that it was time to hit the road.

He watched as his brother took his hat off, ran his hands through his too-long hair, and stuck it back on his head. Then he let go of the blinds and opened the door.

"Well, look what the cat dragged in," he said, watching Worth come up the steps.

"Actually," Worth said, "it's the other way around."

Ford heard an obnoxious howl that he recognized as Oscar's weird meow.

"Claire said to take your fucking cat back," Worth said, thrusting the animal in Ford's face. "This thing does not like riding in a truck."

Ford took Oscar, and the damn thing immediately began licking him and purring sporadically like an old tractor on its last legs. Well, hell. He hated to admit it, but he was kind of happy to see the nasty thing.

"Claire said he meowed constantly and kept trying to get out. She said he misses you."

Ford rubbed Oscar between his ears.

"She also said that meant the cat had shit for brains."

He wanted to hear every last word that Claire said, even the bad ones directed at him, and he had to swallow down the urge to ask Worth if there was anything more.

"How is she?"

"Pissed. Are you going to let me in? It's hot out here."

Ford moved out of the way and let his brother inside. "Want a beer?"

Worth looked around the sparsely furnished trailer. "Nah. Not staying that long."

"You drove all this way to give me my cat?"

"And to call you a fucking asshole."

Ford raised his eyebrows. His little brother didn't often talk to him like this. In fact, this was probably the first time he ever had. And he was on thin ice, because if either of them was an asshole, it was Worth.

"How could you treat her that way?" Worth asked. "You didn't even say goodbye."

"It was bound to happen sooner or later, and you're one to talk."

"What is that supposed to mean? And why didn't you come see me at my last rodeo? You said you'd be there, and you weren't. I guess you can't keep your word to save your soul—"

"I was there, you little shit. And it's a good thing I'm holding this cat, because that's the only thing keeping me from punching you right in your smartass mouth."

Worth's face went blank with surprise. "Did you see me crash? Man, that was the worst ride of my life. Figures it had to be my last."

"I got there after it happened."

"Why didn't you come and find me? I was having a horrible day and could have used the support."

"I did."

Worth furrowed his brow. "Really? I didn't see you."

"I looked for you at Thirsty's."

"I went to Thirsty's, but I never even got out of my truck."

"Stayed in the parking lot?"

"Yeah. I was—"

"I saw you."

"Why didn't you come talk to me?"

"You were indisposed. Are you still stringing Caroline along? If so, you need to break it off, brother. Don't do this to her."

Worth's eyes widened. "What the hell are you talking about?"

"I saw you with a woman. And it wasn't Caroline."

Worth covered his face with his hands and muttered, "Oh my God, Ford. You're a fucking idiot."

"I know what I saw."

Worth looked at him and shook his head. "No. You definitely do not. The woman you saw me with was Aunt June."

What? Aunt June was blond, but why would she be sitting in Ford's pickup with her arms around him?

Worth sighed. "Caroline is being deployed."

"Wow, Worth. I'm sorry. But I don't see what that's got to do with—"

"She called me and told me just before my go-round. And furthermore, she broke off the engagement. Said I'm too young to have to wait on her. I shouldn't have taken the call. I shouldn't have gotten on the horse in the state of mind I was in. But I did. And I missed my mark and then I crashed. I needed to talk to someone. I needed my family, and you weren't there."

"I was just running late—"

"I texted Aunt June, and she came out to talk with me on her break. I didn't feel like being around folks, so I didn't go into the bar. What you saw was our fifty-seven-year-old, three-packs-a-day aunt trying to comfort me."

Worth hadn't cheated on Caroline?

"I thought it was the curse," Ford said softly.

Worth sighed and put his hand on Ford's shoulder. "Brother, I don't know what you're so afraid of. But I don't believe for one minute that it's that stupid curse."

"But it's—"

"Not real. So why did you walk out on Claire when she needed you most?"

Ford's mind ground to a halt. There was no answer to that question. None that Ford could come up with, anyway.

"Do you love Claire?" Worth asked quietly.

Oh, dear Lord. He did. With all his heart. "Yes. But it doesn't matter. Not after what I've done."

"I tend to agree with you. I don't know why she'd take you back, honestly. But people in love do stupid shit."

Maybe Claire had been in love with him at one time. But surely, she wasn't anymore.

"You can't explain anything to Claire until you figure it out yourself. You were looking for an excuse to leave. You thought I gave you one. You thought the *curse* gave you one. But you were wrong on both counts. Why are you looking for excuses, Ford?"

Oscar meowed and clawed his way out of Ford's arms.

"I don't know," he said. "But I miss Claire. I'm walking around with a hole in my heart. And I miss Big Verde, too."

"Then, cowboy, come home. But I wouldn't expect a welcome wagon."

Chapter
Thirty-One

❧

Claire dropped orange and grapefruit slices into a plastic pitcher of sangria while Trista dumped a bag of ice into a galvanized tub for the beer. The noise level in the kitchen was through the roof, and the shower hadn't even started yet.

She hated leaving her mom today. Her dad had had another appointment on Thursday, and it had been a rough few days. Nobody had slept last night.

Claire hadn't been to her own little home in days. Miss Daisy seemed like one of many silly ideas now. Like Petal Pushers and the dream of having her own shop. But the biggest delusion of all had been thinking Ford Jarvis would settle down.

She'd been duped, and then she'd been dumped.

Again.

A foam basketball bounced off her head.

"Meghan!" Trista hollered. "Get that out of the kitchen."

Of all the things littering the kitchen floor—toy tractors,

books, and Barbies—Claire didn't understand why the foam ball was the straw that broke the camel's back. Maybe because Meghan kept throwing it at their heads.

"Do you want this transferred to a pretty glass pitcher?" Claire asked. "Or are we serving in plastic?"

Trista straightened up and blew a strand of hair out of her face. "Do you honestly think there is any glass left in this house?"

"Gotcha. Plastic it is."

The doorbell rang. "Will somebody get that?" Trista yelled.

Suddenly, the house went deathly silent.

"Hey!" Trista shouted again. "Somebody get the damn door!"

"I'll get it," Claire said.

Trista blocked her. "No. Not you."

"But I don't mind—"

"You don't understand. At any given time of the day, every single door in this house is open. I'm talking cabinet doors, refrigerator doors, bathroom doors, and patio doors. My kids are freaking experts at opening doors. They just don't want to open *this* one because I asked them to."

"Okay, so—"

"Bubba!" Trista hollered, right in Claire's ear. "Make one of the kids open the door!"

Bubba entered the kitchen wearing shorts and a T-shirt that said BEER BABY with a downward-pointing arrow.

"You're not wearing that," Trista said.

"It's my baby shower shirt," Bubba said.

The doorbell rang again.

"Did you rinse off all the lawn chairs?"

"Yep. But the cushions are missing."

"What do you mean the cushions are missing?"

A foam ball bounced off Bubba's head. "I mean they're missing. I think the kids took them to the neighbors' place to make a fort."

Someone was now pounding on the door, and Claire snuck off to open it. It was locked, and the doorknob was frantically jiggling. She turned the bolt and opened the door to find a very harried and disgruntled Anna.

"What took you so long? I thought I was going to have to go through a window."

"Sorry."

Anna stopped in her tracks in the foyer and stared in awe at the baby shower decorations in the dining room. Or maybe it was shock. Shock and awe. "Oh. My. God."

"It's fine," Claire said. "You're not in charge of this party."

"But—"

There were spaceships on the tablecloth. Clowns on the napkins. Football streamers, and a boy band poster on the wall. Actually, the boy band might not be part of the decorative theme. Hard to know. The table centerpiece was a cut-out cowboy.

"It looks like Party Town exploded in here," Anna said.

"That's basically what happened," Claire said. "They couldn't decide on a theme, so they went with all of them. There's sangria in the kitchen. Would you like some?"

A foam ball bounced off Anna's head. "Are we mainlining it?"

"No. We're having it in plastic Solo cups because Trista doesn't own glasses."

Anna sighed and put her gift on the table. "Let's hit it," she said.

Twenty minutes later, the party had moved to the Larsons' backyard. Claire sat with Maggie, Anna, Alice, and Trista on the deck—not very comfortable without chair cushions—while the men loitered around the barbecue pit.

"Are Worth and Caroline coming?" Maggie asked.

Trista refilled Claire's cup. "They're supposed to."

"How nice," Claire said. She didn't have a thing in the world against Worth, except that he reminded her of Ford. Actually, everything reminded her of Ford. She took a huge gulp from her cup and then held it out for more. Trista raised an eyebrow.

"She's drinking for two," Maggie said. "That's our agreement while I'm pregnant."

Trista added a bit more, and Claire leaned back against the hard metal chair slats. Either the chair was more comfortable than it had been a few minutes ago, or she was catching a sangria buzz.

"Well, I hope they can make it," Maggie said. "Especially since Caroline's being deployed soon. It will be nice to see her again."

Poor Worth was beside himself over Caroline's upcoming departure. But at least she was wearing that engagement ring again. Worth had worked super hard to convince her that he wanted to wait. That he wanted to support her while she was deployed. They planned to marry as soon as she returned. In the meantime, he'd promised to make a home for them in Big Verde. And Claire believed he'd do it, too. He was a fixture on the ranch, thank God. He'd joined Bubba's bowling league, even though the word on the street was that he couldn't bowl. And it was rumored he'd been to church last Sunday.

Unlike his brother, he was obviously putting down roots, and nothing catastrophic had happened as a result. Just the opposite, in fact. Worth was living his best life, whereas Ford was living his worst.

At least Claire *hoped* he was. Curses of biblical proportion were what he deserved. Locusts. Boils. That sort of thing.

Anna squealed as a foam dart from a plastic gun bounced off her arm.

"Sorry," Trista said, refilling Anna's cup.

"When I leave here, I'm getting my tubes tied," Anna said.

"File that under *Things you shouldn't say at a baby shower*," Maggie said.

"No offense intended," Anna said.

Maggie patted her belly. "None taken. Motherhood isn't for everyone, and that's okay."

"I don't plan to have children," Alice said. "Although I enjoy being around them."

She picked up a faded frisbee and threw it to Henry, who missed it and said, "Shit!"

"Travis!" Maggie yelled.

Travis walked over and squatted next to Henry, presumably to tell him to *cut that shit out*.

"If you don't mind me asking, why not?" Trista said. "Why no children?"

Alice intrigued Claire. She was so independent and happy in her own skin. Claire wanted to be the same, but she'd always had this very strong sense that her "other half" was out there somewhere, and all she needed to do was find him. She didn't really like being alone. She liked having people around to share things with. Maggie had once said, "If Claire is having fun, and nobody is there to see Claire having fun, did Claire really have fun?"

She was like that tree that fell in the forest.

"I enjoy my life the way it is," Alice said. "I don't have to consider anyone else's needs unless I really want to. I don't pick up after anyone else. I'm not responsible for anyone else's possessions or behavior—"

"Please stop," Trista said. "You're going to make me cry."

Alice laughed. "You're a wonderful mom, Trista. You're raising good humans, and the world needs good humans."

"Aw, thanks," Trista said, with her eyes misting up. "Do you think you'll ever get married?"

Oh, dear God. Claire hoped they weren't going to make a party game out of *that* question.

"No," Alice said simply. "I'm not interested in that. And if I were to ever change my mind about having kids, well, there are lots of ways to make a family. JD and Gabriel are prime examples of that."

"Yep," Maggie said. "Look at how I became Henry's mom. As Grandma Honey used to say, there is more than one way to skin a cat."

"That's a horrible saying," Claire said, watching JD and Gabriel argue grilling tactics with Bubba. "But I have to admit, it's comforting to know that I can have a family without a partner, if I want."

"There you go!" Alice said. "Who needs Prince Charming? You're enough all by yourself, Claire."

Maggie nodded. "We all are."

"Holy cow," Trista said, looking toward the gate to the front yard. "Look who's here!"

"Oh my God," Maggie whispered. "Claire, honey, don't stop drinking."

Claire turned to see who they were looking at. At first, she didn't recognize the guy wearing khaki shorts, a yellow polo shirt, and holding two gift bags. But then something clicked, and she realized it was Ford Fucking Jarvis.

* * *

Ford had almost turned around about a hundred times. And now, as he stood quietly while an entire party ground to a halt, he wished he had.

Showing up after what he did to the Kowalski family would have been bad enough. Doing it in the first pair of shorts he'd worn in twenty years was downright unbearable. Even though Bubba and Gabriel were both in shorts, too.

A wolf whistle rang out—probably Bubba—and then everyone started talking at once.

Trista came over and took the gift bags. Bubba put a beer in his hand. JD offered him a seat. But all he wanted to do was see Claire.

The tugging around his midsection had started in earnest as soon as he'd entered Verde County. "Is Claire here?" he asked JD, even though he knew she was. *He could feel her.*

"Yes," JD said, glancing over Ford's shoulder. "And, oh, look. Here she comes now."

Ford slowly turned to look over his shoulder, and his breath caught in his throat. She wore a light green sundress and strappy sandals, and her hair was piled up on top of her head like a cinnamon bun. She was gorgeous, and as he watched her stomp toward him with exaggerated steps, he realized she was also a bit drunk.

And armed with a Nerf gun.

"Oh, dear," Trista said. "Sorry, Ford. She wasn't expecting you to show up."

Bubba pounded him on the back. "You've got balls, man. Even in those shorts."

"She looks murderously pissed off," JD said.

Folks parted like the Red Sea, and Claire marched right up to Ford.

"Let's give them some privacy," Trista said.

"Ah, hell no," Bubba said.

Claire poked the gun in Ford's chest. "Who invited you?"

"I did," Bubba said, stuffing a chip in his mouth. "Trista sent me to the post office with the invitations, and I dropped them in the box."

"I forgot to take Ford's out," Trista said apologetically. "I addressed them, you know, before."

Ford's face became hot with embarrassment. Worth had warned him there would be no welcome wagon, and he was right. None of these folks wanted him here. And yet, he so desperately wanted to be here. With these people he'd come to think of as friends.

"I'm sorry," Ford said. "This was a mistake. I should go."

"Ya think?" Claire asked. Then she pulled the trigger and six Nerf darts bounced off his chest in quick succession.

"Do you need another cartridge of darts?" Trista asked in a stage whisper.

Claire nodded. "Bring me all the ammo you've got."

Ford just stared at her, and suddenly he was overcome with the urge to laugh. He was so happy to see her that he didn't care how many Nerf darts she shot at him. Hell, he was happy to see *everyone*.

"How far is that drive from West Texas?" Gabriel asked.

"A little over nine hours," Ford answered.

"You came all this way to be with us at the shower?" JD asked.

"Yes. And well…"

Here was the hard part. The part that had kept him up all night last night.

"I'm planning to stay here in Big Verde if I can find a job."

Trista handed Claire another cartridge of darts, and she reloaded. "Oh, I don't think so, cowboy."

Maggie walked over with Travis. "What have we missed?" she asked.

"Claire just told Ford that this town is not big enough for the two of them," Bubba said.

"And this party definitely isn't," Claire said, glaring at Ford. "So, you need to be moving on down the road."

"Neither one of you is going anywhere," JD said. "You're both our friends, and we want you here. We're going to have cake and open gifts. Nobody has to talk to anybody they don't want to talk to, and nobody is going to shoot anybody."

Claire pulled the trigger again, and this time she'd aimed the darts lower, at his knees.

"Claire," Ford said, trying to dodge the last dart. "Can we talk?"

Everyone but Bubba started to drift away, and Trista grabbed him by the arm and dragged him off.

"I don't have anything to say to you."

"I know I don't deserve—"

"My time," Claire said. "You don't deserve my time. And JD said nobody has to talk to anybody they don't want to talk to, so…"

She walked away, and Maggie sidled up next to him. "Not that I care, but are you okay?"

"I shouldn't have come."

"But you did. You drove nine hours to bring us a gift."

"It's nothing much," Ford said. "Just a package of those little blanket things. The lady at the store said you can't have too many."

Maggie smiled and rubbed his arm. "Thank you. I'm sure she's right."

Laughter came from the barbecue area, but Ford had the feeling that everyone was on edge. He'd ruined the party.

"Why *did* you come?" Maggie asked.

"Believe it or not, I miss y'all."

"We miss you, too. But your actions had real consequences for the people you care about. I don't know what
your deal is. I don't even know if *you* know what your deal
is. But you can't toy with Claire's emotions this way. She's
a strong woman, but she's not invincible."

"I thought I was doing what was best for her."

Maggie furrowed her eyebrows. "No. I suspect you were
doing what you thought was best for yourself. I don't need
to understand all the subtle nuances of whatever is going on
with you to know that much. And furthermore—"

A foam ball bounced off Maggie's head, and she kicked
it back over to the kids.

"And furthermore," she continued, "you left the Kowalskis in a real bind."

"How's Gerome?"

"Pretty dang sick. He's on chemo."

Ford's stomach took a dive. "I thought he wasn't going
to have to do that."

"The cancer was worse than they'd thought. He's been in
bed for weeks."

"Well, who's running the ranch?"

"The drunk girl."

"By *herself*?"

"Beau and Bryce are helping. Worth is helping. The
other ranch rats—Manuel and the rest—jumped ship to the
Kelsey Ranch."

Those fuckers. "But what about her store?"

"Didn't happen. I don't know if you heard, but their
foreman *done run oft*, as Grandma Honey used to say."

Ford stared at the beer in his hand and felt sick to his
stomach.

"What did you think would happen?" Maggie asked.
"Best-case scenario—without you—was still pretty bad."

"I thought that Claire and I had gotten the ranch in decent shape. And that she had a marketing plan—"

"That got shot to shit because somebody has to feed the cows, Ford. Somebody has to be the foreman, and while Gerome's down, the manager. That's Claire."

"I just thought—"

"Stop saying that. You didn't think. You *felt*. And that scared you, so you ran."

He stared at his feet. They looked stupid in sneakers. "I thought you said you didn't understand all the subtle nuances of what was going on with me."

"Oh, that's not subtle. That's obvious as hell. And I suspect it's just the tip of the iceberg."

Ford sighed. She was probably right.

"Look around, Ford. Do you see all this?"

Ford looked at the messy backyard, the kids running around, the men flipping burgers on the grill...

"Claire wants this," Maggie said. "And she's going to get it. I want you to think about that. About who she might get it *with*. Because as of right now, it's not going to be you. Not until you can figure out what you want."

"I know what I want," he blurted, surprised by the fierceness in his own voice. "I want this. And I want it with Claire."

Because Jesus, he really did. He loved that woman. He loved her family. He loved the ranch, and he loved this stupid, quirky-ass town.

And he'd thrown it all away.

"You're going to have to work hard for it," Maggie said. "And you still might not get it."

Chapter
Thirty-Two

❦

Ford sat in his truck and stared at the Kowalskis' ranch house. Claire had been very clear about not wanting to have anything to do with him, so he'd waited until he knew she'd be gone. Maggie had told him that they were having a Boots and Ball Gowns committee meeting today at the Village Chateau.

He clenched the steering wheel. He hadn't turned the engine off yet, maybe he could just turn around and leave...No. He definitely couldn't do that again.

He got out of his truck. His boot had barely hit the first porch step when the front door opened. Miss Lilly stood there, looking only mildly surprised to see him, and also tired and strained.

"Hi there, Ford," she said. "I saw you pull up. Gerome and I heard you were back in town."

Oh, he bet she'd heard, all right. And Claire had probably been cursing up a storm when she'd told them. But Miss

Lilly's face was pleasant, as always, and he heard nothing in her voice but kindness. He relaxed a little and went up the rest of the steps. "It's nice to see you again," he said, meaning every word.

"Come on in the house," she said. "Can I get you some iced tea?"

"No thank you, ma'am."

Inside the foyer, he held his hat in his hands and looked around. There was a walker in the corner. Prescription bottles on the coffee table. And a silence he wasn't used to experiencing at their house. "I'd like to see Gerome, if he's up to it."

"Of course he is," Miss Lilly said.

Ford breathed a sigh of relief and headed for the stairs at the back of the house.

Miss Lilly touched his arm. "He's in the den. Been having a hard time with the stairs, so he's in there for the time being."

Gerome couldn't get up the stairs? And he had a walker? Ford nervously twisted and untwisted the brim of his hat. When he'd left, you couldn't even tell Gerome was sick by looking at him. He braced himself for whatever he was going to see.

Miss Lilly gave him a nudge. "Go on in. He'll be happy to have some company."

Ford wasn't so sure about that, but he walked past the kitchen to the den, where Gerome Kowalski sat in a chair looking out the window. Ford could only see the back of his head, but he couldn't miss the changes. Gerome looked smaller. Frailer. And he'd lost all his hair.

Ford's hands started to sweat. His heart stuttered. And his feet wanted to turn around and walk right back out the door he'd just come in.

Miss Lilly offered a sweet, encouraging smile, and Ford walked over to Gerome's chair and cleared his throat. Gerome jerked his head—he'd been dozing—and looked up at Ford. His face was thin and pale, but his eyes were sharp and aware and intensely focused.

Recognition kicked in, and he almost smiled. "Well, look who's back," he said. "Pull up a chair."

Ford pulled a stool over and sat on it. "You're looking good, Gerome."

"Liar," Gerome said. "But believe it or not, I looked worse a couple of weeks ago. I'm starting to feel a little better."

"Oh? That's good news."

Gerome nodded, and they just sat there for a minute, looking at each other.

Ford wasn't here to talk about crops or cows or the weather. So he cleared his throat again. Best to just spit it out. "I owe you an apology."

"No kidding."

"I don't rightly know what to say. I guess I just—"

"Apology accepted," Gerome said.

"But I—"

"I figure you've got your reasons. I don't know if they're any good, but they're not my reasons, so I don't need to concern myself with them."

Ford started to say more. Gerome might not need to know the reasons he'd left, but he deserved to know them. But what came out of Ford's mouth was, "How's the ranch doing?"

"As well as can be expected."

Without a foreman while you've got cancer and your hands are jumping ship.

"Claire is running things. The poor girl is burning both ends of the candle, that's for sure, but she's holding it together. I'm right proud of her."

Ford was, too.

"And your brother is a big help. He's a good man, even if he does need a damn haircut. Did you know he puts that blond mane in a ponytail? I never heard of such a thing on a ranch."

Ford wanted to tell him it was worse than that. Worth had been known to don a man bun under his hat. But Ford didn't want to have to explain what a man bun was.

"Your look is sharper," Ford said with a wink. "And I bet it's easy to care for."

Gerome smiled. It was the equivalent of a belly laugh, and it warmed Ford to the core.

"Worth says you raised him from the time he was a toddler."

"Well, I don't know that I *raised* him."

"He says you did."

"Our dad left. We have different moms, but they kind of banded together, so from the time Worth was about three years old, we lived in the same house—or houses, rather. We moved around a lot. Anyway, our moms both worked all day, and I'm ten years older than Worth, so I took care of him and our sister, Abby."

"I've heard about Abby. And I'm sorry for what happened. This flood must have brought back a few rough memories."

Ford swallowed, but didn't say anything. A stack of catalogs on Gerome's TV tray caught his eye.

"Those are Claire's," Gerome said. "Lotions and soaps and whatnot. Texas wildflower scents. And she says they're going to have our cattle brand on them. Isn't that the silliest thing you ever heard?" He pointed a bony finger at the catalog. "But do you know what? We made a profit off those non-beef items in the grocery stores last quarter. Thanks to the flood, it was our only profit for the quarter. So, we're going to be raising a herd of toiletries now."

"Claire has a mind for business."

"That she does. How long are you going to be in town?"

"Forever."

Gerome raised an eyebrow. "That's a big step for a fella like you."

"Yes sir. I know."

"You got a job?"

Surely, he wasn't going to offer—

"Because I hear the Kelsey Ranch needs another herdsman."

Ford swallowed. "Thank you. I'll head over there next."

He hadn't expected Gerome to offer him a job after what he'd pulled, but it still hurt. And he didn't want to work for Mr. Kelsey, but he damn well would if it kept him in Big Verde. Close to his brother, close to these folks, and close to Claire, even though she'd be crazy to have anything to do with him.

"Where are you staying?"

"At the Big Verde Motor Inn."

Gerome nodded. Rocked back and forth in his chair. "Nobody's going to believe you're staying, including me, unless you show that you're really trying to make a home here. You need a place to live that isn't a motel or a bunk-house. You have any money?"

"A little." Actually, he had quite a lot.

"I know of a small piece of property if you're really serious, but we can talk about that later."

A small piece of property? As in a small piece of property *to buy*?

What would it be like to have his own place? A place to really call home?

"Once you've got a place to live, you've got to unpack your suitcase. You don't leave your belongings in a box or in the back of your truck or horse trailer, you hear? You unpack. And you hang a picture on the wall. Put a tea kettle on the stove. Buy yourself a welcome mat."

Ford smiled. "I can do that."

"A cow dog is a nice addition, but I understand you've got that other four-legged situation—"

"A cat," Ford said.

"Yeah. One of those." Gerome shook his head as if owning a cat was the craziest thing he'd ever heard. "And then you have to give something to the community. Maybe you paint a church. Maybe you plant flowers at the park, or give money to an organization that needs it. You've got to invest in your town."

"Yes sir."

"And join a club."

"A club?"

"Yes, a club. You go to pointless meetings once a month. Nothing much gets done, but it means you belong. You have an instant group of folks you have something in common with, even if it's just bad coffee, stale doughnuts, and a random line at the end of your obituary."

Ford laughed.

Gerome studied him for a few seconds. "I'm not kidding about that club. Also, I've got one other thing to tell you."

Gerome's manner completely changed. His eyes bored into Ford, filled with fire and fury. And Ford didn't care if Gerome was on chemo and had a walker, at this moment, he had no doubt the man could totally kick his ass. Ford was wishing he'd accepted that glass of tea from Miss Lilly, because he'd started to sweat.

"Have you seen Claire?" Gerome asked.

"Just once. She shot me with a Nerf gun."

Gerome didn't look the least bit surprised. "I don't know what that is," he said. "Did it hurt?"

"Mere flesh wound," Ford said, trying not to grin. "She might have been a little bit drunk at the time."

"You don't want to let a redhead get drunk, son."

"I wasn't consulted."

Gerome gave him a half grin, but then it slipped away and he became serious again. "While I'm fairly happy to see you, it appears that Claire was not. So, if I hear about you going near my daughter or pestering her in any way when she does not want to be pestered, I will string you up from the nearest tree. Do you understand me?"

"Yes sir," Ford said.

"If she happens to change her mind," Gerome added with a twinkle in his eye that indicated he thought she very well might, "then it's none of my business."

"Yes sir," Ford repeated. He sure hoped that twinkle in Gerome's eye meant there was a chance.

"Get on out of here now," Gerome said. "I imagine you've got a few things to take care of."

God. He loved this man.

* * *

Claire sat in the empty ballroom of the Village Chateau, nervously pinching the seam that ran down the leg of her pants with her thumb and finger. She was the first one to arrive at the Boots and Ball Gowns committee meeting, and the space felt huge and lonely.

Since the night Ford had left, *every* place felt huge and lonely. But now he was back, and it somehow felt even worse. She could *feel* him. And she knew he was staying at the Big Verde Motor Inn, because she could see his freaking truck parked there every time she drove by. Which was nearly every damn day.

How long was that idiot staying? He'd said he was "coming home."

Ha! This was her home, not his. And he'd better not start encroaching on her territory. It was bad enough that he'd come to the baby shower.

"Hey, there, Claire. You're early."

Claire looked up to see Jessica Acosta, the manager of the Village Chateau's restaurant, Chateau Bleu. She flipped a switch and the chandeliers overhead burst into sparkling light.

This was going to be a gorgeous venue for the gala.

Claire looked at her watch. "The others should be here shortly. Are you staying for the meeting?"

"You bet," Jess said. "Carmen is super pumped to support this fund-raiser. She's filming in Bali right now, or she'd be here herself."

Carmen was a celebrity chef with her own TV show, and she owned several restaurants, Chateau Bleu being her latest acquisition.

"Oh! That's great news! Does this mean we can count on a discount for the food?"

"It means," Jessica said with a beaming smile, "that you can count on *free* food."

Claire gasped. The hotel was donating the ballroom, and now Carmen was donating the food? "Are you kidding me?"

The sound of high heels tapping a Morse code across the dance floor announced Anna's arrival. "Kidding about what?" she asked.

"The restaurant is donating the food," she said.

"Well, praise Jesus!" Miss Mills said from the doorway. "He answers prayers."

It had actually been Carmen, but Claire wasn't going to argue Jesus with Miss Mills.

Jessica and Claire started setting up chairs in a circle while Anna watched. She squinted in Jessica's direction. "Just so long as you donate the good stuff. We don't want the C-class appetizers."

Anna had had it in for Jessica ever since the two of them had been forced to share the role of head cheerleader their senior year, and then insult had been added to injury when Jessica had been crowned homecoming queen.

"We don't have any C-class appetizers, Anna," Jessica said. "But you might have to accept *käseigel* instead of goose liver pâté."

Trista Larson limped in with a little girl wrapped around each leg. "Get *off*," Trista said, shaking a leg to no avail. "What on earth is *käseigel*?"

Anna shrugged. "Beats me."

"It's a gorgeous appetizer consisting of fine cheese," Jessica said. "You'll love it and everything else I have planned for the menu."

Anna's eyebrows rose over the word "planned." She pulled a journal out of her bag, sat in a chair, and crossed her legs like she meant business. "Okay, ladies. This thing is happening in a mere three weeks. Let's get busy."

The rest of them sat down just as Maggie and Alice arrived. "What have we missed?" Maggie asked.

"We're having *kerfluffel-muffel*!" Trista said, badly mispronouncing the word. "Which is a fancy way of saying cheese."

Jessica laughed. "And other things. That's just to get us started."

"Cheese and I have a deep and meaningful relationship," Maggie said. "So, I'm on board."

"Maggie, when is the baby due?" Jessica asked. "You still look so tiny."

"Ha!" Maggie said, patting her belly. "Short and tiny are not the same thing."

Anna sighed. "First order of business," she said, "is the rest of the menu."

She wasn't going to tolerate baby talk since she, herself, was not pregnant.

"I'm thinking finger foods," Jessica said.

Anna's right eye twitched.

"Oh, Bubba's not going to like that," Trista said.

"Neither are any of the other men," Anna added. "They're going to want something more substantial."

"Well, he might like it when he tastes it," Jessica said. Then she clapped her hands loudly and shouted, "Hope! Roll it in!"

Anna stood. "Roll *what* in? We haven't even discussed—"

Hope, Jessica's eleven-year-old sister, pushed a cart into the room. In the center was what Claire's mom would call a *cheese porcupine*, a round loaf of bread covered in toothpicks with cheese and olives and whatnot. This one was exquisite with various cheeses, mushrooms, vegetables, and shrimp.

Everyone ooh-ed and ahh-ed appropriately, except for Anna, while Hope beamed.

"Hope, did you help make that?" Claire asked.

"Yes ma'am," Hope said, pulling out a toothpick and popping a cherry tomato in her mouth.

"Hope, I told you to wait until after," Jessica said.

"I forgot," Hope said with a glint in her eye that indicated otherwise.

Jessica shook her head, but she was grinning. "The kids at Hope House would love to make some of the decorations for the ball. I've talked to Sally Larson about it—"

Anna produced an audible *harrumph*. When everybody looked at her, she said, "We want tasteful decorations."

Hope House was a community center for folks with physical and developmental disabilities, or *extra special* abilities, as Hope and Jessica liked to say. Hope had Down syndrome, and the center was started by her grandmother, Mavis Long.

Everyone collectively glared at Anna.

Hope handed out toothpicks while Jessica pointed out the other items on the tray. "Fried Brie with a red currant sauce, albondigas with a pepper cream sauce, chorizo and mushroom tapas, crepes with camembert and chives..."

"This is divine!" Claire said.

Because it really was. Like, totally more than they could have hoped for.

"Does this mean we're not doing the nacho bar?" Trista asked. "Bubba was really looking forward to it."

"No nacho bar," Anna said. "This is going to be classy, and Bubba is just going to have to deal with it. No hot dogs. No cheese from a can. No big bags of chips on the table."

"What about beverages?" Claire asked. "Open bar is out."

"That means a cash bar is in," Maggie said.

Miss Mills crossed her legs at the ankles and her arms over the giant purse on her lap and said, "I'd like it to be known, for the record, that I am against serving alcohol at this event. I have a delightful punch recipe that calls for lime sherbet. It's a real people-pleaser at funeral receptions."

Anna just looked at her.

"Go ahead," Miss Mills said, nodding at Anna. "Write it down in the minutes."

"There are no minutes being kept—just notes—and I'm not writing it down. I wrote it down at the very first meeting, right here on the same page where I have the quote from the DJ. It says, 'Cumbia Outlaw, music from the sixties to today, $475 for four hours, Miss Mills is officially opposed to alcohol.'"

"It wouldn't hurt to write it down again," Miss Mills said stubbornly.

"It wouldn't help, either," Anna said. "Jesus heard you the first time."

Miss Mills yanked her daily devotional out of her bag and commenced to angry-fanning. "There will be drunkenly misconduct, mark my words."

"Oh, absolutely," Maggie said.

"And possibly Nerf gun battles," Alice said quietly, with a glance at Claire and a wink.

Claire had practiced various scenarios for how she'd react if Ford Jarvis ever showed his face in Big Verde again. None of them had included a plastic gun and foam darts. And yet...

She'd never forget the sight of him jumping around as she'd aimed for those knees. *Knees! He'd been wearing shorts!*

"What are you grinning about, Miss Kowalski?" Maggie asked.

"Nothing."

"We've got that rampage model Nerf gun," Trista said. "It slams out twenty-five darts at a time if you want to enter the gala locked and loaded."

"I don't know what y'all are talking about," Jessica said. "But it sounds fun."

It wasn't fun. It was humiliating.

Also maybe a little fun.

"On the first Thursday night of the month we let the teens do Nerf battles in the library," Alice said. "The stacks make it really challenging, and they get to blow off steam and play like kids again."

"That sounds absolutely wonderful," Claire said. "As soon as the new library is open, they'll be able to have even bigger and better battles."

"I sure do hope so," Alice said. "And I want y'all to know how much I appreciate this. How much I appreciate each of *you*."

Chapter
Thirty-Three

❧

Claire concentrated as she applied sparkly pink polish to the nail of her pinky toe. With all of the endless ranch work and committee meetings and back-and-forth discourse with suppliers, she hadn't had time for a professional pedicure before the Boots and Ball Gowns gala.

"Thanks for letting us get ready at your house, Alice."

"No problem! It's fun, and we're just a mile away from the Village Chateau."

Like Claire and Maggie, Alice was wrapped in a fluffy white bathrobe.

"If you two don't mind," Alice said, "I'm going to go get my gown on. Feel free to use the guest room or bathroom when you're ready to slip into yours."

"Some of us will be squeezing rather than slipping," Maggie said.

Claire set the nail polish bottle down and admired her handiwork. "Not too shabby."

"I don't know why you bothered," Maggie said. "You're just going to stick those piggies in a pair of boots."

"You're jealous because you currently can't even see your piggies," Claire said, glancing at her gorgeous new white and silver cowboy boots resting in a box. "And there's no way I can put unpolished toes in those boots. They don't deserve it."

"For what you paid for them, you'd better get married in them," Maggie said.

Claire just sighed and shook her head. She'd always dreamed of getting married in a big, fluffy wedding gown and a pair of fancy cowboy boots. It was a Texas thang. But now, her wedding dreams seemed childish and immature.

Prince Charming didn't just come along because you wanted him to. And sometimes he came with baggage he couldn't unpack. And then, you had to let him go.

After shooting him with a Nerf gun.

What Claire had learned from the flood and her dad's cancer—and all that had happened since—was that life was unpredictable. It didn't follow some kind of storybook outline. You didn't know what chapter you were in, and nobody was guaranteed a happily-ever-after at the end.

"Actually," she said to Maggie, "I'm probably going to put these fancy boots on tomorrow and castrate some bulls."

"Is it because of the mood you've been in? Or is it just time?"

Claire laughed. "It's just time."

And yes, she was in a mood.

Maggie pointed to a box on the coffee table. "What's in that?"

Claire opened the box and lifted out a pair of rhinestone-studded spurs. "Fully functional," she said.

"Holy cow! Those are insane! Where on earth did you get them?"

"Relic from my rodeo queen days," Claire said. "I also have a—"

"Shh," Maggie said. Then she whispered, "What is that sound?"

Loud moaning and gasping came through the door of Alice's bedroom.

"Is there a man in there with Alice?" Maggie asked, eyes wide.

Claire listened closely. "Spanx," she finally said. "She's worming her way into a pair of Spanx."

"I don't know what those are," Maggie said.

"Wow. That was really spoken from a place of privilege."

Maggie furrowed her brows. "But what—"

At that moment, Alice burst out of her bedroom, cheeks pink and huffing as if she'd just run a marathon. She wore a champagne-colored, heavily beaded, one-shouldered gown.

Maggie and Claire gasped.

"What's wrong?" Alice asked, turning her head and looking over her shoulder.

"You're stunning!" Claire said.

Maggie nodded. "You're red carpet and paparazzi material."

Alice blushed. "I possibly went a little overboard, but this gala is for my library, after all."

"The gown is perfect in every way," Claire said.

"Thanks, guys. But you'd better get yours on now," Alice said. "We need to leave in about twenty minutes."

Claire and Maggie hustled down the hall to the guest room. "You first," Claire said.

Maggie unzipped a bag on the bed and slipped off her robe. Her pregnant body was stunning, and Claire felt a lump forming in her throat as Maggie stepped into a flowing red dress with an empire waist.

"Oh, Maggie," Claire whispered.

Maggie stood in front of the full-length mirror and cupped her baby bump with both hands. When she looked up at Claire, her eyes were glistening. She let go of her belly and fanned her face with her hands. "Oh gosh. My eyes are leaking."

Maggie had always been the town's tomboy. *One of the guys.* But she sure didn't look like one now.

Claire wrapped her arms around her friend. "I'm so happy for you. You know that, right?"

Maggie smiled. "I do know that." She turned to gaze at her image in the mirror again, eyes drifting down to her belly. "Never in a million years did I believe this would ever be me."

"I did," Claire whispered. "I believed."

"Thank you," Maggie said, letting go of Claire and wiping her eyes. "Now, let's get you into your beautiful gown."

A few minutes later, Maggie zipped Claire into her blue satin gown. "You're stuffed in there like a sausage," she said. "But what a freaking gorgeous sausage."

Claire looked at herself in the mirror. The sleeveless dress had a dramatically flared skirt—lined in tulle to make it swirly—that flowed into a slight train. Beaded pearls accentuated the waist and hem. Claire twirled around and said, "Wait for the best part...Pockets!"

"Oh my God," Maggie said. "It's like the Holy Grail of ball gowns. And you look just like Cinderella."

Claire gasped. "It *does* look like a Cinderella gown. What was I thinking?"

"Consciously, that you look kick-ass in blue. Subconsciously, that you're a princess and you're ready for your happily-ever-after."

Claire put an arm around Maggie. "I absolutely *am* ready for that," she said. "But I'm writing my own story, and this princess does not need a prince. Because I'm enough, Maggie. All by myself."

"Oh, honey," Maggie said, giving Claire a squeeze. "Are you just now figuring that out?"

* * *

Ford helped Gerome into his truck and then climbed into the driver's seat. Gerome had called him earlier in the day and asked if he felt like taking a small drive to see the pretty piece of property he knew of for sale.

Since Ford was terribly tired of living at the Big Verde Motor Inn (Oscar seemed tired of it too), he had rushed right over. "You sure seem a lot stronger, Gerome," he said as they pulled away from the ranch house.

"That's because I am," he said. "And continuing to improve every day."

There was no more chemo scheduled, and hopefully Gerome would be back to his old self in another few weeks. "Which way are we headed?"

"Across Wailing Woman."

Across Wailing Woman? There was nothing over there but Miss Daisy, the foreman's cabin, and Ruben's place. He raised an eyebrow at Gerome.

"We're going to see Ruben," Gerome said.

Gerome hadn't been getting out much. And Ford wasn't going to begrudge him a drive around the ranch, especially since Ruben's place at Oak Meadow was the prettiest spot on the property.

They drove across the bridge and past the lane that led to Miss Daisy. Ford intentionally didn't glance at it. He'd promised Gerome he wouldn't bother Claire, and he hadn't. But he never stopped thinking about her.

She had no reason to forgive him for what he'd done, and he didn't expect her to.

He hoped she would though.

They passed the foreman's place next.

"I'm about to fill that cabin," Gerome said. "For good, or for at least a good long while."

Ford swallowed, heart hammering away. Gerome wasn't going to offer it to him, was he? Maybe the pretty property he was talking about was the foreman's cabin.

"Beau and Bryce," Gerome said. "They're good, loyal men. And they've shown their grit these last few weeks. I couldn't choose one over the other, so I figured I'd just promote them both."

"And what about Claire? You can't just kick her out of the position without something else to offer her."

He heard the defensiveness in his voice, but he couldn't help it. Claire had more than proven herself, hadn't she?

"She's going to be my new vice president of marketing," Gerome said. He smiled and added, "How about that?"

Ford smiled. He wished he could be there when Claire got the news. "I think that will make her very happy. And you know she'll be good at it."

He was a bit disappointed not to be taking part. The ranch was headed in new and exciting directions. But he'd had his opportunity, and he'd blown it.

"I hear you're doing a fine job for Mr. Kelsey," Gerome said.

"Yes, sir." The Kelsey Ranch wasn't a bad gig. It's just that it wasn't what he wanted.

"I wouldn't expect anything less."

Ford turned onto the road that led to Oak Meadow and Ruben's place.

"There's a bit of smoke," Gerome said. "I wonder what Ruben's burning."

"God knows," Ford said. "The last time I saw him burning something, it was for a weird ritual after the flood."

"Homecoming," Gerome said. "And cleansing. He told me."

"It's crazy talk, if you ask me."

"No crazier than flipping over a horseshoe or not setting a hat on the bed," Gerome said. "And by the way, I never set my hat on the bed. It'll burn your house down."

Ford grinned.

When they got to Oak Meadow, he turned the engine off and rolled down the windows. "Would you like me to help you out, Gerome?"

"Oh, I'm not getting out. It's you who needs to talk to Ruben."

Ford gawked at Gerome, then realized it and closed his mouth. "I don't need to—"

"He's waving you over," Gerome said.

Ford sighed and got out of the truck. Ruben was standing near a fire. God knew what kind of nonsense he was up to. "What are you welcoming now?" he asked.

"Nothing," Ruben said. "Just burning brush. But I'm not surprised to see you here."

The sun was starting to set, and the smoke from Ruben's fire swirled in the air, twisting and turning like an exotic dancer.

Boo came over, and goddammit, he circled Ford's legs twice, counterclockwise.

"I see you're still cursed," Ruben said simply, staring at Boo, who'd now plopped down on his side in the dirt.

"No such thing," Ford said, although a bit of unease crept up his spine. He reminded himself that it didn't matter. Even if the curse was real—which it absolutely wasn't—he had nothing left to lose. He'd already lost Claire.

"You know," Ruben said. "The only curses that have power over us are the ones we put on ourselves. The others aren't real."

"None of them are real."

"Okay," Ruben said. "If you say so."

Ford didn't appreciate the patronizing tone. "Are you trying to say I've cursed myself? Why would I do that?"

Ruben shrugged. "Loss, usually. Maybe you lost something in the flood when it displaced you."

The wind shifted slightly, and smoke blew into Ford's face. It burned his eyes, and he moved to the other side of the fire. "We've been through this, Ruben. The flood didn't get anywhere near the foreman's cabin. I know you did that smoke mumbo-jumbo, but I was not displaced by the flood."

"The smoke doesn't lie. It brings in those displaced. Welcomes them home. And you came with the rest of the animals."

Ford shook his head. Ruben was going to Ruben, and that meant he'd spout nonsense until the cows came home.

Ruben cocked his head and looked at Ford. His gaze was unwavering, despite the smoke that made both their eyes water. "You know," he said. "Maybe it wasn't this flood. Was there another one?"

Ford took a step back, and Ruben raised an eyebrow.

This was stupid. And yet...

"There was another flood," he said softly. "A long time ago. And I lost my little sister."

Lost her. It was such a strange way of putting it. Abby

hadn't been misplaced or left behind somewhere. She hadn't slipped through a hole like change in your pocket.

She'd died.

"She drowned when I was supposed to be watching her."

Ruben nodded as if everything made sense. He reached out and touched Ford's shoulder, and Ford didn't step away, even though he wanted to. In fact, he wanted to run. He wanted to get in his truck and drive far, far away.

It's what he always did when the feelings got too big.

"I'm sorry," Ruben said. "That's an unbelievably deep loss. No wonder you cursed yourself."

"I haven't cursed myself, Ruben."

Although he'd been running for an awfully long time.

"No roots. No ties. No home. You don't want to get close to anyone, because you're afraid of the responsibility that comes with loving them. Were you with your sister when she drowned?"

Ford squeezed his eyes shut.

He'd told Abby not to get too close to the water, and then he'd busied himself with searching for grasshoppers for his fishhook. The creek was really running because of all the rain, and he'd wanted to drop a line in it.

He was only twelve. How could he have known they were under a flash flood watch?

The water had come with a roar.

And Abby was gone.

Ford, you were supposed to have been watching her!

"There's always a chance we'll lose what we love," Ruben said. "It's easier to stay alone. You can't lose what you don't have."

A wistfulness had entered Ruben's voice, and Ford opened his eyes to see Ruben gazing into the distance with watery eyes. Maybe it was just the smoke.

"Believe me," Ruben said. "I get it. And you're cursed, brother."

Ford thought about all the ranches he'd worked. About how he'd worn loneliness like a comforting blanket.

Ruben seemed to snap out of it. He shook his shoulders and leaned over and rubbed Boo's belly. "Well, you know what to do if you want to lift the curse."

"I do?"

"Yeah. You do. You've got to take a risk, *muchacho*."

"I've already lost the only thing that mattered," Ford said. "I've lost Claire."

"Oh, I wouldn't say that," a deep voice said from behind them. Both men turned to see Gerome standing there.

"Gerome, let me help you." Ford grabbed the older man's arm so he wouldn't fall. The ground was uneven and scattered with rocks, and he shouldn't be walking unassisted as weak as he still was.

Ford's face was hot with embarrassment. How much had Gerome heard?

"Believe it or not, I was young and dumb once," Gerome said. "Thought I knew what I wanted. Didn't have a clue as to what I needed. But I thought for sure that it wasn't this ranch."

Ford stared at Gerome. "You didn't want this place?"

"I wanted to see the world," Gerome said. "I thought I was too big for Rancho Cañada Verde. Too big for this town. And I was terrified of a pretty little schoolteacher who seemed hell-bent on roping me."

Ford grinned. "It looks like she roped you, though."

"She had to chase me first," Gerome said. "And when she caught me, well, let's just say that I'm lucky she didn't have a Nerf gun."

Ford shook his head and held in a laugh.

"It turns out I wasn't too big. I was too small."

Even ill, Gerome Kowalski was larger than life. "But, Gerome—"

"I rose to the occasion, son. Accepted my responsibilities and all of the curses and blessings that came with them. And you can, too. I wouldn't be standing here next to you if I thought otherwise."

Ford knew he should say something. Maybe just a simple *Thank you for believing in me* would suffice. But the words were stuck in his throat, and his chest felt tight. It was embarrassing.

"You two better finish up your business," Gerome said. "Or Ford won't make it to the ball on time."

Had Gerome been on his feet for too long? Was the sun too hot? Because he sure as shit sounded confused.

"I've got no business with Ruben," Ford said. "And I'm not going to the damn ball."

Gerome raised an eyebrow as if he knew differently. "Ruben is selling his little house and five acres. I thought you might be interested."

Ford couldn't believe his ears. Ruben was selling?

The western sky looked like glowing embers in a campfire. Lightning bugs flickered; the frogs were croaking with tentative, sleepy voices; and the Rio Verde snaked lazily through the valley below.

It was the prettiest spot on the ranch, but that's not what had Ford's mind racing and his pulse pounding. It was the sense that he was meant to be here. Right now. At this very moment. With these people who felt like family. And on this ranch that felt like home.

Only one thing was missing, and that was Claire. Was it possible that he still had a chance of having everything he'd ever dreamed of? His pulse slowed as the walls started going up.

You don't deserve it.

"You're squeezing my arm pretty tightly, son," Gerome said.

Oh dear God. He had the poor man in a death grip, but Gerome didn't seem to mind. His eyes twinkled.

Ford looked at Ruben. "You're selling?"

"It's time."

"But this land has been in your family since forever. Why is it time?"

"The smoke led you here. This is your home."

Gerome snorted a little, and Ford shook his head. "Cut that crap out, Ruben. Why are you doing this?"

"Let's just say I've got my own curse to deal with."

"A woman?"

Ruben shrugged. Smiled a little. "A daughter in Chicago."

Boo walked over to Gerome and sniffed his feet. Then he walked back to Ruben and plopped down in the dirt.

"Well, that's good news," Ruben said. "Boo didn't sit on your feet."

Gerome chuckled. "I'm mighty relieved."

Ford's mind felt foggy and numb, but he figured he and Ruben had a few details to work out. What if he couldn't even afford this place? "How much are you asking, Ruben?"

Gerome nodded at Ruben. "He got this place for next to nothing, and I'm assuming he'll sell it for a reasonable price."

Ford swallowed. Was this really happening?

"You've got about five minutes to settle your business," Gerome said, turning to walk back to the truck.

"Why five minutes?"

"You've got a ball to get ready for."

"I told you. I'm not going—"

"There was a fancy gray tuxedo delivered from a rental

company yesterday. Claire said she forgot to cancel the order. It has your name on it, so I figure you might as well wear it."

The idea of going to the Boots and Ball Gowns gala made Ford's blood run cold. He didn't really like dressy events. But Claire would be there.

Neutral territory. Presumably void of Nerf guns.

It would be a good place for groveling.

He swallowed down a lump of anxiety, because he had to take a risk, didn't he? Curse or no curse.

"Aw, hell," Ford said. "Gerome, can I change at your house?"

Gerome grinned and headed back to the truck. "Finish up your business, Romeo," he called over his shoulder. "And then we'll get you cleaned up."

A short while later, Ford stared at himself in Miss Lilly's mirror. The tuxedo fit pretty well, but he couldn't help but tug at the collar.

Miss Lilly fussed with brushing imaginary lint off the jacket. "My, but you are a handsome one," she said.

Ford couldn't help it. He blushed.

"Make sure you're back by midnight," Gerome said.

"What happens if I'm not? Will I turn into a pumpkin?"

"No. But you might be late for work in the morning. And I won't stand for that."

This was confusing as all get-out. Gerome had hired Bryce and Beau to be the foremen. "Work?"

"I've got two foremen. I've got a vice president of marketing. And now I need a ranch manager so Lilly and I can take a damn vacation."

"Are you asking me to be your ranch manager? Permanently?"

"I sure as hell am. Are you interested in coming back to Rancho Cañada Verde as the big boss?"

Ford took his hat off and held it in his hands. He didn't feel too big for this ranch; he felt too small. But if Gerome Kowalski thought he could manage it, then he damn well could.

Gerome was never wrong.

"There is nothing on God's green earth that I'd like more."

It felt as if the curse—the one that didn't exist—had already lifted.

Chapter
Thirty-Four
❦

Claire could hardly believe her eyes. The last time she'd seen the Village Chateau transformed to this extent, Anna had turned it into a haunted house for a Halloween gala.

"You know how much I hate to give Anna credit," Maggie said, gazing at the ceiling, which was covered in a million sparkly lights. "But this place looks like it's straight out of a fairy tale. Did you see the Cinderella carriages lined up outside?"

Miss Mills walked up. "That's the church's doing," she said. "We rented them from Yellow Rose Pony and Buggy. Twenty dollars per person. The library gets one half, and the youth group gets the other. And it was my idea."

"It was a good one," Claire said. "And don't you look lovely!"

That might be a bit of a stretch, but Miss Mills did look slightly less dour. She wore a green Sunday church dress and, in keeping with the theme, sturdy black ankle boots.

"You girls look nice, as well," Miss Mills said. "Although aren't you cold? All those bare shoulders. Why don't ladies wear shawls anymore? One would come in especially handy for you, Alice, seeing as how you're missing about half your dress."

"Oh my word," Alice said, eyes sparkling. It was clear that she was so thrilled with the evening that she'd barely heard Miss Mills. "I'm beside myself. Look how many people are here!"

The lobby and ballroom—and probably the courtyard outside—were filled to capacity. The women wore gorgeous gowns and men wore...

Everything.

While a few were dressed formally, there were plenty of stubborn asses walking around in jeans or Western leisure suits.

Well, that was Big Verde for you. Claire wasn't going to let it spoil her evening. What mattered was that people had turned out. Big time.

"Everyone looks wonderful, don't they?" Alice asked.

"Well, except for RB Wright," Maggie said. "He's in overalls."

Sure enough, RB Wright stood at the buffet table wearing denim overalls and loading things he couldn't pronounce onto his plate.

"As long as he paid to get in, what do we care?" Claire said.

"I started counting heads earlier," Alice said. "I gave up."

"How many tickets did we sell?" Maggie asked.

"Four hundred," Alice replied. "And we've reserved a few for the door. If we sell out, we'll only be about six thousand dollars shy of our goal."

Alice could hardly stand still, and she looked absolutely gorgeous. "What if we can actually build the library even better than it was before? Wouldn't that be something?"

Claire loved seeing Alice so happy.

And speaking of happy, Maggie was also suddenly beaming. Claire didn't need to look behind her to know what—or who—was making her face look like fireworks going off. Travis must have arrived.

"Oh my God," Maggie said. "Would you look at my cowboy?"

Travis was so dang handsome even Claire got a little tickle in her tummy. He wore a black Western tuxedo jacket over a deep burgundy embroidered vest. Jeans on the bottom, but it was perfectly fine, because *sexy*. Big silver belt buckle. Dressy black boots. And a black felt hat on top.

He wrapped his arms around Maggie. "Well, if it isn't Little Red Riding Hood," he said, leaning over and nuzzling her neck. "Fancy meeting you here."

"Hey, knock it off," a low voice said, and they all looked up to see Bubba, with Trista on his arm. "If you folks can't control yourselves, you'll need to take it outside. This is a classy party. You can tell it's classy by its lack of a nacho bar."

"Yeah," Claire said, raising an eyebrow. "There's a shed out back if y'all need privacy."

Maggie blushed until her cheeks were nearly the same color as her dress.

"Y'all hush," she said.

Bubba wore a plain old suit that was probably reserved for weddings and funerals, and Trista wore the bridesmaid dress from Maggie's wedding. Maybe they'd never grace the cover of a fashion magazine, but Bubba looked at Trista as if she'd hung the moon, and a small seedling of jealousy waved its little leafy hands at Claire again.

Bubba started bouncing on his feet as a popular Tejano song came on. Nobody loved to dance more than Bubba, and as Mexican *gritos* rang out across the ballroom, he looked at Trista and grinned. "Come on, Mama. Let's cut a rug."

Trista grabbed his hand, and the two of them headed for the dance floor.

"I suspect this is the last time I'm going to be this dressed up for a long while," Maggie said. "Possibly for forever. It's a shame that I don't really feel like dancing."

"We need to find you a seat where you can put your feet up," Claire said.

"Good idea," Travis agreed.

Just as they turned to head for a table, George Streleki walked up and tapped Maggie on the shoulder. "Guess what? We've got an offer on Petal Pushers."

Claire's heart nearly broke. In fact, it pretty much did. She thought she heard it crack.

Maggie stopped in her tracks. "Oh? That's great news. How much?"

"Asking price. Earnest money in hand."

"Wow. That's fantastic!"

"They want to walk through the building again tomorrow morning. You should probably run by and tidy it up a little."

"You bet," Maggie said.

Claire squared her shoulders. "I'll help. What time?"

Maggie looked at George. "Buyers are coming around nine," he said.

"Yikes," Maggie said. "That means we're going to have to get there early."

"Oh, and Claire," George said, turning his eyes on her. "Tell your daddy I'm drawing up papers to accept that offer."

Claire stared at George. Surely, he hadn't just said what she thought he'd said. "Papers? What offer?"

"It has to do with the ranch. He'll know what I'm talking about. Offers galore!" he said. "It's been a good day in real estate."

And with that, he walked off, leaving Claire devasted and shaking in his wake.

"What offer is he talking about?" Maggie asked.

Claire's eyes filled with tears. How had this happened? After all her hard work, her dad was selling? And he hadn't even told her. "I don't know for sure," Claire said. "But I think Dad just sold Rancho Cañada Verde."

"No," Maggie said.

Travis furrowed his brow. "That can't be right, sweetheart. I don't even...Hell. I don't know what to say. My brain can't accept it."

Two years ago, when Travis discovered his father had left him a ranch burdened with back taxes, Claire's dad bought the lien, just to give Travis time to save Happy Trails. How could that same man now be giving up his own ranch?

And he hadn't even talked to Claire first.

The upbeat Tejano music stopped, and a screech of feedback made everyone wince and cover their ears. Alice had taken the stage.

"Excuse me," she said. "Can I have everyone's attention please?"

"That's Alice?" Travis said. "Holy shit. She cleans up well."

Beau and Bryce joined the group. "She sure as hell does," Beau said.

He'd said it under his breath, but he was close to Claire's ear, and she'd heard it. She raised an eyebrow at

Beau. He blushed furiously and then continued looking at Alice like he was a puppy and she was a warm saucer of milk.

Poor Beau. Did he and Bryce know about the ranch?

Alice tapped the mic and blew in it, even though it was working just fine. "I want to thank all of you for coming and supporting the library. As of fifteen minutes ago, we were still six thousand dollars shy of our goal. But we've just had an anonymous donation, and we're completely funded!"

The room erupted in deafening cheers and applause. Beau stuck his fingers in his mouth and whistled shrilly, making Claire wince and cover her ears. She wanted to join in the celebration. This was what they'd been working for! But her heart was too heavy.

While everyone hugged and cheered and cried, she quietly slipped out to the courtyard.

Nobody would miss her. They were too busy having all their wildest dreams come true and their wishes granted and their hearts filled.

Meanwhile, her dreams had been crushed. Her wishes remained unfulfilled. And her heart was completely broken.

Again.

She found a small bench beneath a giant magnolia tree and sat down. She sighed and sniffled and tried to hold in the tears. But they came anyway.

She covered her face with her hands and crossed her legs. One of her stupid rhinestone spurs caught on the hem of her dress, and she yanked it loose, not caring if it pulled the satin or tore the tulle.

How had she ever believed she could write her own story? Fate—and men—kept getting in the way.

* * *

The tuxedo felt awkward and was a little over the top. Ford might as well have just stepped off the set of an old Western, because the outfit was pure *Gunsmoke*, right down to the bolo tie. The jacket was gray—gunslinger style—with a super-fancy yoke. A black vest and black hat completed the look.

Claire had picked it out, so that meant she liked it.

He straightened the bolo tie, tilted his hat to just the right angle, and scanned the room.

He'd been here for about fifteen minutes, and in that time, it seemed like he'd seen everybody and his damn dog. But he hadn't seen Claire.

"Did you find her?" Alice asked. "We were all talking to her earlier, so I know she's here."

"No," he said. "And I'm a little worried, because I'd expect her to be the belle of the ball. Did something happen to upset her?"

Alice cocked an eyebrow. "You mean recently?"

Ford lowered his eyes. He'd upset Claire plenty, but probably not in the last fifteen minutes. "Yes."

"Not that I know of. Why don't you check the courtyard again? I'll go look in the ladies' room."

"Thank you, Alice," Ford said. "And congratulations on reaching your goal."

Alice smiled and clasped her hands in front of her heart. "I still can't believe it. If I ever learn who the anonymous donor is, he's getting a big old kiss."

Ford's cheeks heated, and he hoped Alice couldn't see the blush. Gerome was right about investing in your community. It felt good.

He had his town. And thanks to Gerome and Ruben— and a quick call to George Streleki—he had his ranch. The only thing missing was his woman, and nobody seemed to know where she was.

God knew he didn't deserve her, but this was a magical night. Anything could happen.

He was just about to go back inside when he felt it.

Tug.

He turned just as Claire stood up from a bench hidden in the shadows.

Her beauty took his breath away. Knocked the air right out of him. And it wasn't the dress, although he could see how lovely it was. And it wasn't her hair, which was piled up in curls on top of her head.

It was just *her*. The very essence of her. Tough, yet soft. Strong, but vulnerable.

Nobody's princess.

His woman.

When he was finally able to inhale, his hand was over his heart, clenching at his vest.

Beau walked by. "Hey, bud," he said. "You okay? You look like you're having a heart attack."

"I'm—"

What was he supposed to say? That he was *fine*? There wasn't a single word in the dictionary that could possibly express what he felt when he saw Claire.

The only word that came close was *home*. He wanted to rush to her, bury his face in her hair, and stay there forever.

"Fine," he said. "I'm fine."

Beau pounded him on the back. "If you say so. Want a beer?"

"No thanks. You go ahead."

Claire's eyes met his with a wary gaze. Who could blame her? What could he ever say to her that could possibly come close to an explanation for the heartache he'd put her through?

I love you.

That's what he would say.

The music from the ballroom floated out to the courtyard, and the DJ was playing "Bless the Broken Road."

It was their song.

Claire's face softened. Ford took a few steps toward her, tilted his hat, and then he tentatively held out a hand. "Would you like to dance?"

Claire headed his way with small, hesitant steps. As she came out of the shadows, Ford could see that her nose was red and her eyes were shiny. A small trail of mascara ran down her cheek.

"Darlin'," Ford said. "What's wrong?"

In a blur of blue motion, Claire stumbled toward him. He opened his arms to catch her and hold her, but...

She ran right past him.

"Claire!" he called, turning to watch her flee. "Wait!"

He took a step, and something crunched beneath his boot. He bent over and picked up a pretty silver spur, set with rhinestones.

He'd crushed it.

It had to be Claire's. He ran after her, but just as he rounded the corner, she climbed into a horse-drawn carriage and rode away.

Chapter
Thirty-Five

&

Claire blew her nose into a tissue and watched Maggie sweep the floor. This was probably not what helping your pregnant friend should look like, but Claire hadn't slept at all last night and was totally useless.

Maggie stopped sweeping and stared at her, eyes filled with mischief. "Let me get this straight. He asked you to dance, you rushed toward his open arms, and then swerved at the last second?"

That was pretty much it. Although she hadn't done it intentionally. The last-second swerve had surprised even her. She'd wanted so desperately to fall into his arms.

"Stop being so impressed by my cruelty, Maggie."

Maggie put her hand up. "It's just that that is such a classic Big Moment Move. I mean, Claire. Seriously. The arms were out and open..."

"And whoosh," Claire said. "Blew right past him."

"And he looked so hot," Maggie said. "I saw him talking to Alice when he first came in."

"You did?"

"Yeah. And then I saw him chatting with George—"

"Ugh. George. I wonder if he blabbed to Ford about Dad selling the ranch."

"What did your dad have to say for himself this morning? Did you let him have it?"

"He's bald from chemotherapy, Maggie, so no, I did not *let him have it.*"

Maggie shrugged. "I didn't know. You did that swerve move with Ford, and I thought maybe you were targeting chemo patients next."

Claire sighed. "He wasn't up yet."

"Oh?" Maggie furrowed her brows. "Is he feeling poorly again?"

"He's fine. He's just discovered the joy of sleeping in."

Maggie's face relaxed, and she put the broom down and walked over to Claire. "Hey, I'm sorry if I'm flip and irreverent. It's what I do when I get nervous. Which is very unfortunate. You deserve a friend who can provide real comfort instead of just farting out of her mouth."

"I realize it's a nervous thing for you," Claire said. "Like how you giggle at funerals."

"Which is also really unfortunate," Maggie said.

"What are you nervous about?" Claire asked.

"Well, there's this," Maggie said, pointing at her pregnant belly. "And there's the fact that my store is closed. And sold. And therefore, not mine anymore. And then there's my best friend, who's in a lot of pain."

"I'll be okay," Claire said. She wasn't sure she believed it, though.

Maggie sighed heavily. "This is all such crap timing. If

you'd known your dad was going to sell Rancho Cañada Verde, you could have bought Petal Pushers."

No kidding. Claire had lain awake last night thinking about it. She'd given up her dream. And for what?

Nothing.

"It's too late now," she said.

"Maybe they'll back out," Maggie said. "Or maybe it's not too late for me to back out—"

Claire put her hand up. "No way. It's asking price. They've put down earnest money. And honestly, now I don't even…"

"What?"

"I don't even know what I want anymore."

Or even who she was.

"You shouldn't let your dreams die," Maggie insisted.

"A dream is just a wish your heart makes," Claire said. "And wishes don't come true."

Maggie patted her awkwardly on the head. "Now you're just being morose."

Claire snorted. Because that's exactly what she was doing, and it felt good. She'd spent the first twenty-nine years of her life spewing rainbows and looking at the bright side of things. But it turns out the glass was half empty all along, and she'd just dumped it over.

"I feel empty," she said.

Maggie hugged her. "Aw, Claire. You're breaking my heart. But on the upside, you're probably really rich now."

Claire pulled away from Maggie's embrace and put her head on the counter. She had no idea how much the ranch was worth. Probably a lot. But she didn't care. She looked at her hands and thought about how the Rio Verde no longer ran through her veins.

"I can't stop seeing Ford's eyes," she said. "He looked so utterly devastated when I ran past him."

"Swerved," Maggie corrected. "You swerved at the very last second."

"Even after everything he's put me through, I don't feel good about it."

"That's because you're an inherently kind person. And because you're in love with Ford, and it hurts to hurt the ones you love."

Claire groaned. "How can I still be in love with Ford after all he's done?"

"I don't know. How could I still have been in love with Travis after what he did? Remember how he kept that big secret from me? Even though he knew that brutal honesty is the cornerstone of my personality?"

Claire remembered. After their anonymous hookup, Travis had figured out Maggie's identity. And then, out of a fear of losing her, he'd kept it to himself. She hadn't known that he was the masked man she'd had sex with at Anna's Halloween gala.

"You and I sat right here, at this very counter," Maggie said. "And you convinced me that sometimes things aren't at all what they seem, and that Travis deserved a second chance."

"Ford has had his second chance. And he messed it up. Pulled the exact same stunt he pulled the first time."

"Not entirely," Maggie said.

"How's that?" Claire asked. "He led me on, and then he left."

"Except he's still here," Maggie said. "And he's in Bubba's freaking bowling league."

"He is?"

"Yep. And don't forget he's wearing shorts to baby showers and tuxedos to galas, even though we both know he probably hates shorts, baby showers, tuxedos, and galas."

Most definitely.

"I don't know what demons he has, Claire. But I think he's at least trying to outrun them. And it's because he loves you."

It would be so easy to accept that Ford could change if she hadn't already made that mistake once. But she had. And guess what? No change.

"I don't want to keep talking about Ford," she said. "Aren't you curious about who is buying Petal Pushers? I can't believe George didn't tell you who they are."

"Maybe they're the same people buying Rancho Cañada Verde. Maybe they're buying the whole freaking town."

The bell over the door jingled. "Ah, we forgot to take that down," Maggie said.

"Is that the buyers?" Claire asked, peeking over Maggie's head.

"No," Maggie said. "It's just your dad."

"My dad?"

"And Ford."

Great. What the heck were they doing there?

* * *

It had been a quiet ride over to Petal Pushers. Ford didn't know why he had to come, but Gerome had insisted. *You're the ranch manager, and this whole thing was your idea.*

Yesterday, when he'd dropped Gerome back at the house after visiting with Ruben, he'd asked to see the quarterly business reports. And then he'd made a big suggestion. *Buy Petal Pushers and turn it into a ranch store.*

They'd stood in awkward silence while Gerome considered the idea. Ford had grown so uncomfortable that he'd almost taken the suggestion back. But then he'd thought about Claire.

She'd given up her dreams for her family. She deserved to finally have her store and be back in town, where she could flourish and thrive. And besides, buying the store was a damn good idea.

Gerome apparently thought so, too, because after a few minutes, he nodded his head and called George Streleki. And while he'd had the man on the phone, Gerome had set up the sale for Ruben's property, as well.

Everything was moving right along, so why was Ford so nervous and uptight?

Because last night, Claire had taken one look at him and run. What would she do this morning? And was any of this worth it if the woman he loved could never forgive him?

Life was no fucking fairy tale.

They entered the empty store to the sight of Maggie holding a broom.

"Gerome!" Maggie said. "Look at you! It is so good to see you out and about."

"It feels good to be out and about."

"Hi, Dad," Claire said.

Her voice sounded cold and distant, and Gerome raised an eyebrow.

"Good morning, princess."

Ford backed up and moved out of the way. Then he took his hat off and stared at it. Neither he nor Claire said a word to each other, and it was agony.

"Are you two just out for a joyride?" Maggie asked.

At least she'd noticed Ford was in the room. Claire was still pretending he was invisible.

"No, ma'am," Gerome said, walking behind the counter to perch on a stool. "We're here on business."

"Business?" Claire asked. "What kind of business?"

"Ranch business, of course."

Claire bit her lip. Scrunched up her eyebrows. "Do we even still have a ranch?"

"Of course we do. Why would you ask such a thing?"

"Because George Streleki told me he'd drawn up the papers for the sale."

Gerome almost smiled. "I didn't sell a damn thing. I'm just buying."

Maggie snapped her fingers. "You're buying the store!"

"Yep. On the advice of our new ranch manager, we're opening a ranch store to sell our branded merchandise."

"But we don't have a ranch manager."

Claire snapped her head around to glare at Ford.

"You've got to be kidding," she said. "Him?"

Good Lord. Ford felt like shrinking into the small crack in the floor at his feet.

"I've also got a new vice president of marketing," Gerome said.

"And who would that be?" Claire asked. "Darth Vader?"

"No," Gerome said with a snort. "More like..." He snapped his fingers, trying to come up with the name.

"Leia!" Maggie shouted. "Claire, you dummy. It's you!"

* * *

Claire leaned against the counter so her knees wouldn't buckle.

Her dad hadn't sold the ranch! And she had a store!

Her emotions were going to give her whiplash.

And speaking of emotions...

Ford.

He was across the room, leaning against the wall. His hat

was pulled low, and he appeared to be examining a crack in the concrete floor. But he was grinning to beat sixty.

Claire's heart wanted to respond to that grin, but it was being held hostage by a frozen nugget of anger and resentment. She could feel it pounding against her rib cage like a prisoner beating against the bars of a jail cell.

I want out!

George showed up, and while he and her dad and Maggie started discussing details, Claire sneaked out to the patio and sat on a whisky barrel. Her mind hummed along.

She'd renovate the outside of the store to look like an old ranch house. And inside, there would be themed rooms, according to the merchandise. The cookware, spices, and kitchen gadgets would go in Lilly's Kitchen. The fashion (because of course there would be fashion!) would go in Claire's Closet. Soaps, linens, and toiletries would go in the Washroom...

The door opened, and Ford walked out, holding his hat. "Want some company?"

Did she have a choice? Her dad had hired him as ranch manager. They were going to be working together from here on out.

And yes, she wanted company. She wanted to talk for hours about everything she was going to do to make the ranch store a one-of-a-kind experience, and she wanted to do it with someone who would listen patiently, soaking up every word, while his hazel eyes silently said, *I believe in you.*

She'd missed this man, but she wasn't ready to let him back in, and she didn't know if she ever would be. Much to her heart's dismay, the frozen nugget of anger and resentment had made itself pretty dang comfortable over the past few weeks.

"This was your idea?" she said.

"No, darlin'. It was yours, remember?"

She wanted to tell him he could drop the *darlin'* business and call her Ms. Kowalski from here on out, but it would be silly, and besides, the way he said *darlin'* with that Abilene twang was somewhat pleasing to the ears.

She'd allow it.

"I thought I'd lost the ranch, so this is all a bit overwhelming, to be honest."

"I told you I'd help you hold on to it, didn't I?"

"You told me that, and *then you left*. Don't forget that part. You left me with plenty of worries. More than you can ever know."

"I'm so sorry," he said, taking a few steps toward her.

Her legs were itching to stand up. To meet him halfway. But the frozen nugget in her chest wouldn't let her.

Ford sighed and his shoulders slumped. "I thought I was doing what was best. Jarvis men are—"

"If you're going to mention that ridiculous curse, you can haul yourself out of here right now," she said.

"You know about the curse?"

"Caroline told me. And it's no excuse for what you've put my family through."

Ford removed his hat and came to stand in front of her. She stood, because she didn't want him towering over her.

"You are absolutely right. And any apology I offer for the way I've treated you and your family is going to fall way short. I don't think there are any words I can come up with to do it justice. But I am sorry, Claire. More than you can ever know."

"My dad seems to have forgiven you."

"I didn't earn it, but yes—"

"Don't expect me to be a chip off the old block," Claire said. "I'm not that easy."

She crossed her arms over her chest, hoping to protect the frozen nugget nestled inside. She liked it there. It was steady and reliable and not nearly as sensitive and vulnerable as her dumb heart.

"I can't go through this again," she said. "You can apologize if you feel it's necessary, but it won't change anything between us."

You are locked out, buddy.

"All I'm asking is that you listen," Ford said. "I know you don't want me anymore, and I promise not to pester you after today. But I owe you an explanation, if you'll hear me out."

It wasn't true that she didn't want him anymore. She wanted him with every fiber of her dang being. That was the problem.

She sighed. "Go ahead."

Ford took a deep breath. "I've spent my whole life trying to outrun my feelings. And I was pretty good at it, until I met you. You made me feel all kinds of crazy things I thought I wasn't supposed to feel. Mostly, you made me happy, and that was the one emotion I didn't think I deserved."

"Everybody deserves to be happy," Claire said.

Ford shook his head as if he didn't quite believe it. "I'd already broken myself, Claire. And I figured I'd break you next."

"You did break me. Can't you see that?"

"I can see it now, and I'm so sorry, darlin'."

None of this really explained anything. Curse be damned, all it amounted to was that Ford Jarvis couldn't keep a promise.

"When Abby died, I was responsible—"

Claire held a hand up in front of Ford's face. She might be confused about a lot of things, but this was not one of them. "No. You were a child yourself. It is not your fault that Abby drowned."

"She died on my watch," he whispered. "Do you know what that does to a boy?"

Claire looked into Ford's eyes and saw that little boy. The one accepting all the blame and guilt for an accident that was nobody's fault. No wonder he felt cursed.

The outer layer of the ice nugget started to sweat a little.

Ford swallowed. "She was my light. The one thing that was pure and good in my life. And I let her die."

"No, you—"

Ford gently put a finger to her lips. "I carry it with me every second of every minute, and every hour of every day. There's no respite, even when I sleep. I ran from you, because I couldn't handle the responsibility of loving you. The very notion that something could happen to you, and that it could happen on my watch—"

Ford hadn't left because he didn't care. He'd left because he cared too much.

"I'm a grown woman. I don't need protecting."

Ford grinned. "You give me fits."

The ice nugget was no match for the grin. It was for sure going to embarrass itself and melt all over the place.

"I don't expect forgiveness or for you to return my affection," he said. "But I'll always save a space for you; in case you can ever change your mind about me—"

She placed her forehead against his. "You have to forgive that broken little boy inside you. Can you do that?"

"I can try. Because I love you, Claire. I'll do anything for you, even if it means learning to forgive myself."

"You've never said you love me before."

"I was afraid to say it out loud, in case it invited bad luck…"

"You're not cursed, Ford," Claire said.

"I know. And I love you, Claire. You're my whole world, and dammit, that's terrifying. But I'm here for it, and I'm never leaving again."

Claire's heart was splashing like a little sparrow in the puddle left behind by the nugget of ice. "I've been waiting for you my whole life," she whispered.

"I'm sorry it took me so long to get here."

Claire smiled and wiped away a tear, because apparently she wasn't done melting. "It's been a long, broken road, cowboy. But all that matters is that you're finally home."

Ford pulled Claire close and pressed his warm lips to hers.

And they lived happily ever after in one town, on one ranch, and with each other.

The End

Epilogue

❦

Claire drove her Mini Cooper over the Wailing Woman low-water crossing, noting with satisfaction that there wasn't a cloud in the sky. It had been two years since the dreadful flood, and the community of Big Verde was one hundred percent back to normal.

All of the shops and cafes on Main Street were up and running. The library was bigger and shinier and even more amazing than Alice had dreamed it could be. And Rancho Cañada Verde was still the gem of the Texas Hill Country ranching community.

Today had been a busy day at the ranch store, simply known as the RCV Mercantile, but Claire had finally finished setting up the new baby nursery section. The merchandise—a crib, monogrammed bedding, diaper bags, and clothing—was finally prepped, priced, and on display. And she'd had so much fun setting it all up that she'd lost track of time.

She looked down at her tummy. "We're running late to our own party, Peanut."

Talking to Peanut was her new favorite pastime.

She drove past the lane that used to lead to Miss Daisy. The little trailer had been uprooted by Claire's parents, who dragged it on near-constant adventures to "see some other countries," as her dad liked to say whenever he and her mom left Texas. Luckily, they were back from Yellowstone National Park in time for today's festivities.

She drove past the gate to the foreman's cabin before turning onto the road that led to their house at Oak Meadow. Everyone still called it "the old Luna house," even though she and Ford had been living in it since they got married.

Today was their one-year anniversary.

She smiled thinking about their wedding, because how could she not?

The photographer had asked for a photo of Ford being "roped." It was meant to be a silly stunt, but after Beau had successfully tossed a rope around Ford (he'd clearly been trying to impress the photographer), he'd tightened it and, at Bubba's goading, had literally dragged Ford down the aisle.

The wedding guests had hollered and clapped as Ford passed, blushing and grinning in his gray tuxedo and black felt cowboy hat.

After he'd taken his place, Beau had shouted, "Should I untie him?"

Claire, who'd been standing at the entrance of the old stone chapel, had shouted back, "Are you nuts? Not yet!"

Folks had nearly gone insane with laughter, and it was to this joyous noise and the melody of "Bless the Broken Road" that the bridesmaids—Maggie, Alice, Trista, and Caroline—had walked down the aisle with Travis, JD, Bubba, and Worth.

Next had come the showstoppers.

Henry had pulled little Miss Brianna Castro-Mayes and her trusty sidekick, Maisy Mae Blake, down the aisle in a wagon. As toddlers, they were basically loose cannons. But they'd been darling and had mostly remained in the wagon, distracted by their gigantic blue tulle gowns (Maggie had said they looked like blue Pomeranians) and the petals they were supposed to be tossing from their baskets.

After that, Claire had finally walked down the aisle on the arm of her father, wearing a Vera Wang gown and her white and silver cowboy boots with the rhinestone spurs (she'd had the broken one fixed). Her dad lifted her veil, kissed her on the forehead, and then untied Ford with a stern gaze, causing more laughter to ripple throughout the chapel.

But that hadn't even been the best part.

Unbeknownst to Claire and Ford, Beau and Bryce had placed bright orange Nerf guns beneath each guest's chair, and the newly married couple had been forced to run down the aisle through a barrage of foam arrows.

Best. Wedding. Ever.

She arrived at the top of the hill and the Oak Meadow clearing to a herd of pickup trucks parked around her house. She pulled up next to Bubba's truck, which was somewhat routine since he and JD were there nearly every day to oversee the extensive renovations being done to the house. Claire barely recognized the building Ford used to refer to as "Ruben's hut."

Alice rushed out to meet her.

"Oh my God," she said, opening Claire's door. "Hurry up. I literally can't stand this for one more second. Seriously.

This has been the worst thing anyone has ever asked me to do."

"You volunteered!"

"I wish I hadn't," she said, yanking Claire out of the car. "It has taken years off my life."

Claire was hustled into the house, where Ford took her bag and enveloped her in a hug. "Welcome home," he whispered in her ear.

Claire smiled and took a moment to sink into him.

"I noticed that dang horseshoe is upside down again," she said. "Alice practically threw me through the door, so I didn't have a chance to straighten it."

Ford kissed the top of her head. "I don't care," he said. "I'm the luckiest man alive."

"Oh yeah?"

"I might even toss my hat on the bed."

"Don't go crazy. We'd hate for this place to burn to the ground just as JD and Bubba are putting the finishing touches on it. And sorry I'm late. I don't even have an excuse. Time just gets away from me when I'm at the store, and we had a busy day."

Ford gave her a squeeze before letting go. "Sounds like a *good* day."

"It was. And thank you for getting ready without me."

"I hardly did a thing. Maggie and Lupe got here two hours ago, and all I've done is try to stay out of their way. Everybody's outside. I fired up the grill earlier, and Bubba and JD are already fighting over when to put the steaks on. JD is wearing Brianna in one of those baby backpack things, and she's eating goldfish crackers out of the brim of his hat. It's the cutest thing you ever saw. And did you know that Henry already taught Maisy to say *shit*? Oh, and your portobello mushrooms are marinating in the fridge—"

Claire kissed him. "I love you, and you're rambling."

"I'm nervous," he whispered. "I don't know how I'll react in front of all these people."

"These people are our friends and family, and however you react will be the right way to react."

Ford smiled. "I love you, too."

Maggie walked up and put a glass of iced tea in Claire's hand. "Nice of you to show up. Now come on outside, before Alice explodes and makes a mess."

The new French doors to the patio opened, and Anna stuck her head in.

"Good Lord," she said. "You were late to your own wedding, so I don't know why I'm surprised, but we're going to have to call an ambulance for Alice in about five minutes if you don't hurry up. Just thought I'd let you know."

Anna shut the door and rejoined the party.

"Who invited Anna?" Claire asked.

"You did," Ford said.

"Why did I do that?"

"Because you're too nice," Maggie said. "Now come on. Let's get this show on the road."

Together they walked into the backyard, where Alice was trying to hold Bubba and Trista's kids off the piñata. "Oh, thank God!" she said when she spotted them. Then she climbed on top of a folding chair and screamed, "Let's do this thing!" at the top of her lungs.

Everyone quieted down. For one thing, they weren't used to a screaming Alice. For another, this was a highly anticipated event, and the air was saturated with a hushed excitement.

Claire's parents joined them, and then Worth did, too, and the five of them stood together, arms intertwined.

"As all of you know," Alice began, "Claire and Ford do not know the gender of their baby."

Ford put his big, warm hand on Claire's tummy and kissed her on the cheek.

"They had the doctor write the sex of the baby on a piece of paper and place it in a sealed envelope, which they gave to me exactly ninety-six hours and thirty-one minutes ago. This was apparently ninety-six hours and thirty minutes too long, so..."

"Spit it out already," Anna said. "Why does this have to be such a production?"

"Because that's literally what gender reveal parties are," Maggie said, holding her camera up. "Productions. Now...Action!"

Anna rolled her eyes.

"Without further ado," Alice said, "we're going to break this piñata! The color of the confetti will reveal the gender of the baby."

Claire and Ford approached the piñata, which was in the shape of a giant cowboy hat. Together they grabbed the piñata stick, and after the partygoers counted to three, they swung.

The stick connected solidly, but no hole was torn, so they repeated the process two more times and then...

The piñata exploded in a cloud of colorful confetti.

Claire's heart beat frantically and her eyes widened to take it all in. This was the reveal! This was the moment! And...

Everyone quieted down in confusion, because the color of the confetti was yellow.

Alice screeched and clapped her hands. "Congratulations!" she shouted.

"Um, Alice?" Claire said. "We don't know what yellow means."

Alice put her hand on her forehead. "Oh! Of course not. I'm sorry. I was trying to avoid gender stereotypes, because they're social constructs, and honestly, I find the concept of these reveals to be somewhat problematic. Anyway, I decided to avoid the typical pink and blue, so I went with yellow and purple and—"

"Alice!" everyone shouted collectively.

"It's a girl!" Alice shouted back. "Congratulations!"

Claire thought her knees might give out, but Ford held her up, as everyone cheered. *They were going to have a daughter.*

Ford lifted her face to his, and then his trembling lips were on hers. Soon, they were surrounded, and for the next few minutes it was all hugs, tears, and laughter. It was the warmest blanket of love and support Claire had ever felt, and she knew things were going to be okay. With Ford by her side, and these folks lifting them up, she could do this.

She could be a mom.

Her heart was so full she thought it might burst.

"Do you have a name picked out?" JD asked.

Claire looked at Ford and together they said, "Rosa Abilene."

"I know that Abilene was your sister's name," Gabriel said. "Is Rosa a family name, too?"

Not too many folks knew that the old stone chapel had once had a name—the Santa Rosa Chapel—and that their daughter had narrowly escaped being named Hay Barn.

Ford grinned and winked at Claire. "It's more of a family tradition."

Don't miss the next book
in Carly Bloom's
Once Upon a Time
in Texas series!

Must Love Cowboys

Available Spring 2021

About the Author

Carly Bloom began her writing career as a family humor columnist and blogger, a pursuit she abandoned when her children grew old enough to literally die from embarrassment. To save their delicate lives, Carly turned to penning steamy, contemporary romance. The kind with bare chests on the covers.

Carly and her husband raise their mortified brood of offspring on a cattle ranch in South Texas.

You can learn more at:

CarlyBloomBooks.com
Twitter @CarlyBloomBooks
Facebook.com/AuthorCarlyBloom
Instagram @CarlyBloomBooks

For a bonus story from another author you may love, please turn the page to read *Rocky Mountain Cowboy*, by Sara Richardson.

Everyone wants a piece of Jaden Alexander. Ever since the famous "Snowboarding Cowboy" took a near-fatal spill on live television, he's been hounded by the media. Every reporter in the country wants an exclusive interview with the chiseled Olympic heartthrob. But only one of them has the easygoing charm—and breathtaking beauty—to knock Jaden off balance . . .

Kate Livingston isn't looking for a scoop. As senior editor for *Adrenaline Junkie* magazine, she's testing out camping gear on the Colorado Trail when Jaden's rescue dog Bella seeks refuge in her tent. Before she knows it, Kate is face-to-face with the world's sexiest snow-riding cowboy—and the biggest opportunity of her career. But getting close to Jaden isn't just about her job, and for the first time ever Kate has no idea how this story will end.

ROCKY MOUNTAIN COWBOY

Sara Richardson

To Jenna LaFleur

CHAPTER ONE

In a small town like Topaz Falls, Colorado, the grocery store was the last place you'd want to go if you didn't want to be noticed. But when your diet consisted mainly of Honey Nut Cheerios and you'd run out of milk, you had no choice but to show up at Frank's Market in full disguise.

Jaden Alexander pulled his blue Colorado-flag stocking cap farther down his forehead so that it met the top of his Oakleys. Not that the sunglasses were inconspicuous. They were a custom design, made exclusively for him when the company had courted him for sponsorship six years ago after he'd made his Olympic debut. No one else would know that, though. To other people, he hoped he looked like just another ski bum who moonlighted as a bartender or waiter during the off-season. With any luck, no one in town would realize that J.J. Alexander—dubbed the Snow-boarding Cowboy by the media—had come home.

The door still chimed when he walked in, the same way it

had when he'd done the weekly grocery run for his grandma twelve years ago. In fact, it looked like Frank hadn't changed much of anything. The same depressing fluorescent lights still hummed overhead, casting bright spots onto the dirty linoleum tiles. He passed by the three checkout stations, where two bored cashiers stood hunched behind their registers, fingers pecking away on their phones.

One of them looked familiar enough that a shot of panic hit Jaden in the chest. But the woman didn't even look up as he slipped into the nearest aisle, so maybe he was just being paranoid. Death threats on Twitter would do that to a guy. Ever since the accident, going out in public wasn't exactly his favorite thing to do. He'd been ambushed by photographers, reporters, and fans who'd written him off, and he was not in the mood to deal with any public showdowns tonight.

"J.J. Alexander? That you?"

Anyone else and he would've shaken his head and kept right on walking, but he knew the voice behind him. He'd never get away with walking on past without a word. He turned around, and right there at the end of the aisle stood Levi, Lance, and Lucas Cortez. Back in high school, Jaden had bummed around with Levi until Cash Greer passed away. After that, Levi had gone to Oklahoma to train as a bull rider, and Jaden had finally been accepted to train with the U.S. ski and snowboard team.

"Holy shit, man." Levi sauntered over the way a bull rider would—all swagger. "I didn't know you were back in town."

"Hey, Levi." Jaden forced his jaw to loosen and nodded at each of the brothers in turn. "Lucas. Lance." Now, those three had changed in twelve years. They'd all cleaned up. Still cowboys in their ragged jeans and boots, but each of the brothers was clean-shaven and more groomed than he'd ever seen him. Wasn't a coincidence that they all had rings on their left fingers now too. Jaden slipped his sunglasses onto his forehead, grateful the store seemed empty, so they shouldn't attract too much attention.

"Actually, I'm not back." His voice had changed since the accident. These days he had to fight for a conversational tenor instead of slipping into defensive mode. "Not permanently anyway. I'm only here to consult on the new terrain park at the resort." The Wilder family had been looking to expand their ski hill outside of Topaz Falls for a few years now. He'd never been a fan of the Wilder family—no one in town was—but the job had offered him an opportunity to lie low for a while.

"Heard that's gonna be quite the addition up there," Levi said. "I also heard your grandma sold the ranch a few years back. You got a place to stay?"

"I rented a place on the mountain." He didn't acknowledge that bit about his grandma. Hated to think of her stuck in that facility in Denver. He hadn't had a choice, though, once the dementia started. She'd taken care of him—raised him—seeing as how his dad had been a loser and his mom a free spirit who'd rather live the gypsy lifestyle than hang out with her kid.

Four years ago, the roles reversed, and he was the one taking care of Grams. Back then he couldn't do much for her. He was too busy splitting his time between Park City and Alaska, chasing the snow so he could stay in shape. After she'd started wandering off, he'd moved her into the best facility in Denver and dropped in a couple of times a month to visit, even though she no longer knew him.

"Sorry to interrupt, but I need backup." Lance moseyed over. As the eldest Cortez brother, he was serious and stern.

He used to scare the shit out of Jaden when they were kids, but from the looks of things, he'd mellowed out. "Jessa didn't tell me there were a thousand different kinds of tampons. I have no clue what to get. Any ideas?"

Uhhh...Jaden looked around, realizing for the first time they were in *that* aisle. The one he never set foot in. On purpose anyway.

"There's regular, super, super-plus..." Lucas shook his head as he examined the products stacked on the shelves. "I thought we were buying tampons, not gasoline."

The brothers laughed, and even with the anxiety squirming around his heart, Jaden cracked a smile. "So this is what happens when you get hitched, huh?" Oh how things had changed. Used to be, on a Friday night, he and Levi would drive up to the hot springs on the Cortezes' property, share a few beers, have a bonfire, and get to at least second base with whatever girl looked good that night. Now these three spent their Friday nights shopping for woman-stuff.

Levi glared at his eldest brother like he wanted to string him up by his toenails. "We were out for a beer when Lance's wife called with an"—he raised his hands for air quotes—"emergency."

"She was in tears," Lance said defensively. "And quit bullshitting us. If Cass had called, you'd be doing the same thing right now."

That seemed to shut Levi up.

Lucas looked at his brothers with humor in his eyes. "Naomi loves me too much to put me through that."

"Yeah?" Levi shot Jaden a sly grin. "That why she sent you to the store for hemorrhoid cream after Char was born?"

And that was Jaden's cue. There were some things you couldn't unhear, and he definitely didn't want to know anything about having babies and hemorrhoids. "Well, it was good to see you guys. Maybe I'll see you around."

He made a move to slip past and leave them all behind, but Levi walked with him. "Hold up. How're things going?"

The familiar anxiety slipped those cold fingers around Jaden's heart and squeezed. He'd been conditioned. Anytime someone looked at him like that—used that overly sympathetic tone of voice—he wanted to turn and bolt before they could bring up the accident. "Things are fine," he lied. Things had fallen apart after that race. In his life and in his head. Three months later, he still didn't know how to put it all back together.

"I saw the crash on TV."

Yeah, Levi along with the rest of the world. If they hadn't witnessed it during live coverage of the race, they'd seen it in the extensive news analysis afterward.

"You all healed up?"

Did it matter? "Pretty much. I've got a few pins in my arm, but who doesn't?" The joke fell flat, and the anxiety squeezed harder, shrinking his heart in its suffocating grasp.

"Haven't heard much about the other guy in a few months." Questions lurked in Levi's tone and in his eyes. Jaden could see them surfacing.

Had he done it on purpose? Had Jaden intentionally taken out his biggest competition on that last turn when it looked like he wasn't going to win the gold? Everyone had already made up their own answers, so why did it matter what he said?

Breathe. Keep breathing. Never thought he'd have to remind himself to do things like that. "Beckett is still in a rehab facility." Scarred and broken. Still trying to relearn how to walk...

"Damn. Sorry to hear it."

Jaden already knew sorry wasn't enough. Not for Kipp Beckett, not for the reporters, not for the officials. Not for fans of the sport. Not even for himself.

"For what it's worth, I didn't think you did it on purpose." Levi was trying to be supportive, but the fact that he said it at all meant he'd thought about the possibility. Same as everyone else.

"I didn't," Jaden said simply. "I wouldn't." In the replays, it might've looked like he'd lunged into Beckett—who'd been his rival in the snowboard-cross event since they'd both started out—but the truth was that he'd caught an edge and it had thrown off his balance. He couldn't recover. He couldn't stop the momentum that pitched him into Beckett, that sent them both careening through the barriers, cartwheeling and spinning until the world went silent. When the snow had settled, Jaden had gotten up, and Kipp Beckett hadn't. His body lay twisted at an angle, and he was unconscious, maybe dead.

Shock had numbed Jaden to the fact that his arm was badly fractured. He'd fallen to his knees next to Beckett before officials had raced in and forced him away. The papers and news shows and magazines all said Jaden was sneering as the medics tended to him. He wasn't. He was crying.

"I would've taken the silver." If no one else believed him, maybe Levi would. "I didn't care that much." He didn't value the gold more than someone's life. Did he? God, the news reports had made him question himself.

Levi gave him a nod. "Looked to me like you caught an edge. Could've happened to anyone." He clapped him on the shoulder. "Hey, why don't you stop over for a beer sometime? I just finished building my new house. Need to break it in."

"Sure." Jaden said it like he did that all the time—

stopped by a friend's house for a beer. But it had been months. Months since he'd had a real conversation with another human being. Months since someone had actually smiled at him. When he wasn't working on the mountains, his days consisted of sitting silently on the back deck with his chocolate Lab, Bella, sprawled at his feet while he tried to figure out how everything had collapsed.

"What about tonight?" Levi shot a look toward his brothers. "Since my evening got interrupted and I'm now free."

"I've gotta head back up the mountain tonight." They were discussing the possibility of lighting the terrain park for night boarding. "But I'd definitely like to hang sometime. Let me know what else works." Levi was the first person who'd actually heard him when he said he didn't mean for any of it to happen.

Maybe he had one ally in a world full of enemies.

* * *

Up until this very moment, Kate Livingston thought the worst thing about camping was the bugs. No, wait. Actually, the mosquitos in Colorado weren't nearly as bad as she had anticipated. So far she'd seen only one medium-sized spider, which wasn't even hairy like some of them in L.A. So, before this moment, maybe she would've said the worst thing about camping was the dirt. Yes, definitely the dirt. She could feel it sticking to her skin, grainy and disgusting as she lay swaddled like a baby in the brand-new sleeping bag that still smelled like synthetic fluff.

Another flash of light split the sky above her flimsy nylon tent. Which had cost about $450, by the way. And now the damn thing was sagging underneath the weight of a rain puddle that had collected right over her head. *Water-proof my ass.*

She squirmed to unearth her arms from the sleeping bag and typed in a note on her phone. *Extreme Outdoors Light-weight Backpacker Tent—Sucks.* Unsatisfied, she underlined, highlighted, and changed the word *sucks* to all caps.

When she'd landed the position as a senior editor for *Adrenaline Junkie* magazine, she had envisioned herself sitting in a corner office overlooking the hustle and bustle of Beverly Hills while she sipped frothy lattes and approved spreads and attended photo shoots with male models who cost upward of a thousand dollars for one hour of work.

But there had been some budget cuts recently, Gregor, her managing editor, had explained on her first day. They weren't working with as many freelancers, and the editor who was supposed to do a gear-test backpacking trip on the Colorado Trail for the fall issue had suddenly quit, so . . .

Here she was, on an all-expenses-paid trip through hell.

The ceiling of the tent drooped even lower, inching toward her nose. A drop of rainwater plunked onto her right eyebrow right as a crack of earsplitting thunder shook the ground.

Now she knew. She knew that the worst thing about camping was not bugs or dirt but a thunderstorm in the mountains. In fact, she would probably die tonight. Either from getting skewered by a lightning bolt or from a heart attack, whichever came first.

"I went to Northwestern journalism school," she lamented over the pattering rain. After she'd walked out of there with her master's degree, she'd assumed she could have her pick of jobs. But nope. Anyone could call themselves a journalist these days. It didn't matter if they had interned at the *Chicago Tribune* or if they knew AP style or even how to use a fucking comma. If they had fifty thousand followers on their blog, they were in.

Let's just say respectable jobs in the world of journalism weren't exactly knocking down her door. So when the opportunity at *Adrenaline Junkie* had come up, she'd done more than jump on it. She'd immersed herself in it. So what if she'd never actually camped? It wasn't her fault her father was a yuppie attorney and her mother a neurologist. They didn't believe in camping. But she could read all about it on the Internet.

Who cared that the one time she'd felt a surge of adrenaline in the great outdoors had come when she'd lost her Gucci sunglasses in a rogue wave on the beach? She'd never swam that fast in her life. It was a job—a senior-level job—and she could finally move out of her parents' basement and away from her role as the butt of every family joke. Both her older sister and her younger brother had become doctors too. Just to make her look bad.

If only they could see her now.

Bringing the phone to her lips, she turned on the voice recorder. "Day one. The Extreme Outdoors Lightweight Backpacker Tent appears to be made out of toilet paper." She wondered if she'd get away with making that an official quote in her four-page spread. "I've worn a rain poncho that repels water better than this piece of—"

A scratching sound near her feet cut her off. The walls of the tent trembled. Yes, that was definitely a scratching sound. A claw of some kind? "Mary mother of God." The whisper fired up her throat. She wasn't sure if it was the start of a prayer or a curse. She'd have to wait and see, depending on how things turned out.

Scrunching down farther into her sleeping bag, Kate held her breath and listened. There was a huffing sound.

An animal sound. A bear? Yes, this definitely called for a prayer. "Oh, God, please don't let it eat me." She squirmed to the corner of the tent where she'd stashed her overstuffed backpack. Yes, she'd read all about how she was supposed to empty the food from her backpack and hang it from a tree in a bear-proof container, but she hadn't actually had the time to find a bear-proof container before she left L.A. Surely bears didn't like freeze-dried macaroni and cheese... did they?

Quickly and silently, Kate dug through the gear until she located her copy of *The Idiot Guru's Guide to Hiking and Camping*. The binding was still crisp. She'd meant to open it on the plane, but she'd forgotten that she'd downloaded *Sweet Home Alabama* on her phone, and God she loved that movie. And Reese. She'd waved to Reese once, across the street on Rodeo Drive, and she'd actually waved back! Well, she might've waved back or she might've been pushing her hair out of her eyes. It had been kind of hard to tell.

But anyway. The bear...

Using her phone as a flashlight, Kate flipped through the pages in search of a chapter about bears while a dark shadow made its way slowly around the tent. "Come on, come on." Hadn't the Idiot Guru thought to inform other idiots what to do if they encountered a bear?

The shadow paused and swiped at the nylon wall.

"Oh God, sweet Jesus." Kate ducked all the way into the sleeping bag, taking the book with her. If nothing else, maybe she could use it as a weapon to defend herself. It was thick enough to do some serious damage. Yet somehow there was no chapter on what to do when a bear was stalking you from outside your tent.

Okay. Think. When she'd first gotten this assignment, she'd read something on the Internet about animal encounters. Was she supposed to play dead? Make loud noises?

She fired up the satellite phone again—waiting for what felt like five years for the Internet to load—and searched *bear encounter*.

Big. Mistake. Apparently, bears did eat people. There were pictures to prove it. Adrenaline spurted through her in painful pulses. How could anyone *like* this feeling? Adrenaline junkie? More like adrenaline-phobic. It made her toes curl in and her skin itch. Alternating between hot and cold, Kate crossed her legs so she wouldn't pee in her only pair of long underwear. Lordy, she had to go so bad...

A whimper resonated somewhere nearby. *Hold on a second.* She hadn't whimpered, had she? No. She was pretty sure her voice wouldn't work right now. Did bears whimper? She wouldn't know because the Idiot Guru had left out that critical chapter...

The creature outside her tent whimpered again, softly and sweetly. Kate peeked her head out of the sleeping bag. The shadow was gone, but the whimpering continued.

Holding the sleeping bag around her like a feeble bubble of protection, she squirmed over to the zippered flap that the company had touted as an airflow vent and inched it open until she could see. The rain had slowed some, but it still sprinkled her nose as she peered outside. The shadowy figure of an animal lay a few feet from the tent, still whimpering weakly. But it appeared to be much smaller than she'd originally thought. Way too small to be a bear. It looked more like...a dog.

"Oh no. Poor thing." Kate fought with the sleeping bag until it finally released her. She unzipped the tent's main flap. After slipping on her boots, she slogged through the mud and knelt next to the dog. It was a Lab. A chocolate Lab just like the ones she'd seen playing fetch on Venice Beach. "Are you lost?" she crooned, testing the dog's temperament with a pat on the head. The dog licked her hand and then eased up to a sitting position so it could lick her face.

"You're a sweetheart, aren't you?" She ran her hand over the dog's rain-slicked fur. The poor love shook hard, staring at her with wide, fearful eyes. "I'll bet you don't like the storm, do you?" she asked. "Well that makes two of us. Come on." She coaxed the dog into the tent. "You can wait out the storm with me." And . . . seeing as how she couldn't stay out here harboring a fugitive dog . . . "First thing tomorrow morning, we can head into the nearest town so we can find your owner."

Then she'd find herself a nice hot shower, a real meal that didn't require boiling water on a camp stove, and a plush queen-sized bed where she could finally fall into a dry, peaceful sleep.

CHAPTER TWO

Bella!" Jaden jogged down the hall of his rented ski chalet, hoping to God that his dog was simply hiding under the massive king-sized bed in the master suite.

He tore into the room, flicked on the lights, and hit the floor next to the bed. His heart plummeted. *Damn it.* He should've brought her up the mountain with him tonight. Or at least locked the doggie door so she couldn't get out. If he would've known a storm was coming, he would have. And he would've kept her right by his side. Though it'd been only a month since he'd gotten her from a rescue in Denver, he'd already learned that lightning and thunder sent her over the edge.

Back in the hallway, he stopped at the closet to grab his raincoat and pull on a headlamp and his hiking boots. As soon as he'd heard the first clap of thunder, he'd told the crew he had to get home, but he wasn't fast enough. It had taken him a good hour to navigate the ATV down the steep slopes in the rain, and Bella could cover a lot of ground in an hour, especially if she was running scared.

Jaden slipped out the French doors and onto the back deck. The rain was drizzle now, but thunder still rumbled in the distance. He cupped his hands around his mouth and yelled for the dog again. The echo of his voice sounded hollow and lonely—small in the woods that stretched out on all sides of him. Hundreds of thousands of acres of pine and spruce and clumps of aspen trees. There were jagged cliffs, rivers brimming with snowmelt, and predators—mountain lions and bears. And his poor dog started shaking at the sight of a rabbit crouched in the grass.

Panic drove him down the steps, and he jogged into the woods, whistling and yelling her name. He hadn't counted on getting attached to a dog. Lately it'd been hard enough to take care of himself. He hadn't slept a full night since the accident. Hadn't felt much like eating, either. The lingering depression brought on by the knowledge that he'd ruined someone's life.

But the last time he'd gone to visit Gram, he'd driven by one of those fancy local pet stores. They were doing an adoption event outside. As soon as he'd seen Bella hiding in the corner of the pen, he knew she'd be coming home with him. They had the same struggle. Anxiety. He'd recognized it right away. According to the worker, Bella had been rescued from a farm where they'd found over thirty emaciated dogs that had been abused and neglected. And that was it. Over. Done. No decision to be made. He knew she needed him as much as he needed her.

"Bella!" The wind made his shouts sound so futile, but he had to do something. It killed him to think of her out there in the overwhelming darkness, terrified and cold and running blind. He knew how lonely it was. That's what he'd been doing since the accident—navigating an endless darkness. The dog had been the first light he'd seen in a while. She'd taken the edge off the silence that had consumed his life.

After the dust had settled, friends had stopped calling. Fans had stopped seeking him out. His grandma had started talking to him like he was a stranger. And there were times he felt like he had no one in the world.

But then Bella would come and lie at his feet. She would trot by his side while he wandered the trails in search of freedom from the burden that always seemed to weigh him down. Every morning, she would whine at him from the side of the bed, coaxing him back to life because she needed him.

She needed him to feed her and play ball with her. She needed him to protect her and to show her that there was good in the world. That not everyone would kick her or lock her in a cold, dingy basement or use a chain to strangle her when she peed on the floor out of fright. She still wore the marks of violence on the fur around her neck. It had taken a few weeks for her to trust him, for her not to cower in front of him when he'd call to her. It had taken her a few weeks to realize he wasn't going to hurt her or leave her. And now she was alone again. He'd fucked up.

"I'm sorry!" he yelled. Maybe the wind would carry the sound of his voice right to her. "Come on, Bella, I'm sorry!" Mud slurped at his boots as he tromped straight up the side of the mountain. "I won't leave you out here." It didn't matter if it took all night. He'd rescue her the same way she'd rescued him.

* * *

Amazing how sunshine could make everything look so different. In the radiance of a bright morning, even the piece-of-shit tent looked pretty.

Above Kate's head, the blue nylon seemed to glow with a happy optimism. She turned on the phone's voice recorder and brought it to her lips. "Day two: waking up in the Extreme Outdoors Lightweight Backpacker Tent doesn't suck. It's actually a very pretty color." Maybe she wouldn't write up the tent as the worst creation since tiny backpacks hit the purse market. (Seriously, how could Kate Spade have jumped on that bandwagon?) She was feeling generous this morning. Almost giddy.

The dog licked her cheek. At some point during the night, Jane Doe—as Kate had come to call her after discovering the dog was a lady when she'd taken her outside to pee at four o'clock in the morning—had snuggled right up against her in the sleeping bag. Now they lay side by side, spooning like a happy couple. "You saved me, Jane," Kate murmured to the dog. "You know that?" Today, there would be no bugs or dirt, and she'd get her first real meal since the cab had dropped her off at the trailhead…Wait. Had that only been yesterday? Huh. It seemed like eons ago.

In the sleeping bag, Kate could feel the dog's tail wagging against her leg. "I know, I know. I'm ready too." She glanced at the time on her phone. Seven o'clock in the morning wasn't too early to get up and at 'em when you were in the backcountry. Right? With any luck, she could be sitting in a cute little coffee shop in town by eight o'clock with her new best friend Jane Doe curled up at her feet.

On that note…She shimmied out of the sleeping bag and pulled on shorts and a tank top, which she had to rip the price tags off of since she'd had to purchase all new clothes for the trip. Once she was dressed, she dug out a stale bagel from her backpack and gagged down half before holding the other half out to Jane.

The dog sniffed warily before taking a hesitant bite.

"I know. They're much better toasted and served with flavored cream cheese." Strawberry. Or maybe with just a touch of honey. Kate's mouth watered. "Don't worry, girl. We'll find some real food in town." There had to be a deli or a diner nearby.

Speaking of town...She rifled through her things until she located her topographical map. Not that she had any clue how to read the lines that supposedly told you how steep the terrain was. "But I do know how to find the closest town." She pointed out the small black dot to the dog. "Topaz Falls, Colorado. Sounds like the kind of place that might have a really nice spa, don't you think?"

Jane panted happily.

"All we have to do is head down the trail to where it meets up with the highway; then we'll be home free." Easy enough. She folded up the map, stuffed it back into her pack, and then shoved her feet into the brand-new hiking boots that had given her blisters yesterday. She stood gingerly, stiff from a night on the thin foam pad, which was supposed to be the best on the market. (More false advertising.)

Jane whined as Kate unzipped the tent. Then the dog bounded outside like she couldn't wait to get started. Kate couldn't either. Over her shoulder, she eyed the nylon structure that had taken her the better part of three hours to set up. (The packaging had boasted a twenty-minute setup—what a scam.) Would it hurt to leave it behind? She'd tried it out for one night. And she'd also gotten to try out the camp stove and the sleeping bag and the foam pad and the collapsible lantern. Did one really truly need to spend seven days on the trail with those things to get a good read on the gear? She'd drawn her conclusions in one night—it all sucked.

"Come on, Jane." Kate slipped on her backpack and set off down the trail, not looking back at the tent. She'd tell Gregor it hadn't survived the storm. That she'd spent the rest of the week building her own shelters out of sticks and logs and leaves. Maybe he'd give her a promotion.

Hiking with a dog was actually fun. Jane would run ahead with her nose to the ground, and then find a stick and bring it to Kate with her tail wagging. She'd toss the stick, and the dog would take off, leaping and running as though this were the best day of her life.

The feeling was contagious. Having company made Kate slow down and actually enjoy the scenery. Yesterday, she hiked the few miles to her campsite with her head down, faltering under the weight of her thirty-pound backpack, cursing the day Gregor had been born. But today she noticed things. Like the way the sun glinted off the new green aspen leaves. And how when she passed a certain kind of pine tree—she didn't know which—the scent of butterscotch would trail in the air.

The mountains were much prettier than she'd given them credit for yesterday. Purple and yellow and white wildflowers dotted grassy meadows that flourished under the shelter of the trees. It was peacefully quiet but not silent. Birds trilled and somewhere water shushed and a pleasant breeze sighed through the thick branches. So basically, if it wasn't for the dirt and the bugs and the thunderstorms, the mountains would be perfect.

They reached the trailhead much faster than she'd thought they would. But then again, she'd never been good at judging distances on a map. The trail broke through the trees and into an open space flanked by the dirt parking lot where the cab had dropped her off yesterday. A few cars sat in the lot but not a soul was around. "Okay." Kate swung her backpack to the ground and found the map again.

Jane trotted over and plopped down, panting like her lungs were on fire.

"Just have to figure out which way to go," Kate said reassuringly. Which way had she come from in the cab again? When she'd first looked at the map, she'd assumed they had to go west, but now she wasn't so sure. She stared at those little lines, but they all seemed to blur together. Her head felt a little funny. "Water," she gasped. She'd forgotten. Gregor had reminded her that she had to stay hydrated in the high altitude of Colorado. Letting the map fall to the ground, she uncapped her water bottle and guzzled half of what was left.

"Hi there."

Kate turned toward the pleasant, somewhat shy voice of a woman.

"I noticed you were studying a map. Is there anything I can help you with?"

The woman walked over, and she looked like she knew what she was doing. Her hiking boots and lightweight pants were worn and dusty, as though she headed out on the trail every day. She wore a wide-brimmed straw hat, and her golden auburn hair hung in two braids down her shoulders. The kindness in her eyes instantly put Kate at ease. Jane, too, judging from the way the dog stood and started to wag her tail.

Kate picked up the map, realized she'd been holding it upside down, and turned it around. "I'm trying to figure out how to get to Topaz Falls from here."

Even when the woman frowned, she looked friendly. "That's a good ten miles down the highway." She seemed to assess Kate's attire. "It'd be a long walk. I'd be happy to give you a ride if you want."

Kate pulled her sunglasses down her nose. "Seriously?" She didn't mean to gawk at the woman, but Kate had once stood on the shoulder of the 405 in L.A. with a blown-out tire and cars had whizzed past like she was a statue. No one had even stopped, let alone offered her a ride.

"Sure." The woman shrugged like it was nothing. "We do that kind of thing all the time around here. We get tons of long-term hikers coming through. A lot of them hitchhike into town."

Kate sized the woman up. Normally she'd never get into a car with someone she didn't know, especially in L.A., but there was no way a psychopath could smile like this woman.

"I'm Everly Brooks."

Everly—what an angelic name. "Kate Livingston." She held out her hand for a professional introduction, even though she really wanted to hug the woman's graceful neck. Maybe even give her a kiss of gratitude on the cheek. "I work for *Adrenaline Junkie* magazine and was out doing a gear-test run." Was that what the real adrenaline junkies called it? No matter. "This sweet dog wandered into my camp last night during the storm. So I thought I would head into town to find her owner."

"Oh…" Everly's pretty eyes grew even bigger. "Then you're in luck. My friend Jessa owns an animal shelter just outside of town. I'm sure she'd be happy to help."

"Perfect." Things could not be more perfect right now. Kate could take Jane to the shelter so she could be reunited with her family—a good deed for someone else. Then she could find a place to stay and get a head start on writing her gear-test article from the comfort of a hotel—a good deed for herself. Gregor would never know that she hadn't spent a week out on the trail.

"I'm parked over this way." Everly led her to an old-fashioned Ford pickup truck that was spotted with rust. Kate climbed in, and Jane jumped into her lap as though she knew she was going home.

It took a few tries to get the old clunker started, but soon enough they were on their way, and Kate relaxed against the seat. "Thanks again for going to all of this trouble." Nothing like this had ever happened to her. A complete stranger going out of their way to help...

"It's no problem," Everly said. The truck puttered down a two-lane road bordered by thick, earthy-scented forest on both sides. "So you must do a ton of backpacking with your job, huh?"

Kate startled. "Oh. Yeah. Sure. You know..." She hoped Everly knew because she sure as hell didn't.

"Where's your favorite place to go?"

"Hmmm." She drummed her fingers against her thigh, pretending to mentally compare the many incredible places she'd backpacked. "I guess I would have to say Banff." That was somewhere in Canada. Someone had raved about it at the office last week. Surely it had a lot of trails and scenery.

"Oh my God, I love Banff." Everly's head tipped as though she were picturing it. "Did you do the Consolation Lakes Trail near Moraine Lake?"

"Of course," Kate said, and then quickly added, "It's beautiful."

"I know," her new friend agreed. "It's one of the most beautiful places I've ever been."

"So what do you do?" Kate asked before Everly could get another question in. She'd pretty much run out of ideas for any additional discussion on spectacular backpacking destinations.

"I run a small organic farm and operate a farm-to-table café that barely breaks even." Everly laughed as though embarrassed. "Doesn't sound so great, but I love it."

"Actually it sounds amazing." Kate could picture it. A cute little farmhouse against a mountain backdrop. It sure beat her tiny apartment that looked out on an alley back in Burbank. There were probably animals and wildflowers and the same beautiful aspen trees she'd seen in the forest. "I'd love to see it."

"Sure. After we take the dog to Jessa's, we can swing by my place on our way back to the trail."

Kate shifted Jane so she could see the woman's face. "The trail?"

"Yeah." Eyes on the road, Everly turned the truck off onto a dirt driveway and drove underneath a framed wooden sign that said CORTEZ RANCH. "I figured you'd want to get back to your trip after you get the dog settled."

"Right. The trip." The lonely, miserable, dirty camping trip. There was one problem with that scenario. Kate no longer had a tent. And she seriously doubted her ability to ever find that thing again. "Actually, I might stick around town for a few days," she said thoughtfully, as though the idea had just occurred to her. "Restock on supplies and stuff." Enjoy a few meals, maybe a massage or a day of pampering to recondition her skin. "Do you know of any good places to stay on short notice?"

"Sure." Everly drove them past a couple of rustically elegant houses with wide stained logs held together by heavy steel brackets and accents of stone. The kind you'd see featured in *Adrenaline Junkie* as the perfect adventure ranch destination.

"The Hidden Gem Inn is the best accommodation in town." Her new friend parked outside of what looked to be a refurbished barn. The modest sign above the double doors announced it as the HELPING PAWS ANIMAL SHELTER.

"Jessa's sister-in-law Naomi and her husband opened the inn almost two years ago," Everly went on. "It's a beautiful bed-and-breakfast right in town. Best food outside of the café." She smiled humbly. "And gorgeous. It's a historic home, built during the silver rush, but it's been all redone inside."

Kate could almost feel the warmth of a luxurious shower. The softness of a brand-new mattress. Geez, she was practically tearing up. "It sounds like exactly the kind of place I'm looking for."

CHAPTER THREE

Ditching the tent on the trail was hands down the best decision she had ever made. Kate sipped her high-priced cabernet sauvignon and popped a dark chocolate truffle into her mouth.

Who knew that a small town like Topaz Falls would have one of the best wine bars she'd ever had the pleasure of experiencing? The Chocolate Therapist was something out of a fantasy—all streamlined and modern and classy without crossing the line into pretentious. After meeting with Jessa Cortez and discovering that no one had contacted her about a lost dog, Kate had offered to keep Jane with her—a fostering situation, if you will—while Jessa checked around. It wasn't only that she wanted an excuse to stay off the trail. She happened to love Jane Doe, too, so it was a win-win.

Once that had been settled, Everly had driven Kate and Jane Doe straight over to the Hidden Gem, where Naomi had upgraded her into their best suite at no charge. Then

Naomi and her husband, Lucas, even offered her an extra car they currently weren't using, just in case she needed it while she stayed in town to help locate Jane's owner.

It didn't matter what she needed; Kate's new bestie Everly would say, "I have a friend for that."

After Kate had enjoyed an extended time-out in the marble-tiled steam shower of her new suite, Everly had insisted they walk Jane Doe to Main Street so she could show Kate around and they could have an afternoon treat. Her new friend had brought her straight to the Chocolate Therapist, where the owner, Darla Michaels, had hooked them up with the best wine and chocolate pairing that could possibly exist in this world.

"I can't remember the last time I felt this happy." Kate took another sip of wine. She and Everly were sitting outside at a bright orange bistro table—with Jane Doe contentedly curled up underneath. The patio looked out on a downtown area where quaint shops with striped awnings lined the cobblestone sidewalks. Baskets of bright-colored annuals hung from the wrought-iron streetlamps, and the mountains hovered in the background like a beautiful barricade constructed to keep reality out. It was something straight out of a storybook fairy tale, safe and fictional and untouchable. "I might never leave Topaz Falls," Kate told Everly, popping another truffle into her mouth.

Everly laughed. "Watch out. That's exactly what happened to me. I showed up here thinking I might stay a few months, and over two years later, I can't seem to leave."

"I can see why." It wasn't only the mountains and the whimsical small-town charm. It was also the people, all connected, all watching out for each other—and even for the strangers who found themselves in their midst. "I can't thank you enough for—"

"What the hell are you doing with my dog?"

The angry male voice came from behind. Kate turned at the same time Jane Doe shot to her feet, whining and yipping.

A man stalked toward them, his chiseled features locked into a punishing scowl. He dodged people on the sidewalk, looking as out of place as Oscar the Grouch at Disney World.

The dog immediately hurdled the fence and made a bee-line for him, ending the dramatic scene with a leap directly into his midsection.

"Bella." The man caught her and knelt, setting her paws on the ground as he wrapped his arms around her. "Jesus, pup. Where have you been? I looked for you all night."

Kate glanced at Everly and mouthed, "Do you know that guy?"

Everly shook her head with a pained expression. Yeah, he didn't seem like a very personable man, but that had never stopped Kate before. She pushed back from the table and stood, calmly letting herself out of the patio's gate before ambling over to where the joyous reunion was still taking place.

"Ahem." She cleared her throat.

The man looked up at her, and immediately the soft relief on his face tightened into anger. Even with the tension that pulled his cheeks taut, there was something vaguely familiar about his features. Though he wore a stocking cap and sunglasses, she could swear she'd seen his square jaw and that exquisite mouth before...

"Why the hell was my dog sitting under your table?" he demanded, standing upright. He was half a foot taller than her, easy, and had broad, fit shoulders, she couldn't help but notice through his T-shirt.

"How about you thank me for rescuing your dog from the woods during the storm last night?" Kate asked cheerfully. No one would ruin this perfect afternoon for her. "She wandered into my camp."

"Your camp?" He flicked his glasses off and swept an irritatingly skeptical look from her head to her toes. "*You* were camping?"

Okay, sure. She would be the first to admit she didn't exactly look the part right now. On the way to the Hidden Gem, Everly had driven past a boutique and Kate had seen this lovely sundress in the window. What could she say? It was love at first sight. The soft pink dress had layer upon layer of delicate, embroidered lace with eyelet trim at the neckline. You couldn't find things like that in L.A. It was both modern and sentimental at the same time. And, since she would be staying in town for a few days, she couldn't resist a few purchases. "Yes, I was camping." Her smile dimmed at the smug look on his face. "In fact, I was on a seven-day backpacking trip," she informed him, glaring right into the man's eyes. They were steely and blue. Whoa. Unmistakable eyes. Famous eyes…

Well, what do you know? J.J. Alexander—disgraced Olympic snowboarder—was walking the streets of Topaz Falls. She knew she'd recognized him!

Kate kept her expression in check. He obviously did not want to be identified, given the hat and the sunglasses, which he'd quickly slipped back on.

"So, what? You were going to keep my dog forever?" he asked, backing down a bit.

"Of course not." She gave him the dutiful smile of a Good Samaritan. "I hiked all the way down the mountain and brought her to the Helping Paws Animal Shelter first thing this morning." And look where that had led her. Right to Jaden freaking Alexander. He'd hidden from the media ever since a reporter tried to accuse him of assault right after the accident. The accusations turned out to be bogus, but after that, J.J. had disappeared. No stories, no interviews, nothing. And now here he was, standing in front of her like some ruggedly wrapped gift from God. If she could score an interview with J.J. Alexander, she'd never have to go on another backpacking trip again.

"I'm Kate Livingston, by the way." She stuck out her hand, but the man simply stared at it.

He hesitated, obviously not wanting to share his name.

"Your dog is such a sweetheart," she went on to compensate for his silence. He couldn't walk away. Not yet. Not until she figured out an excuse to spend more time with him. "Bella is it? I was calling her Jane Doe. Anyway, she slept in my sleeping bag all night. Curled right up next to me and kept me warm. Didn't you, girl?" She knelt and scrubbed behind Bella's ears.

The dog gave her a loving, slobbery lick across the lips.

Laughing, Kate stood back up and wiped her mouth. "We definitely bonded."

"I can see that." J.J. didn't seem to appreciate it much either, judging from his frosty tone. "Well, thanks for bringing her back." He turned. "Come on, Bella."

"Wait." Kate flailed to catch up with him.

The man stopped and eyed her like he was considering making a run for it.

Humiliation torched her cheeks, but she muscled through it. Typically she didn't chase men down the street, but this was an emergency. "Why'd she run away?"

J.J. seemed to debate whether he was obligated to answer the question. Finally he sighed. "She hates storms. And I'm working long days at the resort. Sometimes nights too.

I didn't know there'd be a storm, so I didn't lock her dog door."

Long days at the resort, huh? "Poor thing." Kate petted the dog again, seeing the perfect opening into J.J. Alexander's world. Thankfully, the dog ate up the attention, wagging her tail and whining for more. "When we were hiking this morning, she never let me out of her sight. She seems to get lonely easily."

"Yeah." J.J. watched her interact with Bella. "She's a rescue. Doesn't like being alone."

Kate turned up the wattage on her sunny expression as if an idea had suddenly lit up inside her. "Well, I love your dog, and it just so happens that I'll be in town for a few days, so maybe I could help."

"I thought you were backpacking." J.J. obviously didn't want to take the bait, which meant she'd have to use another angle. Something other than *her* love for the dog.

"My tent was damaged in the storm, which means I'll have to finish out my vacation in town." She nearly gagged on the word *vacation*. Maui was a vacation. Hell, she'd even consider Miami to be a decent vacation. Camping was so not a vacation. "I'd love to watch Bella while you work. Like a doggie day-care thing. I can pick her up in the mornings and spend the day with her so you don't have to worry about her running off."

"That's okay." The man still stared at Kate like she was a lunatic. "She's fine."

"It would be better for her than sitting around a lonely house all day," Kate prompted. If the earlier reunion was any indication, this man loved his dog. So all she had to do was convince him it would be best for Bella. "I'll take her on hikes, and we can play fetch. She can play with my new friend Naomi's dog at the Hidden Gem. Oh, and I bet she'd love swimming in the river at the park."

His torn expression revealed that, yes, Bella did indeed love to swim. What Lab didn't?

"So you'd pick her up in the morning and drop her off after I got home?"

"Yes. I'd love to spend more time with her while I'm in town," she assured him. "You don't even have to pay me." Getting to know J.J. Alexander, aka the Snowboarding Cowboy, would be all the compensation she needed.

* * *

There had to be a catch. Why would some hotter-than-sin woman offer to watch his dog while he worked? For free?

Jaden eyed Kate Livingston from behind the anonymity of his dark sunglasses. She sure didn't look like she belonged anywhere near a backcountry trail. Her silky black hair had that perfect beach-wave thing going on, which he suspected she'd paid good money for. And her skin...it was rosy and flawless. Not lined from the sun like his. Her eyes were the most striking feature about her, though, so dark they were almost black and narrowed slightly in the corners like she had some exotic mix of genes.

His body's swift reaction to her raised his defenses. He'd met women like Kate. All sunny and rosy and completely fake. He'd even had a good time with a few of them, but those days were long behind him.

To get his eyes off the temptation in front of him, Jaden glanced at Bella. His dog had attached herself to Kate's side as though trying to convince him to close the deal. He could see the plea in those sorrowful eyes. *Aw hell.* He was such a sucker. Bella would love having the company. He'd worked almost eighty hours this week, and his poor dog had been on her own.

What would it hurt? The woman—Kate?—hadn't seemed to realize who he was. Bella liked her. And he liked the fact that he wouldn't have to worry about the dog running off again, which would mean he wouldn't have to spend another night tromping all over the mountain searching for her.

Last night had been hell. He hadn't slept at all. He'd hiked until dawn, yelling and whistling and searching until he'd had to go up to work. As soon as the crew had quit for the day, he'd gone home to print some of those lost dog posters he'd seen plastered to lampposts when he was growing up. Which now he wouldn't need.

"So what do you think?" Kate persisted. Yeah. Persistent. That was the only way to describe her. She looked like a woman who had no trouble getting what she wanted.

"I guess it would work."

"Great! Oh, that's so great." A smile made her eyes sparkle. Something about her seemed so young. She was happy; that's what it was. Happy all the way down deep, like Gram used to say.

"We can start tomorrow," Kate said as she hugged the dog again. "We'll have so much fun, Bella! We'll play all day! I'll pick her up at eight. Okay? Make sure to send along everything she'll need for the day. Food, her leash, any toys she'd like to bring, treats."

"Uh…" Jaden blinked at her. Damn Kate had a lot of energy. It felt like she'd boarded a speed-of-light train and he was hanging on the back. "Sure. Okay. That's fine."

"I'll need your address. And I didn't catch your name."

"Jay," he blurted. "My name is Jay." He quickly rattled the address for his rental so he could get the hell out of there.

"Very nice to meet you, Jay." Kate leaned over and gave Bella a kiss on the top of the head. "I'll see you both tomorrow." With a twinkling wave, she sashayed back to her table, where one of her friends was waiting.

"What the hell just happened there?" Jaden asked Bella on the way back to his Jeep. "Did you have to crawl into *her* sleeping bag?" Out of all the sleeping bags in the backcountry, his dog had somehow found the one that held a tempting, aggravating, overly cheerful Disney princess.

"Couldn't you have found some transient guy?" he muttered as he helped Bella jump into the passenger's seat. "That would be a lot less complicated." Something told him he wouldn't be able to keep himself in check forever when Kate Livingston was around. And he'd eventually want to do more than look, seeing as how it'd been a damn long time since he'd had the opportunity. The first sight of her in the strappy little dress had him rubbernecking in a bad way. Not that he'd admit it to anyone else, but that was the only reason he'd seen Bella. He'd noticed Kate first.

Jaden started the Jeep and drove away from Main Street, his eyes sticky with fatigue. All he wanted to do was go home and eat his bowl of Honey Nut Cheerios and then fall into bed. Maybe he'd actually sleep tonight. For once he felt tired enough. But unfortunately, he couldn't go home. Not yet.

"We've got big plans tonight," he announced, trying to muster some enthusiasm.

Bella stuck her head out the window, her lips flapping as she sniffed the air.

"Levi was an old friend of mine. Back in high school. He invited us over for a beer, if you can believe that." Bella probably couldn't, seeing as how they hadn't visited anyone's house since he'd adopted her.

He turned off the highway and onto the familiar dirt road where he used to race bikes with Levi. The Cortez Ranch had gotten a major upgrade since he'd been gone. Originally, there'd been only one house on the property. Now there were four that he could see. Two were newer, one right across from the corrals and one farther up the hill tucked into a stand of aspen trees. That would be Levi's house. He'd described it over the phone but hadn't done it justice.

It wasn't obnoxiously large like the house Jaden had rented near the resort, but it was impressive all the same. Hand-hewn logs stacked one on top of another, stone siding coming halfway up the structure, and a copper roof that must've set him back a good hundred thousand.

Jaden parked the Jeep and let Bella out, taking his time on the stamped concrete stairs that led up the front porch. Stupid that he was nervous. Levi had been pretty mellow at the store, but still…his team had turned on him. When he was winning competitions, they'd become like his family, but after the accident, they'd quit calling, quit inviting him out, quit acknowledging they ever knew him. As his ex-girlfriend and fellow USA team member had reminded him, it wasn't personal. They simply couldn't afford the bad publicity.

His teammates hadn't been nearly as bad as the random strangers, though. The people who had verbally attacked him on social media…and on the streets. It had all made him withdraw from everyone, everything. Social anxiety, they called it. He'd finally looked it up on the Internet.

Bella whined and scratched at the front door, coaxing him onward as usual.

"Yeah, yeah, yeah. I'm going." If it weren't for the dog, he'd probably never get off the couch.

Levi's front door was as grand as the house—stained

wood with an inlaid frosted window. He knocked, half hoping his friend wouldn't be around. Maybe he'd forgotten or maybe something had come up—

The door swung open, and Levi greeted him with a hearty handshake. "Glad you could make it."

Jaden kept his grip firm. "Me too."

Bella jumped up on Levi. "Happy to see you too, pooch." He stepped aside. "Come on in."

Jaden walked into an open-concept living room with high arched ceilings, dark plank floors, and a stone fireplace that took up one whole wall. Even being brand-new and so extravagant, the place still had the cozy touches that made it a home—clusters of pictures and books strewn on the coffee table and some of Levi's bull-riding memorabilia on the walls.

"Let me grab you a beer," Levi said, heading for the kitchen on the other side of the room.

"Sounds great." Jaden wandered closer to the fireplace to get a better look at the framed photographs arranged on the mantel.

An image of a blond woman in a wedding dress—Cassidy, he presumed—stood out from the others. She was dancing barefoot in a grassy meadow, laughing, looking past the camera, presumably at her new husband. "That's a great shot." Not posed or unnatural, but spontaneous and full of emotion.

Levi handed him an IPA and studied the picture with a tender expression. "That's my wife." He said it like it still surprised him. "Cass. Remember her? Cash's little sister."

He vaguely remembered, but Cash had made sure that none of his idiot friends had come within a twenty-foot radius of her, so Jaden hadn't known her well.

"She's a nurse in Denver. Working today." He grinned. "Still have no idea how I got her to marry me."

"You lucked out, I guess." That was a joke. Judging from the other wedding pictures, Cassidy looked as happy and in love as Levi. Something told him luck didn't have much to do with it.

The doorbell rang, sending Bella into one of her happy-barking fits. For being so anxious, she sure seemed to like meeting new people.

"Hope you don't mind," Levi said over the noise. "I invited some other friends."

Tension laced up his spine, pulling his back tight. "Nope. Don't mind at all." It was crazy how casual he could force his voice to sound even when that feeling of dread crawled up his throat.

He hung out by the fireplace while Levi opened the door, and Bella greeted the two new visitors with a nose to their crotches.

"Bella, off," he commanded.

She obeyed but whined until they both gave her some attention.

"This is Mateo Torres and Ty Forrester," Levi said, waving Jaden over. "We trained together forever, and now we run a mentoring program when we're not on the road."

"Nice to meet you." He shook each of their hands briskly. Gram would've been proud of him remembering his manners, even when his throat seemed to shrink.

"J.J. grew up on a ranch a few miles from here," Levi told his friends. "We used to raise enough hell that his granny thought about sending him to boarding school."

"Not true." Gram never would've sent him away. "She couldn't get rid of me." He forced a grin. Maybe after enough pretending, it would eventually start to feel real again. "There would've been no one to do the work on the ranch." But Gram had loved him too. The way a mother was supposed to. He'd never doubted that.

"I bet you've got some awesome stories," Mateo said. "I'm always looking for new material that I can use to humiliate Levi."

Jaden took a sip of his beer and nodded. "I can help you out with that."

"I've got plenty on you." Levi directed the words to Mateo as he went to get more beers from the fridge. He handed them out while the three men compared who had the worst dirt on who.

Jaden stayed out of the conversation. If they'd watched the news in the last three months, they all had dirt on him, and he didn't want to talk about the accident.

Eventually, the pissing match ended, and Levi led them all out to the back deck. Bella followed behind and then trotted down the grass. It seemed his friend had chosen the prettiest spot on the property for his house, right up against the mountain, hidden in a stand of aspen trees. Evening sunlight filtered through the leaves, making everything seem calm.

"House looks good," Mateo said, examining the stone fire pit before flicking a switch to turn it on.

"Yeah. Real fancy, Cortez." Ty kicked back in one of the reclining chairs. "Let me know if you want a roommate."

"Yeah, Cass would love that." Levi pulled two more chairs over and gestured for Jaden to sit.

He had to admit...it wasn't half bad sitting there on the deck with these guys, watching the sun start to sink behind the peaks. It was easier than he'd thought. No questions about the accident. No judgment in their eyes.

"I'm thinking about buying some land so I can build," Mateo said. "Got my eye on a piece of property right on the edge of town. What about you?" He glanced at Jaden. "You sticking around Topaz Falls or you got something else in mind?"

"I'm still deciding." Originally, he'd planned to take off as soon as they'd finished up the project at the resort. He owned a condo in Utah and a cabin in Alaska, but he didn't have a home anywhere. "I guess I wouldn't mind sticking around." The statement surprised him as much as it seemed to surprise Levi.

"That'd be great," his friend said. "Just like old times."

Jaden couldn't resist. "Only now you have a wife who wouldn't take too kindly to you going up to the hot springs to drink beer and skinny-dip with Chrissy...what was her last name again?"

They all laughed.

"Cass would kick your ass," Ty said.

"True statement," Levi agreed. He turned to Jaden. "But seriously, you'd love it here. Small town. Great community. Old friends. You'd be welcome."

Welcome. That one word sparked hope. Maybe Jaden didn't have to live in hiding forever. Maybe he could come back to the place he'd always thought of as home.

CHAPTER FOUR

So this is where a professional athlete went to hide.

Kate climbed out of her borrowed Subaru and walked up the driveway of what could only be described as an ultra-sleek modern take on a ski chalet. The squared structure had been built right into the side of the mountain, constructed mostly of stained concrete and floor-to-ceiling windows, which must've been made from some special type of glass because you couldn't see anything inside.

Standing in front of the heavy glass door, she suddenly felt an agonizing attack of insecurity. Since Jaden had judged her attire yesterday, she'd dressed more carefully for the part she was about to play. Immediately after their encounter, Kate had asked Everly to take her shopping so she could pick out a couple more earthy outfits. Today she wore fitted hiking capri pants with a bright pink moisture-wicking tank top. She'd pulled up her thick, wild hair, taking an extra half hour to make sure the bun looked genuinely carefree and messy. Which it wasn't, of course. There must've been two hundred bobby pins holding it in place. But she'd hidden them carefully. Outdoorsy chicks wouldn't spend an hour on their hair. They wouldn't have changed clothes four times either.

It wasn't that she was nervous to see J.J. Alexander, necessarily. Though the man did have a certain presence that made it difficult to look away. It was more the fact that she had a very limited amount of time to convince him to do an exclusive with her. He didn't seem especially open to interviews at the moment.

But this was it. Her chance for a big story. The story that could make her career. She'd show his personal side. She'd take off his mask for the entire world and dig deeper and deeper until she captured his every emotion, the true heart of who Jaden Alexander was.

"Jay," she reminded herself in a whisper. She had to call him Jay. It didn't bode well that he hadn't even given her his real name, but he would open up. People loved talking to her. She made sure of it. Once, in journalism school, she'd gotten a three-hundred-fifty-pound college lineman to cry during an interview when she'd asked him about his favorite childhood pet.

That in mind, she patted her messy bun into place and rang the doorbell.

Squinting, she watched for a shadow to emerge from behind the glass door, but nothing happened. Tapping her foot, she rang it again. The distant sound of barking could be heard somewhere inside. Within a few minutes, Bella was bouncing and lunging against the door. Where was J.J.? *Jay,* she quickly corrected. Had he changed his mind about their arrangement?

Right when she was about to turn around and stalk

back to the car in defeat, the door opened. Bella hurtled outside, yipping and whining and covering Kate's bare arms with kisses.

When Kate looked up, she nearly fell over, and it wasn't from Bella's weight against her legs either. J.J.—Jay, God, that was going to mess her up—looked a lot different than he had in his stocking cap and sunglasses. His light brown hair was mussed into spikes, and he still had the sleepy eyes of a little boy. Except he was shirtless. And there wasn't anything boyish about his bulletproof pecs and tight abs. Either he did five hundred sit-ups every day or the man had some crazy good genes. Or maybe he had a distant relation to the mythological gods...

"Sorry I didn't answer right away." Drowsiness lowered his voice into a sexy tenor. "I guess I overslept."

"It's no problem." She hiked her gaze up to his eyes. How long had she been staring at his shirtless torso? And more importantly, had he noticed? "I oversleep all the time," she babbled. "It seems like I'm always the last one rolling into work."

His head tilted as he studied her. "What do you do?"

Oops. She had to be careful with questions like that. Lucky for her, he still seemed a bit groggy. "Boring stuff. Really boring." She'd already made herself a vow that she would tell the truth as much as possible. "I edit stuff. Unimportant stuff that no one reads." At least, that could describe her first few weeks at her new job. But once she wrote this story, things would change.

She swept past him and walked into the house before he could fire off more questions. "Wow. This place is amazing. Seriously impressive." A little cold for her taste with the gleaming white walls, uniform leather furniture, and the glossy, seemingly unused kitchen.

"It's the only place I could find on short notice."

Kate made the mistake of turning around to smile at him. He still hadn't put on a shirt, the jerk. "So what did you say you're doing at the resort again?" she asked, running her hand along the white marble countertop in the kitchen.

"Actually, I didn't say." His voice was no longer deep and sleepy. Now it was just dull.

She waited out the awkward silence until he gave in with a sigh.

"I'm on a crew that's helping build the new terrain park."

"Sounds fascinating." She kept her gaze even with his. *Don't. Look. Down.* Or she'd get all weak-kneed and woozy at the sight of his hot body again. She couldn't afford to let Jay make her weak-kneed and woozy. "So you must be into snowboarding, then."

His eyes dodged hers. "I guess."

Wonderful. He was very informative. Getting him to open up and agree to an interview wasn't going to be easy. Good thing she had a whole week. She would have to get creative about making excuses to spend time with him. He didn't seem overly thrilled with the fact that she currently stood in his kitchen. *Well get used to it, buddy.*

Kate turned and started opening the grayish glass cabinets.

"What're you doing?" Jaden walked over and closed one. "Why are you going through my stuff?"

"I'm looking for the dog food," she told him, opening another cabinet. Which was completely empty. "Remember? I'll have Bella all day. I'm sure she'll get hungry. Or did you already feed her?"

After he shook his head, she opened yet another cabinet. Wow. The man had about six boxes of Honey Nut Cheerios stacked above the sink. And he was looking at her like she was crazy? "When's the last time you ate a real meal?"

"I eat." He stiffly marched past her and disappeared into a pantry for a minute. When he came back, he had a dog dish and a bag of food. "She eats twice a day. Once in the morning and once in the afternoon." He shoved the stuff into Kate's hands. "Think you need anything else?" He clearly wanted her to go, and that was probably best since he refused to put on a shirt and she couldn't stop ogling his body.

"Nope. I think this is it. We're good. Right, Bella?" With a bright smile, she turned and headed for the door. "I'll have her home at five o'clock sharp."

Jay followed behind her. "If I'm not here, you can just let her into the house through the garage. The code is one-two-three-four."

She laughed, caught between amusement and a nervous giggle. "Wow. It's like Fort Knox."

He shrugged, tensing those broad shoulders. "Don't have much to worry about way up here."

That was true. Well...the normal person didn't have to worry about much, but J.J. Alexander had just given her the code to his house. Which meant he'd basically handed her an all-access pass into his life.

* * *

Was it just him or were the days getting longer? Jaden shouldered his backpack and started the hike back to the ATV he'd left at the base of the mountain. Eight o'clock. Damn. Late again. Good thing he had someone to watch Bella. Even if the woman happened to be overly chipper and obnoxiously nosy at eight o'clock in the morning. At least all that energy should be good for wearing out his dog. Hopefully Bella had gone to sleep after Kate dropped her off.

"Hey, J.J., hold up." Blake Wilder came sprinting down the hill, and Jaden swallowed a groan. The man had never been his favorite person, but he had to admit—begrudgingly—Blake obviously knew what he was doing. Since the man had taken over resort operations four years ago, they'd almost doubled in size.

Jaden strapped his backpack to the ATV and waited.

"Looks like things are coming together ahead of schedule," Blake said as he approached. "I called out the inspectors for the end of this week. Think we can make it?"

"With the hours we've been putting in? Definitely." A few more twelve-hour days and they'd wrap up this project. The thought didn't thrill him as much as it seemed to thrill Blake.

"You got any idea what you'll do next?"

That question had haunted him for the last few days. "Haven't thought about it much." What options did he have except to go hide somewhere else? Last week, that would've been his first response, but Levi's optimism the other night had made him think twice about picking up and leaving again.

"I'm going to level with you here, Alexander." Blake only seemed to be able to remember people's last names. "I want a bigger focus on snowboarding around here. That's the direction we need to go. And I think you're the guy to get us there."

Jaden couldn't remember the last time he'd laughed, but he was this close. "I'm not exactly well loved in the snowboarding community anymore," he reminded him.

"But you still have a name. You still have the knowledge and experience I need." That was the other thing about Blake Wilder. When he looked at people, he saw only how they could meet his needs. "I could create a position for you here. Manager for the terrain park. I need someone out here every day during the winter season."

"You're offering me a full-time job?" Was this a joke?

"You're the perfect candidate," Blake insisted. "You'd be responsible for daily risk assessments, inspections, and the maintenance and testing of all the features."

Which meant he'd have to get on a board again. Anxiety skittered through him, headed straight for his heart, and dug in its claws. That's where it always hit him, deep in the chest, poking and taunting and squeezing until the palpitations started. He couldn't even think about getting on a board again.

"The salary wouldn't be what you're used to making. But you'd get full benefits. And there'd be bonuses if you were willing to do some public events to help with publicity."

Public events? Hadn't Blake seen what a train wreck his life had become? Jaden would show up for the public event, and there'd be hecklers and media and the same shit storm he'd been trying to escape. He climbed onto the ATV, ready to start the engine and get the hell out of there. "Thanks for the offer, but I don't think it'll work out." He'd never strap his boots onto a board again.

"Think about it." Blake backed away. "Offer stands for a while. But I'd need a commitment by the end of the project. If it's not you, I'll have to find someone else."

He wanted to tell him he didn't need to think about it. He'd never be able to do it, even if he wanted to. Instead, he gave the man a nod, put on his helmet, and then drove down the mountain.

By the time he made it to his street, the sky was nearly dark, but he could make out a faint outline of a car parked next to the curb in front of his house. Had the media found him somehow? Instinctively, he slowed, but as he got closer he realized it was only a small SUV that looked suspiciously similar to the one Kate had been driving.

What the hell was she doing at his house at eight thirty?

He parked the ATV in front of the garage and cruised through the front door, looking around the empty rooms.

"Hello?" Not even Bella ran to greet him.

Just when he was about to go out front and search Kate's car, he noticed the French doors to the back deck had been left cracked open. He jogged over and slipped outside.

"Oh, good. You're finally back." Kate stood at the grill wearing a white apron and wielding a huge set of stainless steel tongs. "Perfect timing."

Jaden looked around once more to make sure he was in the right house. Yep. It seemed to be his rental. His deck. His grill that she was leaning over. What was he missing here? "What're you doing?"

"Making you dinner," she said as though this were a normal everyday occurrence. "Filet mignon with grilled asparagus." She flipped the sizzling hunks of meat. "Oh! And mashed potatoes with bacon and garlic."

Uh… "Why?" That was the only word he could seem to manage from the fog of shock. He couldn't deny that Kate Livingston was gorgeous. Even more captivating under the soft glow of the globe lights strung overhead. Captivating in a way that triggered his anxiety. For the last couple of months, he'd done his best to feel nothing. It was easier. But she stirred something. A craving that ached all the way through him.

"What do you mean why?" She seemed to laugh so easily. "Okay. I admit it. This is a pity dinner."

"A pity dinner." He couldn't seem to do much more than repeat her.

"All you have in that lavish kitchen of yours are six boxes

of Honey Nut Cheerios." She shrugged and turned back to the grill. "I feel sorry for you. How long has it been since you've had steak and potatoes?"

"Eight years." He hadn't eaten potatoes for eight years. They had too much starch, and he'd had to keep his body fit.

She spun and gaped at him, those standout eyes wide with a look of genuine shock. "Eight. Years?"

"I've had steak. Just not potatoes." But he'd loved mashed potatoes growing up. That might've been his favorite food. Gram used to dump in butter and real cream and fresh herbs from the garden...

"God, really?" she repeated. "Where have you been? In prison?"

"No." But actually, these last three months had felt like exile. Not that he could tell her that.

"Well, I hope you're hungry." Kate walked over to the patio table, which had already been set with dishes and silverware. "Because we have a ton of food. And Darla insisted on sending me home with some wine and truffles." She uncorked a fancy bottle and poured the red wine into two glasses.

Jaden stood right where he was. He had no clue what to make of Kate Livingston. She seemed friendly and innocent. Or maybe that was just the dimples in her smile. Maybe she only *looked* friendly and innocent. Maybe she'd go all *Fatal Attraction* on him any minute. "Why are you here?" he asked again, and this time he wasn't being polite. "Why are you in my house making me dinner?"

Kate set down her wineglass, her shoulders slumping from confidence to surrender. She seemed to think a minute and then turned and walked toward him as though giving up. She stopped a foot away, her mouth no longer smiling. "I'm lonely. Okay?" Her chipper voice had mellowed. "Things in my life aren't awesome right now. I'm not exactly in a place I want to be. And after I saw your house this morning, I figured maybe you were lonely too."

Now, that he could understand.

"Okay, then," Jaden said, taking his place at the table. "Let's eat."

CHAPTER FIVE

Well, what do you know? All those things her mom said about the truth being the best policy were actually legit.

Kate pushed her plate away. As soon as she'd admitted to Jaden that she happened to be lonely, too, everything changed. He still wasn't a Chatty Cathy by any means, but during their dinner, she'd managed to make small talk, and he'd answered all of her questions about the new terrain park in impressive detail.

Unfortunately, he didn't seem interested in talking about anything else, and all the effort she was making to carry the conversation while doing her best to ignore his smoldering good looks was starting to wear on her.

Kate checked him out again. Was it possible that Jay had gotten even hotter as they sat there across from each other? Or was that the wine talking?

"Thanks for dinner." Jay tossed his napkin onto his empty plate. There was something magnetic about his eyes when he wasn't so sullen. They were focused and open. Good listening eyes.

Kate looked away. "I'm glad you liked it." It'd been a while since she'd cooked for someone who actually appreciated it. The last guy she'd dated would head straight for the television and turn on the latest football game after they ate, leaving her to do the dishes. But she wasn't *dating* J.J. Alexander. Ha. That would be…ridiculous. She wasn't here to get lost in his magic eyes or sigh with rapture when he smiled, which was so rare that the shock of it made her heart twirl every time.

She was here to get a damn story.

"You seem cold." Jay eyed the goose bumps on her arms.

Cold. Right. Sure. That's what it was…

"Want me to turn on the fire?"

She looked past him to the dark outline of the mountainous horizon. When the sun had slipped behind the peaks, the temperature had dropped about twenty degrees, but she hadn't noticed until he'd said something. A fire already burned low in her belly. "Uh. Sure. Yeah. A fire would be great."

Jaden bent and opened a small door on the side of the table, and as if by magic, flames illuminated the decorative rock piled in the center of the table.

In any other situation, it would've been intimate and romantic, with the stars glistening overhead, the shushing of the wind in the pine trees. But this was an interview. So instead of settling back into her chair and enjoying the peaceful night more than she should, she leaned forward and folded her hands on the table, ignoring the way the fire made Jaden's face glow. "So, Jay…" She smiled, summoning her impeccable small-talk skills. "What do you do when you're not working on terrain parks?"

"In the past, I've competed." His eyes hardened again, as though petitioning her to leave it at that.

Only she couldn't. "You don't compete anymore?" She figured he'd come back eventually, like all those other professional athletes who were mandated to take a short time-out after a scandal but then eventually came back and made their victorious reappearance.

"No. I can't compete anymore."

He can't? That's not what all of the news reports had said. It sounded like his injury had been relatively minor, all things considered. "Why not?"

"I crashed." His face remained perfectly still. There wasn't even a twitch in his jaw. "Got injured."

It seemed she wasn't the only one who excelled at telling the partial truth. What could she expect, though? He didn't know her, didn't trust her. She'd have to earn that over time.

"So what about you?" The fact that Jaden was actually asking her a question obviously meant he wanted to change the subject. "Do you like being an editor?"

"No." Huh. Had she ever admitted that out loud to anyone else? "I mean, after graduate school, I always saw myself doing something different," she corrected. "Something more important."

His eyes softened again as he gazed across the fire at her. "Like what?"

She didn't even have to think. "Writing stories that change the world." That had been the reason she'd pursued journalism in the first place. She could've become a doctor like her brother and sister, but she loved words. She saw power in words. "I wanted to be another Gloria Steinem. A journalist. A political activist."

"So why aren't you?"

Easy for him to say. He probably still had millions of dollars squirreled away somewhere. But she hadn't wanted to fulfill her parents' prophecies that she'd have to live in their posh Beverly Hills basement in order to survive. "I had to find a job." It was more than that, though. It was the rejection. She'd written a couple of pieces, figuring if she couldn't get hired at any of the prestigious publications, she could work her way there by freelancing.

So she'd written a profile about a girl she'd met on the Metro. After seeing her for a few days in a row, Kate struck up a conversation with the young teen and learned that she'd recently joined a gang. Once she got to know her, Kate had written an article detailing the plight of young women in poverty and why more and more are turning to gangs in order to survive.

All total, she'd amassed forty-three rejection emails from various publications, telling her that either no one wanted to read about girls in gangs, or the article wasn't exactly what they were looking for at the moment, or she had a bland writing style. Kate sighed. "According to the rejection letters, I'm not good enough."

Jaden shrugged. "Then you make yourself good enough."

"I don't know how." She'd done everything. She'd aced journalism school. She'd gotten in touch with all of the contacts she'd built over the years. No one wanted her.

"Well, you shouldn't give up."

He'd given up, though. "Why can't you go back to competing, then? Athletes overcome injuries all the time."

"It's more complicated than that," Jaden said, staring into the fire. "And anyway, we're not talking about me. We're talking about you, Kate." He raised his eyes to hers.

She actually shivered when he said her name. At some

point, she'd lost control of the conversation, and worse, of her heart. It beat hard and hot and fast. *Shit.* She couldn't do this. Couldn't fall for him. "I should do the dishes." Clumsily, she gathered up their silverware and plates and slipped into the house with Bella following at her heels. Easing out a breath, she carted everything to the kitchen sink.

Unfortunately, Jaden did not head straight for the television set to turn on whatever sports match would be playing in May. Nope. He came right into the kitchen and stood behind her. "I can do the dishes."

"That's okay," she sang as she turned on the faucet. "I've got it." She'd intended to use the few minutes of rinsing and washing to regroup, but it was obvious that she wouldn't be able to recover. She could feel him standing behind her, feel her body being drawn to his...

"Sorry if I said something that made you uncomfortable." Jay reached around her and turned off the faucet.

"Oh no, not at all." She didn't know what to do with the wet plate in her hands. It wasn't anything he'd said. It was the way he'd started to look at her. The way he was looking at her now. Like he saw much more than she'd ever intended for him to see.

"I didn't mean to overstep." He inched closer, his gaze settling on her mouth. "But I think, if you want something, you should go after it."

"Mmm-hmmm." Kate carefully set the plate back in the sink before she dropped it. This was happening. Even with the warning lights of panic flashing behind her eyes, her body was moving closer to him.

Jaden's hand reached for her, fingers gentle against her cheek as he turned her face to his. The touch melted into her, softening her hesitation right along with her knees. Jay looked at her for a moment, and all she saw was a man. Not

J.J. Alexander, or a snowboarding champion, or a die-hard athlete who'd taken out his competition.

He was a man as caught up in the currents of seduction as she was.

This is a terrible idea. The thought flitted through her mind but found no place to land before Jay's lips came for hers and everything fell silent. The power of him overtook her senses. In the darkness of her closed eyes, she saw sparks of red. She smelled a subtle hint of aftershave—scents of rosemary's spiciness.

A sound come from his throat, an utterance of want, need, hunger.

She answered with a moan when the stubble of his jaw scraped against her cheek as his lips fused with hers.

And the taste of his tongue...It was wine and notes of chocolate, ecstasy in the hotness of her mouth. A helpless sigh brought her body against his, and he held her close in those strong arms as though he wanted to keep her right there. "This is even better than dinner," he breathed, lips grazing her cheek before teasing their way down her neck.

"Better than dessert too." Her whisper got lost in another moan. His lips left a burning mark on every spot they kissed—between her jaw and her ear, the base of her throat, the very center of her collarbone.

"Even better than dessert," he agreed, his voice low and gruff. He raised his face to hers, and that rare smile hiked up one corner of his seductive mouth before he kissed her again, deeper this time, leaving no question that he was taking his own advice and going after what he wanted.

She wanted it, too, so much she was lost in it—the rush of passion and emotion he brought rising to the surface. She could kiss this man forever. Every morning and every night. Every time he offered her the gift of his smile. Except...the word clawed its way through the exhilaration of a first kiss, a potential new love.

Except.

He had no idea who she really was, what she was really supposed to be doing here. The thought rushed in as cold as the mountain air outside, forcing her to break away from him.

Holding her fingers to her lips, she stepped out of his reach, struggling in vain to catch her breath. "I have to go."

"Go?" Jay looked as dazed as she'd been ten seconds ago.

"Yes." She rushed past him before he could touch her again. She couldn't think when he touched her. "I'm late."

"For what?" he asked, following behind her.

"For...book club." She hastily packed up the cloth market bags Naomi had loaned her. There were other things too—the apron she'd taken off outside, the corkscrew for the wine. But she would have to get those later. "Everly and her friends invited me," she said. "It's at Darla's place. I totally lost track of time. I'm so sorry." Before she could make it to the front door, Jay slipped in front of it, blocking her escape.

"I'm the one who's sorry. I think I misread something."

"No. You didn't." He definitely hadn't misread her attraction to him. "This just...caught me off guard." She'd made him dinner to get him to talk to her. Instead she'd ended up seducing herself.

"Yeah, it was pretty unexpected." He seemed to search her eyes. "But I don't mind being surprised once in a while. Do you?"

"No. I don't mind being surprised." Not normally. She loved surprises. But she liked them better when they came without a dagger of guilt stabbed right into her chest.

"Good." He stepped aside and even opened the door for

her. "Thanks for making me dinner, Kate. It's been a long time since anyone's done something like that for me."

The words twisted the knife. "You're welcome," she murmured before she slipped out into the night.

"See you tomorrow morning?" he called behind her.

No. She should say no and walk away from this right now. But what would that look like? Her going back to search for her tent and resume her week on the trail? She'd already told Gregor about the detour, and he'd told her to get an interview with J.J. Besides, maybe it would help Jaden too. From what she'd seen in the short time she'd spent with him, he had some unresolved issues surrounding the accident. Maybe talking about them would help.

With that in mind, she forced herself to turn around and even dredged up a smile. "See you tomorrow."

CHAPTER SIX

Kate drove straight to the Chocolate Therapist. Yes, indeed, she needed some serious therapy.

Once again, she'd mostly told the truth. She happened to know her new friends were having their book club meeting tonight, and book club meetings were a great place to talk, right? To get advice on what to do when the subject of what could be the biggest, career-defining story of your entire career ambushes your plans for an interview with a sexy kiss that could've easily led to more. So. Much. More.

With a screech of tires, Kate swerved to the curb in front of Darla's wine bar and hit the brakes, scrambling to get out of the car. The effect of Jay's very capable lips had yet to wear off. Her hands hadn't trembled like this since she'd once mistaken her Uber driver for Zac Efron. He was a dead ringer.

The restaurant sat empty and dark except for a glow coming from a back hallway.

Kate rapped her fist against the glass. This was a disaster. Jay had gone from being distant and unreadable to kissing her in the span of one dinner. And that kiss... it was unforgettable. She couldn't pretend like it didn't happen. The memory of his smile, his lips—softer than she'd imagined they would be—had already burrowed into the section of her heart where her favorite moments lived on forever.

After another hearty knock, Darla finally came jogging out from the back room. The woman happened to be knockout gorgeous. A few years older than Kate maybe, with jet-black hair streaked with red and cut into a stylish pixie. Her skin had that youthful glow women paid good money to achieve, but Kate had a feeling Darla didn't care that much. Her clothes were stylish but subtle, too, as demonstrated by the chic tunic she wore over black leggings and fabulous leather boots. Where did she find those in Topaz Falls anyway?

Kate shook her head. She could not get distracted by a pair of boots right now.

On her way to the door, Darla waved as though they'd known each other for years instead of two days and quickly unlatched the lock. "So glad you could make it!" She waved Kate inside. "Naomi said you couldn't come because you had other plans."

"I did." And they'd been thwarted by a shunned snowboarder who apparently was not the monster everyone wanted him to be. "But my dinner got a little out of hand and I need some advice."

"Then you're definitely in the right place." Darla linked their arms together as they walked down the back hallway. "You don't know how happy I am to see you." She leaned closer. "We were supposed to discuss *Mind-Blowing*

Intimacy tonight. Can you believe it?" They paused outside an open door. "Things have really gone downhill around here since Jessa and Naomi both married."

"We can hear you," Jessa called from inside the room.

"It might be good for you to discuss a book on healthy relationships," Naomi added as Kate and Darla walked in.

The coziness of the space instantly put Kate at ease. It was set up like a living room that could've been featured in an HGTV episode. Jessa and Naomi sat on a sagging old Victorian couch while Everly occupied one of two over-stuffed chairs on the other side of a rectangular coffee table that looked like it had been made from an old door. The pops of color in the bright paintings on the walls and the polka-dotted pillows had as much personality as the women in the room.

"I'm not interested in a relationship that lasts more than twenty-four hours," Darla informed Kate with a wicked smile. "I'm all for simple, uncomplicated sex."

"Hear, hear," Everly agreed.

"Does that exist?" Kate couldn't help but ask. Because in her world, even a simple kiss came with complications.

"No. It does not," Jessa insisted. "In chapter eight of *Mind-Blowing Intimacy*, it says, and I quote, 'Every act of sexual intimacy leaves its mark on the human soul. Sex does more than bring two bodies together. It also unites their hearts and spirits and intellects, bringing the two into one.'"

"Good Lord," Darla muttered. "She's got the whole damn book memorized."

"It's a very insightful book," Jessa shot back. "Even Lance thinks so. We read it together. He really enjoyed it."

"Ha!" Darla led Kate to the open chair and then wedged herself between Jessa and Naomi on the couch. "I don't think it was the reading he enjoyed. How many times did you and Lance have mind-blowing sex after reading a chapter in *Mind-Blowing Intimacy*? Hmmm?"

Jessa's face turned red. Kate didn't know a woman could blush that much. "That's not the point."

"Lance is no idiot," Everly commented, helping herself to a cookie from a platter that sat on the coffee table. "A chapter in some boring book is a small price to pay for good sex."

"What do you think?" Jessa directed the question to Kate like she'd decided to give up on Darla and Everly. "In your experience, are sex and intimacy mutually exclusive?"

Kate considered the question. Not that she had a ton of experience with either. In fact, her most recent kiss would rank right up there with the most intimate experiences of her life, and she'd only met the man yesterday. How sad was that? "It's probably different for everyone. I'm sure when you're married to the person you love the most in the world, sex feels a lot more intimate." She smiled at Darla to show she meant no offense. "Some people don't want that, but I wouldn't mind having it someday."

"Oh, speaking of sex…how was your dinner?" Naomi asked with an interested smirk.

"Dinner? Who'd you have dinner with?" Everly demanded.

"She made dinner for J.J. Alexander tonight," Naomi informed the room. An echo of girlish excitement went around.

"I heard he was back in town," Darla murmured. "Or at least back near town. Working at the resort. How the hell did you score dinner with him?"

"It's a long story." And it didn't show Kate in the best light. "I'm watching Bella for him while he's working on the mountain."

"Smart move," Jessa said with admiration. "The way to every man's heart is through his dog."

"So did you two enjoy more than dinner?" Darla scooted to the edge of the couch as if the suspense were killing her.

"No." A sweltering blush contradicted her. *Yes, yes, yes.* "Well, kind of. He kissed me."

More cheering ensued, but she muted it with a shake of her head. "It's not good."

"The kiss wasn't good?" Everly asked.

"The kiss was good." So tender and meaningful. Something told her J.J. didn't kiss just anyone. She let her head fall back to the cushion with a sigh. "But I was only having dinner with him so I could get an interview. Except he doesn't know that yet. I was too afraid to tell him I worked for *Adrenaline Junkie*. I wanted to get to know him first. So I wouldn't scare him off..."

"Sounds to me like you got to know him." Darla elbowed Jessa and Naomi with an amused smile.

"So what's he like?" Everly reached over and handed Kate a cookie.

She ate the chocolate chip goodness, still trying to process the last two hours of her life. "He's...different than I thought." She wasn't expecting a snowboarder to have so much depth. Sure that was a stereotype, but in her experience, stereotypes existed for a reason. "And he's definitely a different person than the media made him out to be." Kinder. More thoughtful.

"The media made him look like a bona fide asshole," Darla said.

"Only he's not." Kate was pretty sure her eyes had gotten all dreamy and pathetic but it couldn't be helped. "He's actually a really good person." A little surly maybe, but he'd been through a lot.

"Oh boy," Naomi muttered. "I've seen that look before."

"She's smitten," Jessa confirmed.

Smitten? Despite her current predicament, Kate laughed. She definitely wasn't in L.A. anymore. "I like him," she admitted. "But I also have to get this story."

Her four new friends traded around perplexed glances.

"All right," Darla finally said. "Here's what you should do. Spend more time with him so he'll know you're not a threat."

"But don't wait too long to tell him the truth," Everly added. "And when you do tell him, make sure he knows you have his best interests in mind. That you want to help him repair his image in the media."

"That sounds like a good plan." She had a whole week here, so she could spend a couple more days with Bella. Maybe hang out with J.J. too—on the condition that there was no more kissing until he knew the truth.

* * *

"What do you think, Bella?"

Jaden rearranged the orange gerbera daisies in a vase he'd found stashed in the pantry. The flowers reminded him of Kate. Bright and cheerful, but delicate too. They definitely made a statement on the patio table, much like her. She'd left an impression on him last night with that dinner, and now he intended to do the same by making her breakfast.

The dog took a curious lap around the table, her neck stretching and nose sniffing at the very edge.

"Sorry, pooch. The bacon's for the humans." Jaden pushed the platter of meat and pancakes farther to the center so they'd stay out of reach. After spending so much of her life hungry, Bella had a tendency to get wild about food. "But I promise you all of the leftovers if you behave."

Could he behave? That was the real question. Last night's kiss had stoked something he hadn't experienced in months. Emotion. It'd shocked him to feel something when Kate had looked at him all unsure and shy from across the fire. The flames had made her face lovely and soft. Then, when he'd gotten so close to her in the kitchen, desire had surged hot and fast, triggering him to act before he could think it through.

Sometimes it was good not to think. He hadn't thought about Kipp or the accident the whole evening. It'd been nice to focus on someone else's problems for a change.

After that, though, he couldn't stay away from her. Kissing her had roughed him up on the inside, chipping away at layers of detachment he'd built until his heart felt raw and exposed and alive again. This morning, he'd woken with a craving for more. Which is why he'd hauled his ass out of bed early enough to make a grocery run so he could surprise her the way she'd surprised him.

The doorbell rang at 7:59. Right on schedule. Bella went crazy, leaping and scratching at the door as though she somehow already knew her new best friend was there to play. "Easy, girl." He gently nudged her out of the way and opened the door.

Kate didn't look as cheerful this morning, but she didn't have to smile to hold his attention. The fireworks between them last night had already changed the way he saw her. She wasn't just an attractive woman anymore. She was downright arousing, especially in a blue hiking skirt that hit midthigh and her white tank top. She'd left her black hair down, wavy and soft around her tanned shoulders. Jaden couldn't look away. Yeah, he was at full attention. "Morning," he finally managed.

"Hi." Her indifferent tone and focus on Bella instead of him dismissed his greeting. "Are you ready for a fun day, Bella? Come on, girl. Let's go."

The dog started for the door.

"Sit, Bella," Jaden commanded in his *I mean business* voice. She did, but she definitely whined about it. "You can't go yet," he said to Kate. "I made you breakfast."

The woman glared at him the same way she had last night when he'd told her it had been eight years since he'd eaten mashed potatoes. "Is it Honey Nut Cheerios?"

Oh yeah, he'd surprised her. "It's pancakes, actually. And bacon. Fruit." That used to be Gram's special Sunday morning breakfast on the ranch. He hadn't made it since she'd moved into assisted living, but what could he say? This was a special occasion. "Isn't that what normal people have for breakfast?"

Her lips tightened as though she was trying a little too hard to look annoyed. If you asked him, she looked spooked. "I wasn't aware you were normal."

He wasn't. Or at least he hadn't felt normal until she'd pressed her body against his last night. "Have breakfast with me, and I'll show you how normal I am." She was the one who'd made him feel normal, who'd given him the chance to be someone other than J.J. Alexander, the Snowboarding Cowboy.

Kate glanced back at her car. "I don't think I can stay. I have a lot planned for Bella today, so we should probably get going."

"You have a lot planned for my dog?" he asked, making sure his skepticism didn't go over her head. "Like what?"

"Well...you know..." How could he know when she

didn't even seem to know? "I'm bringing her to the inn to meet Bogart," Kate said, looking satisfied with herself. "That's Naomi's dog. He's really sweet."

Jaden resisted the urge to smile. "Do you have reservations to meet Bogart?"

"Um...not exactly, but I don't know Naomi's schedule." Kate's cheeks were pinker than they had been when he'd first opened the door. That was good, right? She didn't seem to be hesitating because she couldn't stand him. She just seemed to get nervous around him.

He opened the door wider. "All the food is made. Table is set." He'd even picked out flowers.

"Okay. Fine." She stalked past him and followed Bella to the kitchen. "I'll have breakfast with you."

"Perfect. Everything's out on the deck." Jaden led the way and carefully gauged her reaction as she stepped through the door.

Kate's dark eyes widened when she saw the flowers on the table, but she didn't mention them.

They each took the same seat they'd sat in last night. The ambiance was different, though. Bright and warm and relaxed. Actually, scratch that. Kate's bare shoulders looked tense.

"Nothing like starting the day off with a good breakfast." Jaden took the liberty of serving her pancakes and syrup, along with a helping of fruit and a few slices of bacon before he filled his own plate. She didn't answer, but silence with Kate didn't press into him like it did with some people. It was...easy.

Bella wriggle-crawled her way underneath the very center of the table as though she couldn't decide who would be most likely to drop her a crumb.

Kate took a bite of the food and chewed slowly. "Wow." Her face perked up. "These pancakes are incredible."

"Mmm-hmmm." He tried one too. They were light and airy, exactly the way he remembered. "It's my grandma's recipe. She always whipped the egg whites forever. Then she would carefully fold them into the batter."

"They're so fluffy." Kate seemed fascinated, inspecting them as she cut another bite.

"So this breakfast isn't as painful as you thought." He'd intended the words to make a point, and Kate seemed to take it in stride.

"No. It's not painful at all." The first hints of a smile relaxed her face. "The food isn't half bad. Way better than Honey Nut Cheerios. I'm glad I stayed."

Jaden set down his fork and held her gaze. "Only for the food?" Because he wasn't enjoying the pancakes as much as he was enjoying sitting across from her, sharing breakfast with someone.

"Not only because of the food," she murmured with an unsure glance. "But…my life is a little complicated right now."

Join the club. He seemed to have secured a lifelong membership. "So is mine. That's why it's nice to have something uncomplicated. Dinner. Breakfast." He needed that. Something normal. Another presence in his world. Conversation. He hadn't realized how much he needed it until last night. For some reason, he found it so easy to be honest with Kate. "I like you. Spending time with you is…simple. And nothing in my life has been simple for a long time."

"I like you too." Kate's smile grew, finally resembling that quirk of her lips she'd shown off when he'd kissed her last night.

"So let's not complicate it," he suggested. "Let's have dinner while you're in town. And breakfast. Maybe lunch once in a while. Whatever works."

"That sounds perfect." She poured herself a glass of orange juice. "So what's complicating your life right now?"

A familiar tension crowded his gut. "Let's make a pact not to talk about our complications."

Kate tilted her head as she studied him. "What are we going to talk about, then?"

"Um…" Talking had never been one of his talents. "Our families?" That would be a short conversation on his part. "Funny stories from when we were growing up?" He had plenty of those. "But why don't we start with our most embarrassing moments?" That should be good for a laugh, keep things light.

Kate dropped her head, suddenly extremely interested in her food again. "Um…no thank you."

"Ohhh…you must have a good one."

"I hardly know you." She hastily helped herself to more pancakes, drowning them in syrup. "Why would I tell you my most embarrassing moments?"

"I think you're being dramatic," he teased. "I bet your most embarrassing moment isn't even embarrassing." She'd probably gotten toilet paper stuck to her shoe or something lame like that.

"Oh, it went way past embarrassing," she assured him. "It was humiliating."

"Now I have to know." Jaden refilled his mug of coffee from the pitcher he'd brought out. Though for once he didn't feel like he needed it. He'd slept better last night than he had in months. "I swear I won't tell anyone else."

"Fine." She left a dramatic pause. "My sophomore year of high school, I asked a boy to homecoming."

"That doesn't sound so bad."

Kate narrowed her eyes. "My friends convinced me I should decorate his car. So I skipped our last class and spent an hour covering his beloved Mustang in flowers and streamers and balloons and cute little signs."

"Uh-oh." He had a feeling he knew where this was going.

"Yeah." She crossed her arms and leaned back. "So when the bell rang, the entire school walked out to the parking lot and there I was, sitting on the hood of Tommy's car with a rose in my mouth and this huge, obnoxious, glittery sign asking him to go to the dance with me."

A laugh was brewing. He could feel it starting way down deep. Jaden held his breath so it wouldn't come out.

"When the guy came out and saw me," she continued, "he was horrified. He kept yelling about his car. How could I touch his damn car?"

"Ouch." *Don't laugh. Whatever you do, don't laugh.* It was hard, though, considering she told the story in a way that made him picture every detail.

"He said no, by the way. He said he wouldn't even go to Taco Bell with me."

That did it. Jaden could no longer hold back. But at least she laughed too. "See? I told you it was humiliating. Now you have to make me feel better about myself and tell me yours."

"Right. A promise is a promise." Even though his didn't even compare to the scene she'd just detailed for him. "My most embarrassing moment was in high school too." Wasn't everyone's? "I was in English class screwing around, being loud and obnoxious, and the teacher made me get up to apologize to the whole class."

"I have a hard time seeing you as loud and obnoxious."

"Oh, trust me." Before a couple of months ago, he'd been a lot more outgoing. He'd always preferred to think of it as extroverted and friendly rather than obnoxious. "Anyway, in front of the whole class, Miss Tolbert said, 'You come up to the front of the room right now and tell the class you're sexy. I mean sorry!'" He mimicked the old woman's voice for effect.

Kate did not look amused. "That's it? You're telling me that the most embarrassing moment of your life has to do with you being hot?"

Yeah, he had a feeling she wouldn't be impressed. "Miss Tolbert was a hundred years old. And that's all anyone could talk about for weeks. You should've heard the rumors that went around about us."

"I'm sorry." She shook her head, her sleek black hair swooshing around her shoulders. "That doesn't count as an embarrassing moment."

"Why not?"

"Because it probably made you a legend in your school," she grumbled. "It sounds to me like that was Miss Tolbert's most embarrassing moment, not yours."

Jaden laughed. "I never thought of it that way." But the woman had a point. "If it makes you feel better, I would've gone to homecoming with you."

"Right." She made a show of rolling her eyes. "Sure."

"Why don't you believe me?" Seriously. He would've killed to go to homecoming with someone as intriguing as Kate Livingston.

"You were this big-time snowboarder jock, and I was a newspaper nerd." She huffed. "I highly doubt you would've gone to homecoming with me."

"Maybe I would've surprised you," he said, eyeing her lips. The same way he'd surprised her last night...

"You've definitely accomplished that, Jay." Kate stared into his eyes with a slow smile. "I think it's fair to say I've never been more surprised by someone in my life."

CHAPTER SEVEN

"Today's the day, Bella." Kate uttered a heart-cleansing sigh and gazed at the dog, who sat with her ears perked in rapt attention in the passenger seat of the borrowed Subaru. They'd been sitting in Jay's driveway for ten minutes, but Kate hadn't been able to get out and face the man.

"I have to tell him." Time was running out. Over the last week, Gregor had called and texted roughly twenty times, asking how the story was going, checking in to see if she'd finished a draft yet. She'd been putting him off, telling him that Jay had been extra busy so she hadn't collected all the facts yet. Which hadn't been a complete lie. Jay had been extra busy this week. She'd simply neglected to tell Gregor that Jay had been busy with her.

Since he'd made her breakfast that morning, they'd settled into something of a routine. She would arrive at the house around eight to pick up Bella, and Jay would make her breakfast before she and the dog went about their day.

At five, she'd bring Bella back to the house and either pick up dinner on the way or cook something on the grill. They'd sit out on the back deck under the stars, wrapped in blankets while the fire flickered between them, and entertain each other with stories late into the night. He hadn't told her anything about the accident yet, but that was okay because there was so much more to him.

He'd told her about being raised by his grandma, who took over the ranch when her husband died in his early forties, about how she was a better shot than any of the men in the county, about how he hadn't heard from his dad since his sixth birthday, and how his mom moved around the country in an old Airstream trailer, sometimes sending him postcards from wherever she happened to be living at the moment.

Kate had told Jaden things too. She'd told him about the time she'd done an undercover investigation on the recycling efforts at her middle school. It turned out they weren't recycling at all. At the end of the day, everything from the recycling bin got dumped into the garbage, and she'd exposed their deception in the center spread of their extracurricular newspaper.

She'd told him about how, when she'd declared writing as her major in college, her parents, along with her brother and sister, had staged an intervention dinner where they took turns telling her all of the reasons she would fail to find a career. Then she'd told him how her family had been all too happy to reiterate those reasons, along with a hearty round of *I told you so*, when she couldn't find a job.

Those were the real Kate Livingston stories. The ones that hid behind the happy smile. The ones that made her who she was. She couldn't remember the last time she'd shared them with anyone else.

By day three, breakfast had turned into one big flirt fest, with Jaden teasing her and touching her a lot, placing his hand on the small of her back or brushing her hair over her shoulder when she pretended to be offended by one of his jokes. Dinner had turned into rushing through the food part to get to the make-out portion of the evening, where they'd lie entwined on the couch, kissing with an intensity that seemed to grow stronger every day.

"God, how am I going to tell him?" It would ruin the alternate reality they'd created together. With him, she suspected, escaping from horrible memories about the accident, and her finally allowed to simply be Kate. Not a screwup in her family's eyes or an outdoorsy badass in her colleagues' eyes. It had been strange at first, being herself, but she'd started to love the feeling.

Bella yawned with a squeak and curled up in the seat as if she figured they'd be there awhile. Oh, how Kate wished they could be, that she could put this off a little bit long—

The front door of the house opened, and Jay stepped out, looking like an enticing cross between a cowboy and a mountain man in his boots, jeans, and a threadbare gray T-shirt. Even from this distance, his smile summoned hers as he slowly walked to the car.

"Hi," Kate called through the open window. It sounded more like a dreamy sigh than a greeting. Heart thudding in her throat, she scrambled to let Bella out before climbing out of the car herself.

"Didn't realize you were already here." Jaden knelt to pet Bella, who was whining and pawing at his legs like she hadn't seen him for a month.

Kate tried to keep her smile intact. "Just pulled up a minute ago." Now that was a lie.

"Perfect." The man stood, and she couldn't believe how

different he looked than he had the first day she'd met him. His face had relaxed, and his lips loosened into a smile whenever he saw her. Even his posture seemed stronger, taller, and less reserved.

"I want to take you somewhere." Jaden eased an arm around her waist and brushed a kiss along her temple. "I've got dinner packed," he whispered in her ear.

Even with regret and guilt swelling through her, she couldn't resist leaning into his touch, savoring it. Once he found out about her story assignment, he might never touch her again. "Maybe we should eat here. So we can talk." She couldn't tell him the truth in public. The setting for this conversation had to be perfect. They had to be alone.

"We can talk where I'm taking you." Jaden released her and strode up the driveway. "It's kind of a hike, so we'll take the Jeep." He punched in the garage code. Then he walked back to her and took her hand, guiding her to the passenger side and opening the door for her.

He did things like that all the time. Small gestures like moving aside to let her go first through a doorway or always leaving the last bite of dessert for her. In the evenings, he'd walk over and slip her sweatshirt on her shoulders when he could tell she'd gotten cold. Kate closed her eyes as Jaden let Bella into the backseat and then strode to the driver's side and climbed in.

How was she going to do this? She'd rehearsed the words a hundred times. Before she'd pull up to his house every morning, she would say them again. But then he would greet her and kiss her and he was so happy that she didn't want to ruin it. She didn't want it to end.

"You okay?" he asked, backing the Jeep down the driveway.

"Fine," she murmured, close to tears. "Just a little headache." Heartache.

"Here." He reached back into a small cooler and pulled out an ice-cold water bottle. "Water usually helps. It's easy to get dehydrated at this altitude."

"Thanks." Her throat felt raw. She opened the water bottle and took a long sip. She had no idea where they were going, only that it was up. Up the street, then up past the resort, and then up higher still on some lonely dirt road that cut through the wide spaces between trees that Kate assumed were ski runs. Patches of snow still dotted the mountainside, but there was grass too—new and green. Luckily, they didn't need to talk. With the Jeep so open on top, wind whistled between them, which meant Kate didn't have to force the words that churned in her stomach. He wouldn't have heard them anyway.

While the Jeep bumped along, Jaden brought his hand over to rest on her thigh. "Feeling better?"

Nodding, Kate closed her eyes and breathed in the cooling air. She loved the feel of his hand on her, warming her, reassuring her.

After one more switchback, he parked the Jeep, and she raised her head. They were above the trees. There was more snow up here, but she hardly cared about the temperature. The view to her right consumed her. It was endless. A blue-hazed vista of snowcapped peaks hovering above a watercolor of reddish cliffs and green, tree-studded mountainsides that came together in long, lush valleys. There were little round lakes so far off in the distance that they looked like puddles. "This is incredible," she breathed.

"One of the reasons I loved boarding so much." Jaden gave her thigh a squeeze and then got out of the Jeep. "That view never gets old."

He let Bella out and started to rummage through things in the back of the Jeep before meeting her on the passenger side. "It's colder up here," he said, helping her put on a fleece jacket. It smelled like him—like male spice. The same scent that always filled her senses when they were kissing.

Taking her hand, Jaden led her a few steps away from the Jeep, where a large snowfield still smothered the grass. The view once again stretched out in front of them, a painting she wanted to jump into.

"This is the snowfield where I started out," Jaden said. "My buddies and I would hike up here, out of bounds, and we'd board as long as we could. All the way through June some years."

She threaded her fingers through his, holding on to his hand tighter. "You never got caught?"

"Nah. They didn't keep a close eye on things around here during the summer months." He couldn't seem to look away from the snow. "Even as a kid, I loved it. Being out here made me feel so free."

"I bet you miss it," Kate said quietly. She could see it in the sad slump of his shoulders, hear it in the shaky tenor of his voice.

"I almost killed someone." He paused and swallowed hard like the words had the power to strangle him. "A few months ago. At the Olympics." Jaden faced her as though he wanted her to see the pain on his face. "I was trying to take the lead, and I lost control. Plowed right into my rival and took him out."

Kate looked up into his eyes, and she couldn't lie to him anymore. "I know."

"You do?" He dropped her hand and stepped back. The sudden uncertainty in his glare cut off the rest of her words. She couldn't tell him about the article. Not yet. "I kind of put it together. Jay—J.J. You're a snowboarder. You've been in an accident..." He had to realize that she would've heard about it. Everyone had heard about it.

"You never said anything." His expression was guarded, the same way it had been when she'd met him on the street.

Kate eased closer to him, looking intently into his eyes so he would remember she wasn't a threat. "You didn't bring it up, so I figured you didn't want to talk about it."

"I haven't." The rigidity in his shoulders seemed to give way. "Not with anyone. The days after were so intense. With the media, and surgery to reset my arm." He turned back to the snowfield with a blank stare. "Then they told me Kipp had a spinal cord injury. That he wouldn't walk again. And I couldn't function. I couldn't sleep or eat. I had nightmares constantly. Everyone was saying I'd done it on purpose..."

"Of course you didn't do it on purpose." She turned him back to her. God, he was so tormented by it. She couldn't stand seeing him that way, so lost. "Tragedies just happen sometimes. You didn't cause it. You didn't bring it on him or yourself." She took his cheeks in her hands and guided his face to hers. "You are a good person, Jaden Alexander. You didn't deserve this. You didn't deserve to be crucified in the media." But she could change things. She could tell his side of the story. "You need to stop hiding and let people see who you really are. I can help. I can write—"

"First I need to get back on my board," he interrupted, gazing at the snowfield again. "That's why I brought you here. I can't do it alone."

Kate studied him. That was his total focus. Getting back on the board. And yes, he did need that. So talking about the article could wait. "How can I help?" she asked. "You want me to cheer you on? Take a video so you can remember this moment?"

"No." For the first time, he looked amused. "I want you to board with me."

"I'm sorry, what?" This time Kate was the one who backed away. "As in *snow*board with you?" As in strap a piece of wood or whatever the hell it was made out of to her feet and go racing down a freezing cold snowfield?

Jaden's smile answered the question. That was exactly what he wanted her to do. Which proved he was crazy. The man was nuttier than a five-pound fruitcake. "I can't snowboard," she informed him. "I don't even *have* a snowboard." So there.

"I grabbed one from the rental shop, along with some boots that I think should fit you fine."

Damn his thoughtfulness. "I've never been snowboarding." She eased a few more feet of distance between them. "This might come as a shock, but I'm actually not outdoorsy. At all."

"I know." He approached her, taking her forearms in his hands, and dear Lord his touch wrecked her.

"You do?" she almost whispered. Here she thought she'd played her part of the outdoorsy chick pretty damn well over the last week.

"I kind of put it together." One corner of his delicious mouth lifted higher than the other. "That's one reason you were so eager to help out with Bella, right? Because you didn't want to go back out on the trail to finish your mysterious trek?"

"I hate camping," she confessed. "I hate the bugs and the dirt and peeing in the woods. Oh, and I hate the stupid tents that suck at being waterproof."

Jaden laughed. "I figured." He pulled her close, locking his hands at the small of her back. "But I don't think you'll hate snowboarding."

"I guess we'll find out." For him, she'd give it a try. She'd do pretty much anything to make him happy, to hear him laugh again. Even if it involved adrenaline.

* * *

"I don't know about this." Kate reached for Jaden's arm and peered down at the snow that stretched out below them.

"I don't know about this either," he admitted. What had appeared to be a pristine, sparkling field of snow suddenly looked a lot more like an icy death trap. Now he knew what could happen. He knew he had no control out here. Life could change in seconds if he made one wrong move or caught an edge.

But he also knew that things could be restored, that there could be healing, if he found the courage to seek it out. Kate had reminded him of that. She'd proven there could be light at the end of his tunnel of despair, but you had to work for it. So here he was, slowly inching toward that light, sweating and sick to his stomach.

He'd purposely chosen this spot because it wasn't as steep as some of the other areas he used to frequent, which meant it should be an easy place for Kate to learn. But he couldn't seem to move his legs. Might as well be honest with her. "I'm not sure I can do this." Stay standing. Glide over the snow the way he used to without a thought. Even just the feel of the frozen ground beneath him was enough to trigger the memories of kneeling at Kipp's side, seeing him unresponsive...

Grunting in her cute, soft way, Kate inched her snowboard toward him until she was close enough to squeeze his hands. "You can. Let's do it together." A brave willingness came out in her smile, which meant he couldn't wimp out now. He'd told her everything, and she still looked at him the same way. The ugliness of his story didn't shock her, or overwhelm her, or even make her question his integrity. He'd never been given a greater gift.

"Okay." Jaden locked his weak knees and then held her steady with an arm around her waist. It was awkward with both of them on their boards, inverted sideways on the mountain, but she would need his help.

"First, you want to find your balance." He assumed the position so she could see—weight centered, knees soft.

She emulated his posture. "Like this?"

Taking her hips in his hands, he set her back slightly. "Perfect. How does it feel?"

"Awkward." Her body wobbled. "I don't like having my feet strapped into something."

"You'll get the feel for it." And he would do his best to keep her upright. Maybe that would distract him from the sudden surge in his blood pressure. "Make sure to keep your center of gravity low, then put more weight onto your downhill leg." He let go of her and showed her what he meant, sliding down only a foot so he could catch her or break her fall if he had to.

"Whoa…" Kate eased her weight onto the downhill leg, arms flailing. Somehow, she caught herself and balanced, inching the board down to where he stood.

"You're a natural." He couldn't resist touching her, taking her hands and seeing the color rise to her face.

She looked up at him from under those long eyelashes. "I don't know about that, but this isn't as terrible as I thought it'd be."

"It's not as terrible as I thought it would be either." She kept his mind off the fears. "I meant getting back on a board isn't as terrible," he clarified. "Not being here with you." He eyed her mouth, trying to decide how hard it would be to kiss her when they were both standing on snowboards. "I like being here with you."

She smiled softly at him, still holding on to his hands. "Thank you for letting me be here. For trusting me." The last words wobbled out, full of emotion.

Screw keeping our balance. He leaned over and kissed her, securing one hand on her forearm to keep her upright and stroking her cheek with the other.

When he pulled back, Kate seemed to be breathing harder, though they hadn't actually gone anywhere.

"So we have to go all the way down to the end?" She moved her gaze down the slope.

It was either that or ditch the boards and hike back to the top. "If you're up for it."

"I guess," she muttered, but she also smiled.

"We'll take it slow." He released her and eased into the board again, sliding it slowly down the hill in a path she could follow.

Kate started out behind him, but her balance was off.

"Low center of gravity," he called.

"I don't know how!" She started to panic, body lurching, her arms flailing, the board going vertical. She picked up speed, coming straight for him.

Uh-oh...

Just before she plowed into him, he opened his arms, catching her against his chest. The momentum knocked them both backward, and Kate landed on top of him.

Bella barked and ran circles around them, as though she wanted in on the game.

Jaden grinned at Kate. "At least I broke your fall."

"Oh my God, you should've seen your face." She shook

with laughter, which made him laugh too. It felt good to laugh. Felt good to be out here on the mountain, lying in the snow, feeling this woman against him. There was nothing quite like feeling Kate against him.

When they would lie on the couch after dinner in the evenings, their legs tangled as they kissed and touched and murmured about how enjoyable it all was, he felt normal and whole. Part of something again. The last time she'd pulled away and said she'd better get going, it almost killed him, but he hadn't wanted to push her. He needed her to want him as much as he wanted her.

Did she? Did that growing hunger gnaw at her the way it did him?

He closed his arms around her. "Will you stay with me tonight? I don't want you to leave."

She propped her chin up on her fist. "That depends... how comfortable is your bed?" She was teasing him again. And damn he loved it.

"The bed is okay. But you should see the tub in the master bathroom."

"Big enough for two?"

"I'd hope so. It takes up half the bathroom." When he first saw it, he'd thought it was a ridiculous waste of space, but now he could see the benefits of having a huge tub.

"Perfect." Kate moved her face closer to his, her eyes full of everything he needed in his life—humor and fun and depth too. She seemed to see so much in him. The good. What he thought had been lost.

"I'd love to stay," she murmured. "I'll need a good hot soak after this little adventure."

"In that case, let's cut this run short and hike back up." He snuck his hand into her fleece coat and felt his way up her chest.

She rolled her eyes in mock annoyance, but her heart beat faster under his palm. "We just got here."

"Snowboarding is overrated." Especially compared to sex.

She wriggled away and maneuvered to a sitting position. "We can head back soon. But first I want to see you ride all the way down there." She pointed to where the snow tapered off into wet, soggy grass. "You need to finish this run, Jaden."

He loved the sound of his real name on her lips. "What about you?"

"I'll watch. That's how I learn best anyway." She took his face in her hands and pressed her lips to his, brushing them softly, waking him once again. "Go. Alone. Do what you came here to do." She obviously understood how much he needed this, to rediscover peace out here.

He reluctantly stood, surprised to find the dread was gone. There was nothing but anticipation. Starting out slowly, he eased his weight onto his downhill foot, cutting across the mountain before leaning into a turn. Slushy snow sprayed all the way up to his face, cold and familiar. He let himself pick up speed, taking the turns quicker, carving a wavy line into the snow. Wind sailed across his face, stinging his nose the way it always did when he really cut loose and flew.

"Woohoo!" Kate cheered behind him, clapping and whistling. He crouched lower, using the momentum and speed to cut and jump, feeling lighter than he had in three dark months.

CHAPTER EIGHT

They didn't even make it inside the house before Jaden started to kiss her. He moved swiftly around the Jeep and opened her door, taking her hand.

The captivated, aroused look on his face heated Kate all the way to her core.

Seeing him on that mountain—facing whatever demons had chased him through the last few months—had done something to her. She no longer cared about the article. Or Gregor. Or her stupid job as a senior editor. She wanted Jaden. All of him.

Bella scooted out of the Jeep after Kate, barking as though she didn't understand what was happening.

Jaden seemed to ignore the dog. His eyes were intense on Kate's, speaking all sorts of hot, scandalous things without saying a word. He pinned her against the side of the Jeep, kissing her lips, sweeping his tongue through her mouth. Then he pulled back, stealing a glance at her, smiling that private, sexy smile.

Bella wedged herself between their legs and whined.

"It's okay, pup." He reassured her with a quick scratch behind the ears before Kate directed his gaze back to hers by threading her fingers into his hair and holding his face in place so they could take the kiss deeper. So much deeper. His lips were fused to hers with a heat that set her skin ablaze and made her body burn for him. "Inside," she managed to gasp. "Take me inside."

He hoisted her into his arms, and she wrapped her legs tightly around his waist as he carried her through the garage door. Kate was so busy kissing him that she caught only a glimpse of poor Bella tagging along behind them.

Jaden brought her through the kitchen and then the living room, all the way to the master bedroom, kissing her mouth with a recklessness she happily matched.

He paused near the bed. "We forgot all about the dinner I packed."

"Later," Kate gasped. "We can have dinner in bed."

"I love that idea." He carried her across the room and set her feet on the floor just inside the bathroom.

He hadn't been exaggerating. The bathtub in the master suite was enormous. A freestanding rectangle that was tucked into a marble-tiled alcove in front of a large picture window that looked out on the mountain. It was straight out of a fantasy—gleaming white porcelain with a crystal chandelier dangling overhead.

"Holy mother," Kate murmured, staring at the beauty over Jaden's shoulder.

He held her close. "Are you using me for my bathtub?"

"Yes," she said with fabricated certainty. Then she worked her hands up his chest underneath his T-shirt and leaned into him, running her tongue along his neck until she'd reached his ear. "Is that a problem?"

"Nope." He jumped into action, plugging the drain and turning on the water, holding his hand under the faucet to test the temperature.

The running water seemed to spook the dog. Bella scampered out of the bathroom and plopped herself on a cushy pillow next to the king-sized bed. Obviously the dog was not a fan of baths.

Jaden left the water running and came at Kate again, lifting her back into his arms. "It feels so good to hold you," he whispered against her shoulder. He carried her to the king-sized bed and set her on the very edge, standing close enough that she could raise his T-shirt and kiss his tight abs.

His breath hitched each time she pressed her lips to his skin. As she tasted him, his hands smoothed down her hair. He stepped back and took her right foot in his hands, removing the boot, and then her sock, watching her eyes the whole time. He did the same with her other foot, caressing her toes with his thumb until she lay back on the bed, moaning like she was already halfway to an orgasm. "Wow. You're amazing."

"Are you using me for my massage skills?" he asked, running a single finger down the length of her foot.

"Yes," she whispered. She loved the way he touched her. His hands were so strong, knowing and perceiving, taking their cues from the sounds she made, the movements of her body.

Jaden grinned. "Use away." He inched closer and caught the waist of her yoga pants in his fingers, tugging them down her hips, efficiently taking her lace underwear with them. Moving even closer to the mattress, he edged his body in between her legs and leaned over to unzip the coat she was still wearing. He worked slowly, watching her face between long gazes down her body like he didn't want to miss one detail.

Gently, he pulled one of her arms out of the coat and then the other, shoving her jacket aside before securing his hands to her waist under her T-shirt. "You're so beautiful, Kate. Such a good person." The words were almost solemn, as though he didn't think he deserved this, deserved her. But he didn't know.

She cupped her hands on his shoulders, bringing him down to lie over her. "You're a good person too. Strong and thoughtful and funny." So profound in his thoughts, tender in his touch. "I've made mistakes." The biggest one lately not telling him everything the first day she'd met him.

"Mistakes can be forgiven." He slid his hands higher up her rib cage, pulling off her shirt and letting it pool behind her.

"I hope so." She drew in a long, sustaining breath as his finger traced the very edge of her lace bra.

One of his hands eased under her back and popped the clasp, and then he shifted onto his side next to her and pulled the garment away. His gaze swept over her, dark and greedy. Jaden kicked off his own boots, pushed off the bed, and pulled her up to stand with him, pressing her body to his as he maneuvered back to the bathroom. He broke away only long enough to shut off the water, and then he had her back in his arms.

Kate took over, peeling his shirt up and over his head, letting it fall to the floor next to them. She kissed his neck, his chest, sliding her tongue seductively over his skin while she unbuttoned his jeans and pushed them down, taking his boxers with them. "Actually, maybe I'm using you for your body." She stood back to admire him—all that hard, angled muscle tensed into perfection.

"Like I said... use away."

"Oh, I plan to." Keeping him in anticipation, she stepped into the tub and slowly lowered her body to the water. Resting her head against the side, she closed her eyes. "Ohhhhh."

"That good, huh?" Jaden climbed in and settled his back against the opposite side to face her.

"I can think of something better." She shifted to her knees, opening her legs to straddle his hips.

His chest expanded with a long breath. "You've changed so much for me." He gazed steadily into her eyes. "It's been so long since I've felt anything..."

"What do you feel now?" She ground her hips into his, moving over his erection, feeling it slide against her, slick and hard.

"You." He held her tighter against him. "I feel you. Everywhere. In my head. In my heart. In my arms." He kissed her so torturously slow, as though he wanted to make it last as long as possible. But there was too much passion surging through her, too much want nudging her closer to the edge.

She stilled her body, and Jaden sat up straighter, bringing his mouth to her breasts, nipping and kissing his way from one to the other. Her head fell back, the ache for him driving deeper into her.

He traced his lips up her chest and back to her mouth while his hands caressed her back. He paused and looked into her eyes. "What are you thinking?"

"How much I want this," she murmured. "How much I want you." It had all happened fast but he'd let her see everything, his pain, his heart. Way more than any other man had ever allowed her to see.

Kate stood on weakened legs and stepped out of the

tub. Within seconds, Jaden stood with her, kissing her as he slowly eased her backward toward the bathroom vanity. He lifted her and set her backside on the marble countertop and then opened a drawer and found a condom. She leaned over and kissed his shoulder while he put it on. "I need you inside of me," she whispered, tugging on his hips and arching her back to bring him in deep.

Jaden wrapped his arms around her as their bodies came together, moving in a rhythm that loosened her feeble grip on control. He angled his hips on each thrust to graze that magic spot, again and again until she was gasping and throbbing and too close to pull back. Bracing her hands against the countertop, she pushed up to meet his thrusts, welcoming the explosion of sensations as it burst forth inside of her, moaning his name so he knew he could let go too.

"God, Kate, you're amazing," he uttered between jagged breaths. Jaden held her tighter, rocking his body, reigniting her climax until he trembled with release.

He hunched over her, his forehead resting on her shoulder.

"Wow," she murmured into his hair.

He raised his head and kissed her softly, still out of breath. "Wow."

"I'm exhausted." She could hardly hold herself up anymore.

Jaden straightened and took care of the condom before wrapping a towel around his waist. Then he came back and lifted her into his arms and carried her to the bed.

They both fell to the soft mattress, lying side by side. His fingers stroked her bare arm. "I wasn't just saying that earlier. You really have changed things for me."

Kate entwined her fingers with his and brought his knuckles to her lips.

"You're the first person who's bothered to see me," he

went on. "No one else cared what happened. Everyone wanted a fallen champion, a villain, so that's what they turned me into."

Kate propped herself up on her elbow and looked at him for a long, beautiful moment. "I see who you really are." And she would make sure everyone else saw it too.

* * *

Waking up had never been Jaden's favorite thing, but it had been especially brutal since February. Most mornings he would've much rather kept his eyes closed than face the world, but not when he had Kate in his bed. Since the sun had come up, he hadn't been able to stop looking at her.

He still held her in his arms, her body curved against his, their legs tangled together. Kate was asleep, her face still somehow just as stunning as it was when she smiled at him.

At some point during the night, Bella had snuck onto the bed and curled up at their feet as though she couldn't stand to be left out.

A lazy contentment weighted Jaden's body. He wanted this. Waking up with someone every morning. Feeling the silkiness of her hair over his arm, feeling her breathe so peacefully against him.

In so many ways, Kate was still a mystery. All he really knew about her was that she lived in L.A. and worked as an editor. But she didn't seem to love it there. He wouldn't either, not with the constant crowds and the paparazzi everywhere. Maybe she'd be open to moving. For the first time since the accident, he could see settling down, sharing his life with someone. And he wanted it to be here in the mountains. At least if he took the job at the resort, he'd have stability, a beautiful place to live where the community had seemed to accept him back. He would have something to offer her.

Kate stirred and stretched her arms. Her eyes opened, and that gorgeous smile of hers bloomed when she looked at him.

"Morning, beautiful."

"Morning." She wriggled closer and wrapped herself into him.

He couldn't resist playing with her long, soft hair as she laid her head back down and closed her eyes.

"Not a morning person?" he asked innocently.

"Normally I am, but we didn't exactly get much sleep last night." She kept her eyes closed, still smiling.

"Sorry." He wasn't. Not at all.

"I'm not sorry." She peered up at him as though her eyelids were too heavy. "It was the best night I've had in a long time."

"Me too." This whole week had been some of the best moments of his life.

"What time is it?" Kate asked through a yawn.

Unfortunately, he'd been keeping an eye on the clock. He almost lied, but she could easily see for herself. "Nine."

"Nine?" She shot up to a sitting position. "Aren't you late for work?"

He sat up, too, leaning over to kiss her neck. "Yep."

"Then you should go." The words didn't have much conviction.

"Don't want to." He pulled the comforter away from her chest and admired her full breasts. "I'd rather stay in bed with you all day."

Kate lay back down and turned on her side to face him. "Aren't they doing inspections?"

"Mmm-hmmm." He couldn't seem to pry his gaze away from her body.

"Then you need to be there, mister." She pushed at him playfully. "Go. Right now. They won't be able to sign off on everything if you're not there."

Yeah, yeah, yeah. Blake had already sent him three panicked texts. Jaden scooted off the bed. "What about you?"

"Bella and I will be fine. Won't we, sweetie?" Kate reached down and petted the dog's head.

"You'll be here when I get home?"

"Yes. I have some work to do today too," she said cryptically. "But I will most definitely be here when you get home."

"As long as you promise." He pulled on clothes and his boots but couldn't resist going back to the bed where Kate still lay watching him. Her black hair was mussed and gorgeous, her eyes still sleepy and innocent.

"I'll see you later." He kissed her, and she held on to him a little longer.

"Hurry home," she murmured. "I'll make a special dinner."

"Can't wait." He forced himself to leave then, before he started taking off the clothes he'd just put on.

The drive up the mountain didn't ease the ache that had tortured him since he'd left Kate in his bed. When he made it up to the site, Blake jogged over, looking more relieved than pissed.

"Glad you're finally here," he said.

"Sorry. Got a little hung up this morning." Could've gotten more hung up if it hadn't been for his damn responsibilities.

"The inspector is taking some pictures." Blake pointed to a man who was currently sizing up the towrope. "I hope it passes."

"It'll pass." Jaden had no doubt. Every detail had been well thought out and executed perfectly. He'd made sure. That was the only thing he'd had to focus on for the last month. And now that the project was ending, he knew what he wanted to do next. "By the way, I'll take the job," he said to Blake.

The man nodded as though he wasn't surprised. "This have anything to do with the woman you borrowed the snowboard for?"

"Yeah." But it was more than that. "I want to be part of a community again too." He wanted to start over in the same place he'd started out.

CHAPTER NINE

Kate hadn't been this nervous since that fateful day when she'd asked Tommy to homecoming. She finished setting the table and stood back to admire the simplicity.

After the embarrassing car decorating debacle, she'd learned that sometimes subtlety was best, so no balloons or flowers or cheesy *Please forgive me!* signs on the table tonight. No humiliating rejection either. It would be different. She and Jaden may not have known each other long, but he seemed to get her. He would understand why she'd kept certain things from him. And once he read the article she'd written, everything would be okay.

"Right, Bella?" she asked, kneeling to give the dog some love.

Gregor had texted her early that morning to tell her he needed a draft of the article by noon or there'd be serious consequences. "Not that I care about the consequences," she explained to Bella. Writing the article had become something bigger. She'd spent the whole morning pouring her heart into her keyboard, and the words had flowed. She'd likely get fired for writing a personal exposé on what an incredible person Jaden Alexander turned out to be instead of capturing what everyone expected, but it would be worth it.

Sure, Jaden would be surprised, but she could explain everything over dinner. It was a simple meal—lasagna and a hearty Italian salad. She liked to think of this as half an apology dinner, half a makeup dinner. Or at least she hoped they would make up after they had the inevitable conversation she'd been avoiding for a week.

"He'll forgive me," she murmured.

Bella licked her cheek in agreement.

"He'll understand just like you do." Once Jaden read her words, he would see how much she cared about him.

"Hey, gorgeous."

Kate straightened and spun to the French doors. "Hi." The sight of Jaden standing there in his jeans and boots sent a wave of heat crashing through her. "You're home early." She thought she had another half hour to prepare for this.

"We finished up ahead of schedule." He took a step toward her but was blocked by Bella, who wanted his attention first. "The inspector was impressed," he said, giving his dog a pat on the head.

"Well good. That's great." God, she already sounded guilty, and she hadn't told him anything yet.

"I may have gone twenty over the speed limit all the way back here too." He wrapped her in his arms and lowered his mouth to hers. Nope. Uh-uh. She couldn't get distracted now. She had yesterday, but enough was enough. Gently, she pushed him away. "Why don't you sit down? I'll go see if the lasagna is ready."

Without giving him a chance to respond, she hurried to the kitchen, opened the oven, and peeked under the tin foil. The cheese had bubbled to perfection. *Okay. Whew.* She was really going to do this. Kate patted her pocket where she'd stashed the printout of the article. After a quick explanation of the situation, she'd hand him that right away. Before he could even ask questions. The article would make everything okay.

When she finally carted the lasagna outside, Jaden was throwing the ball for Bella.

"Dinner's ready," she called, setting the casserole on the trivet she'd put out earlier.

"Looks good." He jogged over. "But not as good as you." His gaze slowly trailed down her body. "Maybe we should eat later…"

No, no. They had to do this now. Kate scolded him with a little smirk as she sat down. "We don't want it to get cold."

"Right." Disappointment tugged at his mouth, but he sat too. "So what'd you do today—" His phone buzzed. "Sorry." He dug it out of his back pocket. "Guess I'll turn it off. I've been getting calls from weird numbers all afternoon."

Kate paused in the middle of cutting him a generous slice of lasagna. "Calls?" Her heart glitched. Coincidence. It had to be a coincidence, right? She'd sent Gregor the article at noon, just for his opinion, but it wouldn't go to print for a few more weeks…

"Now I got a text." Jaden was squinting at his phone. "'What's your response to the *Adrenaline Junkie* article?'" he read. He looked up at Kate. "I had no idea *Adrenaline Junkie* was doing an article."

Oh no. No, no, no. Kate couldn't seem to move. Her body had frozen to the chair. Instead of beating, her heart was zapping in her chest. "Oh God."

"I know." Jaden rolled his eyes. "They've left me alone for a long time. Why are they all of a sudden interested again?"

Tears flooded her vision as she stared at him wide-eyed. "I'm sorry. Jaden, I'm so sorry." Regret burned through her, thawing the shock, letting her move. She got out her phone and went to *Adrenaline Junkie*'s website. Sure enough, her article had been posted on the blog, and it already had 14,253 shares on social media.

When she looked up, he was staring at her. "Why?" His voice hollowed as though he was afraid to know. "Why are you sorry?"

"I wanted to help." She dug the folded papers out of her pocket. "To tell your side of the story."

"Wait." His eyes narrowed into that distrustful glare she recognized from before. Before he knew her. Before he'd kissed her. Before they'd made love. "You sent them an article about me?"

"No." *Don't cry.* She couldn't let herself cry. "I work for them. I'm a senior editor there."

"What the fuck?" He pushed away from the table and stood. His eyes had hardened like he didn't want her to see the pain behind his anger.

Kate stood too. "I printed out the article so you could read it. I was going to show you tonight. I had no idea they'd post it today. It wasn't supposed to go to print for a couple of weeks." As if that made any of this better.

Hand trembling, she handed him the papers, but he ripped them into pieces and tossed them into the wind. "I can't believe this. You played me. You never told me you worked for *Adrenaline Junkie*."

"I was afraid to." She eased a few steps closer to him, but he backed away. "I knew you wouldn't even talk to me if I told you where I worked."

Jaden shook his head. Closed his eyes. When he opened them, the anger had been replaced with indifference. "Go. Get out."

"Wait. No." He hadn't even read the article yet...

"You got what you wanted out of me." His jaw went rigid. "Now you can go."

"I'm not like that." He knew her. He knew the real Kate Livingston almost better than anyone else. "I don't use sex to get stories." She inhaled, calming the desperation in her voice. "I really feel something for you, Jaden. And I think you feel something for me too."

"I don't." His tone was as dull as his eyes. "I feel nothing for you."

The apathy in his gaze tempted her to look away, but she refused to give in. "Nothing? Really? Because you said all that stuff. About me changing things for you...about wanting to trust someone again."

"And you proved I can't trust anyone."

No. She'd proved that he could get back on his board. That he could come out of hiding. That he could feel something again. He just needed to remember that connection they'd built. "I'm sorry I didn't tell you about *Adrenaline Junkie*. I should have. But spending time with you wasn't only about the story for me."

He studied her for a minute, as though trying to judge her sincerity. "Why did you offer to watch my dog?" he finally asked. "Did you know who I was when we met on the street that day?"

Before she even answered, she knew she would lose him. But she couldn't lie. "Yes."

"And you saw an opportunity to use my trauma to your advantage."

"No," she whispered. "I didn't know..." How deeply

he'd been wounded by all of it. How it haunted him so much. "I never meant to hurt you. I only wanted to help. If you would just read the article—"

"You're the fakest person I've ever met." Anger simmered beneath the words. "You're worse than the reporters who ambushed me on the streets." Jaden turned and strode down the deck stairs, heading for a trail worn into the tall grass at the edge of the forest. "Bella, come." The dog looked at Kate and whined.

"Come, Bella," he commanded again.

Head down, the dog trotted across the yard to follow him.

Kate wanted to follow him, to force him to read what she'd written about him. She'd put her heart into that article. But it was too late. She'd lost him.

Before Jaden disappeared into the trees, he glanced at her over his shoulder once more. "You need to be gone when we get back."

* * *

If Kate had learned one thing about the women of Topaz Falls, it was that they were always prepared.

When she pulled up at Everly's adorable café on the outskirts of town, Jessa, Naomi, Darla, and Everly were all there to greet her. They ushered her into the old converted farmhouse where they'd already claimed a booth, and they were armed with enough comfort food to feed a whole cast of brokenhearted rejects from *The Bachelor*.

"We've got chocolate and scones and muffins and wine and brick-oven pizza," Darla announced.

"We wanted to cover all our bases," Jessa added, patting the open seat next to her.

"Thanks." Kate slumped into the booth, unable to look

any of them in the eyes. She'd given them the gist of what had happened with Jaden via text so she wouldn't have to relay the story in person.

"It's a great article," Everly said, pushing a plate across the table. "Very heartfelt."

"Has he read it?" Naomi asked quietly. Her baby girl was sleeping contentedly in a wrap secured around her shoulders, and she obviously didn't want to wake her.

"No. I printed it out for him but he ripped it up." Kate winced at the sting the memory brought.

"Well that's dramatic." Darla popped a truffle into her mouth.

"I'm sure he'll calm down when he reads it," Jessa offered.

"I don't know." His eyes had been cold and dull. Not full of feeling like they were when he'd looked at her before. "He has every right to hate me." Though she hadn't exactly meant to, she'd tricked him. He was right. She'd seen an opportunity, and she'd selfishly pursued it, never considering how it might hurt him. Or her. "I should've told him a long time ago." Like her new friends had recommended. They could all be sitting there saying *I told you so*.

"It seems like people are really connecting with the article, though." Everly glanced at her phone. "Up to 24,953 shares already. It's going viral."

Yeah, she'd heard. On her way over, she'd called Gregor to have a few words with the man about posting something before she'd approved it, but he'd been too busy counting hits on their website to care much.

"So what are you going to do now?" Jessa asked, cutting a slice of pizza into petite bites. "Head back to L.A.?"

"I don't have much to go back to. I quit my job." She hadn't planned to, but when she was talking to Gregor, Jaden's words had echoed back in her head. *You're the fakest person I've ever met.* He was right. She didn't want to be a fake anymore. Even if it meant she had to slink home with her tail between her legs and move back into her parents' basement for a while.

"In that case, you can stay in Topaz Falls." Naomi's excitement woke the baby. She quickly stood to sway Charlotte back to sleep.

"Yes!" Everly, Jessa, and Darla whispered in unison.

"Stay?" She had a feeling there weren't a ton of jobs for unemployed writers in a small town like Topaz Falls. "But I have to work."

Darla's face brightened. "I've been thinking about hiring a manager so I can have a little more freedom to pursue my hobbies."

Everly grinned. "She means so she can have more time to date."

Darla ignored the snickers. "You'd be perfect management material," she said to Kate. "You're friendly, a good communicator, detail oriented..."

"Not to mention gorgeous," Jessa added. "That'll be good for business."

Kate looked from face to face with another round of tears brewing. "It sounds incredible." She had never fit anywhere. Not really. Not in her scholarly, overachieving family, not in her job. And here were these women she'd met only a week ago making a place for her.

"We're not fully booked until July." With Charlotte back to sleep, Naomi slid into the booth across from Kate again. "So you can stay at the inn for another month until you find your own place."

"And if you need more time, I've got an extra bedroom," Everly chimed in.

"Wow." A job, a place to live. But more importantly

than either of those things, it came with the most generous, lively, compassionate friends she'd ever met. "Okay. I'd love to stay."

Excited squeals woke the baby again. Naomi stood and swayed while Darla poured everyone a celebratory round of prosecco.

"Cheers!" Jessa held up her glass, and they all clinked away.

"I can't believe I'm moving to Colorado." Maybe Jaden would stay too. Maybe after time, he would give her another chance to prove to him that he could trust her with his heart.

"And you won't have any problem building a freelance writing career now," Jessa pointed out. "Not after the article goes viral."

That was true. With all of the exposure the article was getting in the mainstream media, she'd have a more recognizable name. "But that's not why I did it."

"Of course not." Everly reached over and squeezed her hand. "But maybe now you can focus on the kinds of things you've always wanted to write. You'd be great at profile pieces. Diving past the surface to really capture someone's heart."

Gratitude welled up in Kate's eyes once more. "Maybe I'll start with a profile on the extraordinary women of Topaz Falls."

CHAPTER TEN

Secluded Mountain Cabin on 30 acres! Exceptional privacy! Hidden driveway!

Jaden clicked on the real estate listing that promised the escape he needed. *Perfect.* The place was in No Man's Land, Canada, which sounded like paradise right now, considering it had been almost three days since that article had gone viral and the influx of calls and texts from reporters all over the world hadn't even started to slow down. Some paparazzi idiots had even camped out at the end of the street just waiting for him to leave.

At the moment, moving out of the country looked like a pretty damn good option. Except Canada might not be far enough away. Maybe Siberia...

Bella slunk into the office with the same forlorn posture she'd moped around in since Kate had left three nights ago. Didn't matter that Jaden had taken the dog on two hikes a day via their secret trail out back, or that he'd thrown the ball for her, or even that he'd given her extra treats. She still gave him those sad, pathetic eyes every time he looked at her.

"Come here," he said through a sigh. The dog trotted over. Was it just him or did she look more guilty than sad this time?

Bella came and sat at his feet, and sure enough, she had something in her mouth.

"Drop it," he commanded.

The dog complied all too happily. Didn't take him long to figure out why. It was a hair tie. Kate's hair tie. The one Jaden had tugged on to free her soft, long hair when she'd spent the night with him, when it felt like nothing could damage the connection they'd built.

Except for lies. Those could pretty much destroy anything.

The ache that had taken up residence in his gut sharpened. "You've got to get over her, Bella." Yeah, sure. He was telling Bella. Not himself for the thousandth time. "I know it's hard being here." Seeing as how this is where the three of them had played house for the better part of a week. "But we'll move on."

He scrubbed his hand behind the dog's ears until she leaned into him with a purr-like growl. "I'm looking for a place to go right now. We can start over." Again. He was getting pretty damn good at it. "Then it won't be so hard to forget." And yet he already knew how that logic worked. He hadn't seemed to forget either one of his parents, even though they'd pretty much abandoned him the day he was born.

Jaden turned back to the computer screen. What choice did he have, though? When he and Kate were messing around about her using him for his bathtub and massage skills, he had no idea how much truth hid inside those jokes. While he'd been thinking about a future with her, she'd been carefully taking notes on his story so she could expose him to the masses. How could he have been so stupid?

A sound outside the window forced him to leave that question unanswered.

Bella's ears perked.

Awesome. Just what he needed. The paparazzi sneaking around his backyard. Jaden shut his laptop and crept along the office wall, staying just behind the curtain. He almost laughed when he peered out and saw Levi Cortez tromping across the back deck like some kind of criminal.

The dog saw, too, judging from the mad swing of her tail. Bella scratched at the window, barking and whining at the prospect of company.

"Easy, girl." Jaden nudged her out to the living room, where they met Levi at the French doors. "What're you doing here?" he asked as he let him in. He had a feeling he already knew.

Levi sauntered past him in his cowboy's gait. "Haven't heard from you for a while. Figured I'd check in. And I saw the photographers outside, so I came around back." The man sat on the leather couch in the living room and leaned back like he had all day. Bella followed him, nosing his hand as though she'd been starved for attention the past three days.

Jaden stood where he was. "You could've called."

"I have called. You haven't answered."

Yeah, he hadn't even looked at his phone in a good twelve hours. After getting a text that had asked if he planned to marry Kate Livingston, he'd thrown the damn thing in a drawer. But Levi wasn't here to simply check up on him. And Jaden had had enough bullshit for one week. "Why are you really here?" He positioned himself in the chair across from the couch so they were facing off.

Levi grinned. "You haven't had the pleasure of meeting my sisters-in-law, Naomi and Jessa. But they're about as obstinate as a bull that's lost his balls. And they happen to like Kate. So here I am."

Jaden shook his head to stop Levi right there. "You're wasting your time," he informed his friend. "I can't stay here now. I've already found a place in Canada. You have no idea what it's like to have to hide in your house."

"So quit hiding. Who cares if they take pictures or write more stories?" Levi leaned forward, resting his elbows on his knees, still casual but also more determined. He obviously still had that stubborn streak. Typical bull rider.

"According to Jessa and Naomi, Kate's pretty broken up about everything."

"She's good at pretending." Jaden knew that for a fact. He'd replayed every scene of their tryst in his head. Every kiss. Every story she'd shared. Not once had he suspected she'd turn on him. That was the worst part. After everything he'd been through, he'd become an expert at sniffing out ulterior motives, and she'd completely snowed him.

"I get why you're pissed off," Levi said. "But it seems to me you used her too."

The anger that had only started to recede churned again, growing bigger, stronger. "How do you figure?"

The edge in Jaden's voice didn't seem to faze Levi. He simply shrugged. "When we talked on the phone last week, you told me you didn't think about the accident when Kate was around. So you used her as a distraction. Or did you screw her that night for *her* benefit?" The obvious sarcasm confirmed Levi already knew the answer. It also confirmed that word about him and Kate had gotten around Topaz Falls faster than Jaden could've dreamed.

"I guess that's it, then. We were using each other." That

wasn't how it felt, though. He hadn't intentionally used her. It wasn't about the sex for him. It was that he thought she'd made the effort to see him. The real him. The one no one else cared to notice.

"She wasn't using you." Levi sounded so sure, but how could he know? He hadn't been there. He hadn't seen how good Kate was at drawing information out of him. How she'd lured him into telling stories that she'd probably written up in the fucking article.

"Maybe she was using you at first," his friend acknowledged. "But that's not why she wrote the article. Have you even read it?"

No. He hadn't been able to stomach the thought of staring at her words. Words that had been taken from him without his consent.

His silence must've spoken for him because Levi nodded. "You really need to read it. Hell, it almost made me choke up."

"I can't read it," Jaden said simply. He'd read plenty of articles that had torched him, and he hadn't cared. But Kate's words would matter more.

"Guess I'll have to read it to you, then." His friend shifted and pulled his cell phone out of his pocket. "At least the good parts."

"No thanks—"

"'When I first met J.J. Alexander,'" Levi interrupted, "'I saw what the rest of the world had seen—a cocky, bitter, fallen hero—'"

"You can stop now." Pain roiled in Jaden's gut. He knew her words would sting.

"Sorry. I shouldn't have read that part. It gets better." Levi turned his gaze back to the phone. "'After spending a week with him, I realized I was wrong. We were all wrong.

J.J. isn't bitter or closed off or arrogant. He's wounded, haunted by regrets just like the rest of us. In one split second, his board caught an edge, and that tragic accident didn't only change Kipp Beckett's life, but it also changed J.J.'s life forever. He hasn't been able to escape it. He thinks about Kipp every day.'" Levi glanced up at him. "See? She's obviously trying to help, to get people to see your side of the story."

"I don't need people to see my side of the story." He hadn't made excuses for any of it. The accident might not have been intentional, but it was still his fault. It was all on him. "The article will only make things worse." She'd put him back in the same spotlight he'd been running from for months.

"There's more." Levi bent his head and went back to reading. "'Instead of exposing Jaden as a disgraced athlete like I had intended to do in this article, I fell for him. I fell for his subtle wit and his thoughtfulness and his profound depth. I fell for the way he loves and protects the dog he rescued from abuse and neglect. And yes, I even fell for his emotional scars because they are what make him so real. In one week, I discovered that J.J. Alexander has more empathy and strength and compassion than I ever will.'"

Her words roused hope, but he couldn't quite hold on to it. "Maybe she wrote it that way on purpose." Everyone wanted a good love story. "Maybe she wanted it to go viral so she'd have a recognizable name." What if she didn't care about him at all? No one else except for Gram ever had. Not his parents or his teammates. When he had been competing and winning, everyone had wanted to stand by him, but after he had fallen, he stood alone.

Levi shoved his phone back into his pocket and glanced around, a sure sign he was changing his approach. "Growing up, you and I didn't exactly have the greatest example of what love should look like."

"That's an understatement." When your parents left, love pretty much looked like abandonment. Levi knew that as well as he did.

"I was like you for a long time," his friend said. "Happy with a hookup here and there. But everything was different when I reconnected with Cass. It didn't matter what she did to me. How angry she got or how many times she pushed me away. I couldn't let her go. Not because I wanted anything from her either. I just loved her."

Jaden stared out the window. Had he ever just loved anyone? He didn't know how.

"Look..." The first signs of frustration showed in Levi's narrowed eyes. "I'm not as good at this lecture thing as Lance is. All I know is, I couldn't picture my life without Cass. I guess you need to decide if you could have feelings like that for Kate. Or for anyone. Maybe not now, but someday."

The feelings were already there. That's why he hurt like this. Somehow, the last two days had been lonelier than all twenty-four years of his life before he'd met Kate because now he knew what he was missing. "I already screwed it up." Jesus... had he really told her she was the fakest person he'd ever met? It wasn't only the words he'd used, though; it was also the venom behind them. She'd never forgive him for treating her that way.

"Believe it or not, I have some experience in begging a woman for forgiveness." Humor returned to Levi's voice. "But before you can ask for it, you've got to get yourself in a better place so you don't need a distraction anymore. Or things will never change."

The words were like stones sinking into his gut. Nothing would ever change if he didn't work for it. He'd put too much on Kate. It couldn't be her responsibility to pull him out of the pit he'd been living in. It shouldn't be. She deserved more. "I did use her." He cared about her, too, but that didn't change the facts. He'd only wanted her there because she made him feel something. She'd given him the courage to face the mountain again. All that had mattered was what she could offer him.

"Well, my work here is done." Levi stood and gave Bella a good scratch behind the ears before he opened the back door. "We've got a poker night at my place next Tuesday if you're up for it."

Jaden simply stared at him. How could he think about next Tuesday right now?

"You can let me know after you get this shitshow cleaned up," Levi said with a grin. Then he slipped out the back door, leaving Jaden to sit and wallow in his own stupidity.

Seeming to sense his misery, his dog walked over, sat down, and laid her head on his knee.

"Damn, Bella." He rested his hand on her head. "How are we gonna fix this?"

* * *

The Craig Hospital gift shop was stocked with flower arrangements, stuffed animals, and inspirational books and plaques. Jaden wandered down an aisle past shelves of trinkets inscribed with clichéd messages: *Get well soon! Healing thoughts and good wishes!*

The sentiments turned his stomach sour. What could he say to Kipp? What could he bring him that would make any of this better? He'd been trying to figure that out for two days, and he still had nothing.

Hands empty, he ducked out of the gift shop, dragging

three months of guilt along behind him. When he'd emailed a request to visit Kipp in the hospital, Jaden fully expected him to decline, but he hadn't. *Come on by anytime,* Kipp had written. *I'll make sure you're on the list.*

It was surreal walking down the hall now. He'd imagined this place would look like a dungeon—dark and depressing—but windows everywhere let in the bright sunlight. Two young women pushing themselves in wheelchairs rolled toward him, chatting and laughing like they were in the hall of a high school. They smiled as they passed, and somehow he found a smile too. They looked happy. Healthy. He hoped the same was true for Kipp.

Jaden continued down the hall, following the directions to the rec center where Kipp apparently spent most of his afternoons. The room looked nothing like he imagined. There were low Ping-Pong and pool tables and a huge television screen mounted on the wall with video game consoles lined up underneath.

"What's up, Cowboy?" Kipp wheeled himself over, a Ping-Pong paddle sitting in his lap. He looked...the same. From the bandanna tied around his head to the sturdiness of his broad shoulders to his confident grin.

The sight stung Jaden's eyes. "You look...good." He didn't mean to sound so shocked, but all of the mental images he had of Kipp were still from those first few days after the accident when the media had plastered pictures of him being loaded into the medevac.

"I feel good. Just kicked Jones's ass in a game of Ping-Pong." He gestured to another man in a wheelchair who'd moved on to the Xbox. "You want to be next?" Kipp asked with that signature spark in his eyes. Without waiting for an answer, he wheeled over to the Ping-Pong table and brought Jaden a paddle.

He almost didn't know what to do with it. "You want to play Ping-Pong?"

"Hell yeah. I'm undefeated." Kipp trucked to the other side of the table and got into position. "Zeros," he said one second before he nailed a killer corner shot that Jaden of course missed.

"I wasn't ready." He wasn't ready for any of this. He hadn't even told the man he was sorry yet.

"Better get ready, Alexander. Because I've had a lot of time to practice." Kipp found another ball on the floor nearby and rolled back to the table. "One–zero." He served another zinger that whizzed by Jaden's right shoulder.

"Wait. Hold on." Jaden set down his paddle. "I didn't come here to play Ping-Pong. I came here to tell you I'm sorry. I'm sorry you got hurt and not me. I'm sorry I'm not the one sitting in that chair." It could've been him. "You don't have to pretend this is easy." He got that Kipp didn't want his pity—Jaden wouldn't want pity either—but the man's life would never be the same.

Kipp rolled his eyes as though he'd been dreading this conversation as much as Jaden. "It's not easy," he acknowledged. "But I've had three months to process things. At first I was as pissed as hell about it. Some days I still am. But I've also learned my life isn't over. Hell, I've already been invited to be a commentator for the X Games next year."

He should've been competing in those games, though. Jaden didn't say it. Kipp already knew what he'd lost. Somehow he seemed to be on the road to accepting it. So why couldn't Jaden? Why couldn't he release the guilt? "You let me know if you ever need anything." Maybe that would help. If he could just do something for Kipp, maybe he could forgive himself. "I'll be there for you. I'll help you out however I can."

"You don't have to be sorry, J.J. I've seen the footage." His old rival mocked him with a smirk. "It's not your fault you're not as good on a board as I was."

Same old trash talk from one of the greats but this time Jaden didn't return fire. He couldn't. "I should've pulled back." He'd been moving too fast, too recklessly. He'd wanted to win. That was the truth of it. If he'd backed off, the accident never would've happened.

"I would've been offended if you had slowed down," Kipp said. "We competed. We're athletes. That's what we do." The man's expression sobered. "The last three months have sucked but I've got a lot going for me. That's what I want to focus on now. The future."

And that's what Jaden would focus on too.

CHAPTER ELEVEN

Welcome to the Chocolate Therapist." Kate greeted the older couple with the same enthusiasm as she had greeted every other couple and family group and friend group that had walked through the doors for the last nine hours.

Her feet, which were stuffed into her favorite pair of black Manolo Blahniks, ached like a mother, but even the pain couldn't dim the excitement of day four in her new life. All within less than a week of the big falling out with Jaden, she'd managed to fly home, pack up her apartment, and say farewell to everyone before she'd driven straight back to Topaz Falls.

When she'd driven into town, the sun was setting over the mountains in a fiery red welcome. So far it felt like this place had always been her home. Even with long days of learning the wine and chocolate business, the shininess of her new venture still hadn't dulled.

"Would you like a table?" she asked the couple, gracefully

withdrawing two menus from the hostess stand. "Or would you prefer to sit at the bar?"

Darla appeared behind her. "I can take over, Kate. Your shift was over a half hour ago."

"That's okay. I'm having so much fun." Even with achy, swollen feet, this was better than going back to her room at the Hidden Gem to spend the evening by herself. Despite the homey decorations, loneliness echoed between the walls.

"All right." Darla drifted back to the bar. "But at least sit down after they're seated."

Ignoring her friend, she turned back to the elderly couple.

"We would love a table near the windows, dear." The woman appeared to be in her early seventies with white wispy hair and jewel-like blue eyes.

Her husband was a head shorter than her and just as adorable with a rim of frizzy gray hair around a shiny bald spot. "There's something going on down the street, and we'd like to see how it turns out."

"Of course," Kate sang. "Right this way." Ignoring the pinch in her toes, she led them to a quaint table for two that looked out on Main Street. Darla had been right. She was good at this. Good with people. They always smiled at her, and even though she'd only been working here for a few days, she'd managed to defuse three grumpy patrons' complaints and had them all smiling and laughing again within a matter of minutes.

"Here we are." She tucked the menus under her arm and pulled out each chair with a charming smile, patiently waiting until the couple had gotten situated before she handed them the wine and chocolate list.

Instead of opening his menu, the man craned his neck as though trying to see down the street. "Any idea why all that trash is piled onto the car out there?"

"It's not trash, Gerald," his wife corrected. "It's sweet. There are flowers and streamers and balloons..."

Kate choked on a gasp. Flowers. Streamers. Balloons. On a car...

She tried to keep her hopes smothered under practical logic, which had never been one of her strengths. Jaden hadn't returned any of her emails or calls. After a few days, she'd stopped trying.

"It's so pretty," the woman went on. "I saw the man fixing it all up nice. He was tying heart-shaped balloons to the door handles, the sweetheart."

Sweet Lord...

Those darn hopes threw logic to the wind and sent her heart sky-high. Bracing her hands on the table, Kate leaned forward as far as she could without bumping her forehead on the glass. Each beat of her heart thumped harder when she looked down the block to where she'd parked her car earlier. Sure enough, it was covered.

"Oh my God." It had to be him. No one else around here knew that story.

"Um...your waiter will be right with him...I mean you," Kate stammered to the couple. The happiness burning in her eyes made her voice all weepy. She steadied herself against their table once more and pulled off her shoes, letting them dangle from one hand as she hurried toward the door.

"Are you all right, honey?" the woman called.

"I will be." As soon as she saw him—as soon as she felt his arms wrap around her—she would be. Kate ran down the sidewalk barefoot, her pencil skirt surely making her resemble a waddling penguin, but she didn't care. It was such a lovely sight, her car covered in orange. There were gerbera daisies and orange hearts cut out of construction paper, and yes, even heart-shaped balloons. But she couldn't see the front yet. Would Jaden be there? Had he really forgiven her?

"Pardon me," she mumbled, bumping her way past people.

When she finally broke through the crowd that had gathered, her knees gave. Jaden was sitting on the hood of her car with the stem of an orange gerbera daisy between his teeth.

"Look at you..." She stumbled off the curb, nearly incapacitated by the tears and laughter, sure that the happiness of this moment could fill a whole lifetime.

"Hey, gorgeous." He somehow managed to enunciate perfectly, even with the daisy in his mouth.

The crowd around them grew, pressing in on both sides of the street. Both locals and tourists snapped pictures and selfies on their phones. He hadn't tried to disguise himself. No hat. No sunglasses. Just J.J. Alexander sitting on the hood of her car. None of the attention seemed to bother him, though. He stared steadily at her as she crept closer. "What're you doing?"

"I'm asking you on a date." He took the flower out of his mouth and dropped it on the hood and then reached for her hand. "Kate Livingston, will you go on a date with me?"

"Hell yes, she will," Darla called from behind her. "How about right now? We can set up a nice private table in the back."

Murmurs of approval went around the crowd. Someone even clapped.

Kate shushed everyone with a frantic wave of her hand. This moment was a scene straight out of her dreams, and she didn't want anyone to intrude.

"I'm sorry I was such an ass." He eased off the hood and stood across from her. "I'm sorry I didn't hear you out. I'm sorry I ripped up your article."

"Awww. I'll go on a date with you," some woman yelled from the other side of the street.

"No." Kate put her hands on his broad shoulders to make sure this was really happening. "I mean yes. Of course I'll go on a date with you."

Jaden lowered his face to hers, her favorite grin in the entire world flickering on his lips. "Now?"

"Now," she confirmed.

The crowds parted. Cell phone cameras followed their every move as they huddled together and hurried back to the Chocolate Therapist, ducking through the doors so they could leave the rest of the world behind.

"Back here, you two." Darla quickly ushered them down the hall to the room where they met for book club. She'd already had the waitstaff drag in a small round table, two chairs, and a vase with a single orange gerbera daisy she must've swiped from the car.

God, these women. They had the best and biggest and brightest hearts she'd ever seen. "Thank you." Kate brushed away her tears as Darla gave her a wink and disappeared, closing the door firmly behind her.

They both sat down.

"You're crying." Jaden took her cheeks in his hands, using his thumbs to wipe away the tears.

"You humiliated yourself out there." All for her. "That'll be all over the news by tonight." People were probably tweeting and Instagraming and Facebooking the pictures right now.

"I don't care." Something had changed on Jaden's face. The day she'd met him, it had borne the lines of tension and stress, but now his features seemed softer. Relaxed. "I'm tired of caring what everyone else thinks. Except you." He slipped his hand under hers and held on. "You were right. There is something between us. Something…special. Something I've never had with anyone else."

Kate closed her eyes, letting those words soak in to heal all of the wounds he'd inflicted before. She looked at him again, wanting him to cut away that last bit of uncertainty that still dangled from her heart. "What changed?" she whispered. "You were so angry…"

"Yeah." A sigh slipped out. "Levi pretty much put me in my place. Told me I'd better get my head out of my ass and figure things out before I lost you for good."

"Levi, huh?" She smiled, thinking back to Jessa and Naomi's secret little side conversation at Everly's café the day she'd told them what had happened.

"Yeah, Levi." His smirk confirmed her suspicions. "He reminded me that I had issues to work on too. So I went to see Kipp."

Kate tightened her grip on his hand. "That must've been hard. How is he?"

"Still in rehab." Jaden threaded his fingers with hers, and the power of it, the intimacy of that gesture, heated her eyes again.

"But I spent the afternoon with him. He's exceeding the doctor's expectations. He's even taken a few steps with a walker."

"That's great news." For Kipp and for Jaden. No wonder his appearance had changed so much. He'd been set free.

"I read the article too. Actually, Levi read it to me." Jaden brought her hand to his lips and kissed her knuckles, sending an electrical charge all the way down to her toes.

"I'm sorry I betrayed your trust." She'd been waiting to say those words for over a week, but before now, something told her they wouldn't have done any good. "I should've told you. Right away. But I was afraid you'd keep me out. And I loved being with you."

"I loved being with you too," he murmured, leaning over the table until his lips were nearly touching hers. "I think that's why I lost it when I found out about the article. It was an excuse to bail. I figured you'd turn out to be like everyone else." His gaze shied away from hers. "I haven't exactly had much commitment in my life."

She kissed him, hopefully taking away any lingering doubts about her feelings for him. "I meant everything I said in the article."

This time his eyes stayed steady on hers. "I know."

"Levi said you were thinking about moving away." God, when she'd heard that, she'd had to excuse herself so she could cry in the bathroom.

"I was seriously considering it," Jaden said. "Until he reminded me it wouldn't help. I want to stop hiding. I want to make you happy. I want to focus on the future instead of the past."

She rested her forehead against his. "Me too."

Just as his lips brushed hers, the door swung open.

"Don't mind us." Darla traipsed in, followed by Everly and Jessa and Naomi, all carrying something different. They set down truffles and a bottle of wine and glasses and small china plates.

"Carry on," Everly said, herding the others toward the door.

"Those truffles are strawberry-filled dark," Darla called, fighting Everly's hold on her.

"The perfect aphrodisiac," Jessa added before Everly shoved her outside.

"Happy date night!" Naomi said with a sly grin.

Shaking her head, Everly waved at Kate and Jaden once more before closing the door.

Jaden laughed. If she could bottle up that deep throaty sound and listen to it every night before bed, she totally would.

"Levi wasn't kidding about their persistence."

She leaned in to claim the kiss she'd never stop craving. "Sometimes true love takes a village," Kate murmured against his lips.

And they seemed to have found theirs.

ACKNOWLEDGMENTS

Thank you, dear readers, for spending more time in Topaz Falls. I hope you are enjoying this town and these characters as much as I am. It's impossible for me to express how grateful I am for your notes, comments, reviews, and mentions. Your support keeps me going.

As always, I am so thankful to the team at Forever for allowing me to live my dream and write more books. You all continue to amaze me! With each project I learn more from my brilliant editor, Alex Logan. Thanks for everything you do to make me look good.

I will never be able to thank my family enough for their patience and perseverance, especially while I was writing this book under such a tight deadline! Will, AJ, and Kaleb, you will always have my heart.

ABOUT THE AUTHOR

Sara Richardson grew up chasing adventure in Colorado's rugged mountains. She's climbed to the top of a 14,000-foot peak at midnight, swum through Class IV rapids, completed her wilderness first-aid certification, and spent seven days at a time tromping through the wilderness with a thirty-pound backpack strapped to her shoulders.

Eventually Sara did the responsible thing and got an education in writing and journalism. After a brief stint in the corporate writing world, she stopped ignoring the voices in her head and started writing fiction. Now she uses her experience as a mountain adventure guide to write stories that incorporate adventure with romance. Still indulging her adventurous spirit, Sara lives and plays in Colorado with her saint of a husband and two young sons.

Learn more at:
   www.sararichardson.net
   Twitter @sarar_books
   Facebook.com/sararichardsonbooks

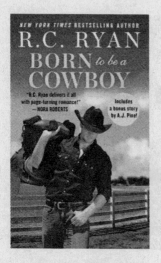

BORN TO BE A COWBOY
by R.C. Ryan

After running wild in his youth, Finn Monroe is now on the other side of the law as the local attorney. Between his practice and the family ranch, his days aren't as exciting as they used to be—until Jessica Blair steps into his office. Gorgeous and determined, Jessie has a hunch her aunt is in trouble, and Finn is her last hope. When she and Finn start poking around, it becomes clear someone wants to keep them from the truth. But as danger grows, so does their attraction. Includes a bonus novella by A.J. Pine!

ROCKY MOUNTAIN HEAT
by Lori Wilde

Attorney Jillian Samuels doesn't believe in true love. But when a betrayal leaves her heartbroken and jobless, an inherited cottage in Salvation, Colorado, offers a fresh start—until she finds a gorgeous and infuriating man living there! Tuck Manning has been hiding in Salvation since his wife died and isn't leaving the cottage without a fight. They resolve to live as roommates until they untangle who owns the cottage. As their days—and nights—heat up, they realize more than property is at stake…

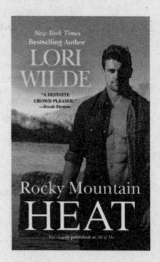

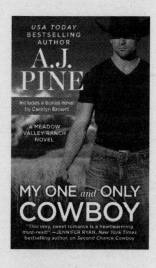

MY ONE AND ONLY COWBOY by A.J. Pine

Sam Callahan is too busy trying to keep his new guest ranch afloat to spend any time on serious relationships—at least that's what he tells himself. But when a gorgeous blonde shows up insisting she owns half his property, Sam quickly realizes he's got bigger problems than Delaney's claim on the land: She could also claim his heart. Includes a bonus novel by Carolyn Brown!

UNFORGIVEN by Jay Crownover

Hill Gamble is a model lawman: cool and collected, with a confident swagger to boot. Too bad all that Texas charm hasn't gotten him anywhere in his personal life, especially since the only girl he ever loved has always been off-limits. But then Hill is assigned to investigate her father's mysterious death, and he's forced back to the town—and the woman—he left behind. Includes a bonus novella by A.J. Pine!

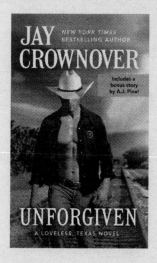

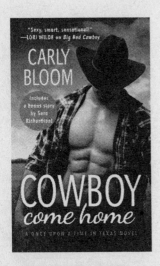
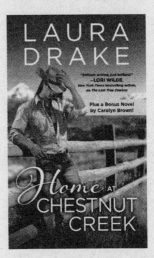